KNAVES OVER QUEENS

The Wild Cards Universe

The Original Triad

Wild Cards

Aces High

Jokers Wild

The Puppetman Quartet

Aces Abroad

Down and Dirty

Ace in the Hole

Dead Man's Hand

The Rox Triad

One-Eyed Jacks

Jokertown Shuffle

Dealer's Choice

The Novels

Knaves over Queens

Double Solitaire

Turn of the Cards

The Card Sharks Triad

Card Sharks

Marked Cards

Black Trump

Stand-Alones

Deuces Down

Death Draws Five

The Committee Triad

Inside Straight

Busted Flush

Suicide Kings

The Fort Freak Triad

Fort Freak

Lowball

High Stakes

The American Triad

Mississippi Roll

Low Chicago

Texas Hold 'Em

KNAVES OVER QUEENS

Edited by
George R. R. Martin

Assisted by
Melinda M. Snodgrass

Written by

Paul Cornell | Marko Kloos

Mark Lawrence | Kevin Andrew Murphy

Emma Newman | Peter Newman

Peadar Ó Guilín | Melinda M. Snodgrass

Caroline Spector | Charles Stross

A Tom Doherty Associates Book
New York

This is a work of fiction. All of the characters, organizations, and events portrayed in this novel are either products of the authors' imaginations or are used fictitiously.

A Tor Book
Published by Tom Doherty Associates
120 Broadway
New York, NY 10271

www.tor-forge.com

Tor® is a registered trademark of Macmillan Publishing Group, LLC.

The Library of Congress Cataloging-in-Publication Data is available upon request.

ISBN 978-1-250-16806-1 (hardcover)
ISBN 978-1-250-16805-4 (ebook)

Our books may be purchased in bulk for promotional, educational, or business use. Please contact your local bookseller or the Macmillan Corporate and Premium Sales Department at 1-800-221-7945, extension 5442, or by email at MacmillanSpecialMarkets@macmillan.com.

First published in Great Britain by HarperVoyager, an imprint of HarperCollins Publishers Ltd

First U.S. Edition: August 2019

Printed in the United States of America

0 9 8 7 6 5 4 3 2 1

Copyright Acknowledgements

to Jane Johnson

Voyager's own ace

who lured us all across the pond

A Flint Lies
in the Mud

by Kevin Andrew Murphy

September 15th, 1946

'AND THEN,' PADDY O'REILLY continued, whisky tumbler upraised, 'we thundered down the mountainside, clutching the canopy poles of our elephant's howdah, a hundred angry Kali cultists behind us, waving their knives and their crimson Thuggee sashes!'

'My darling Timothy Patrick Xavier,' the beautiful Chandra Ratri intoned in her Bengali lilt, 'there were no more than fifty,' she laid a delicate brown hand upon his freckled forearm, 'and half were from the temple of Ganesh.' Her fingers squeezed gently but firmly, flashing a diamond-encrusted wedding ring, 'and most were my relatives and *not*,' she shook her head, making the *maang tikka* pendant on her forehead sway, the pigeon's blood star ruby at its heart winking above her bindi, '*cultists*,' she added emphatically, pouting her coral-painted lips up at him from where she sat nestled in the silk damask loveseat.

'Forgive my Fenian poetics, my lotus,' Paddy gazed down, emerald eyes pleading, 'I meant "worshippers".' Paddy's name and colouring might be Irish, but his accent and demeanour were decidedly American.

Chandra turned away, her tawny topaz eyes flashing. 'I will consider it,' she pronounced, then took a sip of her cocktail, still unmollified.

Brigadier Kenneth Foxworthy sweltered in the armchair nearer the fireplace, puffing his pipe as he observed the couple with considerable amusement. They had retired to the far end of the Queen's Salon for post-prandials. Foxworthy wished he could remove his dress jacket, but it would be unbecoming of an officer of His Majesty's Army. Yet the O'Reillys' company was worth some discomfort: the Irish American animal trapper and the Bengali princess or priestess or some such were easily the two most engaging dining companions he'd found and a distraction Foxworthy desperately needed.

'We Bengalis do not forgive so easily,' Chandra chided Paddy, setting her cocktail on the coffee table. 'Nor forget. I am the elephant's daughter.' She smiled then, flashing teeth white as ivory. 'I will require a kiss.'

Paddy leaned down, paying his fine honourably, while Foxworthy hid his smile with another sip of excellent single malt. Then suddenly the whisky sloshed out of his glass and into his face as Paddy stumbled forward, barking his shins on the table. Chandra's highball glass tipped over and shattered, filling the air with the scent of cognac and champagne.

'Merciful Kali!' Chandra exclaimed. 'What was *that*?'

A purserette ran up and threw a bar towel over the mess. 'Nothing to worry about,' she reassured Chandra, 'just a patch of rough water. Another King's Ruin?'

'That, my lotus, was not "rough water",' Paddy told his bride as soon as the purserette left. 'That was trouble.'

Foxworthy agreed: the *Queen Mary* had slowed, suddenly and precipitously. And if they'd felt the lurch here in first class, the stable centre section, Foxworthy did not like to think how it had been felt in cabin class at the stern, let alone tourist class in the bow.

Foxworthy exchanged a glance with Paddy. The animal

trapper nodded curtly, saying, 'Brigadier, perhaps you might speak with the commodore while I check on my tigers?'

Foxworthy removed his pipe. 'You have tigers on board?'

'In the kennels,' Paddy explained. 'A pair for the Hyde Park Zoo, but young so I was able to reserve the St Bernard crates. Hyde Park New York, not London.'

'Ah,' said Foxworthy, 'last I saw tigers, I was a boy.' Well, living tigers. The bombing of Berlin's Tiergarten had been horrid. 'But a sound plan.' Foxworthy rose, looking up at the American. Paddy was a strapping fellow, standing half a head taller than him for all that Foxworthy stood an even six foot one. 'Reconvene here once we have our intelligence?'

Paddy nodded as Chandra rose. She was no delicate flower either, only appearing dainty in comparison to her husband. 'I shall remain. Gossip has five hundred tongues and a thousand eyes and the monkeys chatter most when they visit the watering hole.' She indicated the bar, her diamonds flashing. 'I will listen with the ears of Ganesh.'

'Very good.' Foxworthy puffed his pipe and left the honeymooners to their parting kiss while he went to see the commodore.

Foxworthy wondered what the trouble might be. The Atlantic, while not particularly calm now, was not notably rough either. He knew that just four years ago, in '42, the Queen Mary, in her zigzagging to evade Nazi U-boats, had hit one of her escort vessels, the Curacoa, slicing straight through. Over three hundred died that day, and all the Queen Mary had felt was a bump. He'd read the reports. And once, while transporting over sixteen thousand American soldiers from New York to England, she had been struck by a rogue wave so great she had almost capsized.

But that was *almost*. If she'd capsized, it would have been the greatest maritime disaster since the Titanic. It wasn't.

That dubious distinction was one Foxworthy was all too familiar with, to his everlasting shame. It had been only a year ago, in Lübeck. The day before, the British Army had taken the city without resistance. That day, in a show of force, the RAF sank three ships in the harbour.

In between the sinking of the first vessel and the second, one of Lübeck's citizens somehow made her way through the gauntlet of junior officers to beg him to stop the bombings. Her son, the woman had cried, was aboard the *Cap Arcona*. Foxworthy rebuffed her pleas: the *Cap Arcona* had not surrendered, and, like the *Queen Mary*, she had been a luxury liner. She could hold battalions. If she disgorged them, the battle for Lübeck would be bloody.

The woman swore only her son and a few other soldiers were aboard, but by the time she told him who else it held, it had been too late. He'd watched the bombs drop.

The *Cap Arcona* was no troop transport but a floating prison, packed with inmates from the concentration camps. The SS *Thielbek* as well. And the *Deutschland* was a hospital ship, her funnels painted white, a red cross on the side. Seven thousand innocents perished at British hands that day.

But the war was over, and the *Queen Mary* was not perilously overloaded with troops, just fully booked for the last days of summer with everyone from American soldiers returning home with British brides to the wealthy resuming their former pastime of taking the 'shuttle' to enjoy the splendours of New York. Which meant over two thousand passengers and one thousand crew at risk.

Foxworthy rounded through Piccadilly Circus, the nexus of luxury shops at the heart of first class, and took the stairs up to the bridge. He hoped he was overreacting, but six years of war bred a certain wariness. Men who relaxed ended up dead, often taking many others with them.

When he arrived at the bridge he found the door closed, but activity could be observed through the windows. Commodore Ford was talking animatedly, his great head looking down at one of the junior officers. Foxworthy was unable to get Ford's attention, or anyone else's for that matter, but it was bright inside and dark out and they were deeply engaged. He rapped sharply, then waited, puffing his pipe.

It had gone out.

He took out his lighter. It had been his father's, carried through the trenches of the Great War, adorned with Edward VII on one side, Britannia on the other, the lighter's sides formed from two pennies from almost half a century ago.

The flint wheel spun expertly beneath Foxworthy's thumb, steel striking stone, a cascade of sparks catching the wick alight. He clenched the amber bit, puffing until the tobacco caught and he was able to pull in a proper draw, savouring the taste of Ye Olde Signe, his favourite blend, a parting gift from his sweetheart, Alice. He wished he could taste her lips instead: Lady Alice Camden, with her chestnut-brown curls and cornflower-blue eyes, whom he would see again at the end of this deplorable journey, whom he could at last ask to be his wife . . .

Then another pair of blue eyes caught his and he snapped to attention.

'Good evening, Brigadier Foxworthy,' said the crewman. He was young, athletic, of medium height, with a public school accent and a peculiarly rich voice. 'Lieutenant Waters. I am afraid the bridge is off-limits to passengers at the moment. 'Commodore Ford—'

'—can speak for himself,' said Commodore Ford, patting the young lieutenant on the shoulder. 'That will be all, Waters.' Waters made his exit and the commodore took his place, looming in the doorframe. 'Brigadier Foxworthy, this is not the most opportune—'

'I've noticed,' Foxworthy said. 'How may I be of assistance?'

Commodore Ford stared down at him. 'Help prevent a panic. We don't want wild rumours circulating.' The commodore glanced around, then said in a low tone, 'The port of New York is closed. Reports as to why are confused to say the least. We may need to divert to Baltimore, but for now we're idling the engines.'

'Confused in what way?'

'You wouldn't believe me if I told you.' He waved a large hand as if he were shooing invisible flies. 'Reports of a bomb but then that the dropping of the bomb had been prevented. A small aircraft colliding with a weather balloon. And some mention of Jetboy.'

'Robert Tomlinson?' Foxworthy asked. 'The boy pilot? Wasn't he found last month on a desert isle having tea with Amelia Earhart?'

'I hadn't heard about Earhart.'

'It was in the *Daily Mail* so take that with a grain of salt.'

The commodore rubbed his temple. 'I feel positively brined at the moment.'

Foxworthy took a puff on his pipe, the meerschaum carved with the face of Charlemagne or some other ancient king (though it might be Hades for all he knew). 'So what should we let people know?'

'Just say that there's a spot of trouble with the propellers. Nothing to worry about, just disengaging the engines while we run some tests. Gives us time to sort out the radio reports.'

'Very good.'

'We'll get things sorted out straight away, I have no doubt. I appreciate your discretion, Foxworthy. And please, be my guest for tea tomorrow at the Veranda Grill. You and the charming Mr and Mrs O'Reilly.'

'I would be honoured.' Foxworthy gave a small salute.

'Thank you, Brigadier.' Ford shut the door and went back to talking with the bridge crew. From the quantity of gold braid present, Foxworthy could see that he had assembled his entire staff: the staff captain, the chief officer, the chief engineer and two more engineers below him, the purser, the chief steward, even the ship's doctor and surgeon.

♣

Back in the Queen's Salon, the band was playing 'Begin the Beguine'. Purserettes circulated with trays of canapés, oysters *à la Russe* and the like. Foxworthy accepted one, ordered a fresh Scotch, and reclaimed his former seat by the fireplace, below the huge gesso frieze over the mantel. It depicted two unicorns engaged in mortal combat, one adorned with gold leaf, the other with bright silver, done in the deco style still popular when the *Queen Mary* had first been launched ten years ago.

He did not see Paddy, but spied Chandra, chatting with a bevy of society ladies before excusing herself and retaking her place on the loveseat. 'That was very interesting,' she remarked. 'One of them overheard the maids saying some criminal had released a gas over Manhattan that's causing mass hallucinations!'

'How would a maid know that?'

'Her husband works in the radio room.'

'Hallucinogenic gas?' Foxworthy shook his head. Probably something cooked up by IG Farben. He imagined Nazi sleeper agents waking around the globe, committing unthinkable acts to avenge the loss of their Führer.

Chandra sipped another King's Ruin. 'Did you learn anything from the commodore?'

'Nothing so lurid,' Foxworthy admitted honestly, 'but he asked me to quell any wild rumours to prevent panic.'

Chandra nodded. 'Hallucinations are how *rakshasas* play their tricks.'

'Rakshasas?' Foxworthy repeated.

'Tiger demons,' Chandra explained. 'They weave their deceptions from *maya*, the flames of illusion.'

'Ah.' Foxworthy sipped his Scotch, considering. As entertaining as Paddy's wild adventure tales were, he couldn't wholly believe them, for despite Paddy and Chandra's gay banter, there was no way they'd escaped the ghastliness of the past few years. War had not been limited to Europe. The Japanese had invaded Burma, and between the refugees, the famine in Bengal, and the policies of the Raj, he had it on good authority that three million had perished in the region.

Three million. It was not six million, but there was a certain level of atrocity that the human intellect might comprehend, but the heart never could. It just became meaningless rows of figures, beads clicking on Death's black abacus, the brutal calculus of war.

'Did the famine completely pass you by?' Foxworthy asked bluntly, for there was no delicate way to put it.

'Of course not.' Chandra's topaz eyes turned sad. 'But famine is no stranger to Bengal. One wishes to speak of babies born, not children buried, weddings, not funerals. I am a priestess of Kali, and I have seen more than my share of death.' She smiled defiantly and took a sip of her cocktail. 'My father thought Paddy was a rakshasa, with his tall tales and flaming hair, but I do not care if he is. Not all rakshasas are wicked, not all lies are unjust, and Paddy smuggled rice upriver to our village, saving it.' She took another sip. 'We had a *fabulous* wedding feast.'

'And then?' Foxworthy asked.

'Oh, it is much as he told you.'

'Your elephant went storming down the mountain pursued by the combined worshippers of the temples of Kali and Ganesh, who are also Paddy's in-laws?'

'I am a high priestess, forbidden to leave the temple complex. I was abducted like Sita.'

'You eloped.'

'That would be sacrilege.' Chandra glanced around, taking a nervous sip of her cocktail. 'I hope Paddy is not having trouble with the tigers . . .' Her tawny eyes turned to Foxworthy, settling on the Crown and Bath stars on his epaulette as she raised a raven eyebrow. 'So, what takes you to America, Brigadier Foxworthy?'

Foxworthy exhaled smoke, felt it burning against the Scotch, and rasped, 'Just meeting some colleagues in Washington.'

He sighed. 'Plus I promised myself I would see New York, maybe find a betrothal gift for Alice, my intended. She's in London.'

'Were you raised in London?' asked Chandra.

'No, Aldworth. Tiny village in Berkshire. Doubt you've heard of it. Nothing noteworthy, but for a fair quantity of elf shot. Legend says it was shot by the pixies. But in truth, it's just Neolithic flint arrowheads. Had quite a collection as a boy.' He gave Chandra a wry smile. 'Never met an elf, though. Though there is a statue of a dwarf at the church. And of course the giants.'

'Real giants? Paddy hopes to catch a yeti one day, but Aldworth has real giants?'

'In the fourteenth century. Now they're all stone like the dwarf.'

'Like Scandinavian trolls?' asked Chandra. 'Did they come with the Vikings?'

'Close,' Foxworthy laughed, 'the De la Beche family came with the Normans. Philip was seven feet tall and served as valet to Edward II along with a dwarf. Their statues are in the church, along with the stone effigies of Philip's giant sons, each of them bigger than the last: John Long, John Strong, John Never Afraid, and John Ever Afraid, the biggest of them all.'

'Why was he afraid if he was so big?'

'Because,' Foxworthy related softly, 'it costs a lot to feed and clothe a giant, so he made a deal with the Devil for worldly wealth, with a stipulation in his contract that when he was laid to rest, the Devil could come for his soul, whether he was laid inside a church or out.' Foxworthy blew a smoke ring. 'So John Ever Afraid arranged to be buried *in the wall of the church.*' He blew another smoke ring. 'But in Cromwell's time, some Roundheads decided the Aldworth Giants were pagan idols so smashed them all – except for John Ever Afraid, who they took as a trophy to Cromwell himself. When they stopped to rest and set the statue down, the Devil appeared, for the wording of John's contract had finally been fulfilled. He'd been laid to rest outside a church. The Devil took John Ever Afraid to Hell – and the Roundheads with him!'

'*Sláinte!*' roared a voice behind him. 'Another round for the *shanachie!*' Paddy joined Chandra on the loveseat, giving her a kiss. 'So, what's the news?'

Chandra shared the fruit of the gossip tree, then Foxworthy related what he'd been told by Commodore Ford, both the official story and the few details he'd been allowed.

'Jetboy?' Paddy guffawed. 'Oh, that's rich. Heard that too, down by the engine room. This poor ugly mug named Harry said he'd heard whispers about a plague that turns people into monsters. Germ warfare from the Nazis.'

◆

The Veranda Grill was the *Queen Mary*'s most exclusive club, situated in the stern on the sun deck – usually only open to first-class passengers with a months-long waiting list, but this day was unscheduled and Commodore Ford could admit whomever he liked. Today his guests included Foxworthy, Paddy and Chandra, and the Fisher family of the Fisher Family Theatricals, hailing from Cheapside and consisting of Francis Fisher, his wife, Edwina, and seven children, ranging from the younger Francis, the eldest at twenty-four, to Bertram, the youngest, at ten. In between were Muriel, Alfred, Colin, Jillian, and Robert.

A grand table had been set up before a colourful mural depicting circus performers: dancers and acrobats, harlequins and clowns, an animal tamer with a tiger and a black panther jumping through his hoop, a green-faced witch with her pointed hat and wand and a Caribbean sorceress tossing a cockerel into the air, a grey-faced fakir and a pantomime horse, an African serpent charmer dancing with her boa, a statuesque ringmistress marching in high-heeled boots bearing a beadle's ceremonial staff as her swagger stick, and Marie Antoinette herself fluttering an ostrich-plume fan, a mouse peeping out of one side of her wig.

The Fisher family had taken to this naturally, dressed in their theatrical finest, with Chandra and Paddy seated at the far end of the table near the animal trainer and his leaping leopard, while Foxworthy was seated beside Ford at the head of the table near Marie Antoinette, next to Mr and Mrs Fisher, and opposite Lady Ermengarde Arkwright, the dowager of something or other. She was old enough to dictate her own fashion, wearing one of those stoles so popular in the twenties composed of at least a dozen ermines, heads, tails, and all, their beady little eyes replaced with beads of jet.

It was a fine day, broken only by a transitory patter of sea mist or light rain from a passing cloud, but Commodore Ford looked anything but happy. 'Brigadier, if you thought last night was madness, you would not believe the insanity coming over the radio today,' he confided to Foxworthy in a hoarse whisper as they were being seated.

'So what are you going to do?'

'I've informed the crew, of course. We don't need to tell the passengers anything other than it's a spot of engine trouble. Extra caviar and champagne does wonders, and for those who find those insufficient, discounts on future trips. But we'll still need to keep pootling about until the New Yorkers come to their senses and open the port.'

Lady Arkwright, oblivious to the captain's mood, was nattering on to Chandra, Paddy, and the Fishers. 'I was on the maiden voyage of the *Queen Mary*, you know. Hard to get tickets, but you can always weasel something if you know the right people. And oh, don't those look lovely!' her ladyship exclaimed, as the waiter set an ornate silver epergne on the table, its trays laden with strawberries, cream puffs, jam tarts and fairy trifles topped with gooseberries.

Mrs Fisher, seated beside him, screamed.

'Francis!' she cried. '*Francis!*' Referring not to her husband, but her son. Young Francis Fisher was dressed in his army uniform, a proud young Tommy just returned from the war, and had been in the action of reaching for one of the trifles on the epergne when his hand touched the silver. That hand was now silver as well, shining like a mailed gauntlet. The Brigadier thought for a moment that the man had suffered an injury during the war and was using a costly prosthetic, when he looked at Francis's face and saw that his face was silver too, every eyelash and feather of hair perfectly sculpted, like the Silver Swan of Barnard Castle. But unlike the famous automaton, Francis sat frozen and unmoving, lifeless as a silver statue.

Then Lady Arkwright screamed as well, her false teeth falling from her mouth, forced out by the sharp fangs of a mustelid. Her eyes turned jet black and the wreath of dead winter weasels about her throat came to life, screaming as one, waving their tiny claws as they writhed to escape but could not, fused to her like the tangled tails of a rat king or, perhaps, ermine queen, savaging her ladyship's own clawed hands as she reached up to touch them.

Mrs Fisher fainted dead away or fell dead, Foxworthy was not sure which, slumping to the floor, while her husband began to choke, gooseberry-green froth bubbling from his mouth. The froth coming from Commodore Ford's mouth, however, was red, the colour of blood that Foxworthy was all too familiar with. Then blood began to issue from his ears and his eyes, pouring from his nose.

The waiter standing nearby, poised in shock with a jug of iced tea in one hand, suddenly turned as thin and translucent as a saint's icon from a stained glass window, then fell backwards and shattered, the tinkling of broken glass muffled by a sound in the distance like a bomb going off. Then a great wall of water slammed into the restaurant, gushing through

the windows and doors as the customers continued to transform and die, to writhe and change, or stand or sit stricken
with horror, still human for the moment.

The wave subsided, only the edge having reached the table
at the back of the restaurant, and Foxworthy stood up as Mr
Fisher dissolved into green sludge stinking with the anise reek
of absinthe. Paddy was standing and Chandra as well, staring
at the horror that had replaced Robert Fisher. The thing still
wore the tatters of the boy's clothes, but his body had become
that of an ape with a dozen arms and a gorilla's face. Hairy
tarantulas with twice as many legs as they should have began
crawling from the gorilla-shaped husk.

Of the remaining children, Jillian still sat in her chair, her
mouth agape with horror, while little Bertram had fallen dead
like his mother. Muriel lay on the floor, twitching and writhing,
caught in the throes of death or transformation, while Alfred
and Colin, one fair, the other dark, had drawn together in
fright, fused into one being, but not one that could live.

Chandra held up her hand, blood pouring from her finger
around her wedding band as she cried, 'Aiyee! It is the curse
of Kali!' But it seemed, in fact, the curse of Ganesh, for her
delicate hands were puffing up and swelling, turning grey and
growing larger until they resembled the stumpy legs of a baby
elephant, the left one cruelly scarred and weeping from where
her wedding band remained embedded. Her face retained some
semblance of its former self, but the whole of it was covered
with rough grey hide, the setting of her maang tikka pendant
fused with her flesh, its ruby star winking on her forehead.

Paddy struggled to support her as she wept with pain. He
remained unchanged, as did Jillian. 'Help your family,'
Foxworthy ordered her. She was only thirteen and a girl, but
there'd been younger soldiers before, that damnable Jetboy at
twelve, and Jillian Fisher had lived through the Blitz. 'Remain
here. I'm going to check outside.'

Outside, chaos reigned. A puddle of blood slicked the deck,

spilling from a skeleton in a woman's coat and mixing with seawater. People lay writhing and contorting into things that were not people or not alive and mainly both, twisted corpses strewn everywhere, but Foxworthy's attention was drawn to the starboard bow where those passengers and crewmen who remained alive and human, for the moment, had gathered.

The rogue wave that had slammed into the Veranda Grill had swept many overboard, not all of them dead or dying of whatever evil had overtaken the *Queen Mary*, but all of them surely drowning in the Atlantic if they did not get aid. All except one, for the wave was still there, but frozen like aspic or some fanciful moulded jelly as big as an iceberg and shaped like the head of Neptune, his kingly beard trailing off into streamers of froth and foam, his eyes twin vortices of phosphorescent sea fire.

Yet in the blue of those giant watery eyes, Foxworthy thought he recognized the young officer he'd encountered on the bridge the night before, Lieutenant Waters. As King Neptune gazed down upon the human and inhuman flotsam he'd created, two smaller waves, their crests curling like fingertips, swept passengers and corpses back towards the ship.

Both passengers and crew were tossing lifebelts over the side, lowering lifeboats, some dying as they did so, but apart from the nightmare transformations, it was a dance Foxworthy knew from the battlefield. Blind panic transmuted to the stone-cold certainty of doing what needed to be done. 'Someone get a rope!' Foxworthy cried, but the seas were too rough, the passengers slamming fatally against the side of the ship except when Neptune or Waters, or whomever the watery monster was, pushed people away.

Then a miracle occurred.

A blond crewman stood at the railing, stretching his arm out and crying vainly for some figure floating towards the horizon. 'James!' he cried and 'James!' again and a third time '*James!*' But then his arms stretched out, further and further, extending like twin telescopes until his hands reached his friend, the farthest of those being swept out to sea, and grabbed the drowning man by the collar as he bobbed and gasped for air.

The crewman pulled back, his torso telescoping as well, spiring taller and taller like a ship's mast until it towered over the smokestacks of the *Queen Mary* herself, his back braced against the wall of the promenade, his feet against the railing, as he hauled the drowning man onto the deck. James coughed up water, but did so quickly, seeing as he had three heads. But he was alive, which was what counted, and his saviour, the telescoping crewman, had done his duty and gone on to pluck others from the waves.

Foxworthy found his hands drawing out his pipe on habit, for he felt a desperate craving for a smoke, to calm his nerves and allow him to think. The danger looked ever so slightly more under control, but the madness still unexplained, and at this point he didn't care if the face on his pipe *were* Hades. He shoved the king's crown full of tobacco, and then, with trembling hands, took out his father's lighter. His fingers, usually so adept, fumbled at the flint wheel, and his father's lighter, carried through two wars, slipped from his fingers and skittered across the deck, tails up, Britannia with her trident and shield spinning anticlockwise, an ill omen if ever there was one, then disappeared over the railing.

Foxworthy almost swore, but a gentleman never swore, especially a middle-class boy desperately working for promotion. Nor did one flash a two-finger salute, no matter how much he might like. And so he did as he had trained himself to do, holding his wilful fingertips back with his thumbnail, forcing his fury and rage, his hurt and horror, into a painful but secret gesture of regret and consternation.

There came a *snap!* as his rebellious fingers broke free.

It stung and it felt as if he'd cracked his thumbnail, but then he looked. His nail had become as grey as the flints he'd hunted as a boy, his thumb as well, and from the tip, in the place of blood, oozed a tarry black substance like bitumen. But it was burning, with a literal flame. And Foxworthy still desperately wanted that smoke.

Not questioning the nightmare logic of it all, he held his thumb to his pipe, drawing the flame until the tobacco caught, then sucking in. He was pulling too fast, the smoke scorching hot, but the fire soothed his lungs and it was, in fact, what he needed. Foxworthy examined his thumb, which was still burning like an oil lamp. He snuffed it out against his jacket. It extinguished like any ordinary flame, leaving a scorch on the wool, but he was more concerned for his thumb. The bituminous blood scabbed over, hard and black on the grey stone, but though the greyness had spread down his thumb and was progressing to his palm, his thumb was still flexible.

He turned to the three-headed crewman who had got to his feet and was exchanging glances with himself in a shell-shocked daze. 'You, sailor,' he barked, 'James, is it?'

There was an instinctive posture to a trained military man when he heard a commanding officer's voice, no matter the branch of service. 'Yes, sir!' the three-headed man cried from all three of his mouths, saluting, his hand only raised to his rightmost head upon his ridiculously broad shoulders, his uniform rent asunder.

'I'm a brigadier in His Majesty's Army, and I'm taking this as an act of war and declaring martial law. So, name and rank?'

'Seaman Gully, sir!'

'Commodore Ford is dead. Who is the next ranking officer?'

James Gully's heads swivelled, looking in all directions. 'Maybe Eddy?' said the leftmost, pointing out to the watery bulk of Neptune. 'Lieutenant Waters,' the right corrected him. Then the middle head, still wearing his sailor's cap with the CUNARD band, said, 'All the officers save the Commodore were on the bridge, sir. We were all swept overboard.'

'Then barring any new information to the contrary, I'm declaring myself captain of this vessel. Is anyone manning the bridge?'

All three of Gully's heads looked in unison, then all of them shook. 'No, sir. But Commodore Ford set us on autopilot. Our course is set on a very slow circle in order to conserve fuel.'

'We'll need to loop back faster to sweep for survivors.'

'Should we radio for assistance?' asked Gully's left head.

'Good God, man, no!' Foxworthy cried. 'I don't know whether this was caused by Nazi gas, an alien plague, or Madame Blavatsky going to Atlantis to reopen Pandora's box with the Thule Society, but we dare not expose other ships. Just go find any men fit to helm the bridge, and when you have enough, loop back.'

'Aye aye, Captain . . .' the three-headed man trailed off, staring.

'What is it?' Foxworthy had seen soldiers tongue-tied with shock before, but never one with three tongues who still couldn't spit out what he was trying to say. 'Out with it, man!' Foxworthy snapped his fingers impatiently then watched as sparks flew and a chip of stone broke off his thumb, flying off like a flake of Neolithic elf shot, but burning with fire as it lodged itself in the woodwork five feet away.

He then saw what all three of James's heads were staring at: his whole hand had turned to stone, not just his thumb, like a sculpture expertly flaked from flint, still betraying the sharp edges and tiny traces and ripples left by flint knapping. 'It's flint . . .' Foxworthy realized.

'Aye aye, Captain Flint!'

Foxworthy saw no reason to correct the three-headed sailor. 'To your work, seaman,' he whispered and stalked off, hoping Paddy was still alive. The animal trapper was a resourceful fellow and more importantly, not yet dead.

Paddy was not in the Veranda Grill, so Foxworthy headed for the purser's desk. On the carpet before it lay a gigantic speckled egg, big enough to hold a man. The desk itself lay abandoned save for the corpses of bellboys and one thing that resembled an enormous nudibranch, its colourful frills and tentacles lying limp, its mouth gasping where it had struggled out of the skirt and stockings of a purserette's uniform. 'I'm sorry,' Foxworthy told her softly, but when the thing extended a plaintive but poisonous-looking fluorescent-orange-spotted violet tentacle, he snatched the guest book and retreated.

Paddy and Chandra had taken the Windsor Suite. Foxworthy's new hand at least worked for knocking. Paddy opened the door, looking sick with worry but still human.

Foxworthy held up his hand. 'Yes, it's happening to me too.'

Chandra lay on the bed. Her shapely brown feet that only yesterday had been learning the foxtrot, today were the ungainly grey feet of an elephant. 'The curse of Ganesh has touched you as well . . .' she sobbed.

'Yes,' Foxworthy agreed, 'but my hand is not elephant hide but flint.'

'Then it must be the curse of Kali.' She held up her left arm with its elephant foot, the wound weeping from where her wedding band had cut through warped flesh and bone. 'The Divine Mother's wrath has cursed New York and now struck us here!'

'Chandra, if we do not take control of this ship, we will be doomed. I need you to lend me Paddy.'

'Don't I get a say in the matter?' Paddy asked.

'Not if you want to save your wife's life and yours into the bargain.'

There was a silence broken by Chandra. 'He is right, Paddy. Go help him.'

Paddy nodded, then bent to kiss Chandra until she finally pushed him away with her elephant feet. 'Go, my darling. Go. Save us both.'

Paddy nodded and ducked out of the cabin. Foxworthy

followed, not ducking but feeling the doorframe was nearer. In the hallway he asked, 'Am I taller?'

Paddy glanced at him. 'Maybe, but I think you have bigger problems. The stone's spread to your neck.'

Foxworthy felt with his still-human left hand, finding that what Paddy said was the truth. 'Bugger,' he swore. He shook his head then led the way onwards. His right eye burned and then his left as the petrification swept over them, but his vision sharpened to crystal clarity so he didn't complain. They made their way back to the bridge past vistas of surreal horror, worse than anything he'd seen in the death camps save in their sheer multitude.

The only sight that truly disturbed Foxworthy beyond what he'd already seen was what he glimpsed in the first class children's playroom. There, among the twisted bodies, stood a pretty rocking horse with a real horsehair mane and tail, but rocking by itself, with no child riding it. But then he realized the rocking horse was looking at him with a child's brown eyes, pleading, weeping, rocking faster and faster as it tried to follow them but could not because its horse's hooves were fused to curved runners bent from human bone.

By the time they were back at the bridge, the petrification had become complete and Foxworthy not only stood taller than Paddy, but his knife-edged flint feet had cut themselves free of his shoes and his uniform was ripped at the seams.

Gully, the three-headed midshipman, snapped a salute. 'Captain Flint!'

'*At ease,*' Foxworthy said . . . or tried to say. His voice was gone, and only a stony whisper escaped his lips. He looked down at the motley crew that Gully had assembled. Well, looked down on all but one. Gully's rescuer was there, his torso still three feet longer than it should be, with his left arm hanging down to his knees and his right arm hanging to the ground. His head was identical to James's three. The two were identical twins . . . or at least had been until this afternoon, and quite young. '*Brothers?*' Foxworthy assumed, his voice hoarse and whispery.

James Gully pointed his thumb up at his telescoped former twin and his side heads nodded while his central head said, 'Yes, sir. That's John.'

Foxworthy surveyed the rest of his men. Along with the twins were four other crewmen and two gentlemen from first class. One of the first class gentlemen had skin and hair striped vibrantly blue and gold like a tropical fish while the other appeared untouched. Suffering the opposite horror to James but still having his shirt ripped open, one of the crewmen had no head but a giant face upon his chest, exactly like one of the monstrous men found in foreign lands in medieval manuscripts but never seen until now.

The other three crewmen appeared fully human, and in fact, the mechanic in the grease-stained overalls was almost impossibly handsome, tall, with Grecian features, wavy golden hair, and a figure so finely sculpted that it made even a mechanic's rags look fashionable.

'Ugly Harry?' asked Paddy. The Adonis nodded sadly. 'Damn,' Paddy swore, 'at least someone found a prize in the bottom of Pandora's Cracker Jacks.'

'You don't understand.' Handsome Harry had a gorgeous voice but a thick Cockney accent. 'I'll never find a woman who'll want me. My face may look nice now, but I'm a freak. My navel's disappeared. I ain't got no nipples neither.'

'You'll find women who can overlook those flaws,' Paddy reassured him.

'No,' Harry moaned wretchedly, 'I'm sexless as a doll!'

'*Considering the alternatives, you are still very lucky,*' Foxworthy told him, '*but let us compare horror stories when we are not in danger of dying.*' He glanced at John Gully. '*Has everyone been rescued who went overboard?*'

'Yes, sir.' John Gully sounded exactly like his brother James.

'*Who's tending to the wounded? Has the ship's doctor survived?*'

'The doctor and the surgeon are both dead, but a couple of the nurses are fine, for now, sir,' John Gully reported. 'They're tending to the victims.'

'Some on the wireless said it's an alien plague,' his brother's leftmost head told him, then the right one added, 'It's all over New York.'

'Sir,' added the middle head.

Foxworthy exchanged a glance with Paddy, but everything that could be said in their defence did not change the fact that they'd been wrong. *'What's the chance it's a Nazi gas?'* he asked. *'Do we have someone on the radio to find out?'*

'Everyone in the radio room's dead, sir. It's like the Blitz.'

'My family survived the Blitz, but they didn't survive this,' said a girl's voice as Jillian Fisher stepped onto the bridge. 'Bertie just died. Muriel too. Mama died at the start.'

'All of them, Jillian?' asked Paddy.

'All of them, Mr O'Reilly,' said the girl. 'There are horrid spiders that used to be parts of Robert, but they're just spiders. Frankie's a statue, but not alive.' She glanced up. 'Brigadier Foxworthy?'

'That's Captain Flint,' James corrected, but Foxworthy nodded and said, *'Yes.'*

'What do I do now?'

'Go and help the nurses. I've no time to play nursemaid and we need to get the radio working.'

'I'm clever with mechanical things,' she offered. 'I've taken apart a crystal set.'

'I could do with some help,' Handsome Harry admitted.

'Then you have your assignment,' he told her, then asked John Gully, *'Do we have enough fuel to return to England?'*

The rightmost head checked a gauge. 'Barely, sir,' he reported, 'but we could make it with the currents.'

'Then let's do so,' Foxworthy commanded. *'This is Mr O'Reilly. I'm deputizing him as my second-in-command. I feel an urgent*

need to sleep, and if I do not return in the morning, he is your captain.'

'Aye aye, Captain Flint!'

♠

When Foxworthy woke, he found his grey legs dangling off the bed that he'd broken. When he stood up, he was hunched over against the ceiling, like Philip de la Beche crammed into his crypt. He stood over seven feet, if not closer to eight. His uniform lay shredded.

He was also craving Scotch, and saw no reason to deny himself given the circumstances. He tore open his steamer chest. The bottle of Glen Grant Alice had slipped him as a parting gift tasted like nectar and he drained it. Then he realized he'd bitten off the bottleneck too. But the shards didn't cut his mouth, only felt like a mouthful of boiled sweets, but tasting savoury, like lobster lozenges as they melted.

Foxworthy regarded the broken bottle with horror, but still swallowed. Then he belched, a small gout of fire shooting out of his mouth like a dragon. Or a demon. Or John Ever Afraid returned from Hell.

He glanced at the dresser mirror. His face still looked like his face, if larger, but sharper, more chiselled, as if a brutalist artist had hewn his portrait from solid flint, down to the waves of his hair. His eyes, always deep-set, were now pits to the fires of Hell, flames dancing in their recesses. But when he rubbed them in horror, he found he still blinked, and that his eyeballs were now made of some transparent mineral, like isinglass in the windows of a stove.

His teeth were like diamonds as he took another bite of the delicious bottle. Then he stopped himself. '*Oh Alice,*' he whispered, '*what will you think of me?*' He flung the bottle away, glass smashing against the panelling. Then he gritted his teeth,

worked out the plague part because his tigers weren't touched. The Americans are calling it the Wild Card Virus.'

'*Wild Card?*'

'From poker,' she explained. 'You call a card wild and it can be anything, and you make a virus wild and it can be anything too, from the sniffles to turning a man into King Neptune. Nine times out of ten it kills you, and of those who survive, nine out of ten are turned into something horrid.' She grimaced. 'No offence.'

'The lucky ones get something good, even if it's not what they wanted.' John gestured, extending his forearm by three feet.

'*Then why are you afraid you're going to die?*' Foxworthy asked Jillian.

'Mr Philips changed when he heard the news from New York,' John said, pulling his arm back in and shuddering. 'We all thought he'd been spared.'

'*I'm sorry.*' Foxworthy's heart felt as heavy and black as the stone it undoubtedly was. '*How far are we from England?*'

Gully squinted out of the window, his neck extending several inches. 'Not far at all, Captain Flint. We won't win the Blue Riband for passage west, but we should break the speed record east at least from where we were.' His neck went back to its proper length while his legs extended, keeping his head at the same level, and Foxworthy saw the grey irises of the boy's eyes whirl like spyglass lenses. 'The *Queen Mary* never had King Neptune to help with the crossing before. We should be in Southampton in a few hours.'

'We've radioed ahead,' Jillian said. 'They want us to anchor offshore for quarantine. When they're sure it's safe, they'll send doctors, maybe take us to London Hospital.'

Which was hours by train. Foxworthy felt an awful premonition in his stony heart, made worse by the fact that he had seen this story before: Three ships had gone down in Lübeck's harbour, seven thousand lives lost.

All the ritual phrases had been said: *errors were made, an unforeseeable tragedy, a sad, sad day, etc.* Hands that were wrung in one instant had been washed the next.

It wouldn't be an RAF bomber. Too blatant. Maybe a stray mine, something that could be denied. Or a torpedo from a captured U-boat. The Nazis had been trying to sink the *Queens* for years, but they were too fast. But anchored off Southampton for an indefinite time? The *Queen Mary* would be a very large sitting duck, and to abuse the bird metaphor further, it would kill two birds with one stone to sink the plague ship and blame the deed on Nazis who'd flown south to Argentina.

Churchill would have done it quickly. Attlee? It might take a few more days, but Foxworthy knew what foul deeds could be contemplated then ordered for sake of security and safety. He felt a stone-cold certainty now. '*That will not be happening,*' he decreed. '*We will go straight to London, closer to the hospital.*'

'Why?' asked Jillian. 'They were very clear.'

He told them, glad for the moment for his new whispery voice. They were appalled, but not disbelieving. They'd been through the war themselves.

'Where do we go, sir?' asked Gully.

'*The further in, the better. The Isle of Dogs if we can make it. We can be quarantined, but in London, they dare not sink us. They won't risk plague victims fleeing into the city.*' He glanced to John. '*Our King Neptune – can he talk?*'

'No,' said Gully, 'but Lieutenant Waters taught me semaphore.'

'*Good. Then let us break that record. To London.*'

♣

The Thames flooded its highest since 1928. Ships fled the *Queen Mary*, but those vessels too slow to avoid the onrushing ocean liner found the watery enormity of Lieutenant Edward Waters rising up, but with longer, wilder, literally flowing hair and whiskers, not King Neptune but Father Thames as depicted by Gustav Doré. The crowned titan pushed the ships out of the way with a far more defined set of translucent hands.

Around the bends they went, past Canvey Island and Cliffe Pools, past Gravesend and Grays, past Purfleet and the Dartford Marshes, past Erith, then around the bend to the Isle of Dogs, straight to the infamously noisy bascule bridge miraculously spared by the war. Father Thames reached into his river and pulled out a geyser shaped like a trident, sweeping cars off the bridge and down Manchester Road each way, like a croupier clearing chips off a gambling table.

The drawbridge began to rise, groaning mightily, but it soon became clear that the bridge's aperture was far smaller than the *Queen Mary*'s beam. Her draught, however, was narrower. Father Thames dropped his trident back into his river where it dissolved into bubbles and put his watery arms under the *Queen Mary* and lifted, sloshing right, like a man attempting to manoeuvre an awkward parcel through a narrow gate. He himself stepped through the north end of the bridge, a giant man-shaped wave crashing over it in slow motion, then set the *Queen Mary* down on the other side.

The ship washed into the lock leading to the West India Docks, everyone aboard clutching the railings. Sparks flew from Foxworthy's fingers as he gripped the rolled steel joist beside his head, then he ducked down to see out of the window. Lieutenant Waters stood, tottering, thigh-deep in the river, fluid leaking from his sides where the bridge had passed through him, not so much a wave passing over a rock as a hot knife cutting through gelatine. With a look of distress in his swirling blue eyes, he dissolved into water. Foxworthy braced himself as the wave slammed into them.

Sparks flew, people screamed. 'Aiyeee!' wailed Chandra from her wheelchair, Paddy behind her, bracing it. 'O wise Varuna, Ruler of all the Waters, do not let your most blessed and faithful servant perish!' She raised her elephantine stumps in praise. 'I have failed in my duties to Ganesh and Kali, and for that I accept my rightful punishment, but heal him! Lend him your strength! His name is your name! His fame is your fame! May the Waters heal and be praised!'

Tears flowed down her cheeks, staining the elephant hide of her once-beautiful face, while Paddy laid a comforting still-human hand on her shoulder.

Jillian Fisher was also crying, but not so much as the Gully twins, bawling from all four heads, and Handsome Harry and the headless crewman whom Foxworthy had never learned the name of had anguished expressions on their handsome and horrible faces.

Foxworthy stood like a stone. This was not the first time he'd seen a brave man die, nor, he feared, would it be the last. But then the waters of the West India Docks' outer lock began to boil and bubble like something out of Shakespeare's plays.

'Praise Varuna!' Chandra cried, waving her stumps to the Thames. 'Praise the blessed Waters!'

A wave rose up, frozen like the tip of an iceberg, then two more on each side and two again, the tines of Father Thames's crown as Lieutenant Waters rose up even larger than all his previous manifestations, a watery titan swelling with the inrushing tide into an aqueous colossus.

He lifted the *Queen Mary*, like a child picking up a large toy boat, and stepped over the lock to the main pool of the West India Docks, waded a few paces as he drew in more water, growing even larger, then stepped over the Marsh Wall and the sluice gate shattered in the Blitz, stepping into the upper elbow of the Millwall Outer Dock. As if he were picking his way through tidepools, he manoeuvred carefully to the larger lower elbow, now half-drained, and sat down in the rectangular pool as if it were a royal bath, holding the *Queen Mary* steady as if it were his favourite bath-toy. He glanced over his shoulder to the west, to where the old channel to the Thames had been filled in twenty years ago, the ground now pocked with bomb craters. He gave a jerk of his head and the waters of the Thames flooded over the lip, refilling the pool around them. Lieutenant Waters leaned back, the cataract of water erasing the war's scars, his whiskers flowing with the incoming tide. His left hand pushed the *Queen Mary* drifting gently towards the South Dock. Then he waved and slid into the pool, disappearing into the water he was.

A great cheer came from the port bow. Foxworthy followed as everyone rushed there, seeing a crowd of dockers, waving and tossing their hats in the air, then one of them taking to the air himself, screaming as he drifted away on a light southerly breeze like a child's lost balloon. Another screamed, sinking into the dock as if the wood were quicksand, then a third fell forward, his head breaking off, bowling across the planks as it changed into a coconut and dropped into the water, more coconuts rolling out of his clothes.

The remaining dockers ran away, most still on two legs.

◆

Foxworthy dozed unpleasantly, but that was nothing compared to the past week: the *Queen Mary* had docked, the crew lifted down by Lookout to secure her anchor chains, but they had remained for quarantine, especially once Jillian had restored her radio repairs and given the authorities a load of codswallop about fears of a hull breach which is why they had come to London rather than anchoring off Southampton.

That a thirteen-year-old girl raised by theatricals could lie like an army requisitions officer should not have come as a surprise.

Foxworthy affirmed Jillian's false story, then left it to her and Paddy, equally skilled in confabulation, since the radio room was cramped for his new stature and his whispery voice made him hard to understand. He'd then gone outside to smoke, one of the few things that still gave him pleasure or, it seemed, nourishment.

Over that week, he'd sneaked a few nips of Scotch and swallowed a shot glass, but even once he'd succumbed to his monstrous appetites for alcohol and glassware, it was like trying to survive on sugar water and crisps. The contents of the on-board tobacconist only sustained him by chain-smoking.

Other virus victims were starving as well. Lady Arkwright could pretend her tastes had not changed while letting her lei of ravenous ermines gorge themselves on steak *tartare*, but others were not so fortunate. Foxworthy saw a woman with flowers rooted in her hair swear she would die if she could not go to Kew Gardens. They had prevented her, then watched as she fainted, withering like a cut tulip in the sun.

More victims joined them – dockers they'd infected and soldiers who'd strayed too close to the quarantined Isle of Dogs. Others came from across the city, sent with food, medicine, and promises that doctors would come once they knew how to sanitize the alien spores.

Foxworthy had retired early, still hungry, but mainly cold. He had drifted into a dreamless sleep, but he was awake now.

He heard voices somewhere, one of them a woman's, familiar. Alice? No, not Alice. He tried to open his eyes, but could only force them open the barest crack, seeing light and then a skeleton. '*What fresh Hell can this be?*' he tried to say, but couldn't. He realized his jaw was numb, his arms as well, all of him save the tips of his ears and his eyes, numb as when he was a lad and nearly froze in the blizzard of '33, the winter his father had died.

Foxworthy then realized that while he couldn't feel his feet he was standing up, as was the skeleton opposite him. A skeleton only a couple of inches shorter. At first he took it for another victim of the virus, until he saw a sign in eighteenth-century lettering:

Charles Byrne 7′7″
'The Irish Giant'
Acquired 1783

Behind the giant's skull was a railing displaying a collection of horns and antlers, and beyond that was the walkway of a gallery lined with bookshelves containing volumes going back centuries.

Foxworthy shifted his gaze to the left, seeing the head of some long-necked dinosaur, then glanced right, at a Doric column on top of which sat the silvered form of Francis Fisher the younger, still in his army uniform, forever frozen with his hand outstretched. He looked more like a beatific icon of St Simeon Stylites, reaching out in benediction, than a young Tommy who'd been unfortunate enough to touch a silver tray just after he'd inhaled an alien virus.

Beyond Francis stood another column topped by a pyramid of coconuts and a small potted palm and beyond that hung a giant speckled egg sitting in a chandelier ring like an enormous egg-cup, suspended like the roc egg in the palace dome in *Aladdin*. It shone, a dozen lamps trained on it, not just illumination but incubators.

It was the heat from the lamps that had woken him, Foxworthy realized, the warm air circulating in the upper level of the museum, liquefying the bitumen that served as his blood, but only in the top of his head. He was like a stove with the ashes banked, perhaps a few smouldering embers left within him, but not enough fuel for a fire. Pipe smoke and Scotch were not enough to sustain him.

He also realized where he was: the Hunterian Museum at the Royal College of Surgeons, the biggest collection of freaks and oddities in London, at least dead ones.

'*I'm not dead!*' he tried to yell, but nothing came out. '*I'm still alive!*' Again, no words came out of his mouth, not even the faint crackling sound his voice had become, the whisper of flames in a furnace. '*Please, somebody, hear me!*'

Somebody did. The familiar voice sounded close, somewhere beneath the plinth he must be standing on . . . and it sounded not like just any woman's voice, but his mother's. 'Lord Webb-Johnson, I don't care if your man from Pompeii was shattered during the Blitz,' Foxworthy heard his mother say, 'you're not exhibiting my Kenneth as a statue – and naked no less!'

'*Mother, I'm here!*' he tried to call, but again, no words emerged.

'Please, Mrs Foxworthy, think of it this way,' said a cultured man's voice. 'We are a research institution, yes, but we also subsist on donations from the public, including medical oddities. Your Kenneth is gone, but the wild card virus has left behind a very grand statue. Consider it a monument to him. It's what he would have wanted.'

'*I'm alive and I don't want it, you bloody toff!*' Foxworthy screamed in his head.

'I'm a better judge of what my son would want than you,' his mother said.

'Your son wanted to save lives,' the lord pleaded, 'and so do we!'

'How?' his mother asked. 'You declared him dead!'

'By every objective medical standard, yes. He has no heartbeat, no pulse, no brain activity – but this wild card virus is entirely new territory!'

'I live in the old territory. The real world, not some castle in the air! I trust you will see things my way and release my Kenneth's body to me so I may take him back to Aldworth to be buried beside his father.'

'*No, mother! No!*' Foxworthy tried to yell. '*I'm alive! I'm still alive!*'

'As you wish, Mrs Foxworthy,' said Lord Webb-Johnson, admitting defeat.

♠

The last thing Foxworthy recalled was losing consciousness in the back of a cold lorry. He awoke to a drop of sweet fire on his tongue, trickling down the back of his throat. His vision swam, then resolved itself to show him a familiar freckled face. 'Just a drop of poteen,' said Paddy. 'Brought it for the wake, but saved you a taste.'

'*More,*' Foxworthy croaked weakly. '*More . . .*' But no sound came out of his lips.

Chandra joined Paddy, who protested, 'Dear, you shouldn't be out of your wheelchair.'

'I can stand,' Chandra told him. 'It would pain me more to not say goodbye.' Her baby elephant foot touched Foxworthy's cheek. 'Paddy is taking me back to Bengal, but I am the elephant's daughter and I shall never forget you. Sleep well.'

His mother smiled down at him next. 'My Kenneth,' she said sadly. 'My brave boy.' Tears rolled down her cheeks. 'When you returned from the war, I thought you were safe. A mother shouldn't have to bury a son.'

'*I'm alive,*' he tried to say, but couldn't. '*I'm still here.*'

She smiled then, as if she had heard, and his stone heart leapt, but then she said, 'King George knighted you. Star of India and the George Cross too. I couldn't be prouder. But I don't know what I'll do without you . . .'

'*I'm not gone!*' he tried to scream. '*Get Paddy to give me more of that damned whisky!*'

His mother left, and after the glittering of the sun, he saw Alice standing over him, a vision of loveliness and grief, a veil over her cornflower-blue eyes. She caught her breath, covering her barberry-bright lips with her glove. 'Oh, Kenneth, what did those monsters do to you?' She leaned down, whispering, 'You never asked me, but I know you wanted to. I thought you were going to when you came back. But I wanted you to know, I would have said yes.' She bit her lip, her lipstick smearing as her tears rolled down. 'Even like this, I would have said yes.' She kissed his cold stone lips. 'I love you, Kenny. Goodbye.'

Alice stepped away, and after a last glimpse of sunlight, the coffin lid was shut. Not even the hellish light from his eyes illuminated the darkness. The fire in his heart was extinguished.

He felt the coffin lurch and then lower, heard the mumbled prayers which could only have ended in *ashes to ashes, dust to dust*.

He heard the earth hitting the coffin lid.

The Coming
of the Crow

by Peadar Ó Guilín

Donegal, 1951

DADDY DIDN'T LIKE IT when Anya looked inside the puppies. He stood at the door of the shed, eyes wide, mouth open as though to shout or weep.

'I can stitch them back together,' she offered.

It wasn't enough, and never could be, because Daddy . . . Daddy had *moods*. The one called 'sadness' made his eyes glisten. It set him to drinking from the bottle under the stairs and Anya's life became difficult for days on end. All that fuss to bring him around again! Fighting to make sure he didn't lose his job for drunkenness. And now, the loss of some troublesome pets had brought him down again.

She distracted him for a while with chess, allowing him to win, although she kept the game close enough that he muttered, amazed, 'You'll be thrashing me soon and you're only twelve! Your mam would have been so proud.'

And later, when he was changing her bandages, sopping up the blood, removing scraps of rotting skin from her face or inside her elbows, Anya used her brave voice to tell him, 'Oh no, Daddy, it doesn't hurt me at all. Will you read me a story?'

'Of course, my love! My poor pet. Of course!'

The two of them had a big house all to themselves: a mould-spotted warren with rattling sash windows that sucked in every draught from across the bog and the sea beyond. Daddy's breath clouded the air when he read to her by the light of a gas lamp. Anya liked the old legends best, for what better way was there to plumb the mystery of emotions? Of fury so strong it warped a hero's body? Of a love deep enough to kill Deirdre stone dead? Of Gráinne's lust, and Diarmuid's failure to suppress his?

She wondered if she would ever feel such things herself; if she would have 'moods' that would control her and allow her to be controlled by others.

Who am I? she often wondered. *What am I?* She asked those questions every day. Perhaps adolescence would provide the answers, although the chances were her condition would kill her first. How unsatisfactory to die before finding out.

On the day after the puppies were buried, Daddy left to go teaching with the usual warning: 'Stay in the house, my love. Nobody is to see you, remember that. I couldn't bear it if they took you from me. Promise you'll be good?'

'I will, Daddy.' She widened her eyes to display sincerity. He wanted to believe her, she thought. Yet, as she watched him from her bedroom window, he paused several times on the lane, as though uncertain. Then, he straightened and walked out onto the road, scattering a flock of crows along the way.

She had seen this happen a hundred times and yet today something about the birds' behaviour caught her attention. Chickens ran from people. She knew this from personal experience, but for some reason, she had thought crows were different. Why should they be? And why should she think so?

She crawled over her bed to the flaking window. Daddy believed her too fragile to open it, yet when she pulled, all that happened was that skin broke under her bandages, leaking blood. She slipped on the way out, however, landing harder than she meant to. The impact felt like metal spikes hammering into her joints. It was more than the diseased frame of a twelve-year-old child could handle, and for a moment, eyes fluttering, she had one of her visions.

She found herself hovering high over the thirsty bog, counting the missing tiles on the roof below. But the pain eased soon enough, returning Anya to herself, so that she could take stock of the day.

Everywhere lay rock and brown bog, with hard-won pastures rising above the surface. Off to her right, a cluster of famine ruins hid her from the road. Seán Brian Hiúdaí had been using the stones bit by bit to wall his barren fields. There was no sign of him today, however, and she was safe to proceed.

The crows perched on wall and bush and along the top of the shed. They cawed and pecked or nibbled at their own feathers, but as she approached all preening came to an end and they turned to watch her, in that curious way birds have, from one side of their heads. Not one of them flew off or backed away.

'Is it that ye can't smell me with the bandages?' she asked them. Her whole body was covered, after all, other than her sensory organs.

The wind ruffled their feathers and waved the bog cotton growing behind the shed. Two of the birds stood on one of Seán Brian Hiúdaí's chest-high walls. Anya stepped slowly towards them and waved her hand, watching as their heads bobbed to follow the path of her fingers. She picked up the nearest one. It did not tremble as the puppies had done, or the chickens before that. And when she wrapped its warm body in both bandaged hands and twisted sharply, the little crack failed to drive the others away.

'Come here,' she said. And they did, they all did, an entire flock descending to form a carpet of black feathers that remained calm, no matter what she did to them, until at last she said, 'Leave me,' at which point the survivors scattered.

Fascinating.

She hid the crows she had killed lest they cause another mood in Daddy. Then, she experimented further, calling out to a nearby robin. It ignored her. As did starlings, wrens, and cows. She was considering sneaking over to find Old Brídín's donkey when she realized something was wrong. A stillness that shouldn't be there.

'Well, well,' came a man's deep voice. 'It's all true then.'

A stranger stood right behind her. How did he move so silently? He was big too, her face was level with his sternum, and when she looked up and up again, she saw a wide, snaggly smile over a square, dimpled chin.

Anya found herself leaning back against the wall, feeling the sharp angles there sawing at her bandaged skin. Her head spun as it did when the pain became too much, but mere pain couldn't make her heart beat so fast, or warm the skin of her ears. Was this a 'mood' at last? Love, maybe? Lust? She was the proper age, after all.

'Don't you recognize your own uncle, girl? I'm Séamus.'

Ah. The youngest of Daddy's brothers. She saw the nose now, the sharp beak they all shared.

'I know you're surprised, girl. We're not expected.' He grinned. Her heart beat even faster. His whole face seemed to glow like the picture of a martyr. 'Truth is, your daddy hates me now, but we all have our cross.' Then he shouted, 'Eoin? Eoin? Come and meet your cousin.' And up from the end of the lane came a little blond boy of maybe eight years of age. Uncle Séamus took each of them by the hand, and again, Anya felt her heart speed up. Her hand in his was so tiny, even with a layer of bandages on top of it.

'You all right, Eoin?'

'Yeah, Da.'

'He doesn't speak Irish, I'm afraid, girl. How's your English?'

Anya shrugged.

He paused. 'Can you speak at all? By God, you got a bad dose, didn't you, you poor thing?'

'I speak.'

He grinned, dimpling his cheeks. 'Eoin, this is Anya.'

The boy smiled, either as a signal of happiness or to offer alliance, Anya couldn't tell. Having met several doctors and a priest, she had learned to recognize 'disgust', but she saw no trace of it in the boy's face.

'Good lad,' Séamus said. He ruffled the blond curls as though he couldn't help himself, as though Eoin were a favourite puppy, and at that precise moment, Anya realized she had never looked inside a human before. Would there be a 'seat of emotions' in the brain? Would it tell her, at last, who she was? What she was?

But there was no time for that. Séamus pulled both of the children with him up the lane until they reached the front door. She struggled to keep up, with her sore joints and the old woman's curve in her spine. Her condition had been growing worse. It would kill her soon, she felt sure.

'Keeps the house locked up, I see,' said Séamus. 'Sensible man, my big brother.' He let go their hands and without pausing for even a second, he walloped the door with his mighty shoulder. Once, twice. Splinters fell. And then, with a grunt, he hit it a third time to knock it right off its hinges. 'Let's all have a cup of tea while we're waiting.' But he paused beside the stove to wipe dust from the photograph on the wall behind it.

'By God,' he breathed. 'Haven't seen this in an age. Eoin?' He switched to English. 'Look at this, boy. It's your grandfather.'

'He's got a big nose,' said Eoin and Séamus laughed.

'Sure, we all do! Right, Anya? Even the bandages can't hide yours.'

She could only look at him, still clutching the palm he had held in his only moments before. But then, the man's merriment seemed to die and he crouched down, face-to-face with his boy. 'Your granda gave his life for Ireland. You understand? So the country could breathe free again. And still the English cast their filthy shadow over six counties in Ulster.'

'You'll free them, won't you, Da?'

'I will, son. Or you will. Or your boys if you have any, please God.' He raised his voice and the air seemed to thrum around him. 'Life springs from death! From the blood of patriots! We feed the land from our veins!' His face was shining, his eyes were as sharp as razors that Anya could feel in every inch of her torn and leaking skin. Her cheeks felt hot under the bandages. *Life from death. Blood of patriots.* The kitchen spun around her, and then she toppled right over on her face.

As often happened when she fainted, Anya had a vision.

From above, she saw her cousin, Eoin, pelting down the road towards the school. Men in green uniforms crouched behind the ruined cottages, watching him, but from his position on the ground, Eoin saw none of this. He fetched Daddy out of the classroom and back home.

Daddy also missed the soldiers. He ran like a maniac, but when he found his brother at the front door all he said was, 'How dare you! May the devil splinter your bones! You were never to come again!'

Anya's vision brought her to the roof of the house. Her heroic uncle stood just outside, a head taller than Daddy, his shoulders wide enough to carry a full-grown cow.

'There's no problem, Páidí. I'm fairly sure they didn't follow me.'

'Fairly sure?' Her father's voice rose to a screech. *'Fairly sure?'*

And Daddy did what Anya had never seen him do before, he threw himself at the larger man, his hands around his brother's neck until both went down in a heap while little Eoin, arriving only now, screamed at them to stop.

Anya sat up in bed, breathing like a piston. She was bleeding everywhere and knew that under the sodden bandages entire flaps of skin would be sloughing off like a beggar's rags. She couldn't say why, but she had to see the fight, she had to! The pain in her joints slowed her to a hobble, but she would not be stopped, not by mere agony, nor by the waves of dizziness that followed.

She found them breathing hard, but sitting like civilized men at the kitchen table, with water boiling on the stove and Eoin absent. Sent off to play, perhaps.

'There she is!' Séamus smiled and Daddy tried to match him. But then Daddy said, 'Listen, Séamus, I don't care about your cause.' He spoke English. He must have thought Anya wouldn't be able to understand, despite the fact that it was always on the radio.

Her uncle replied in the same language. '*Our* cause, brother.'

'No. I've paid already. More than any man should have to. Anya is my only cause now. I can trust the doctor and the priest and a few others, but if anybody in Dublin thinks . . .' His eyes slid over to her, moist with the mood of 'sadness'. 'If they think she's a joker . . .'

'But, Páidí, she is a joker. She must be.'

'It's a skin disease,' Daddy hissed. 'There's nothing that can't be explained by that. No . . . no cloven hooves. No wings or whatever.'

'For God's sake, Páidí, her mother *dissolved*. I saw it, I was there when she opened the crates.'

Ah, Anya thought. That's why the grave in the back field had been empty when she'd gone digging last spring.

'If . . .' Séamus continued, 'if your little girl *is* one of them, don't you think she'd be better off getting specialist care?'

'She's not, though. I told you. It's mostly Americans who caught that thing. And a few others. Like the passengers on the British liner that was steaming for New York at the time.'

'Oh, there have been several outbreaks by now,' said Séamus. Then, his beautiful deep voice became a whisper. 'But you know, brother . . . you must know what else was being stored in New York when Jetboy got his comeuppance?'

Daddy didn't answer, his head down as though at prayer.

'That's right,' said Uncle Séamus. 'The guns.' And Daddy was weeping now, with Séamus saying, 'Just tell me where you buried them, Páidí. I'll take them off your hands. We're finally rearming. We're getting ready to take the north back from the Brits and if you want no part of it any more, sure I understand. Just tell me where to find them.'

'I can't,' Daddy snivelled like a child. 'What . . . what if it's true? What if they *are* infected somehow?'

'All the better,' Séamus breathed. He was a god compared to Daddy and Anya's heart still responded to him as though his every breath were food and drink to her. 'We'll gladly risk the virus,' he said. 'Sure, a few of the boys will die for the cause, maybe. They'll give their blood so Ireland may be free. But some of them . . . Some of them might become *aces*. And what would the Brits think of that? Imagine picking up tanks and throwing them across the sea!'

Daddy didn't answer. Instead, he looked up at Anya, and switched back to Irish. 'Is it sore, pet? We need to change you. Come on.'

He led her hobbling back to her room with Uncle Séamus calling after him. 'Just tell me, Páidí. I'll have the lads collect them and we'll be gone! Just tell me!'

♣

The bandages had soaked too long and didn't come away easily. Even Anya gasped and couldn't stop herself blacking out when the dizziness came again.

She found herself wheeling through the sky, watching the house below her no larger than a fist. She saw a convoy of three green trucks moving in from the east. She saw the glistening bog, each tiny pool red with the setting sun. The land was always drinking, and yet, always thirsty too. What could possibly satisfy such an appetite? *Blood*, said Pearse and the other poets. *Blood and life*. The ancients had known as much.

She'd seen pictures in the books kept in the back room of men fed to bogs to bring good harvests.

She wondered then, if her vision would allow her to see her own body. Sure enough, her view of the world swooped down until she was looking through her bedroom window at a stooped and skinny child, dressed in the loosest of clothing and wrapped head to foot in rolls of reddened bandages.

'How can there be so much blood in one little girl?' Daddy was asking. But then, he looked over at the window. 'Dirty crows,' he said. He raised his hand as though to strike her. Anya leapt away, only to fall, it seemed, back into her own body.

'Anya? Did I frighten you?'

'No, Daddy,' she said, although her words slurred and the look of worry on his face said he might be calling the doctor down from Letterkenny again soon. Or perhaps he'd listen to her uncle's advice and send her away altogether.

'It doesn't hurt at all, Daddy.'

◆

That night in bed, Anya heard footsteps and knew immediately who they belonged to. She still felt weak, but an opportunity like this might never come again.

She dressed, careful to put on shoes so as not to leave a trail of blood after her. Then, from behind the wardrobe she fetched the remaining knife Daddy didn't know about.

The front door had already been repaired – the two brothers working together had it back in place in a jiffy. But nothing anybody could do would ever fix all the draughts in this house. She limped, shivering, into the back bedroom to find Eoin sitting in a pile of picture books with a gas lamp for company.

'You couldn't sleep either?' he asked. 'What's the knife for? You didn't think I was a robber, did you?' He smiled at that last part, showing a gap in his front teeth.

Anya studied him, wondering at the best way to do this. Right now Daddy was in bed with an empty bottle, but he would certainly have one of his moods if he caught her looking inside another creature. And who knew how Uncle Séamus would react? In all the stories daddies fought for their offspring.

But sometimes children wandered away from a parent's protection and lost themselves forever. That's what was going to happen here, she decided.

Eoin was still grinning. 'Look at all the books ye have!' Stacks of them towered over him, their shadows pitching about the room as he waved the lamp around.

Anya cleared her throat. 'Let us go out,' she said.

He clapped his little hands. 'Oh, yes! We'll have an adventure. We won't tell anybody.'

She nodded, waving at the window.

'You want me to open it?' he asked.

Another nod. But even as he turned to obey, he spotted something on the floor. 'You play chess? I *love* chess. Daddy says I'm good enough to be a champion one day.'

He went back to the window, but she stopped him with a touch to the shoulder and a nod towards the chess set.

'You want to play, cousin?' he asked her.

Want didn't come into it. Chess was deeper and more mysterious than the bog itself. But it could not be properly explored without an opponent and Anya had yet to meet anybody capable of immersing themselves farther than the depth of an ankle. She had played the angry priest; the doctor from Letterkenny, who perched glasses on his nose; and various friends of Daddy's. All of them became nervous even when she held back and permitted them a win.

But a *champion*? She shivered, the knife forgotten at her side. She could always open the boy later.

He set up the pieces, putting the white queen in the wrong place. For a moment, she suspected a ruse, or a different set of rules. But no. No. Mere stupidity.

And that's when a great crash came from the hall behind them. Boots hammered the floorboards and their own door flew open to smack against the wall.

A man stood there in a green uniform, his face blackened by polish, a rifle in his hands. 'Stay royt dere!' he shouted. It wasn't the English of the radio, by any stretch, but Anya grasped the intent. Other soldiers were checking her room and Daddy was getting quite a surprise by the sound of him. The invader paused for a second, surprised perhaps, by the sight of a little girl covered in blood and bandages. But then he shook his head and demanded, 'Who else is hee-urr?'

'N-nobody,' Eoin said. The man, unsatisfied, shouldered down several of the columns of books and opened the only wardrobe – a haven for yellow, curling newspapers and a tidal wave of dust.

A single volume dropped from the top of the nearest stack to land at Anya's knee. It was a book she knew well. Her younger self, the Anya from before the sickness, had loved this one. That little girl had filled it with drawings of hearts and stick figures holding hands. Some of the pages even bore tiny stains of what might have been tears.

It fell open now at the picture of a glorious woman, surrounded by a flock of birds. *Badb*, the caption read, *Goddess of War*. She took the form of the crows that served her. She who renewed the land through the blood of young men. *But not just any men: heroes.*

The soldier might have searched some more, but right then there came the sound of shouting and a window smashing. 'Stop! That's an order!' and 'He's getting away!' Gunshots echoed down the hallway, followed by a scream. 'He's armed! He hit Tom!'

Anya's sluggish heart began to beat. It was Uncle Séamus, of course. Suddenly, she wanted to be with him. She had to see him! She had to! Nausea came when she tried to stand, like a stranger's fingers shoved down her throat. Pain flared in every joint, and all over her body new lesions ripped themselves open. She had a brief vision of the house, seeing it from the outside with lights in every window, but she forced herself back into her own head in time to see the soldier leave the room.

Eoin's face displayed attributes of both fear and panic, so it was the easiest thing in the world to take charge of him. She pointed at the window. 'Open it,' she told him. He helped her climb outside and then she led him into the night, towards his father.

Soldiers ran everywhere with flashlights. Shouting. Looking in all the wrong places.

'What . . . what's that?' Eoin leapt up in fright as something flapped past his face.

'Crow.'

'There's more of them! They're everywhere! They should be asleep!'

To shut him up, Anya said, 'We find your father. He is this way.'

'How . . . how can you know that?'

That was a good question, for other than the glow from the windows and the flashlights of the soldiers, the darkness was complete. Yet Anya knew where Séamus was the way a compass knows the north. He had run behind the shed, and from there across the bog, probably blundering into every pool along the way.

Anya did not splash even once. She remembered nothing of the years leading up to her mother's death, but since then her mind had preserved entire games of chess, books, diagrams and, yes, the location of every stone and hummock around her home.

She brought Eoin with her, using his strength when her own failed, swallowing the pain that tried to make her faint. Energy drained away with every step. Anya might well die tonight, but she felt the answers were closer than they had ever been, to the mystery of who she was. Of what she was.

Still she couldn't see her uncle. But he was there, all right. The glory of him was like a furnace and she the helpless moth. How was it that nobody else could sense it? The soldiers shouted somewhere behind her, only ever blundering into each other.

She found one of Séamus's shoes and then, just ahead, she heard him lose another, sloshing and whispering a curse.

'Daddy!' cried Eoin. Anya grabbed at his hand, but the boy shook her off, plunging forward only to fall face down in a pool with a massive splash.

'Over dere!' cried one of the soldiers. A whistle was blown. A line of flashlights – at least a dozen of them – swept the area. Every one of those men carried a weapon, Anya knew. They charged and cursed and fell. An army of shadows, panting, equipment jouncing, ready to kill.

And then, the strangest thing happened. Anya's lips rose to form a smile. This was not a decision she had made to influence others, for there was nobody here to see her. It was something her body had decided of its own accord.

'Get away, Eoin!' Séamus cried. 'Get away from me! Stay down!'

'Daddy! Don't leave me!' More splashes came, followed by shots, *crack, crack, crack*, splitting the night. Anya felt the breeze of something whipping past her face. Her knees shook. Her body trembled, but not from cold.

'Dere's sumptin' hee-ur!' a voice cried. It was just another crow – the soldiers were shooting at anything that moved.

Anya's left arm suddenly went numb. She was lying on the wet hummocks of the bog with no memory of falling. Blood seeped out of her faster than ever it had before. Her eyelids fluttered and then, she was in the sky, watching the chaos below her. Her own, twisted little body lay transfixed by the beam of a flashlight as a soldier cried out and splashed towards her. He meant to kill her, she thought, but that mustn't happen! Not yet! Something vital was occurring here and she *had* to see it.

She swooped down at the man's face, like an arrow from the sky, until she smashed right into his left eye.

The pain! The pain! Even Anya had never felt the like before! As though she had snapped in two.

But then she opened her eyes to find herself still alive, still on her back. The soldier lay next to her with the smashed corpse of a crow jutting out of his head. *Fascinating!* But she had little time to ponder the meaning of this, because confused voices told her that the other soldiers had lost her uncle again in the darkness.

He hadn't gone that far – she could point right at him, less than a hundred yards away. She had to help him now, she realized. To get what he wanted, what the *land* wanted and needed more than anything. She couldn't stand, but she still possessed one tool: the crows, of course. *The crows.*

Anya pushed her right hand into the bullet wound on her left arm. It hurt, yes, but she was used to worse, so she pushed harder, deeper, feeling flesh part until the agony drove her out of her own body entirely.

As a crow, she could see no better in the darkness than a human could, but her uncle still drew her. She led the flock down around him and every bird cawed at the same time until the torches of the soldiers converged on their position.

'We see you, McNulty!' came a shout. This time, the accent was cultured enough for the radio. 'Time you handed yourself over. The lad you shot will live, so it's just going to be prison.'

Séamus spat back at them, as Anya knew he must. 'I don't recognize your so-called republic!' he cried. 'Without the north, what are we but lickspittles? Tugging our forelocks for the masters.'

He glittered with sweat in the torchlight, as heroic as Cú Chulainn tied to the rock. His mighty chest heaved, his jaw clenched. Bleeding, wounded, Anya dragged herself closer to him, helpless before his power, but at last she recognized it for what it really was: belief. A conviction so strong that only death could put an end to it. It was glory in its purest form; at the very peak of ripeness.

'Daddy!' Eoin cried from somewhere up ahead. 'Daddy!'

'Tell them, son. Tell them what you saw here today. Spread the word so that all Ireland may be free.'

Then, the great man pointed his pistol and shot towards the flashlights. One of them fell, but answering shots flew out of the night to take him in the leg, the chest, the neck. Anya cried out, as though every wound was a hammer taken to her bones. *Crack, crack, crack.* Light spurted from her uncle's body, or so it seemed to her. Nausea rose in her throat; her belly rioted; her skin . . . her skin burned as though doused in petrol and set alight. And when Séamus McNulty finally fell, she threw her head back and screamed loud enough for soldiers to drop their torches and cover their ears.

♠

Some time later a voice said, 'Take the children back to the house.'

'But . . . those bandages. What's wrong with her?'

'Wear your gloves if you're worried, lads. Get going.'

They returned her to the back room for some reason, laying her next to a weeping Eoin. Her head spun. Her heart was pounding. The smile she'd felt earlier came back and laughter bubbled up into her throat, followed immediately by tears; by a warmth in her groin; by shivers in her muscles.

'What's wrong wit hurr? She one o' dem jokers? You been hidin' hurr?'

She had no idea who was speaking, but Daddy was there to answer.

'She's . . . uh, she just had a fright. I mean, her uncle . . .'

He picked her up. His arms were warm around her and Anya wanted to sink into them. Her own arms, as if they knew exactly what to do, wrapped around him too, squeezing so tightly that she must have opened all of her wounds at once. But she didn't care! She laughed again, then sobbed.

A more cultured voice: 'The men say you've been hiding a joker, McNulty.'

'I told you . . . I'm telling you, it's a skin thing. Just leave us be. Haven't you done enough?'

'I need to see. I'm sorry. Under the bandages. I need to see it now. If you haven't reported it . . .'

Rough hands pulled Anya away from her father, although she struggled and whined to hold on to him. She watched them peel the bandages away, one by one, from the cleanest, softest skin she had ever seen in her life. Not a single wound remained. Even the gunshot to her left arm had left no trace. Beside her, on the floor, the book of Irish mythology still lay open on the page of the goddess Badb, surrounded by her crows. And Anya burst out laughing again. 'Daddy,' she said. 'I feel . . . I feel . . .'

'What, love?'

'I feel *everything*!'

♥

The soldiers left after a few days of fruitless search for a cache of guns, said to be buried in the bog.

In the weeks that followed, Daddy still had moods, but they were mostly good ones and he left the bottle under the stairs alone. He smiled a lot and spoke of Anya's return to school in September. And she laughed, glorying in the way her face flushed with that feeling known as 'happiness'. She even lost once at chess – not on purpose, but through fear of sacrificing the foot soldiers that in English were called 'pawns'.

But less than a fortnight later she woke to find herself rational once more. A lesion on her arm dribbled blood onto the sheets. *Fascinating*.

She wandered into the back room to collect some bandages.

She touched the chess set, wondering if she would ever meet a worthy opponent. Then, she turned to the stacks of books. The volume of Irish mythology had been tidied away, but she remembered the picture with the crows in it and knew now who she was. What she was, even if Daddy did not.

She found him at the kitchen table, planning lessons for the following week. 'Daddy . . .' She used her lost, little girl's voice. 'Where are the guns?'

He froze.

'We can dig them up,' she said, because Daddy liked it when they did things together. 'We can give them to the warriors.'

He displayed all the signs of 'shock' and 'disbelief'. But she would work on him. The land needed heroes, after all. It needed to drink.

♣   ♦   ♠   ♥

But a Flint
Holds Fire

by Kevin Andrew Murphy

March 1952

A FLINT WHEEL TURNED.

It was not a wheel precisely, but served the same function, steel striking flint, spark catching fuel, a tiny pool of alcohol freeze-distilled to sufficient proof. The fire then shone light through two small isinglass windows to illuminate a swatch of stained satin.

Foxworthy awoke, trying to make sense of what he was looking at in the dim illumination: the inside of a coffin blooming with mould.

'*I'm alive!*' he yelled. '*Alive!*'

His whisper echoed inside the coffin, but it *was* a whisper, and he realized his mouth was open, his jaw unfrozen. '*ALIVE!*' he cried, his voice the whoosh of an open chimney flue. He felt air rush into the chambers in the stone that served as his lungs, fanning the flames, catching other fuel, and bringing him fully to life.

No one answered, the cliché of the silence of the grave true except for him. But Foxworthy realized it would soon be completely true. There was a limited volume of air in the coffin, and when it was gone, it would snuff out the hellish flame that had enlivened him.

His stone heart pounded, pumping liquefied bitumen to his extremities, and he dragged his arms up, slicing through a soggy shroud to tear at the coffin roof. The rotted satin shredded instantly but his nails curled shavings from wood that was sound save for one sodden patch around a horizontal gash where the water dripped through, directly above his face, like the splinters left by an axe-blade. Or shovel. He jammed his fingers into the crack, prising. A bit of swollen wood broke off, followed by damp earth falling into his mouth.

He spat it out, then tasted what was on his tongue: cheese. Cave-aged Stilton to be precise, soaked in port. But cold as an icebox. He swallowed the clot of grave-dirt and knew the gnawing hunger inside him had finally found the sustenance it craved. But he also realized, with growing horror, that he would still suffocate, a mountain of food on top of him.

Hades might have devised the torments of Tantalus and Sisyphus, but the wild card had given Foxworthy flint knives as cheese spades. He only had to break through a coffin lid and dig his way through six feet of food to reach air.

The lid was first. He went with what he'd started, working it lower, his stone hands cracking the wood like a walnut shell, then shovelling the freezing, damp earth that rained down to either side in the coffin. He struggled to sit upright upon the growing pile.

The earth collapsed around him, the oxygen grew thin, the fire within him guttered then went out, along with the light from his eyes. He calmed himself as he had as a boy, reciting Rossetti's charm as he continued to worm his way upwards: 'An emerald is as green as grass; a ruby red as blood; a sapphire shines as blue as heaven; a flint lies in the mud . . .' Not the most cheerful rhyme, given the circumstances. He dug in darkness, feeling the languor of the grave begin to enfold him in its cold embrace. It would be so easy . . .

Morris Foxworthy had dug himself out of the trenches of Verdun, dragging himself back to his sweetheart and then wife, to gasp his last in her arms in Aldworth two decades later. Kenneth Foxworthy would not abandon his mother, nor shame his father with cowardice, or lose his chance to see Alice again to sheer stupidity, for if the grave-diggers had buried him the usual six feet under, he now stood far taller. All he would need to do was stand up.

He strained to straighten his legs, pushing against the weight of wet earth on his head and shoulders, and gritted his diamond teeth with the effort till sparks flashed. But if they were sparking, they were not pure diamond . . . The words came in a rush: *'A diamond is a brilliant stone to catch the world's desire. An opal holds a fiery spark – but a flint holds fire!'*

He roared the last as his head broke through the cold earth, air rushing into his lungs, fire catching in his stony heart, only to have his blazing eyes illuminate the iron bars of a prison.

Not a prison: a mortsafe, an iron cage like the Victorians once installed to prevent resurrectionists from plundering bodies to be used as medical cadavers, the bars slick and shining with the drizzling rain melting the snow inside the cage. But once he'd got his arms free, with a spark and a clank, Foxworthy snapped the bars.

He considered the wrought iron in his hand. It felt and smelled like a stick of rock from Blackpool, so he bit a piece off. The cold iron melted in his mouth, tasting sweet and herbal, and he gave a dark chuckle. It was as if the witch from *Hansel and Gretel* had had the bars of her child cage confiscated as scrap for Hitler's war effort and had then crafted replacements from stalks of candied angelica: they were about as effective. But the darkest joke was that he'd starved aboard the *Queen Mary* when she might as well have been the *Good Ship Lollipop*.

Foxworthy took another bite of iron then reached under the snow for a handful of delicious half-frozen earth, tasting even more improbably like a cheese puff from a Christmas party, then levered himself out of the grave by the uneaten mortsafe bars and rolled over into a snow-free patch, laughing with relief and shock, alternating bites of candied iron with handfuls of soft muddy ground which now tasted like fresh brie. He wondered where and what the water biscuits were. The world was mad but the most insane part was that what he'd thought was Hell was actually the Land of Cockaigne.

Finally the hunger, the panic and the shock lessened to the point at which he fully noticed the ground he was lying on was very soft. As soft as newly turned earth.

He sat up and looked around. It was dark and drizzling, the moon hidden behind England's ever-present clouds, but the firelight from his eyes illuminated the stone:

ANNE VIOLET FOXWORTHY

BELOVED WIFE AND MOTHER

JULY 12TH, 1899 – JANUARY 8TH, 1952

Foxworthy bawled like a child, crying tears of fire as he staggered out of the churchyard towards the Old Bell Inn, the village pub.

♣

While the scene that ensued would go down in village legend, to be completely fair, the Old Bell had seen worse rows. After slaking his thirst with half a case of Scotch, Foxworthy allowed the vicar to coax him back to the church where, over tea and biscuits – actually paraffin and several boxes of charcoal tabs intended for the censers – he confessed everything, every horror, all his fear and pain.

A good man of Christ, the vicar simply listened, finally reassuring Kenneth that Aldworth had always taken care of its sons and this time would be no exception, but he needed to talk to the bishop. So after bidding Kenneth to get some rest, he excused himself, leaving Foxworthy to spend a sleepless night with the broken statues of Philip de la Beche and his family, now looking less like funerary sculptures and more like murder victims.

In the morning, the vicar explained the sad facts: Anne Foxworthy had left her worldly goods to the church, and while something probably could be done given the circumstances, the house had already been sold. So, after pressing him to take a small bundle of personal effects, the vicar urged Foxworthy into the back of Seth Marlowe's horse trailer where, with a hay bale as a pillow, he finally got some rest.

He awoke to find Seth poking him with a pitchfork, then stepping back in alarm. 'You're awake. Good.'

Foxworthy emerged, clad in a toga made from horse blankets, and heard the leaf springs creak as he left the trailer. '*This isn't the Isle of Dogs.*' He looked up and down the street, seeing high-end shops mixed with bombed-out buildings. '*This looks like Mayfair.*'

'Which is where you're wanted,' Seth explained. 'Vicar was on the phone all night.'

'Captain Flint!' cried a voice. 'Or should I say "Brigadier Foxworthy"?'

Foxworthy turned to see an absurdly handsome man modelling the finest suit possible standing in a shop door. 'Or "Sir Kenneth"?'

'*Any will do, I suppose.*'

'Good. Come in the back.' Handsome Harry pulled the tape measure from his neck. 'Let's get you fitted.'

◆

Harry stood on a ladder, taking measurements. '*Perhaps you should hire Gully,*' Foxworthy jested. '*I expect he's residing on the* Queen Mary *with his brother?*'

'Oh no,' said Harry, the edges of his Cockney sanded off with his new address, 'Lookout's not a joker like us, he's an ace. But a decent one, not like Spring-heeled Jack.'

'*Spring-heeled Jack?*'

'Another wild card,' Harry explained. 'Fell out of the deck last autumn. Has red eyes that glow like yours, sir, but nowhere near so tall. He flaps around in an opera cape like a great bat, waves steel claws, and scares the wits out of natural folk, but unlike the original, he hasn't murdered anyone. Yet. Largely he just robs jewellers and silversmiths.' He scribbled measurements. 'Whereas Lookout works in Brighton, is a great favourite with the press, but isn't stuck up. He still drops in to visit Jamie, Jim, and Jimmy.'

'*Seaman Gully named his heads?*'

'Well, they *are* different men, sir. They just share a body. Then again, the Jameses are almost as tall as you now so they might be a help. I've fitted them for a number of suits.'

'*The wild card made them grow?*'

'Well, more as a complication,' Harry explained, measuring Foxworthy's arm. 'Three heads means three pituitary glands, so the Jameses suffer from gigantism.'

Foxworthy sighed, then asked, '*So what's this business with aces and jokers and wild cards?*'

'Bit of Polari from the Americans, sir. The aliens who made the virus, these blighters called the Takisians, they named it the *Enhancer,* because it's meant to enhance your psychic abilities. But the Takisians made a botch of it, got a virus that's too random, so chose to test it on us.'

'*Lovely of them,*' Foxworthy sniffed.

'Well, yes,' agreed Harry, 'but if it's any consolation, they're all dead – the bad ones at least – all except this poncy little bugger named Dr Tachyon who, if you believe it, dresses like an extra from a Restoration comedy, can read people's minds, and says he was trying to stop the other Takisians when everything went pear-shaped. Which is something you're decidedly not,' Harry remarked, taking in Foxworthy's shoulder-to-hip ratio and adding notes to his pad. 'But anyway, rather than the Enhancer, the Americans decided to call a spade a spade and dubbed the virus what it is: the *Wild Card*. It can do anything. But it's all random and luck of the draw. Anyone infected with the virus is called a wild card too. And having the virus manifest itself is "turning your card".'

He jotted more measurements down. 'Aces like Lookout got dealt something good from the wild card deck: they look completely normal, except when they use their powers. Jokers like the Jameses got something bad, so have to hide it, if they can.' He paused, clenching one end of the tape measure in his perfect teeth and tensing it, considering, a Pre-Raphaelite pose, making him look like Proud Maisie's brother crossed with a shirt collar advertisement until he released it. 'And the ones who perished are said to have drawn the black queen, like poor Princess Elizabeth – though of course the Palace denies it. But everybody knows.'

'*Oh*,' said Foxworthy, taking the news in. He'd rather liked Elizabeth. '*So Margaret's heir?*'

'No, sir,' said Harry. 'She's Queen. But the coronation won't be until next year since we're still in mourning for King George, who died only last month. Lung cancer. Terrible illness.' He ran the tape measure around Foxworthy's waist. 'What, did no one tell you?'

'*It . . . didn't come up. There were . . . other distractions.*' Foxworthy paused. '*I suppose I don't need to thank him for knighting me now . . .*'

'No, I suppose not.'

'*So, with the wild cards, are there knaves?*'

'I don't know,' admitted Harry. 'It might be a good term for those like us who got dealt a mixed hand. Everyone thought your joker turned into a black queen, sir. Very glad it didn't.'

'*Even more so I*,' Foxworthy confessed. '*So, this Spring-heeled Jack, what is he?*'

'He wears a mask, sir, and even with it off, it would be hard to tell. Few'd guess I'm not a nat unless I dropped trou, and I'm not in the habit of that, now more than ever.'

'*Nat?*'

'Natural person, sir. More American Polari.' Harry paused, rechecking a measurement, then remarked, 'With you back, sir, it gives me hope. Should cheer Jillian even more.'

'*Jillian Fisher?*' Foxworthy asked, glad to hear she was still alive but then asked the other half of the question he'd been dreading, '*Is she a joker?*'

'No,' Harry said brightly, 'so far her card has stayed in the deck. But her brother Francis's silver statue disappeared from the Hunterian last autumn, about the same time Spring-heeled Jack showed up. There was talk Francis was Jack's first theft, but Lord Webb-Johnson claimed not only had Francis come back to life, but he'd flown out of the skylight.'

'*On what? The stuffed camel? The dinosaur?*'

'No, just by himself – the Flying Tommy if you'll believe it. But it's not as silly as it sounds. The Americans have a coloured pilot with a jacket, goggles, and scarf who flies around just like that, with no plane. They call him Black Eagle.'

'*So Francis is alive?*'

'Well, that's just it, sir, we don't know. It was a foggy night when it happened and no one else saw him flying, so most thought it was a load of bollocks and someone stole him. But now you've come back, doesn't seem quite so impossible now, does it?'

'*No, I suppose not.*'

'Jillian should be happy to see you in any case. Glad to say she's doing well. Show people are much like jokers in that they look after their own. She ended up in Covent Garden, at the New Theatre. Jillian turned out pretty like her mum and still acts, of course, but you remember how clever she was with mechanical things? She works as a wire rigger now too, making the good fairy fly, and builds props and such. And she's got me costume contracts. Now arms up, sir, let me get your chest,' he said, whipping the tape measure around and pulling it tight only to have it sliced in two by Foxworthy's chest hair.

Harry didn't complain, only walked under Foxworthy's arm, glanced up at him, remarking, 'I'd suggest a gambeson as an undershirt.'

'*Gambeson?*'

'A padded coat meant to be worn under armour, sir. Or perhaps motorcycle leathers . . .'

'*And what will I owe you for all this?*' Foxworthy sighed, dropping his arms wearily. '*I'm afraid my funds are in a knot what with being thought dead.*'

'Nothing,' said Harry, his handsome face smiling up at him. 'You owe me absolutely nothing, Sir Kenneth. 'Tis I who owe you.' He pulled both halves of his tape measure around the back of his neck and held them like a man proudly tugging a pair of braces. 'I'm the face man, but I've a lot of jokers back at the *Queen Mary* doing piecework. Even cobblers. They'd be honoured to help. We should have this pulled together within a day or two.'

♠

Foxworthy stood before the barracks in Kingston upon Thames, the whole edifice looking smaller than he'd seen it last. Then again, he was larger.

But he had a uniform, the most finely tailored he'd ever owned, and all his pips and bars, saved by his mother and the vicar, the ribbons washed out from whatever disinfecting solution they'd been soaked in. And soldiers saluted anything with enough medals, even a statue.

'*I'm here to see Lieutenant Colonel Henshaw,*' Foxworthy said.

'Yes, sir.' The soldier stared up at him. 'Is he expecting you, sir?'

'No,' said Foxworthy. '*Tell him Brigadier Foxworthy is here to see him. I expect he'll need time to prepare. Please fetch me when he's ready.'*

♥

Henshaw's office looked the same as Foxworthy remembered, if smaller, as did Henshaw. His hair was thinner and his neck fatter, but it was still good old Wally. Or Sir Wallace Henshaw if one were being formal.

'*Good God, Wally, I'm a joker, not a ghost,*' Foxworthy told his frightened friend. '*And it looks as if I still outrank you, so at ease, soldier, pour yourself some Scotch, and while you're at it, pour me some too, because I need it even more.*'

Wally, looking both relieved and terrified, fumbled for a crystal decanter, pouring himself a shot which he slugged, then poured two larger glasses. He handed one to Foxworthy, who drank the nectar, feeling the fire flare inside of him upon his more substantial breakfast of charcoal. Wally poured him more, then raised his glass. 'To your health?'

Foxworthy chuckled. 'Cheers.'

Henshaw sucked at his Scotch, then looked up at Foxworthy. 'Ken, you were buried . . .'

'*Were you at my funeral?*' Foxworthy sipped his Scotch.

Wally nodded, then bit his lip. 'Do you recall that bottle of Warre's we put by, promised to break open together after the war?'

Foxworthy did. A rather wonderful old port. Then he recalled the earth that had tasted improbably of port-soaked Stilton. '*You poured it on my grave, didn't you?*'

'Well, yes, sorry . . .' Wally apologized.

'*I got a taste. Well done, old friend.*'

'That's good then,' Wally said. 'A vow is a vow. After what you did with the *Queen Mary*, half the country wanted to hang you and the other half wanted to see you knighted. You saved everyone a great deal of bother by dying. And since no one wants to speak ill of the dead, King George pronounced you a hero and knighted you posthumously.' He lifted his glass. 'Welcome to the peerage, you enormous toff.'

Foxworthy felt both hurt and perplexed; terrifying as he might appear, it was not like Wally to be a coward, let alone with his best friend. But Foxworthy endeavoured to bear it with good humour. *'I'll accept the "enormous", Wally,'* he told him, *'but you'll always be the toff.'*

'I was born to it,' Wally admitted, 'and even you couldn't quite drub it out of me.'

They had not been friends at first, sparring as rivals for Alice's affections. Then both of them had lost out, and in their commiseration, forged a friendship. And when Alice had broken it off with the other fellow and decided she preferred Kenneth, Wally had been the better man, choosing to retain the friendship and pursue it no further, for all that he'd been smitten with Lady Alice Camden since they were children.

Wally had the wealth and title, but Kenneth had the looks and ambition. And then the war came, and Wally had been the one to reassure Kenneth when he was afraid that Alice had been killed. *'Wally, you know how I could always tell you anything. When I was buried, I couldn't move, but I could still see and hear. Alice was at my funeral. She told me she loved me and she knew I wanted to marry her. And she said she would have said yes,'* he gestured to his stony face with the knives he now had for fingers, *'even with me like this.'*

'She's a good woman, Ken,' Wally said. 'She never stopped loving you.' He then caught his breath and looked away, staring at his desk. Foxworthy saw that his gaze rested on a picture frame, lying face down.

Foxworthy was not a fool, but he was a man, and a man still needed hope. *'Show me, Wally.'*

'Please don't be angry, Ken.' Wally looked up at him, cowering.

'Please, Wally. Just show me.'

Wally snatched up the photograph, hugging it to his chest. 'It wasn't all at once, Ken,' he confessed frantically. 'I was in Washington for months and busy with more work when I got back, but you know the social circles our families run in. We were both invited to Sandringham for a holiday party, so of course we had to attend.' He looked stricken. 'Alice was so beautiful and sad, still in mourning for you, and she just wanted someone to talk to, who remembered you as you, not as a hero or a monster . . .' Wally turned the frame around. The photograph was not as Kenneth feared, of them in their wedding clothes. Instead, it was something more recent: Wally in his uniform, smiling proudly; Alice, in a pert jacket and summer hat, smiling, but both tired and older than Kenneth had last seen her; and cradled between the two of them, a little boy, no more than one year old, looking at something off camera with that intensity only infants could manage. 'We named him *Kenneth* . . .'

Foxworthy raised his hands and heard Wally scream, 'Please don't kill me!'

'What are you talking about, man?'

'You're angry!' Wally cried. 'You've got flames of rage shooting out of your eyes!'

'These are tears, man!' Foxworthy brushed them away, but then saw that his hands were covered with flames and his jacket was on fire where flaming paraffin had dripped. He patted it out, at first only spreading the fire but at last smothering it with his stone hands.

His jacket was a ruin. But there was still one thread of hope left. *'Please tell me that Her Majesty's Army has a place for me as I am now.'*

'I could, but I'd be lying,' Wally confessed. 'We pensioned off all the soldiers who became jokers when they got too close to your plague ship. I could ask the same for you . . .'

'Please do.' Foxworthy covered his eyes with his hand so he

would not again spray fire. *'Give all my love to Alice. Tell her—Tell her I would like to see her again some time, and my namesake, when you both think it right . . .'*

Then he ducked out of the room and stumbled away, his jacket on fire, along with his life.

♣

The *Queen Mary* had passed from a quarantined plague ship to a floating hospital to an embarrassing tragedy everyone tried to ignore, much like the jokers themselves, so no one complained if they continued to live there. At some point it had been repainted with thousands of gallons of random paint requisitioned in the hope of sealing any alien spores remaining. Combined with a dazzle camouflage scheme from the Great War, it looked like harlequin's motley.

Since he no longer fitted in the Churchill Suite, he volunteered to take the boiler room, but James would not hear of it, instead leading him to the end of the Queen's Salon where, beside the fireplace and the frieze with the duelling unicorns, there now stood a confused jumble of couches and thrones carved from grey Portland stone. 'Pick a chair,' Jamie, James Gully's rightmost head, said, waving to the lot with their right arm, sitting down in a peacock-backed throne that fitted his huge shoulders.

Foxworthy found a throne his size and was faintly concerned to note that there were larger ones. *'This is unexpectedly pleasant,'* he remarked, shocked to find a seat that did not shatter or even complain beneath his weight. *'Whom do I thank?'*

'Crispin Barbour,' Jimmy, James's left head, said, pointing with their left hand, 'who's also, oddly enough, a barber.'

Foxworthy looked: reclining upon a stone bench lay the sculptor whom Foxworthy had initially taken to be one of the sculptures, a long, lean gryphon-like gargoyle. Not of stone but of flesh, yet his grey, wolf-like, pointed ears and goshawk-grey wings were the same colour as Portland stone, as were the lion-like paws sticking out of his grey workman's coveralls, looking much like the feet of a claw-footed sofa. His beak and razor-sharp raptor talons, however, were of steel.

He awoke, eyeing them with one red goshawk eye, the sole spot of colour on him, then sat up and yawned, stretching his bird legs and flexing his claws, the steel talons ringing like hairdresser's shears. 'So, it's the famous Captain Flint.' He stood, ruffling his wings. 'Pleasure to meet you.' Both red eyes glanced at Foxworthy's own razor-edged fingers. 'We could shake, but I don't know who'd come off worse.'

'*Have we met?*' Foxworthy wondered aloud. There had been so many passengers aboard the *Queen Mary* . . .

'Ever get your hair cut in Westminster?' the gargoyle asked. 'Worked in my family's shop, then joined the RAF, and once the war was over switched trades to stonemason to repair the Abbey. Then I was up on the roof three years ago when this happened.' He spread his claws and his wings, displaying an immense wingspan. 'But it's not all bad.'

He lofted into the air, light as a feather, then pirouetted with a predator's pounce onto a stone ottoman showpiece carved like the golden fleece, seizing it with his talons and paws, spinning it up and around before setting it lightly before the fire with him perched upon it, wings furled, legs crossed, a feather-tufted tail draped over one knee. 'And I also do trims,' he said, scissoring his talons.

'*Do you also still work on the Abbey?*'

'No and yes,' the joker confessed. 'The Archbishop decided he didn't want any dirty jokers mucking around his precious abbey, especially now with the coronation coming up, but he doesn't know his arse from a hole in the ground, and he certainly can't tell the difference between stonework carved with a nat's chisel and a joker's beak. And I've got a couple of mates who take jobs off site, and if he doesn't give me a pass to the coronation? Who's going to count the gargoyles on Westminster Abbey when the Queen's visiting?'

Security, thought Foxworthy, especially if the grey gryphon had told that story before. But he was thinking like a military man, not a pensioner, and so what if some joker wanted to get a gargoyle's eye view of the coronation?

'*There you go.*' Foxworthy chuckled. '*So, gentlemen, I've been out of circulation. What does one do to pass the time here? And what's been happening in the world?*'

The answers to both, it turned out, were the papers. Jokers might be ignored, but newspaper circulation departments took money from anyone, and the advent of the wild card had done little to change the British press other than to add more lurid stories to the tabloids and slightly raise their credibility, since the wild card had rendered the unbelievable the merely unlikely. Other features remained unchanged: Lady Mabel Fortescue-Harrison, despite now claiming to be an ace, still provided prophecies and horoscopes no more accurate than before, leading to even more amusement. Most of the headlines seemed to be about the continuing manhunt for Spring-heeled Jack, who every week knocked over another jeweller or pawnbroker, leading Scotland Yard on a merry chase before disappearing into thin air and often a puff of smoke.

Lord Webb-Johnson's testimony was pretty much unimpeachable – a peer and wealthy doctor besides, he had little reason to lie. So assuming the younger Francis Fisher had returned to life, now able to fly, what reason would Fisher have to not reveal himself to the world?

Foxworthy knew a very good reason: if a man made of flint needed to eat dirt and combustibles with the odd scrap of glass or metal thrown in, a man made of sterling silver should need similar sustenance: namely silver. What silver tasted like to Francis Fisher was a matter of conjecture – ham, maybe – but it was conceivably something he needed to stay alive.

And being from a family of theatricals, it would be easy for Fisher to costume himself as Spring-heeled Jack – an opera cloak, spare wings from Varney the Vampire. And the shining steel claws sounded like an easy mistake to make for someone seeing fingerless gloves worn by silver hands. Add to that the police reports in which bullets had not stopped him, nor caused him to bleed, which the police had assumed was because he wore armour? Being made of silver also explained it.

Even the glowing red eyes were explicable. According to the papers, some wild card powers were more common than others, enhanced strength being one, which Spring-heeled Jack was said to have . . . as did Foxworthy. But his stone came with a stove inside that made his eyes glow, so it stood to reason that Francis Fisher's silver contained a similar furnace – one that evidently belched smoke at times too.

Foxworthy missed his pipe.

But no one had been killed or seriously injured aside from one man with a broken leg. Frightened, certainly: jewellers had been threatened with metal claws, police bowled over as Spring-heeled Jack flew away, sometimes with fire shooting out of his eyes, and Foxworthy intimately knew the wild card biology behind *that*. The poor young man forced to steal to stay alive rather than go back to the living hell of being a frozen statue. Foxworthy had only had a taste of it, and it was enough to make any man cry.

It was a wonder Fisher wasn't mad.

No one had suffered major harm save some insurance companies. For all the fuss in the *Daily Mirror* about guards being doubled at the Tower of London because of Queen Margaret's fears for the safety of Queen Victoria's ridiculous silver punchbowl, no museums had been burgled apart from the original disappearance of the silver statue at the Hunterian. And honestly, a man couldn't steal himself.

And if Her Majesty's Army had decided that they didn't need the services of a joker? Then they didn't need his services.

♦

Wally was good to his word and the pension arrived. Harry made certain he had a nice change of suits. James located his pipe which had been missing since Foxworthy's body had been packed off to the Hunterian. And Crispin Barbour proved to be as good a barber as a sculptor, chiselling off Foxworthy's stony beard and sculpting his hair, keeping him from looking like a hellish effigy of Swinburne.

That was what was good in Foxworthy's life.

The bad? The Vicar of Aldworth was much better at sending apologies than money, which explained how the Archbishop of Canterbury got word that a joker had the audacity to rise from the dead, then spent his Easter sermon insulting him, preaching how the resurrection of Christ was far better than any false miracles from the wild card.

Foxworthy burned that article. He had no problem with Christ, but compared with what he had gone through, rolling aside a stone and getting greeted by your family and friends sounded like a lovely way to spend a Sunday.

But the worst thing was, apart from the pension, there was nothing further from Wally. Or Alice. And he couldn't even blame them. What were they supposed to do, bring him his namesake, then watch him tear up and shoot the child with flaming paraffin? He was a freak and a monster, and the world had wisely decided it should have nothing to do with him.

His fellow freaks and monsters were of a different opinion, but they had their own problems. John Gully still visited his brothers on Mondays, but had the cruelty to mention that he'd found a sweetheart – a nat, naturally – who was of course fine with the handsome Lookout, but didn't want to visit a plague ship to have tea with his brother, the three-headed giant. And a gryphon gargoyle. And a demonic statue escaped from a pagan altar.

And while Foxworthy comforted the Jameses, the fact remained that James was still mostly human, and it would be easier to find a woman who fancied a three-headed giant than one who wanted an inhuman gargoyle or a razor-edged stone giant who shat flaming bricks.

Or one might have Harry's problem, to be desired by an endless number of women – and no few men – but have nothing to offer them. Or even himself.

But there were still the papers. 'Oh, listen to this,' Jamie began nattering to his brothers about one of the endless parade of vulgar American senators, Joseph McCarthy, who had just founded a group of government aces with the truly pretentious acronym SCARE.

Foxworthy paused his self-pity long enough to ask, '*What does it stand for?*'

Jamie replied, 'Sodding Cunt Americans. Really? Earnestly?'

Jim and Jimmy glanced over, Jim reporting, 'It's the Senate Committee for Ace Resources and Endeavours.'

Jimmy told his triplet, 'Yes, but Jamie's is more accurate. Oh, look, here's a bit about our Ermine Queen.'

Lady Arkwright had become something of a folk heroine among the jokers on the *Queen Mary*. A wealthy eccentric to begin with, once she was allowed to leave, she did. But rather than cloister herself in her townhouse in Holborn, letting the world forget her, she donned a pair of smoked glasses, made certain her living stole of ermines was clean and groomed, and set out to live her life exactly as she had before and damn anyone who got in her way. To that end she had her summer weasels, the nickname the press had given to the retinue of solicitors she used to threaten legal action to any shopkeeper who sought to bar her.

'*Perhaps later,*' Foxworthy said. '*Anything happier?*'

Jamie and Jimmy each grabbed a newspaper, flipping them open so Jim could see too. 'Ooh!' he exclaimed. 'Spring-heeled Jack was seen in Belfast! And not at a jeweller's either. At the lodge of the Society of Nuada.'

Jim added, 'Supposedly a poetry and folklore society.'

'Spring-heeled Jack broke all their arms and set fire to the place,' reported Jimmy.

'*What did he take?*'

'According to this, "their holy regalia",' said Jimmy.

'Sounds like a cult,' Jim concluded. His brothers nodded.

♠

Seasons changed, spring into summer, summer to autumn, then even autumn faded into the Christmas season, the calendar turning to December, and Foxworthy found himself crying.

He patted at the flames, but knew the reason. This wouldn't be his first Christmas a joker, but it would be his first *alive* as a joker. And his first without his mother. It had been a special time for her, even more important after his father died, and with the war over, he'd been planning to spend it with her, with Alice as his fiancée.

Foxworthy took out the snot rag Harry had made him, woven from asbestos fibres and infused with fire retardant. '*Stop it, Kenneth Foxworthy,*' he told himself. '*You won't look like less of a monster blubbering napalm on everything.*'

He forced himself to do ordinary things, or as ordinary as his life was now. Checking the paper for the latest antics of Spring-heeled Jack. Drinking paraffin from a teacup then reaching into the coal scuttle that now served as biscuit tin, the cheaper coal tasting like ginger nuts, because to him, sulphur tasted like ginger. Then he proceeded to empty the scuttle because it was cold – bitterly cold – and he needed to stoke his fire if he didn't want to freeze back into a statue.

Everyone else was keeping warm as well, James Gully with three different scarves around his necks, then Harry came in, wearing a fashionable new coat and carrying a large brown paper parcel. 'Happy Christmas, Captain Flint,' the handsome joker said. 'Thought you might be needing this early.'

'*Thank you.*' Foxworthy cut the string with his finger and opened the parcel carefully, setting the paper aside to eat later. It was a greatcoat, a particularly great greatcoat, considering that it fitted him, in black to hide singes and leather-lined to resist cutting. And it was very warm.

'I'll admit I've never put leather patches on the *inside* of elbows, but yours are rather sharp, sir, and you live and learn.'

'*That you do,*' Foxworthy said with good humour, but soon settled back into his brown study, staring into the electric fire while feeding the real one inside him, one day like the next. And so passed the second, the third, and the fourth, different only in that it was turning even more bitterly cold.

He awoke the morning of the fifth to hear James Gully coughing from all three throats, hacking cruelly with a noise Foxworthy hadn't heard since before his father died. But Morris Foxworthy's lungs had been a ruin from mustard gas, and James was a healthy young man, or men, relatively speaking. '*Are you all right?*' Foxworthy asked.

'No,' gasped Jamie, overlapping with Jimmy who wheezed, 'It's the beastly fog,' while Jim hacked and said, 'So thick I couldn't even see our feet,' then all of them coughed in concert.

Foxworthy smelled something in the air then, a delicious Christmas scent, as when his mother was baking gingerbread, filling the whole house with the promise of its goodness.

But Foxworthy's senses were skewed, and he knew what he now smelled as ginger was in fact the reek of brimstone. '*Stay here,*' he told James, '*and take care of yourselves.*'

He went up, but even towards the doors he could see the tendrils of fog creeping in. Foxworthy stepped outside, into the bank of whiteness, and it was like stepping into the Christmas Country from Seidel's *Wintermärchen*, a tale he'd heard only last Christmas – his last Christmas – in '45, in Lübeck, a story German widows read their starving children about a poor widow's children who once visited Father Christmas in his castle made of gingerbread, and how the closer they came, the stronger the scent of the wonderful sweetmeat grew . . .

Foxworthy took a faint sniff, then breathed deep, filling his lungs, and it was all the wonderful things in the world to him: gingerbread and ginger beer, spice drops and Christmas cakes, air he could live on. But he was a monster, with a chimney flue for a throat, and for everyone else what he smelled was the reek of death . . .

He heard gasping in the fog, the sound from his father's final hours, and the rage in his heart made its fire burn brighter, shining through the windows that were his eyes and cutting through the fog like twin bullseye lanterns. Then he heard the gasp again, its almost perfect musicality, and he knew to whom it belonged. '*Harry.*'

Foxworthy thundered down the gangplank, the metal gonging under his tremendous weight, the boards of the dock as well. He found Harry clinging to a lamppost like a dying moth. 'Captain Flint . . .' he gasped. 'I got turned around and—'

'*Steady on, soldier. I've got you.*' It was like picking up a child. The greatest worry was not breaking the gangplank as they thundered back up.

The air in the Queen's Salon was nowhere near as thick with the gingerbread scent. Foxworthy laid Harry out on Barbour's favourite bench and waited until he could speak. 'It was the smog,' Harry gasped. 'I was going to the Tube, but the fog was a peasouper, then the chimney smoke kept getting stronger. I couldn't breathe. I tried to come back . . .'

'*You're safe now.*' Foxworthy ordered the Gully triplets, '*Put a kettle on. The steam from the hot tea will help him breathe. You three too.*' They all nodded.

'What about you, Captain Flint?' Harry asked.

'*Me?*' he replied. '*I was made for this.*'

♥

He did a sweep of Millwall first, then the Isle of Dogs, rounding up all the strays, both jokers and nats, taking them back to the safety of the *Queen Mary*. It had been a hospital before and could be again, most of the lady jokers trained in emergency nursing from their time with the outbreak, and all of them clamoured to be useful again.

Foxworthy knew that feeling well.

But the Isle of Dogs was a shipping district, and the population of London was greater elsewhere, so he went north and west, to Limehouse and Stepney, the fog growing thinner but only for a time, flowing out from the Thames as the day wore on and growing darker as the air grew colder and more coal was thrown into furnaces.

Then he stepped into horror.

Foxworthy knew the devastation the East End had suffered during the Blitz, but knowing was nothing like seeing the ruins up close. He also knew about the almost two hundred killed at the Bethnal Green air-raid shelter, most of them women and children, not due to a German bomb, but the crush of humanity when a woman carrying a child slipped on a badly lit rain-slicked stair.

The woman had survived, but her child had not. Churchill ordered the tragedy covered up, the grieving mother forced to blame her child's death on a bomb that never fell. The same with the other survivors. Foxworthy wondered if the truth had come out or ever would.

'Help me,' begged a voice in the smog.

'*Where are you!*' he roared, but his voice was still a hellish whisper.

'I'm here!'

He found her, an old woman sitting on the fog-drenched ground, her knees skinned, a scarf clutched over her mouth in a vain attempt to protect against the smog. '*I'm here for you.*'

She struck at him as he reached for her. 'No!' she wailed. 'I've lived a good life! Don't take me to Hell!'

'*I'm taking you home,*' he told her as he picked her up and she beat against him. '*I'm not the Devil, I'm Captain Flint.*'

Either she hadn't heard him or she feared jokers more than the Devil. But fighting was life and his eyes were like searchlights, letting him pierce through the smog that choked her even as it nurtured him.

He pounded on the door of the nearest house. An old couple stared up at him as he ducked inside and set the other old woman on her feet where she stumbled over to the man. 'What—'

His wife was faster in crisis. 'It's Mrs Briggs, Mordecai! Help her!' She then turned to Foxworthy, patting him on the arm. '*Yasher koach*, Captain Flint.'

He didn't know Yiddish, but it felt as if the Queen had pinned a medal on him. '*Thank you, madam.*' She nodded and he went out to do a soldier's duty.

♣

He worked through the night and into the next day, and when he grew exhausted he found a petrol station, discovering that to him motor oil was treacle while petrol was strong black coffee.

Soldiers had survived on less.

And still the gingerbread smog continued, nourishing his transmuted lungs even while it choked London. Adding irony to cruelty, the day was December 6th, St Nicholas Day, when Father Christmas was supposed to sit good children on his knee and listen to their wishes, not carry them through the fog screaming and coughing, thinking him Knecht Ruprecht or Krampus or the giant Hans Trapp or some other Yuletide bogey who'd wandered out of Germanic legend the night before with his sack of coal.

In Foxworthy's defence, the coal was to keep his strength up.

But one parent had a Father Christmas cap with a sprig of good English holly, so he requisitioned it. It didn't fool a single child, but made some pause long enough to realize he was a joker, and moreover, one who was trying to take them somewhere where they could breathe.

Through the day he went and through the night, wandering a hellscape not wrought by Hitler or the Takisians but Mother Nature and John Bull's industry. Foxworthy had seen the bodies of children before, but blasted by bombs or twisted by the wild card, not perfect little angels who looked as if they should wake any moment, but never would, smothered by smog.

There were dead adults as well, mostly the elderly, the infirm, and the asthmatic. Foxworthy watched his father die again as he stood helplessly by in the hospital as a veteran of the Great War, his lungs seared decades ago by mustard gas, coughed up phlegm, then blood, then breathed his last.

Not all the victims of a war died all at once.

He later came upon a woman lying in the street, hacking and coughing, but when he reached for her, she began to dissolve, twists of hellish vapour curling from her clothes as she evaporated. Her tormented face drifted apart and away. Foxworthy wondered if she'd been a passenger on the *Queen Mary*, one like Paddy or Jillian who'd survived until now with her card unturned. He wondered if she still survived, like Lieutenant Waters or himself, transmuted not into water or stone and fire, but a being of smoke and fog.

But the wild card was seldom that cruel or that kind, nor the Takisians that competent. In all likelihood, the black queen had spared the woman a different but equally agonizing death.

Foxworthy kept calm and carried on, for if he rested, there would be a flood of fire down his face that would never stop. He'd wanted a purpose for his useless transmuted life? Well, here it was. But it would have been better for the world to have one more self-pitying joker pensioner than to have Pandora shake this latest evil out of her bottomless box.

But with each person he saved, he felt as if he were dragging a bead of Death's black abacus back to the tally of Life, at least for today.

Foxworthy wandered wherever the next cough or cry led him, and when he heard nothing more, he went west, towards the city centre. Now he found himself in Hatton Garden, London's jewellery district since medieval times. He saw a man emerging from the smog, his face covered by a mask such as chemists sold, and a black scarf worn over that. His eyes, hidden behind a black motorist's mask and vintage goggles, glowed red. His fingers gleamed silver, as did the candlestick sticking out of the sack he had slung over the back of his hooded opera cloak.

Spring-heeled Jack looked up at him. 'I have no quarrel with you, Captain Flint,' the knave said, his voice muffled by the mask and scarf. 'Leave me to my work.'

Foxworthy was no Professor Higgins, but he could still recognize a Cheapside accent. He noted that Jack was not overly tall or short, just middling and slim. 'Francis Fisher,' he told him, 'you need to give this up. You're going to get caught.'

'Francis Fisher is dead!' Spring-heeled Jack cried. Then he leapt or flew, Foxworthy wasn't sure which, five storeys up, disappearing over the top of the roof and into the smog, and it was only on account of Foxworthy's hellish vision he could see even that far.

He shook his head. Francis Fisher would not be the first joker to be driven mad by his transformation, denying who and what he had been, but it was still sad. And it was sadder yet for his sister Jillian who had been so distraught at the death of her whole family. Jillian would be overjoyed to know one of her brothers still lived, even as a silver statue.

Or would she? Foxworthy wondered. The woman he loved and his best friend had gone on with their lives together. And what would happen when he proved to not be dead? It was obviously much easier to continue as if he were.

Was Kenneth Foxworthy dead? Was all that remained Captain Flint?

It didn't matter. The smog still killed, and people wouldn't give a damn who saved them.

◆

The smog persisted three more days. So did Foxworthy.

Thousands died, but he lost count of those he saved.

They hadn't, and they were still telling the papers.

At Christmas, Foxworthy received many lovely gifts from friends and grateful strangers, but the most precious of all was a simple Christmas card inscribed in Alice's hand, ending with: . . . *yet most of all, we are glad to have named our son Kenneth after such a good and brave man. We wish we had been half so good and brave ourselves. Please forgive us and let us make it up to you in the new year. All our love, Lord & Lady Henshaw.*

He held it close, forcing himself to keep back the tears which would burn it, when an arm telescoped across the room, shoving his shoulder, John Gully crying, 'Captain Flint! She's talking about you!' Lookout's other arm extended a mere ten feet, adjusting the volume of the radio on the mantelpiece of the Queen's Salon.

Queen Margaret's voice came across the radio. ' . . . again, Captain Flint, if you can hear us, we would like to thank you personally on behalf of London and the Commonwealth for your actions during the Great Smog. While we still do not fully know its cause, we do know its hero, and for that we are grateful. Happy Christmas to you and yours and we look forward to thanking you in person.'

The jokers at the *Queen Mary*'s Christmas celebration were jubilant, as was the one ace, all congratulating *their* Captain

Flint then continuing to make merry. The sole nat, a pretty lass in a pink coat, stood by John Gully, meekly waiting till the end of the queue when Lookout put his arm around her and drew her close, his upper arm now a few inches longer that it should be, saying proudly, 'Captain Flint, this is my Elsie!'

'Pleased to meet you, sir,' she said shyly, then quickly, 'I know we haven't met, but I wanted to say "thank you" on behalf of my friend Carol. She said you helped her nan in Limehouse, and she's all the family Carol's got left.'

'*Family is important*,' Foxworthy agreed. '*I'm glad you got a chance to meet John's. Happy Christmas.*' Elsie smiled and he smiled back. It seemed every time Pandora freed another evil from her box, she let Hope fly again.

♠

Foxworthy arrived at Buckingham Palace on January 5th of the new year, one month to the day from the Great Smog.

He was escorted to a stateroom. Another man was there, in his mid-thirties, of middling height, wholly unremarkable except for the fact that, when Foxworthy entered, he gave him the barest glance, then went back to studying a painting.

Foxworthy was perplexed. Given his stony skin, flaming eyes, and gigantic looming stature, he generally provoked some reaction. As he approached him, the man asked, 'Which do you say the last brushstroke was, not counting the glaze?'

Foxworthy looked. The painting depicted an unusually lanky man in armour with expressive, heavily lidded eyes and an ermine-lined cloak embroidered with a double-headed eagle. '*He's rather tall*,' Foxworthy remarked, '*or I would once have thought so.*'

'Peter the Great stood six feet eight inches tall,' the man related, 'according to the history books, while you stand precisely seven foot nine.' The man's eyes flicked back to the painting, darting with preternatural speed. 'Unless Kneller was being flattering or his perspective was off, because, calculating by the height of the impost of the niche seen over his right shoulder, Peter here stood six foot nine.'

Foxworthy looked down, and because he stood two feet taller, he could see down the back of the man's shirt. Just as the pink flesh of Peter's neck transitioned to the shining steel of his armour, this man's neck transitioned from pink to silver. But there was no rolled and beaten edge as there would be with armour, no glimpse of an undershirt. '*Peter the Great is not the only one here with a painted face.*'

The man looked up, his make-up flawless in its imitation of natural flesh, his eyes wide in surprise. Then they narrowed, his expression calculating. 'Either the wild card has granted you enhanced vision, which is reasonable given your ability to see through the Great Smog, or—' He paused, his hand going to his shirt collar. 'I made an error using height tables from pre-wild-card army enlistment data.'

'*You're living metal just as I'm living stone.*'

'My skin, at least,' the man admitted. 'The rest I've not yet finished calculating.'

'*You're studying the paintings to find the best techniques to pass as a nat.*'

The man turned his head back to Peter the Great with a motion as cold, fluid, and mechanical as the Silver Swan automaton turning her head to view the silver fish in her glass pool. 'Of course,' the man said blandly, 'and it must be sheer coincidence I picked the tallest, most handsome emperor in the room.' He grinned.

'Ah, I see you've made the acquaintance of our Mr Turing,' said a familiar voice. Foxworthy turned to see Sir Winston Churchill, again Prime Minister, enter the stateroom.

Foxworthy glanced back to the man, who'd seemed unremarkable at first, now wholly remarkable even apart from his wild card. '*Alan Turing, the man who cracked the Enigma code . . .*'

Turing did not respond, but Churchill did. 'We call him our Enigma ace, one of Britain's secret weapons.' Churchill walked up to join them. 'That's a state secret, Brigadier Foxworthy, one you don't have clearance for, but that is a situation we shall remedy. In retrospect, we should not have been so hasty pensioning off all the jokers in the military.'

'You made a miscalculation,' Turing observed.

'And you still might be one, Mr Turing,' Churchill threatened wryly.

Turing responded, 'Captain Flint saw through my disguise.'

'Oh?' said the Prime Minister. 'Your error or some wild card power of his?'

'*I looked down the back of his shirt.*'

Churchill glanced up. 'That would work too.'

'Gentlemen,' said a woman's voice, 'if you have quite finished carping, we have business to discuss.'

'Your Majesty,' Sir Winston said quickly, turning and bowing.

'Let us dispense with the ceremony, Sir Winston,' said Queen Margaret, the doors shutting behind her. 'Please.' She walked forward briskly. Rather than robes of state, she wore a lilac brocade gown. In lieu of a crown, her sole jewellery was a multi-strand pearl choker. 'I've had all the ceremony I could stand over the holidays.' She looked up. 'Captain Flint. Or may I call you Sir Kenneth?'

She was not the sixteen-year-old princess Foxworthy remembered, but even so, she looked terribly small and young as a queen of twenty-two. '*Whichever you like, Your Majesty.*'

'Well then, Sir Kenneth,' said Queen Margaret, 'I feel as if I should have a ceremony, since my late father was kind enough to knight you when you weren't around to enjoy it, and God knows I have enough honours I could heap on you now, but the fact is I'm tired and I need your aid, so I shall do away with the frippery and get down to brass tacks. Britain is a laughing stock. America has had two official groups of agents with wild card powers – first the Four Aces and now SCARE

– while Britain suffers her worse disaster since the Blitz and the only one who comes to her aid is a joker pensioner in a Father Christmas cap.'

'The cap was a brilliant touch,' Turing told him. 'I loved the cartoons in *Punch*.'

The Queen ignored him. 'The nation has had good reason to be distracted,' the Prime Minister pointed out.

'No, Sir Winston,' the Queen differed, '*I* have had good reason to be distracted. I lost my sister and then my father and by all rights I should be tearing my hair out with grief, but somehow I have kept it together. Whereas Parliament has been endlessly bickering, and when it has decided to do something, it's done something stupid, like pensioning off every joker in the military then pretending they don't exist. After the Great War, when we had disfigured soldiers, we painted tin noses to give them their self-respect back. That we've not done the same now is an utter disgrace!'

'I'm not disputing that, ma'am,' said Churchill, 'but this is Parliament.'

'Scotland Yard's done no better,' the Queen pointed out. 'It's been a year, and Spring-heeled Jack has robbed so many silversmiths in London he had to go stealing silver in Belfast before coming back for his spree during the week of the Smog.'

'What do you suggest?'

'What would I suggest?' mused the Queen. 'Well, it's in my power to create orders of chivalry as I see fit, and moreover I could use my knights for purposes other than pointless ceremony. So I could invent an order for wild cards, but since *wild cards* sounds too American, I'll make it British. Spring-heeled Jack keeps stealing silver? Fine, silver is a good heraldic metal. Make it the Order of the Silver . . .'

'Helix,' Turing suggested. 'The Order of the Silver Helix.'

'Why "Helix"?' asked Churchill.

'The DNA spiral's a double helix,' Turing explained.

'Xenovirus Takis-A is a complicated strand that inserts itself, rewriting it and transforming the individual.'

'Excellent,' pronounced Queen Margaret. 'The Order of the Silver Helix it is.' She turned to the Prime Minister. 'Give me a reason I shouldn't take my sword and knight these two chaps right here, right now then march down to Westminster Bridge and wave it around until Father Thames appears and then knight him too.'

'Please don't do that, ma'am,' begged Churchill.

'Why ever not?' asked Queen Margaret. 'I understand Father Thames is actually Lieutenant Edward Waters of the Royal Navy – *my* Royal Navy – or at least would be if they hadn't discharged him. What did they do, throw the papers into the Thames? And in any case, he hasn't accepted them. He's spent the past seven years righting capsized boats, preventing shipping disasters, and catching attempted suicides and putting them back on bridges. Volunteer work by pensioners is fine for old men and invalids, but this is an ace we're talking about, even if not one we can hide by just painting his face. I want to see Waters reinstated in the Navy and given back pay. I don't know what he'll do with it, but I dare say he has relatives. When can I expect Parliament to make this happen?'

'Ma'am,' the Prime Minister began, 'I will do my best. There has been talk of creating MI7 as a special branch for wild cards, and we can certainly call it the Order of the Silver Helix.'

'Far better than the Americans' SCARE acronym,' Turing said. 'Not that they set a high bar.'

'Yes,' Churchill agreed quickly. 'But as I said, these things take—'

'You have until my coronation,' Queen Margaret stated bluntly. 'If Parliament can't get matters attended to by then, my sword comes out.' She turned to Turing and Foxworthy. 'Gentlemen, I will also need someone to run this organization. You're both excellent candidates. I propose a contest:

whichever of you can unmask Spring-heeled Jack by my coronation will head the Order of the Silver Helix. Does that sound fair?'

'Quite,' said Turing. 'I do enjoy a puzzle.'

Churchill appeared ready to say something, but Foxworthy watched the old politician glance at Queen Margaret and bite his tongue.

'Captain Flint?' the young queen prompted.

Churchill gave him a quick glance, half hope and half warning, but Foxworthy did not respond. He hoped his own flaming eyes were unreadable. He nodded to Queen Margaret. He was not enjoying this puzzle at all.

♥

Alan Turing had been a genius even before he contracted the wild card. Now he was a computer with a man's body. But even a computer was only as good as the data it had access to. Foxworthy, on the other hand, despite the coal-fired stone juggernaut his soul now inhabited, was an ordinary man, if with a more-than-average share of ambition, luck, and a soldier's duty to protect his men. And one girl.

But it was seven years since the *Queen Mary* tragedy, and Jillian Fisher was now a woman, one who deserved to know what had become of her brother. Jillian was also Foxworthy's best chance to reach Francis, try to talk sense into him before anyone died.

Not that even deaths were insurmountable. This was an arms race and aces were assets, even knaves mixed with jokers. A taste for silver, while expensive, was well within the government's budget, and metallic skin could be camouflaged with make-up.

Foxworthy wondered what Turing's diet consisted of, briefly entertaining the idea the Enigma ace might be Spring-heeled Jack himself. He had the metallic skin, and while his eyes hadn't glowed, nor had he flown; it was not as if Crispin Barbour flew all the time either.

Foxworthy then considered whether Barbour might be the silver thief. The gargoyle shared Spring-heeled Jack's steel talons and rumoured strength, but his eyes, while red, didn't glow. In addition, Barbour used his wings, even if what made him fly was actually telekinesis.

Of course, given the wild card, one could suspect anyone of being an ace, even Churchill.

All that being said, when enquiring at the New Theatre, Foxworthy found that Jillian Fisher had left abruptly during rehearsals for *Blithe Spirit*, to everyone's great inconvenience. Not only did they need to find someone to do wire-work for the ghost, but Jillian had been understudy for both Elvira and the medium, and was doing effects for the séance too. But this was the least of the production's troubles, since not three days after Jillian left the lighting board had finally shorted out beyond repair, followed by half a dozen minor mishaps, ranging from prop failures to missing costume pieces, leading to the company declaring the play cursed if not outright haunted.

Foxworthy listened to this litany of theatrical woes until he heard what he expected: that Jillian Fisher had left the New Theatre less than a week after her brother's statue had flown out of the skylight of the Hunterian Museum, and no one knew where she'd gone either.

Foxworthy left without leads, but he was not without resources.

♣

James Gully spread out the map. 'Here,' said Jim, 'this is the latest.' He pointed to a spot in Fitzrovia. 'Dr Van Moritz's flat.'

'And here's where you saw Spring-heeled Jack in Hatton Garden during the Smog,' said Jamie, pointing to a **CF** written amid a cluster of red dots.

Foxworthy wasn't certain how the three Jameses managed their two hands, but he was certain that the wild card had produced an excellent intelligence analyst. James had collated all the reports of Spring-heeled Jack since his appearance, documenting both thefts and sightings.

'Pity he sticks to night and fog,' John remarked. 'If it were a clear day, I could just stilt up and look for him.'

'You still might,' said Jimmy. 'Look here. On clear nights, the earliest and latest sightings have all clustered around Holborn.'

'And we're on the Isle of Dogs,' said Crispin Barbour, pointing a steel talon, 'so he nests to the west of us . . .'

'Where the sun sets.' John's neck extended six inches. 'He'll be backlit perfectly.'

'Indeed,' said Crispin, 'and while Spring-heeled Jack is by all accounts a poor flyer – he just hops up to rooftops and glides between buildings – I fly rather well.'

'*How's your night vision?*' asked Foxworthy, puffing his pipe.

'Not as good as yours, sir, and nothing in fog, but if it's a clear night, London's never truly dark. And if there's a full moon, it's even better.'

'I can only get Mondays off,' John mentioned, 'and I'd like to spend some time with Elsie.'

His brother's three heads and Crispin's one beaked one all stared at him.

'It's fine,' Foxworthy said decisively. '*Every man deserves time to spend with his sweetheart. Just check the weather and come up to London when it's fair.*'

◆

Neither the English weather nor Spring-heeled Jack cooperated with Foxworthy's plan. January and February were a mixture of fog and snowfall and the papers reported only one sighting and three thefts. March was mostly dry but quite foggy, and the few fair days worked with neither John nor Spring-heeled Jack's schedule.

Of course, neither Turing nor Churchill was having much luck with their respective tasks either, Churchill having a particularly bad time with Parliament.

Then came April. The clouds stayed until the 19th when it became beautifully clear – on a Wednesday. But the weather held until the next Monday when John finally came up from Brighton – bringing Elsie with him, minutes before sunset, the moon almost full.

'Nice of you to lend us our brother,' Jamie leaned down and said to her after they had come up the gangplank.

'Oh, you are a pet,' responded Elsie, spontaneously kissing him on the cheek. 'Thank you for letting me have John all those foggy days.'

Jamie paused, his hand going to his cheek, while Jim and Jimmy gave him looks of mixed shock and jealousy and even John looked a bit the same.

'All right then, Mr Lookout,' Elsie told her boyfriend, winking. 'To your work. I'll be good.' She stepped a bit closer to Jamie, and Foxworthy was reminded of when Alice had left him and Wally to fight it out for her.

'Dusk is falling,' observed Crispin. 'Join me.' With that, the gargoyle leapt up, his great grey gryphon wings unfurling, winging in an arc until he came to rest on the *Queen Mary*'s forward smokestack.

With a glance back at Elsie, John stepped forward, doubling in height each step until he stood leaning against the smokestack as a man of ordinary stature might lean on a low wall, his neck stretching up like a giraffe's as he brought up his equally elongated arm to shade his eyes with one hand, watching, peering, searching for a long while until Barbour grew impatient. The gryphon gargoyle unfurled his wings and flew up to hover beside Lookout's head.

Foxworthy couldn't hear what they were saying, but it became immaterial, John's left arm pointing like a weathervane as it extended towards the sunset. Crispin used it as his guide, flying faster and faster until he outdistanced Lookout's arm extended across the Thames.

Then came a long silence, Lookout still watching, Foxworthy exchanging equally baffled glances with James's three heads and Elsie.

Then Lookout stood up straight, almost doubling in height, then just as quickly collapsed down, stopping at a more normal but still ludicrous ten feet as he sprinted up. 'Crispin got in a fight with Spring-heeled Jack!'

'Who won?' asked Elsie.

'Jack!' John exclaimed. 'Crispin's a better flyer, but Jack knew the terrain and confused him with his cloak. He flew head-first into a chimneypot!'

'*Barbour chisels stone with his beak,*' Foxworthy said. '*He should be fine.*'

'You don't understand,' said John. 'His head went *through* the brickwork. And Jack's still there!'

With a bravery and foolhardiness that Foxworthy knew well, John Gully ran down the gangplank, tripling in stature with each stride as he ran in the direction of Holborn.

Elsie looked up at Foxworthy and John's brothers, alarmed. 'Do you—'

'No,' said Jamie, 'most of us just take the Tube.'

♠

The only good thing was Crispin was not dead.

They sat in Churchill's office, Foxworthy on the floor so he did not smash the expensive antique furniture, Turing in a regular chair, looking smug.

'So you are saying,' Churchill said, sitting at his desk, 'that the gargoyle is not in fact Spring-heeled Jack but one of your agents.'

'Crispin Barbour,' Foxworthy stated. 'Former RAF. Also a talented stonemason.'

'And a hairdresser,' added Turing. 'One of my prime suspects.'

'Enumerate why, please, Mr Turing,' Churchill asked. 'Succinctly.'

Turing ticked the points off on his fingers. 'One: metallic claws. Two: enhanced strength. Three: resistance to harm. Four: flying. Five: red eyes.' He smiled, gesturing openly. 'And six: found with an object stolen by Spring-heeled Jack.'

'Yes,' said Churchill, checking a paper on his desk, 'a Georgian silver candelabrum, reported missing three weeks ago.' Churchill fixed Turing with a tired look. 'Does that compute, Mr Turing?'

Turing went silent. 'No,' he concluded at last, 'only as a very obvious attempt at a frame, and a sarcastic one at that.'

'And Spring-heeled Jack flies with a cloak, whereas Barbour has sixteen-foot wings.'

'They could be bound and hidden,' Turing said. 'Aces actually fly through telekinesis.'

Churchill ignored him. 'Brigadier, had you considered Mr Barbour as a suspect?'

'Yes,' admitted Foxworthy, 'but I also considered Mr Turing.' In answer to Churchill's raised eyebrow, Foxworthy added, 'He has armoured metallic skin and so does Spring-heeled Jack.'

'I only know that it's metallic,' Turing stated. 'I don't yet know whether it's armoured.'

It was a childish thing to do, but battles had been won with less. Foxworthy snapped his fingers, chipping off a tiny dart of flaming elf shot which pinged off Turing's shoulder, cutting his shirt, and ricocheted into the fireplace.

'Ow!' cried Turing. 'That stung!'

'He's armoured,' Foxworthy stated, then used his flaming thumb to light his pipe before extending it to Churchill.

Churchill clipped a cigar and lit it, then Turing, not to be outdone, took out a cigarette. Foxworthy chose to not be petty and let him light it too before snuffing the flame.

Turing took a long draw on his cigarette then observed, 'I wasn't aware that we were allowed to use other aces as agents.'

'*I wasn't aware that we were allowed to put advertisements in the newspaper offering rewards for tips on Spring-heeled Jack either.*'

'Gentlemen,' said Churchill, 'we are all aware that you both have your own resources and peculiar methods which Queen Margaret and I are evaluating. All's fair, within reason, but to that end, I think we'll be keeping Mr Barbour in custody, if just to let Spring-heeled Jack think his ruse worked and keep matters quiet until after the coronation.'

'*What about Mr Gully?*'

'He used his telescoping arm to punch a bobby. But I'm quite aware that he's a local hero in Brighton and an ace we'd want. We'll let him cool his heels overnight then drop the charges in the morning.'

♥

The press had a fine time reporting Spring-heeled Jack had been unmasked as the Grey Gryphon, though Crispin Barbour maintained his innocence and nothing had been recovered apart from the candelabrum. The actual Spring-heeled Jack lay low, allowing the press to concentrate on the coronation.

As for the coronation, Foxworthy felt a bit like the gargoyle in the cathedral himself. He'd been given a seat at the back of the guest section, specially fashioned for his height and immense weight, but otherwise like the rest, covered with platinum velvet, trimmed with gold braid, and embroidered with a crowned MR as the new royal cipher. While it was an honour to be invited, and a strong statement on behalf of Her Majesty, Foxworthy saw the glances, the outright stares, and the long while the television cameras lingered on him. He was the only obvious joker invited, if not the only wild card.

Beside the Prime Minister sat some handsome young Hooray Henry whom the press had dubbed just that as his ace name. His actual name was Henry Astor and he could yell loudly enough to burst beer kegs. Sir Winston had made him his bodyguard, issued him a scarlet military tunic, and was attempting to get the press to call him Redcoat.

The new ace was the Prime Minister's current favourite to head the Order of the Silver Helix, finally ratified by Parliament but awaiting the Queen's announcement after the coronation. Alan Turing, painted to be indistinguishable from a nat, sat nearby, eyeing Redcoat.

But wild cards were not the only ones there. Three rows up sat Lord and Lady Henshaw. Despite the Christmas card, Wally and Alice had not been in touch since, nor had Foxworthy, but they exchanged awkward glances throughout the ceremony until he looked away, knowing the disaster it would be if he became tearful.

The coronation was regal and beautiful, filled with pomp and spectacle. And then it was over, everyone rising to applaud, then motioned to sit down again as Queen Margaret began her procession back up the aisle.

Foxworthy retook his seat, clapping as softly as possible so as to not pelt the guests with elf shot. Someone turned to smile and wave at him – an old woman in an elaborate hat with white egret plumes with their tips dyed black, perfectly matching her old-fashioned ermine stole. A stole made from incredibly fat, pampered, and drugged-looking live ermines. Foxworthy was not the only joker at the coronation – Lady Ermengarde Arkwright, the Ermine Queen, had managed to weasel another impossible invitation.

Lady Arkwright turned her smoked glasses to the woman two seats over whom Foxworthy immediately recognized as the newspaper astrologer and claimed ace, Lady Mabel Fortescue-Harrison, and the old women began chatting. But between them sat a young woman in a green velvet dress. Not the same dress, but the same shade, and her fair hair had been dyed dark to match her mother's, making her look like the ghost of Edwina Fisher, whom Foxworthy had seen die. It was not the beautiful tragic actress, but her daughter, Jillian.

It all fell into place. A young woman without a job would be hard pressed to find lodgings in London, especially if she were looking for a place to hide her silver-skinned flying knave of a brother. But Spring-heeled Jack had his lair in Holborn, the same place Lady Arkwright had her townhouse. Had Jillian, another survivor of the *Queen Mary*, begged the famed eccentric for an attic bedroom? What better eyrie could there be?

This also had to end. It was only due to his joker physiology that Crispin hadn't broken his neck. Foxworthy rose to his full height, brushing past the ushers motioning him to sit down. He crossed to the Prime Minister, leaned down, and whispered, '*I've found Spring-heeled Jack.*'

Churchill whispered into Redcoat's ear, and they rose and followed Foxworthy, Turing making a snap calculation and joining them. Then there was momentary chaos as the Archbishop motioned for everyone to rise, but Foxworthy was head and shoulders above the crowd and never lost sight of Jillian, who was still boxed in by the two old ladies.

The crowd parted quickly for Foxworthy, then he paused, seeing Wally and Alice looking up at him, waiting, but he loped past them, shaking his head regretfully, and made his way to the trio. '*Jillian,*' he told her, '*we know about Francis. We can help.*'

'Captain Flint.' She looked up at him, brave and defiant as that little girl he'd met only two years ago for him, but seven for her. 'My brother Francis is dead. We were both there.'

'*No, he's not,*' Foxworthy stated, '*and we both know it. You've been hiding him in Lady Arkwright's attic since he escaped the museum.*'

Jillian stared up at him. Her mouth dropped open and then

she burst into peals of maniacal laughter. 'You're wrong. You don't know how wrong you are. But it doesn't matter. You've found me. My fault for wanting to be a girl just once and wear a pretty summer frock . . .'

'What are you talking about, young lady?' asked Sir Winston who then said to Foxworthy, 'I thought you said you'd found Spring-heeled Jack?'

'He has, Prime Minister,' said Jillian, reaching into her clutch bag. 'The only trouble is . . .' She held up her bag, revealing within it a black leather driving-mask with ruby-tinted lenses. '. . . Spring-heeled Jack . . .' she depressed a brass stud and the lenses began to glow, '. . . is Spring-heeled Jill.'

After a long moment of silence, Turing cried, 'The charwoman! I knew it! You're the charwoman too!'

'Yes,' Jillian admitted, 'her too.'

Sir Winston remarked, 'In any case, it appears you're not resisting arrest. I shall expect a full explanation once we get somewhere more private.'

'Don't say anything more, dear,' advised Lady Arkwright, 'until I contact my solicitors.'

'I'm certain that won't be—' Sir Winston began until her necklace of fat ermines awoke and bared their teeth.

♣

'Thank you, Captain Flint.' Queen Margaret lit her cigarette from his thumb. She had exchanged her coronation gown and the Imperial State Crown for a silk summer dress and diamond tiara. She took a long drag on her cigarette, then exhaled, glancing around the stateroom with the portrait of Peter the Great, looking from Churchill, Redcoat, and Turing to Foxworthy, and finally to Jillian Fisher. 'If you could,' the Queen asked, 'as a favour, one young woman to another, explain things simply to me, from the beginning?'

'I repair things, ma'am,' explained Jillian, 'and sometimes

make them better. I was in the radio room with Harry, and he said it was hopeless. The radio was broken and we were all going to die. And then he started crying because he was so scared because of his own transformation, and I was scared too, and I wanted to *do something*. Then I looked at the radio and I suddenly just *knew* what I needed to do to make it work again. So I did it and it did.'

Queen Margaret took another puff. 'Go on.'

'I didn't realize that I'd turned my ace. Then we got into London, and there was the quarantine. Captain Flint died, and he and Francis were taken off to the medical museum. Then finally we could leave. I thought I'd go and find my aunt, but when I went by the New Theatre to ask if anyone had seen her, they were upset because the old lighting board had shorted out, and I looked at it and I just knew what I needed to do to repair it. So I did, and I realized I'd found my place, and I'd never much liked my aunt anyway.'

'And how did all this lead to Spring-heeled Jack?'

'I worked out how to use my power,' Jillian explained. 'I made improvements on theatre tricks. Spring-wound gauntlets that shot retractable wires so you could fly without needing riggers. Smoke grenades. A cloak that let you float like a parachute. Simple stuff.'

'And the complex?'

'The wild card virus, ma'am,' Jillian explained. 'I read up on it and realized it was a machine too of sorts. A broken one. But one that was impossibly intricate, and I visited my brother Francis at the Hunterian and I knew he wasn't dead, not really. He was just stuck mid-transformation, and I hoped if I just worked hard enough, I might be able to get him unstuck.'

'Then you brought him to life and he flew out of the skylight of the museum?'

'No, ma'am,' Jillian said sadly, 'that's just what his lordship thought he saw when a silver man with his arm outstretched suddenly flew outside into the fog. He didn't see the thieves with the rope and the block and tackle and the lorry parked outside the building.'

Queen Margaret drew on her cigarette once more. 'And how did you find out about this?'

'I went to the museum the next day. Lord Webb-Johnson was telling everyone. But like I said, I worked in the theatre, and the men doing the wires and the rigging there are the same ones who carried out the robbery. And a couple of days later, they were at the pub, very drunk and very rich, and they were laughing at me about my brother made of silver, and I realized what they'd done. They'd resented me for being a girl and taking away *their* jobs, so stole Frankie as revenge. So I went back to the theatre, put on some armour I'd modified to enhance my strength, threw on a mask and a cloak, then went and beat the hell out of them until they told me where my brother was. But by the time I got there, they'd already sawn him up and divvied out the parts.'

'And so you decided to burgle every pawnbroker and silversmith in London until you got all the pieces back,' Queen Margaret concluded, stubbing out her cigarette then starting another one which Foxworthy lit.

'And whomever they sold them to.' Jillian nodded. 'There were some lunatics in Belfast worshipping Francis's arm. And they weren't the only nutters. Some Satanists tried to dig up Captain Flint so they could worship him.'

This was the first Foxworthy had heard of this. He didn't know whether to be flattered, embarrassed, or horrified.

Churchill sighed. 'Why didn't you just go to the police?'

'Anyone know how many valuables disappear from police evidence rooms?'

'In which year?' asked Turing.

'Do not ask or answer that, Mr Turing,' snapped Churchill, then looked at Jillian. 'My dear,' he said tiredly, 'you are in a rare position given that Her Majesty is in need of aces.'

'I know,' said Jillian. 'That's why I decided to put my cards on the table.'

'You have nothing with which to bargain.'

'No?' asked Jillian. 'Apart from the fact that you need me, I spoke with Lady Arkwright's solicitors. The conspiracy to steal Francis, cut him up, and sell the pieces involved half the jewellers in London. Peers too. They can all be charged as accessories to murder.'

'Murder?' asked Churchill. 'Your brother was pronounced dead.'

'He was pronounced dead too.' Jillian pointed to Foxworthy. 'By the same doctor.'

'*I was alive,*' admitted Foxworthy. '*It was hellish.*'

Queen Margaret exhaled, shaking her head. 'I can hardly imagine . . . that said, Miss Fisher, what do you want? Justice or revenge?'

'I want my brother back,' Jillian said fiercely, 'and before you say that's impossible, his head is intact. I've got almost all the other pieces. And you have jewellers.'

'The odds are astronomically unlikely,' Turing put in, 'even before the dismemberment. And after? You'd require micro-surgery, perhaps some ace—'

'You've been wrong before, Mr Turing,' Queen Margaret snapped. 'No reason to hammer a stake through Hope's heart just yet.'

'I quite agree,' Churchill said. 'Kindly eschew all dire portents and grisly details, Enigma. Give us helpful calculations.'

Foxworthy knew how military intelligence worked. Jillian Fisher was an asset and a powerful one, but the only real hold the Crown had on her was hope. Take that away and Spring-heeled Jill would vanish into the night. '*I agree as well,*' he said.

Jillian beamed. 'Thank you, Sir Kenneth,' she breathed with tears glistening in her eyes, and the stake that had been taken from Hope's heart was stabbed into his instead. Then twisted. 'Thank you . . .'

'*Please, do not thank me . . .*' Foxworthy whispered as he felt another part of his humanity die. '*Please . . .*'

The girl ace turned to the girl queen. 'Your Majesty,' Jillian said, still beaming. 'Thank you.'

'Think nothing of it,' Queen Margaret said. 'Besides the royal silversmiths, what else might you require?'

'I don't know,' said Jillian, shaking her head. 'The virus is so maddeningly complex, and my power doesn't work with living things, so I don't know if I'll ever be able to puzzle it out.'

'I might help,' offered Turing. 'I like puzzles.'

'I don't, but I'm reasonably good at them,' said Queen Margaret. 'The solution here seems simple. We announce Spring-heeled Jack has been captured, but has been secured in a secret government facility, meaning shut in a wardrobe, only to be released when Britain is in need. We release the Grey Gryphon from prison, clear his name, and hope we can persuade him to join the Order of the Silver Helix. We recruit Father Thames, Lookout from Brighton, and if you insist, his brother, what did you say his name was?'

'*James*,' said Foxworthy. '*His heads are Jamie, Jim, and Jimmy.*'

'Three heads.' Queen Margaret took a nervous puff. 'I think he'll be doing his work inside the building. We'll code-name him "Triskelion" and hope the press never gets wind of "James, the three-headed giant".' She glared at Redcoat. 'And I thought "Hooray Henry" was bad enough.' She turned back to Jillian. 'You, Miss Fisher, I think we will just call 'Miss J—' and as far as anyone will know, you'll just be an anonymous secretary. As for your brother, once I have my silversmiths repair him, I will put him on display in the Tower of London as a monument to the victims of the wild card and the veterans of this last war. It will be secure, and if he wakes up, it will be far more pleasant than finding himself in a grave or a bank vault.'

· 'Thank you, Your Majesty,' said Jillian.

'As for Redcoat and Mr Turing, our Enigma ace, it seems

reasonable to put them in charge of security and analysis.' She glanced at Churchill. 'I understand your reservations, Prime Minister, but I have made my decision.' She turned to Foxworthy. 'Congratulations, Captain Flint. You are now Grand Marshal of the Order of the Silver Helix.'

'Thank you, Your Majesty.'

'You're most welcome,' said Queen Margaret, taking out a third cigarette. 'Now please, give me a light.'

♣   ♦   ♠   ♥

Needles
and Pins

by Caroline Spector

London, 1967

'I'M AFRAID WE'RE GOING to have to let you go,' Teddy Bravo said. He had a posh accent and managed to sound remorseful and condescending at the same time.

'But . . . I don' understand,' Constance sputtered. Her accent came out then, as it often did when she was upset. 'I'm yer best tailor. None of the rest of these fellas have half my skills. *Why?*'

'You're too slow,' he replied as he adjusted his cuffs. He was in full dandy regalia today. A purple velvet suit. White silk shirt with ruffled cuffs.

Constance seethed. She'd made the suit. 'You're a right prick,' she snapped.

'There's no need to get shirty about it,' he replied, then laughed. 'I don't make forever fashion. By the time *you've* finished a piece, it's already out of style.'

Constance's eyes narrowed, and she wished she could stab him with her shears. But she didn't want to get blood on her fabric. Blood was hard to get out. She spun on her heel and went to the sewing room at the back of the shop to get an empty box. He followed her. None of the other tailors were in yet. They usually wandered in hungover from the previous night's excesses. But not Constance. She showed up early and was meticulous in her work. It *did* take her longer, but her work was superior. And sometimes she would add something *special* to a finished garment, but so far only for herself and her friend Glory.

Constance glared at Teddy Bravo, her pale hazel eyes holding his for a moment as she began packing up her materials. The fabric was neatly folded and then slipped, along with scissors and sewing kit, into the empty box that had once contained a case of Persil. It still smelled like detergent.

Teddy Bravo reached out and touched the last pieces of fabric Constance was folding. 'I didn't realize you had so much fabric here. None of this is mine. Is this why you've been so slow? You been working on your own designs?'

She wanted to hit him or cry. 'No,' she said tersely. She tucked her short, mouse-brown hair behind her ears. There was a scattering of freckles across her nose, and though she would never be considered a beauty, she was often called interesting-looking. 'I worked on these during my lunch breaks.'

'Nice colours. I love the fabric. What are you making with it?'

Constance almost slapped his hand away. He hadn't cared about her own work until now. 'It's going to be a party dress.' She was using raw silk in yellow and grey. The fabric had a dull sheen, and Constance had planned on doing some beading and embroidery on the skirt. But for now, the pieces were cut out and ready to be put together. *And yes, it will take me some time to finish it, you wanker,* she thought. *And it will be perfect.*

'I don't know why you wouldn't look at my designs,' she said, trying to get control of her accent. 'I do women's and men's clothes. And you know I can sew.'

He waved his hand dismissively. 'You're a top-notch seam-stress, but it takes a different sort of eye to design. Most women don't have that. And why would you? You're not exactly top drawer, now, are you?'

Constance stopped talking. Her accent would always mark her as lower class. It was supposed to be possible to move between classes now, to become something better than just a girl from the East End. She'd been working like a madwoman for the last two years, trying to become a designer and to rise up in the world, but she had nothing to show for it now. Oh, she had her design sketches and her small wardrobe at home filled with suits and dresses. And then there was the clothing she'd made for herself. But she knew that what *she* wore and what the public would buy, well, those were two different things. She had hoped Teddy Bravo would be a mentor. But he was letting her go, and it was a blow both career-wise and financially. She was angry and scared.

You bastard, she thought.

♣

Constance sat in the middle of her bed. It was just a mattress on the floor of her tiny bedsit. She had to pee, but someone was already in the loo down the hall. She looked around and despaired.

In one corner sat her sewing machine on a rickety folding table. On the opposite wall she had her piles of fabric. The tiny wardrobe was stuffed with her designs. The clothes she'd made for herself were folded and stacked on the floor.

She began unloading the box she'd brought from Teddy Bravo's, then stopped because she started to cry. Tears would stain the cloth, and it had taken her a long time to find fabric she liked at a price she could afford. What little brass she had left over from her wages after food and rent went towards fabric and other sewing bits and pieces.

She didn't know what to do. She supposed she could go on the dole until she found something else, but she wanted to work *now*. Before everything changed again.

When Constance had been a girl, London had still been

grey from the war years, but it wasn't any more. At least not in the West End. Everything had exploded with colour and music. And sometimes other, darker things. And Constance loved all of it.

In the West End, thin mod girls wearing brightly coloured, geometric print dresses and knee-high patent-leather boots strolled arm in arm with skinny boys. Constance burned to dress them in her own designs. But Teddy Bravo was right. Fashion and society were moving fast. And if fashion was the bleeding edge of change, then rock musicians were the knife.

Constance knew she could give it all up and go and live with her mum and dad in Bethnal Green – they'd have her back in a minute – but she didn't want to be a burden. They had a lodger now and they'd have to throw him out and lose the rent money. And Constance couldn't have that.

Besides, she wanted to stay where she was. *Admit it,* Constance thought to herself. *You like the excitement, but you also like screwing musicians.* It was a bad habit she knew she ought to shake.

Brushing her hand across her eyes, she swept her tears away, rubbed her knuckles hard against her cheeks to get rid of the last of them, grabbed her handbag, and stepped out of her room. As she turned her key in the lock, she heard the toilet flush. A rush of smoke followed her neighbour, Alice, as she exited the loo.

'Good Lord, Alice, you dolt,' Constance said, walking to the loo and stepping inside. 'Don't smoke joints in the loo. Go up to the roof like everyone else. Now I'm going to smell like reefer for the rest of the day.'

Alice gave her a doped-up smile, and Constance rolled her eyes. She would ring Glory from the telephone box on the corner. Even this early in the morning, Glory would help her work out what to do.

◆

Glory met Constance at the Paris Café. It was tucked into one of the little side streets in Soho. They were regulars, and it was a place where Glory wouldn't have to deal with people staring at her – or doing and saying terrible things to her.

'Hello, luv,' Glory said as Constance sat down. They kissed each other's cheeks, and Constance inhaled the sweet scent of the blooms on Glory's head – today a tight cap of violets, though she might change them to some other flower as the moment suited her. Her joker brought her as much fame as her photography did. She wore a micro mini-skirt with a peasant shirt and sandals. Her legs were long and tanned from a recent trip to Biarritz. She put her ever-present camera on the table.

'So, you got the sack,' Glory said after the waitress brought their beers. She took a sip of her pint. 'Bit early to be drinking, yeah?'

Constance followed Glory's lead, but with greater gusto. She shrugged and then took another swig. The beer stung in her throat, but in a good way. 'Yeah, bugger him, sodding prick.'

'I wouldn't bugger him with someone else's prick,' Glory said. 'What do you want to do?'

'I'm not sure,' Constance replied. 'Right now, I'm planning on getting pissed as fast as I can.' She took another long pull on her pint. 'I could always try Savile Row. Handsome Harry says there will always be a place for me with my talents.' The *last* thing she wanted was to go to Savile Row to work.

A warm golden glow suffused Constance. It started in her gut and spread throughout her body. Her lips went a little numb. She took another drink. 'I wish Frances were here,' she blurted out, suddenly feeling weepy, nostalgic, and remorseful. Frances, Glory, and Constance had been schoolfriends together, but only Glory and Constance were left now. Constance had tried to save Frances, but she hadn't been able to. She'd been told no one could, but it didn't matter, she still felt guilty. 'Frances would know exactly what I should do,' Constance said. 'She was always good at knowing what everyone else should do.'

'She was a better friend to others than she was to herself,' Glory replied morosely. 'Remember when you nicked that necklace and Frances took the blame when your mum saw it? She said she'd given it to you as a present. But your mum knew Frances couldn't afford it either. She made Frances take it back to the shop and Frances got into so much trouble. But she never told.'

Constance started crying harder. She fished a handkerchief out of her handbag, blew her nose in a very unladylike manner, then said, 'That was pretty bad, but she also put your parents off the scent when they were about to catch you with your knickers down and your arse in the air shagging Jimmy Whe—'

'Hush!' Glory exclaimed. 'I never want to hear his name again.' Her blooms turned the same bright pink as her cheeks.

'To Frances,' Constance said, raising her pint. 'Always willing to help a mate out.'

'To Frances,' Glory said as the violets on her head turned to white chrysanthemums.

'To Frances,' they said in unison.

♠

It had been a shitty, rainy, grey day when they buried Frances. Constance and Glory had stood next to the grave with Frances's mum and da, her brother Frankie, and her husband, Reggie Kray. Frances's brother-in-law Ronnie stood next to his twin. Reggie wasn't even trying to hide his tears. Ronnie looked miserable as he watched Reg, but he didn't shed a tear.

Later, at Glory's mum's house, Glory – her head adorned with lilies – took Constance's hand and squeezed it. Constance squeezed back.

'Slit 'er wrists,' Glory's mum said. 'Blood everywhere. In the tub, on the floor, there was even some on the wall! Never would I have expected such a thing from her. She seemed so happy when she and Reg finally got hitched. Well, it wasn't like he hadn't wanted to. She certainly kept him dangling for years. Poor thing, she only just got out of the sanatorium after her last suicide attempt.'

Glory and Constance looked at each other with dismay.

'Oh, I almost forgot,' Glory's mum said. She bustled out of the kitchen, then came back with a medium-sized card-board box. 'Frances's mum said she wanted you to have this. Frances gave it to her three weeks before she killed 'erself. I forgot . . .'

The girls stared at the box as if it were a snake.

'Well, ain't ya going to open it?' Glory's mum asked.

Constance and Glory shook their heads in unison. 'Can't,' Constance said with a hitch in her voice. 'I just can't.'

'Me neither,' Glory added. 'It's too soon.'

Glory's mum shook her head. 'You girls will want something of hers soon enough.'

'I don't think so, Mrs Greenwood,' Constance replied. 'Don't think I'll ever want to look at it.'

'Well, I'll put it away, and when you girls decide you want it, you let me know.'

Glory and Constance glanced at each other and then grimaced. 'There's nothing but misery in there,' Glory said. 'I don't know why she killed herself with a razor. Last time she tried, it was pills. She never could stand blood.'

'She didn't have much luck with pills the first time,' Constance said, and then hated herself for saying it.

'Girls, you're being morbid,' Glory's mother said. 'Go on with you.' She shooed them out of the kitchen.

They went to Glory's old bedroom and sat on the edge of the bed. It was covered with a mint-green floral patterned chenille bedspread, and Constance started picking at one of the tufts. There was a bright brown-and-orange geometric wallpaper on the walls. It was horrid.

'I still can't believe it,' Constance said softly. It was shock. And dismay. And shame. She felt a sharp pain in her chest every time she thought about Frances in that cold white bathroom turning everything red.

'Let's go and get pissed,' Glory said. 'It's what Frances would do.'

Constance gave a quick, sharp laugh. 'No, she wouldn't. Frances didn't get pissed. She got tipsy.'

'Then let's get pissed for us.'

♥

'You rat-arsed yet?' Glory asked.

Constance was indeed rat-arsed and very proud of herself for not having vomited. 'Yes,' she allowed with a loud belch. Her stomach roiled, and she reconsidered the whole vomit issue. 'What's the latest on the man front? Reggie still won't leave you alone? Mick still screwing everything in sight?'

'Reg invited me to a party he and Ronnie are throwing at Esmeralda's Barn tonight,' Glory replied, ignoring the question about Mick. 'Very posh. Come with me. I'll be bored to tears without you.'

Constance brayed with laughter. 'Why on earth would you go to a party them Krays are throwing? Reg won't leave you alone. I thought you hated him.'

'Lord, all I'm asking you to do is go to a fancy party with me,' Glory said in high dudgeon. Her flowers changed to spiky purple roses that clashed with her outfit.

Constance rolled her eyes and took another swallow of her pint despite her stomach's rebellion. 'I may be pissed, but doesn't mean that I've gone soft in the 'ead.' She peered at Glory and found her a little blurry.

Then Constance had a sudden realization. 'Good God,' she blurted. 'Is Mick going to be there? Of course he is. Those Kray boys like nothing better than to get every high-profile bloke and bird at their parties. And you want to see Mick without it looking like you're *wantin'* to see him.'

Glory glared at Constance. 'That's a right awful thing to say. I broke up with Mick months ago.' Her flowers changed again. This time foxgloves sprouted.

'Oh, my girl, *you* should know better. Mick will fuck anything with a pussy. That's the reason you sent him on his way. Remember?'

There was a long pause. Then Glory said, 'So what if I am? He might not be there at all. And Reg said I'd be the only photographer there.'

'So Reg is bribing you with work? Very canny of him. Mick will be there.' Constance hiccupped. 'He'll think it's a laugh.'

'Ronnie's going to be there, too,' Glory said softly. 'And he scares the shit out of me after what they say he did to Frances . . .'

'What people *think* he did to Frances. There's no proof. It's been over a year now. Those are rumours. Rumours you best not be repeating.'

Glory gave Constance a stare of disbelief. 'Oh, c'mon, luv,' she said. 'Your mum and dad and the rest of 'em pretend the Krays aren't that bad, so they can take their help, but you know better. Maybe we don't know for sure that Ronnie had something to do with Frances, but it's easy enough to believe.'

Suddenly, there was a fiery tinge to the tips of her flowers. She shook her head. 'They're dangerous to know, and yet here we are planning on going to another one of their parties, just like everyone else who gets invited.'

'Then why go?' Constance wasn't in any condition to argue about the Krays. And Glory was right. There *were* rumours about what had happened to Frances. And then there were the rumours that Ronnie had a wild card. 'If it's true,' she said with a shiver. 'That makes it *completely* mad to go to this party. You know I'd kill Ronnie if we knew it was him what killed

Frances. But we *don't* know for certain. But I'll tell you, they certainly make being part of the Firm seem glamorous.'

White roses bloomed on Glory's head, bleeding into the foxgloves, making them fade and disappear.

Constance shook her head in disbelief. 'White roses? You really *are* going because of Mick. You're daft. I suppose I'll have to go along to keep you out of trouble.'

♣

It was dusk when Constance woke. Her head was throbbing, and her mouth felt as if someone had used it for an ashtray. Or to wash dirty socks. There was a knock on the door and she heard Glory say, 'C'mon, let me in!'

Constance got up and shuffled to the door. Glory swept in, her head covered in hot-pink rose petals that mimicked Twiggy's famous short haircut. Thin and vaguely androgynous, Twiggy had changed the way women wanted to look. But neither Glory nor Constance had the requisite body type. Still, that didn't seem to bother any of the men they slept with.

'You look terrible,' Glory said. 'It's going to take a miracle to get you in shape for tonight. Oh, this is for you.' She held out a greasy bag. Constance grabbed it and discovered chips inside – and underneath them, a chunk of battered fish. 'Thought you'd need something to eat.'

Constance wasn't sure she wanted to eat *anything*, but the chips smelled wonderful and were nice and hot. They burned a little as she ate them.

'Look in the wardrobe and see if there's something you'd like to wear,' Constance said as she found a cup of cold tea on the windowsill. She wrinkled her nose at the taste, but drank it anyway. 'I used your measurements when I made most of them.'

'Hmm,' Glory said as she pulled out an iridescent electric-blue sheath dress. An elaborately embroidered phoenix wrapped around the skirt, beginning in the front, coiling around the waist, its tail feathers fanning out over the left breast. 'I love this! Can I wear it?'

'Of course,' Constance said around a mouthful of crunchy fish. 'There's a dress in the same pattern in there, but no embroidery. You see it? It's the grey one in dupioni silk with long sleeves. I'll wear that.'

'Finish those chips, then go and take a shower,' said Glory as she began to undress. Her skin was tanned except where her bikini bottom had been. Her bum was milky pale. 'You reek, my girl.'

Constance narrowed her eyes at Glory, then sniffed her armpit. She *was* disgusting. 'I'll be back in a mo.'

◆

Esmeralda's Barn was definitely posh. Crystal chandeliers threw prisms of light across the room. Everything that could be gilded was. Glory began snapping pictures as fast as she could, which surprised Constance not at all. The women at the party wore tight, short dresses, some adorned with paillettes – some with sequins, beads, faux gems. Constance knew the dresses were heavy with all that embellishment. She didn't care much for any of them.

The dresses sparkled as the women danced. Their male partners were dressed in dinner jackets and danced awkwardly, trying to look cool. Everywhere there was something glittery and bright. Constance felt overwhelmed by it all.

Celebrities and gangsters rubbed elbows with locals Constance knew only by sight. She noticed members of the Firm scattered throughout the crowd. It was clear they weren't there to have fun. There were even a few coppers who had reputations for being bent crammed into one of the booths.

On a stage at the end of the room Dusty Springfield was accompanied by a five-piece band. She was singing, 'The Look of Love'.

'I thought they sold this place years ago,' Constance said to Glory. Before they had left for the party, they'd gone up to the roof at Constance's and smoked half a joint. Constance felt light and floaty. It helped with her fear of the Krays. Reggie seemed nice and her parents had nothing but good things to say about him, but Ronnie, well, he was another matter. They said he was schizophrenic and didn't know what was real and what wasn't most of the time.

'They did sell the club, but Reggie said he missed so they bought it back about six months ago.' Glory was clicking away, taking photos as fast as she could. It was clear she wasn't just photographing the celebrities. Glory was in the process of putting together a new series of pictures, but she wouldn't tell Constance what the theme was.

'This is the reopening party. Hey, over there.' Glory looked through her viewfinder and then snapped with rapid-fire. She stopped and reloaded the film in her camera. Then she began working again.

That was when Constance saw Marilyn Monroe and Frank Sinatra sitting at one of the gilded tables in the centre of the room. Sinatra said something, and Monroe threw back her head and laughed. It had been a few years since *Cleopatra* had come out, and much to everyone's shock, Monroe had been brilliant in it. Half of the women in the club were sporting Monroe's new trademark hairdo: long, platinum blonde, parted down the middle. The rest were trying to be Jean Shrimpton.

If only Mum were here, Constance thought. *She'd be beside herself.* Though if Constance was honest with herself, it was a thrill for her as well. She'd never been allowed to meet the famous customers at Teddy Bravo's. Only the male tailors were allowed to do that, so she'd only seen celebrities from the back of the shop as she peered through the curtains.

'Glory, luv, good to see you. I was hoping you'd be here.'

Constance knew that voice – it was famous now. She turned

as Mick grabbed Glory and pulled her into an embrace. He took the camera out of Glory's hand, and then began kissing her enthusiastically.

Jagger's reputation with women was legendarily indiscriminate, even more so since his ace had manifested. Screwing every woman he met seemed as if it were his life's work. Constance noticed people looking their way, and the level of excited conversation noise ratcheted up.

'Stop it, Mick,' Glory said, pushing him away. But as she did so, white roses covered her head. She grabbed her camera back and took a picture of him. He preened. 'We're friends now, nothing more.'

Mick looked Glory up and down as she lowered her camera. 'Gorgeous dress, by the way, luv,' he said. 'And you look smashing in it. Now, who's your friend?' He gave Constance a broad smile. Charisma and danger rolled off him in waves. His attention was flattering and disconcerting at the same time.

'Constance, Mick. Mick, Constance. She made the dress.'

He glanced back and forth between the girls. 'You're quite talented,' he said to Constance. 'And what you're wearing is cool as well. Do you have any other talents?' He smiled at her wickedly. Then he sniffed the air. 'Ah, you two been havin' a puff, I see. Is it the gear I gave you? I'd've thought you'd used all that up. It's been so long since I've seen you.'

'It hasn't been that long,' Glory said, blushing. Her flowers changed to gardenias, and immediately the air was perfumed by the scent of them. 'Where's Keith? I'd like to get a photo of him.'

'Probably shooting up somewhere,' Mick replied dourly. 'We're going on tour soon and he's going to get us busted. Again.'

'I seem to remember you getting nicked every time you go all lycanthrope in public. Won't that be a problem touring the States?' Glory asked.

'Don't see why,' Mick said with a shrug. 'There are already

bands touring the colonies with blokes like me. The Lizard King and the like. Besides, I've made it chic to be an ace, don't you know. And you, my dear, have done the same for jokers. Well, pretty jokers, at any rate. Though they are rarer than hen's teeth.' He turned back to Constance, his eyes turning a flecked yellow, the pupils growing large. 'Constance, do you think you'd like to howl at the moon all night with me?' His ripe, musky smell mingled with the scent of Glory's gardenias.

'This is why I dumped you, Mick,' Glory said tartly. She spun around and began taking pictures.

Mick continued grinning at Constance, but he kept glancing at Glory's back. The way he looked at Glory now that she wasn't paying attention was all Constance needed to know about where his real desires lay.

It was Mick who had made Glory's career. She had snapped the iconic black-and-white photo of him mid-metamorphosis in concert, catching his lithe body as his feet turned to paws sporting razor-sharp claws and his jeans ripped open, exposing his fur-covered legs. His head had been thrown back as he howled the final verse of 'Sympathy for the Devil', the cords in his neck straining and popping just before he became fully lycanthrope.

Rolling Stone magazine had paid a small fortune for the photo and run it as their cover the next week. Glory, no fool, had reserved the rights to it and done limited edition runs of the image framed as if it were fine art. It was a smash and made her a tidy sum. She'd already treated all of her best photos this way, and after the cover everyone wanted her pictures. Some bands had even asked her to tour with them as their official photographer, but Glory declined. Like Constance, she had a weakness for musicians.

'C'mon, Glory,' Mick said. 'Stop making me look at your bum, nice as it is.'

Glory turned and glared at him. 'You don't deserve to look at any of me, you . . . you trollop.' Constance and Mick both laughed, and Glory went bright red. 'That isn't funny and you both know it.'

'Oh, Glory,' Mick said. 'Come with me and we'll have more fun than either of us can stand.'

'What have we here?' A gruff voice interrupted.

Reggie had come up without their realizing it. He was dressed in a flash three-piece suit of black worsted wool with narrow lapels and a black silk tie done up in a Windsor knot. His hair was slicked back. There were lines around his mouth; his nose was large and a little off-centre. Heavy-lidded dark-brown eyes were sunk into his face. He had brawler's hands, meaty with big knuckles. Ronnie stood behind him, looking almost exactly the same, except for his thick black-framed spectacles.

''Ello, luv,' Reggie said, leaning forward and kissing Glory's cheek.

''Hello, Reg,' she replied. She looked at Ronnie nervously. 'Hello, Ronnie. Reggie, you remember Constance from the neighbourhood, yeah?'

'No love for me then,' Mick interrupted with a laugh. 'And I thought we were going to be mates.' He grinned at Reggie, but when his eyes slid towards Ronnie, they narrowed.

Reggie stuck out his hand and Mick took it. 'You won't get all the attention tonight,' Reggie said, smiling. 'There are fish as big as you here.' He turned towards Constance. 'How're you, luv? Haven't seen you for a long time.'

'I'm fine, Reg,' she replied. It didn't matter how often Constance saw the Kray brothers, they still made her uncomfortable. They dressed sharp, drove posh cars. And they had even been interviewed on the telly. Those things could make them seem glamorous if you forgot about the crimes they'd committed. And then there were the ones they'd been accused of but had never been caught at. Those were far scarier – like the story about Ronnie and Frances. But Constance knew if the coppers had anything on Ronnie, he'd be in custody.

'Hello, Ronnie,' Constance said.

'Hello, Constance,' he replied, but it was curt and certainly not friendly. Then he stared pointedly at Jagger. 'Why are you here?'

'Ronnie, old son, is that any way to confab?' Mick said with a mocking smile. But his eyes remained yellow.

'I told you last time I saw you, I wouldn't be so kind,' Ronnie said.

The tension between Mick and Ronnie made Constance think the rumour about Mick rejecting Ronnie's advances in a most humiliating way were true. Supposedly, the Krays had had to pay off the *Daily Mirror* not to run a story about the incident.

Constance saw Jagger's fingers and nails begin to turn into claws. His fingers elongated and silky brown hair covered them. Ronnie flexed his fingers.

'Mick, it's a real honour to see you again,' Reggie said. 'Ronnie and I are sorry about our last meeting. Some parties get out of hand.'

'Don't apologize to him,' Ronnie said angrily.

Reggie glanced at his brother. 'No need for that, Ronnie. We're all friends here, aren't we, Glory?' He put a protective hand on her elbow. 'Mick, I think you know I'm mad about Glory. You don't mind, do you?'

'It's her choice,' Mick said. There was an artificial brightness in his voice. 'Don't need to force any bird to stay with me. Plenty of them out there.'

'No need to be insulting,' Reggie replied. Ronnie nodded in agreement.

Glory pulled her arm out of Reggie's grasp, then moved closer to Mick. An angry expression crossed Reggie's face.

It was then that Ronnie reached out to touch Glory.

Later, Constance would wonder why she did it. What had prompted her? Was it the rumours about Frances's death? Or was it the cold expression on his face? Whatever the reason, at the last moment, before Ronnie could touch Glory, Constance held out her empty glass between them, and said, 'Oh, Mick, could you get me another pint?'

And Ronnie's fingers slid off the sleeve of her dress.

Ronnie stared, a dumbfounded expression on his face.

'Guess those rumours aren't true, are they, Ronnie?' Mick said as his hands reverted to their normal state. He took Constance's glass and handed it to a passing waiter. 'Thanks for the invite, Reg. Glory, always a pleasure. And you, my dear,' he said to Constance, leaning in and whispering in her ear. 'I can buy you that pint later. And if you decide you don't mind sharing . . .'

Constance laughed nervously. Mick gave them all a toothy smile, then sauntered out of the club letting a puff of cool, damp air inside.

An uncomfortable silence stretched out between the four of them while the party swirled in the background. The doors to the club swung open and the glorious Barbara Windsor entered in a gold lamé dress.

'*Reggie! Glory! Ronnie!* Glory, that dress is magnificent,' she said with a delighted laugh. 'Wherever did you find it?'

'My friend Constance made it,' Glory said as she and Babs hugged. 'Isn't it fab? Constance, I want you to meet Barbara Windsor.'

'I can't wait to see *Carry On Doctor*,' Constance blurted out. Inwardly, she groaned.

Glory, Constance, and Barbara began chatting excitedly about films and clothes. Constance was acting cool, but inside she was giddy. Even with the Krays standing by, she couldn't help but be enchanted. The day had been a pendulum swing from disaster to glamour. Except for the Krays, it was everything she wanted.

Reggie stood awkwardly next to Glory, staring at her as if transfixed when one of the Firm came over and whispered in his ear.

'So sorry, girls,' Reggie said as he checked his shirt cuffs, which were already displayed to the exact right length. 'Must attend to something. Babs, Glory, Constance, I'll be back later.'

Ronnie stayed behind. He stepped closer to the women, lurking on the edge of the group, though not taking part in the conversation. Constance glanced up at him. He was staring at her and she didn't like it. She was glad when he finally went away.

♠

Glory and Constance stood outside Esmeralda's Barn around one in the morning. It was chilly outside and Glory shivered. After Glory had snapped pics of Babs, Sinatra and Monroe had come over wanting to be introduced to Glory. Barbara performed the introductions, then went off to talk to Dusty.

'Have you ever thought about coming to Hollywood?' Monroe asked in her breathy voice. Constance was pretty sure it was put on, since she hadn't had it in *Cleopatra*.

Sinatra nodded. 'Marilyn is right,' he said in his silky voice. He was the coolest thing in the room, 'You got something. Looks. Those flowers. You're a barn-burner, baby.'

Glory started taking pictures again. 'Mr Sinatra—'

'Call me Frank,' he interrupted.

'All right . . . Frank. I'm a photographer, not an actress or a model. I can't act and I can't sit still. Can't sing either. What I'm really good at is taking pictures. Now if you'd put your arm around Miss Monroe . . .'

'Oh my goodness, call me Marilyn,' Monroe said, winking at Glory. 'I really love your photographs. I'm honoured that you'd like a picture.'

'I'll do my best,' Glory said. Constance recognized Glory's I'm-barely-keeping-my-excitement-under-wraps voice.

'I'd expect nothing else,' Marilyn replied. Then suddenly, like a light switch, she turned MARILYN on.

Glory rapid-fired her camera, a huge grin stretched across her face.

♥

'I can't believe she knew who I was!' Glory said excitedly as they waited for their cab to arrive. 'I mean, she doesn't seem the type to know about . . . well, hip things.'

'I think she's full of surprises,' Constance replied. 'Where's that taxi?'

A cream-coloured Rolls-Royce pulled up in front of them. The back door opened, and Mick poked his head out. 'I hear you birds need a lift home.'

'Where did you get this car?' Glory demanded.

'It belongs to John,' Mick replied. 'Borrowed it after I left the party. He's driving the psychedelic Rolls tonight.'

'And you've been waiting all night for us to leave?' Glory sounded dubious. 'I thought you were off to shag someone.'

Mick shrugged. 'I'm feeling chivalrous. Don't be cruel. Get in, please.'

'Don't think you're going to have the two of us. Or even one of us.'

He blushed, which amazed Constance. 'Just let me give you a lift home.'

'Very well,' Glory said begrudgingly. 'Constance, you get in first.'

'Oh, no,' Constance said, shaking her head. 'I'm not getting in between the two of you.'

Glory glared at Constance and then climbed into the car. Constance followed. It was gorgeous inside, far posher than anything Constance had ever been in, including Glory's flat, which was as posh as any home Constance had ever been inside.

There was silence as the car pulled away. Constance tried to do anything but look at Mick and Glory, until she smelled the perfume of roses. She looked over, and Glory's head was covered in white roses. Then Constance saw Mick's hand creeping towards Glory's, taking it into his own.

Shit, Constance thought.

A few minutes later, Glory asked, 'Do you mind staying at my flat tonight, Constance? It's just up the road.'

Constance sighed, but secretly she was thrilled. Glory's flat was so nice it was like being on holiday. That's what the whole day had been – a holiday from her life. She didn't mind it continuing that way. Not even one bit.

♣

Constance slipped the key into the lock of Glory's flat and opened the door. The aroma of incense, cinnamon potpourri, and hash met her. She dropped her handbag and Glory's keys on the coffee table and began to unzip her dress.

She'd always liked the lounge with its Milo Baughman settee and two low-slung chairs in the middle of the room. Large sitting cushions made of kilim rugs were piled in one corner. Next to the settee was a side table with two Royal Dalton teacups and a silver-plated cigarette lighter. One cup was filled with tobacco, the other with chunks of hash. Next to the table was a brass hookah embellished with garnets and quartz. On the walls were prints of Glory's black-and-white photographs. The one of Mick took up one wall all by itself.

She stepped out of her dress, folded it and laid it on the settee. Just then, there was a knock at the door. *What the hell did Glory forget?* she wondered as she went to answer it.

'I'd've thought you and Mick would be screwing in the back of that Rolls already. Forgot the Pill?' she said as she opened the door.

'Hadn't planned on screwing anyone,' Ronnie said, reaching out and swiping his hand across the upper part of her left arm. The shock of the pain stifled any cry she might have made. He pushed her back and slammed the door shut behind him, locking it as he did so. Blood began running down Constance's arm, staining her slip and dripping onto the floor.

'Right,' he said. 'It's not your skin what can't be cut. So what happened at the party? Can you turn it off and on?'

Constance stumbled backwards, staggered, and then fell down hard on the wooden floor. It made her bite her tongue and then she was crying.

'Shut yer gob,' he said, grabbing her right arm and yanking her to her feet. He was strong, and she gave a yelp. 'Shut it, or I'll cut yer face.' He laid his fingers on her cheek. It felt like razors resting there just waiting to slice. 'I guess you heard about me? 'Bout how I have a wild card. Well, they're right. All I have to do is think about cutting, and my fingers do the rest.'

Constance was trembling, but she tried to gently pull her face away. He let her. Her arm felt as if it was on fire where he'd cut her. She glanced down, and the amount of blood staining her slip made her woozy.

'I w-w-w-w-won't say anything,' she stuttered. 'I p-p-p-promise.'

'Sit over there,' he said, pointing to the settee.

'But I'll get blood all over it,' she replied. Her vision was going grey and she felt dizzy.

'Really? Seems sort of irrelevant at the moment.'

Constance went to the settee and sat down. She cradled her left arm in her right and tried not to look at the wound. 'This will need to be sewn up,' she said, her voice sounding far away. 'Soon.'

'I suppose it will,' he said curtly. 'And I can't let you bleed unconscious before I get some answers.' He went to the phone, picked up the receiver, and dialled a number. There was a pause, and then he said, 'Ring the surgeon and send him round to Glory's. You know the place. Reg's been having it watched. What? Well, wake him up.'

He hung up. Then he went into the bathroom and came back out with a hand towel. He started to wrap it around her arm, but then he stopped and stared at the floor.

Constance followed his gaze and saw him looking at her dress. There was blood on the floor under the dress, but none on it.

'What's this, then?' he asked softly.

'It's nothing,' she said, edging away.

He tossed the towel on the settee and then reached down and ran his fingers over the dress. It didn't rip. He picked it up and jabbed at it repeatedly. 'So, it's the dress!' he said, shaking it at her. 'Where did you get it?'

'How did you know I was here?' she asked, trying to change the subject even as her pain increased. 'Don't live here.'

'I followed ya after you got into that Rolls with Jagger,' he replied. 'Now where did ya get the dress?' He dropped the dress and reached for her and she shied back again. 'I can do the other arm.'

'No,' she said, hating the way her voice sounded. 'Please don't.'

There was a horrible moment when a completely mad expression flickered across his face. Then he said all too calmly, 'C'mon, luv, give it up.' He sat down beside her, and flexed his fingers again before laying them on her good arm.

'I-i-i-it's my wild card,' Constance admitted. 'Even your p-p-p-power can't affect the clothes I can make.' She was shaking hard enough it was making her teeth chatter. 'N-n-n-nothing can.'

◆

'Interesting,' Ronnie said. He considered the dress and then got up, grabbed the cigarette lighter, flicked it on, and held it to the hem. The chemical smell of lighter fluid filled the air as he held it there. 'Fucking hell,' he said. After a minute or so, he dropped the lighter and shook his hand. 'Thing got 'ot.'

The blood was getting sticky under Constance's hand. She grabbed the hand towel and wrapped it around her upper arm, and hoped the surgeon would get there soon. It was terrifying being alone with Ronnie. *Oh God!* she thought, sweat running down her back. *Oh my God. He did kill Frances! Oh, Jesus. He's going to kill me now. Did he slit her wrists and watch her die with those cold shark-like eyes? His own sister-in-law – how could he? And what am I to him? Nothing. Killing me would mean nothing to him.*

'Hmm, it really doesn't catch fire now, does it?' He gave her a cunning, sidelong glance. 'What else can't harm it?'

'I don't know exactly,' she said, trying to stop her teeth from chattering. 'I j-j-j-just know it doesn't stain, and knives and f-f-f-f-fire can't hurt it.'

'What about bullets?'

'Lord, h-h-h-how would I know that? I d-d-d-don't know anyone who has a gun. Wouldn't want to know anyone.'

Ronnie opened his jacket and Constance saw a holstered gun under his arm. 'Well, you do now. Does anyone else know about this?'

'No,' she lied. Glory and Frances knew. They had known about it since they were in primary school together.

There hadn't been a big incident that had made Constance's card turn. One day when her mother was teaching her to sew, she just . . . *knew* what she could do. If she concentrated, she could make clothing that couldn't be harmed – at least not by anyone other than herself. Glory said she should keep her power secret, and Frances had agreed. And so she had.

But before long, Glory had gone off to be . . . well, Glory. And Frances had succumbed to the charms of Reggie Kray. So Constance felt as if she was lagging behind. Lagging behind in the greyness of the East End, with the glitter of the West End so close. And she desperately wanted to be part of the things that were changing there. It meant everything to her.

'What difference does it make to you, anyway?' she asked. The pain in her arm had settled into a throbbing ache.

Ronnie vanished into the kitchen. He banged around. Then she heard him running water. It sounded for all the world as if he was putting the kettle on.

'Making some tea,' he said, coming back into the room. 'Honestly, that Glory don't have much in the way of tea in the house, just some Lapsang souchong and I don't care for them smoky teas. I bet she makes tea as bad as Frances did.'

Constance stared at him. She was bleeding through the hand towel while waiting for the surgeon to arrive, and Ronnie was intent on making tea. Now that the adrenalin was wearing off, she thought she might throw up. Again. She leaned over and put her head between her knees. It helped a little, but now there was a nauseating spinning. It had been a day of chundering. *I would not recommend this*, she thought hysterically. *Not at all.*

'Where was I?' Ronnie asked. 'Oh, yes. And how have you managed to keep this secret?'

'It's not exactly something that anyone would notice,' she replied. The spinning was going away, but the fear came slamming back. She sat up. 'You can't see it. It's just there.'

Ronnie cocked his head to one side. 'You know, any number of aces would want to use your power,' he said. 'Any ace, *anyone*, could be as safe as houses. Just like Golden Boy.'

'I don't want to make clothes like that,' Constance said softly. 'I have things I want to do with my life

Ronnie turned and started back towards the kitchen. 'I should get the kettle,' he said. 'Don't want to overboil the water.' He whistled as he vanished again.

♠

There was a knock on the door, and Constance felt a wave of relief as Ronnie answered it. Standing in the hall was Frances's brother Frankie, a skinny drink of water with the same cornflower-blue eyes and brown hair as Frances. He stood awkwardly by the door next to a bland-looking man who carried a brown surgeon's bag.

'I brought the surgeon just like you asked,' Frankie said as they entered the flat. 'Glory all right?' Then he saw Constance. 'What 'appened, Constance? Where's Glory?'

Despite the pain and the fear, Constance was suddenly furious. 'Ronnie 'appened, you twit,' she said hotly. 'Look what he's done to me.' She pulled the towel away from the cuts down her arm, hissing as it stuck to the wound. Fresh bright blood began to flow and Frankie blanched.

'Tea?' Ronnie asked the surgeon. The surgeon looked at him with astonishment. Constance suspected this wasn't the first time he'd had to sew someone up after Ronnie got through with them. Nor, likely, would it be the last.

♥

'Here,' the surgeon said. He fished around in his bag and pulled out a bottle of pills and handed them to Constance. 'This'll help with the pain. Have Ronnie bring you around in a few days so I can see how you're healing. Change the dressing once a day. If it starts looking red and puffy, ring me immediately.'

'Thank you, Dr Smythe,' Ronnie said, rising from the sofa. 'You sure you don't want tea?'

The doctor shook his head and closed his bag. 'Ronnie, take care of this girl. She's not part of your business. Don't treat her as if she is.'

'Now, I don't think you should be interfering in my business,' Ronnie said.

Constance shrank into her chair. She was beginning to know that voice. That soft, mad voice.

'I suppose not,' the doctor replied. 'But Reggie wouldn't like this. You know he wouldn't.'

Ronnie didn't answer.

♣

'I have an idea,' Ronnie said.

Constance was still shivering occasionally now. The pills the surgeon had given her were dulling the pain and made her feel as if she was packed in cotton wool, but they only took a little of the edge off the gut-twisting fear of being alone with Ronnie and his madness again.

'I think you should come to work for us.'

'I can't,' she said softly, shaking her head. 'I can't.' She started to cry. 'I can't.'

'Are you worried about the pay?' he asked, ignoring her tears. 'We'll pay you just fine. In fact, better than you'd make if you worked for them chaps down on Savile Row.'

Constance shook her head.

Ronnie stood up and in a flash grabbed her hair and yanked back her head. Then he leaned in close enough that she could feel the spittle as he snarled. 'Well, it don't matter what you want, now, does it?' He released her and sat back down on the sofa and poured himself some more tea. 'Where do you work? You'll have to pack up your things. Let them know tomorrow. I can send someone around.'

'I was sacked today,' she replied.

'Really?' he said. 'Who sacked you?'

'Teddy Bravo,' she replied.

'His loss, innit?'

Constance looked down at the floor. She knew now what Ronnie was capable of.

'You ought to get cleaned up,' Ronnie said, wrinkling his nose. 'You've got blood all over yerself. Might as well put that dress on again, seeing as how it won't get stained if ya start bleeding. And those sleeves will hide the plaster.'

'Okay,' Constance said quietly. 'Shouldn't be here in my slip anyway. Looks bad, you know.' She was too tired and hurt even to say it sarcastically.

◆

'I'm leavin' now,' Ronnie said, shaking Constance's shoulder. She jerked awake. The codeine and fear had finally knocked her out while Ronnie drank tea and read one of Glory's magazines, waiting for morning to come. 'I'm off to talk to Reg. Frankie's here and he's going to stay with ya. Make sure she doesn't leave,' Ronnie said as he walked out of the door. 'I'll call round soon.'

'Constance,' Frankie said nervously as the door shut. Constance didn't know why he should be nervous. She was the one Ronnie was keeping hostage. 'Been a while.'

'Since your sister's funeral,' Constance said, narrowing her eyes. She pushed herself up, wincing as her stitches pulled. 'I rang you after the funeral to see how you were. I was one of her best friends and I thought you might want to talk.'

'I've been busy,' he replied. A flush blossomed over his neck and up his face. He walked over to one of the chairs.

'No,' Constance said. 'No. Ya don't get to sit with me like we're friends. You keepin' an eye on me like this, you can stand over there by the door.'

♠

'Ronnie here tells me you've got a special kind of wild card that could help us,' Reggie said. Frankie had brought Constance to the Krays' private club after a ring from Ronnie. 'Why didn't you come to us a long time ago?'

'Because I didn't want to be making clothes where I had to use my power,' she replied. The codeine was wearing off and she was beginning to hurt again. 'I want to be *designing* clothes, makin' people look different. Makin' them look like they didn't know how they could look. Letting them see themselves in a different way.' She was on the verge of tears. 'Clothes says something about a person. You know that, look at yer suits. They're saying something about who you are. It sounds shallow, but it ain't.' She leaned towards them, holding her hands out like a beggar. 'If I make clothes with my power, it takes a long time. Longer than it does when I sew without it. I have to think about making my clothes with my wild card. And that doesn't leave any time for what I want to do.'

'Now that makes me sad, it does,' Reggie said. He almost looked as if he was. Almost. 'You're a local girl. And we look after your parents when they need us. We look after the whole neighbourhood.'

Constance wanted to shout at him: *I know how you look after them: with bribery and sometimes fear! And pretending you care about them. They may be turning a blind eye to what you do, but I'm not.*

Instead, she repeated, 'I don't want to use it for anyone, Reg. I never would. Why would I?'

Reggie and Ronnie shrugged in unison. It was creepy. 'You could make a lot of dosh. Wouldn't have to live in a nasty bedsit.'

'I dunno what's wrong with you two!' she almost shouted. 'I'm not gonna do it for anyone. Not now, not *ever*.'

'Oh, luv,' Reggie said, not unsympathetically. 'Yes, you are. We're going to give you everything you need and pay you more than you'd ever make working as a seamstress for anyone else. And you're going to tell your mum and dad you're moving back to Bethnal Green. And you'll tell your friend Glory, too. Or maybe we'll tell them if you won't.'

Ronnie stretched his fingers and wiggled them at Constance. And that was when she began to cry again.

♥

'Are you mad?' Glory exclaimed. She stood in Constance's bedsit while Constance methodically packed up her possessions. It had been two days since the Krays had found out about her wild card. 'Ronnie killed Frances! And apparently Reg doesn't care.'

In the hall outside the bedsit, Frankie stood waiting to move Constance's boxes. Earlier, he had tried to come in and help her pack, but she hadn't let him.

'Piss off, Frankie,' she'd said. 'You're working for Ronnie, and he killed your sister. And that's sick.'

'Them's just rumours, Constance, you know that,' he spluttered. 'Ronnie would never do something like that to Frances. You know she were troubled.'

'Oh.' She rolled up the sleeve on her blouse, exposing the bandage. 'What about this? Ronnie did this.'

'Well, Ronnie's mad, Constance, everyone knows that. You just don't cross him. He wants you to make them clothes, you make them clothes. And look, they're going to give you a place to work and live. And you'll get a lot of money. You can help out your mum and da. What else do you want? You're set for life!'

'And you are a stupid git if you can't figure out what's wrong with that,' she snarled. Being mean to Frankie suited her just fine now. She remembered when he'd been a boy a few years older than her, Glory, and Frances, a sweet lad who doted on his sister. But when he was in his teens and working for the Krays, he'd introduced Frances to Reggie and for that she couldn't forgive him.

Neither could Glory. 'Why are you going back to live at home?' she demanded. 'And to work for the Krays?'

Constance didn't answer and continued packing boxes.
'Constance, why?'

'For the love of all that's holy, Glory, why d'ya think?'
Constance threw a jumper on the bed and put her hands on
her hips.

For a moment, Glory looked at her blankly. Then her eyes
widened. 'How'd they find out?'

'The grey dress. The one I wore to the party. When I made
the dress, I used my power. No one but me would've ever
known. No one but me was ever going to wear it, but when
Ronnie went to touch you . . .'

'His hand slid off the dress,' Glory said, finishing Constance's
sentence. 'How'd you know? How'd you know what he was
going to do? That he could even . . .'

'I dunno. A feeling, I guess. All those rumours.' She shook
her head, then bent over, picked up the jumper and began
folding it. 'Doesn't matter anyway. What's done is done. And
he did this to me.' She showed Glory her bandaged arm.

'Oh Lord. What did he do to you? No, I can see well enough.
But, you can't just go and do nothing but make them bespoke
suits! You'll be giving up on everything you want to do with
your life!' Glory's hands were balled up in fists, and her head
sprouted thorny, angry-looking charcoal-coloured climbing
roses. They tangled as they rose above her head, eventually
looking like a demented Marie Antoinette wig. 'Go to the
police! They're always trying to get something on the Krays!'

'I can't,' Constance said miserably. 'Mum and Dad, well,
they wouldn't be safe.' She didn't mention that Glory was in
danger too. 'And what am I going to do? Tell the detectives
the Krays are forcing me to make clothes for them?'

'You could tell them about your power.'

'Absolutely not,' Constance said, shaking her head. 'That's
what got me in trouble in the first place.'

'You can't do this!'

'Stop it,' Constance said, holding back tears. 'I can't bear this if you're angry at me. You have to be my friend now more than ever.' But Constance knew she was being selfish. It would always be dangerous for Glory to be around her. It was dangerous for Glory even to know her.

'Of course I'm not!' Glory cried as she came and hugged Constance. Constance held on to her so tightly some of the thorns scratched her forehead. 'We'll be friends forever.'

♣

Constance had to admit, Reggie was true to his word. The Krays gave her everything she could have wanted. Except for clients and the ability to do her own work. They gave her two flats over their private club – one as her sewing workshop, the other for her to live in.

The only clients she saw were Reggie and Ronnie, but they were demanding. Their suits had to be as sharp as possible and every bit as perfect as any from Savile Row. And of course, she had to use her wild card ability. They even tested the suits to make certain she was doing as she was told.

'You finished with that one?' Ronnie said, pointing at her most recent work. It was a little more flamboyant than the suits they normally wore, which were usually in dark navy or black. But this suit was grey and single-breasted with a windowpane check and a narrow lapel. The colour and pattern were different from the American Mob style they normally sported. Though the cut wasn't as slim as Constance would have made it, because both carried holstered guns nestled under their armpits.

'Frankie,' Ronnie called. 'Come in 'ere.' Frankie slunk in, giving Constance a hangdog expression. She was unmoved. 'Put that jacket on.' Frankie did so, but he looked miserable. Both he and Constance knew what was coming next.

Ronnie took out his pistol and fired at Frankie's chest. The bullet hit the jacket and Frankie groaned as the impact sent him stumbling backwards. The bullet fell to the floor.

'Lord, Ronnie, why do I have ta wear it when you shoot it?' Frankie asked as he took off the jacket and held it out to Constance.

She stared at him, then said, 'Do I look like yer servant?'

Sheepishly, he rehung it on the mannequin. 'Just making sure,' Ronnie replied. 'Anyway, it's more fun to shoot you.' He walked to the mannequin and ran his hand down the front of the jacket. Nothing happened. Then he dipped his hand into his pocket and pulled out a lighter.

'Ronnie, don't be daft,' Constance said. She smoothed out a navy worsted on her cutting table. 'If the bullet didn't do anything, why would that lighter?'

'I'm not daft,' Ronnie replied angrily. 'Thought I told you never to call me that again.' His fingers wiggled as if he were loosening them up.

A chill ran through Constance. It had been six months, but the scars left by Ronnie's cuts were still an angry pink, and it hurt to touch them. She'd taken to wearing long sleeves. 'It's just a saying, Ronnie,' she replied. 'Just a sayin' is all.'

He snapped the lighter on and held it to the sleeve of the jacket. The flame licked at the sleeve, but nothing happened.

'You see,' she said. 'You can trust me.'

'Don't trust no one,' Ronnie said, looking at her with his cold dead-man's eyes. 'Except Reg.'

◆

'I've been thinking,' Ronnie said. He and Constance were in her workroom so Constance could fit a jacket for yet another suit. She closed her eyes and swallowed hard. Ronnie thinking was bad.

'I've been thinking that we never made right what was done to you. You getting the sack and all. It was a good thing for us, but you weren't treated fair, Constance. And I'd like to make that up to you. Come with me.' He shrugged the jacket off, folded it, and laid it on her cutting table.

Constance followed him down the stairs. It was still morning and the club wasn't open yet. It felt strange without anyone in there and the strip lights off. The club smelled of stale cigarettes. A weak grey light came through the front windows.

Teddy Bravo sat at one of the tables with Reggie across from him. Teddy Bravo shook a cigarette out of his pack and lit it with shaking hands.

'Constance, luv!' Reggie exclaimed as she came closer. 'You know Teddy Bravo, don't you? Right nice bloke. Came all the way here just to say 'ello.'

Warily, Constance eyed Reggie. His voice was too bright. Ronnie passed her and sat down at the table. The Krays flanked Teddy Bravo, and he looked positively green.

'Aren't you going to say 'ello to Constance?' Ronnie asked. He reached out and touched the table top, his fingers leaving scratches in the wood. 'I'm certain she's hurt you haven't been round to visit.'

'I didn't know where she went,' Teddy Bravo said with a tremor in his voice. 'There were rumours about her working for . . . well, you and Reggie, but I guess they weren't just rumours.'

A terrible smile cut across Ronnie's face. 'We wouldn't want anyone to get the wrong idea about that,' he said. 'No one should know about Constance and us. It's a private matter. But Constance here is a nice girl who worked for you a long time. And you gave her the sack without so much as a by-your-leave. Not well done of you, old son.'

'I'm filled with regret, Constance,' Teddy Bravo said. She knew he'd prided himself on his ability to rise above any situation, but she doubted he'd ever expected to be sitting between the Kray brothers being forced to apologize to her.

'You know,' Reggie said thoughtfully. 'I don't think that apology sounded sincere. Can't you do better?' Then he took the back of Teddy Bravo's head in his hand and smashed his face into the table. Constance gave a shriek and covered her mouth with her hands.

Reggie lifted Teddy Bravo's head up. Blood dripped from his nose. He made a whimpering sound.

'Constance,' Reggie said in a calm voice. It was worse than if he'd been yelling. 'What would you like me to do with 'im? We take care of our own here. You know that.'

Constance shook her head. Teddy Bravo looked at her, his eyes dazed and scared. He'd definitely hurt her career, but he didn't deserve this. The Krays were doing worse to her right now, making her watch what they were doing to him.

'Nothing,' she said, choking back tears. And she could feel the bile coming up. But there was no way she was going to vomit in front of them. Showing fear was a mistake, she'd learned. 'You're doing fine, but you should let him go,' she said. 'He's not important. And if he hadn't fired me, well, I wouldn't be working for the two of you now, would I?'

It really was all Teddy Bravo's fault. If he hadn't sacked her, she wouldn't have rung up Glory, and wouldn't have got drunk, and she wouldn't have gone to the party where Ronnie had found out about her power. Everything that had led her here, stuck sewing for the Krays and losing everything she'd worked for, *was* his fault.

But Constance had to admit that one thing was her fault: she'd stupidly revealed her power. *Foolish girl*, she thought. *As if you could save anyone. You certainly didn't save Frances. Or yourself.*

'We can do something more permanent,' Ronnie said. He flexed his fingers. 'If you want us to.'

Constance shook her head.

There was blood on the table.

And the threat of more and worse damage to come. And the threat wasn't just to Teddy Bravo. It was to her as well.

♠

Constance was waiting in her flat for Glory to arrive. Ever since Constance had begun working for the Krays, Glory had made a point of visiting Constance as often as she could. Constance had finally broken down one afternoon and told Glory she was also in danger, but Glory had just given a bitter chuckle.

'Of course I know I'm in danger,' she said. 'Do you think I didn't know it from the moment you told me about your mum and dad? I'm your best – and only – friend now that Frances is dead. But whether I see you or not doesn't matter. I'm in just as much danger either way. And I'd rather see you.' She gave Constance a fierce hug. 'Besides, I'm keeping an eye on you and those damn Krays.'

Despite her situation, Constance's flat was nice. Not as fancy as Glory's. But it had a separate bedroom and a tiny kitchen, and its own loo. Under any other circumstances, Constance would have been thrilled.

She looked out of the window. London, on the whole, had finally bounced back after the war, but there were still places in the East End scarred by the Blitz. Prefabs still dotted burned-out streets. There were bombed buildings looking as if they were about to collapse. Constance saw jokers coming out of some of the huts, tending the small gardens they had planted, tiny bits of green dotting the grey rubble. Her heart ached for the bright colours and the people in Soho. Here, it felt as if the war had just ended.

Constance didn't mind the idea of jokers. After all, it wasn't their fault. However, even she had a hard time accepting the really disgusting ones. Fortunately, the jokers who moved into the East End weren't too repulsive. And they did try to make their area prettier. Potted plants – red carnations and violets – appeared in front of tents and prefabs. Some in the East End sarcastically called the area where the jokers were squatting 'Jokers' Council'.

Occasionally, there were violent attacks against them, but

on the whole, the jokers were tolerated. The Krays found some of them helpful for certain jobs. And that meant some had money to spend, and no one minded that at all. Even jokers were welcome when they turned up in a shop with a handful of notes.

There was a quick knock on the door, and then Glory let herself in with her key as Constance turned away from the window.

'I brought something,' Glory said, putting the cardboard box on the table with a grunt. There were yellow-and-white pansies on her head. She wore a faded azure jumper, low-slung jeans embroidered with flowers up one side, and new Mary Janes with surprisingly chunky heels. 'It's heavy!'

Constance recognized the box immediately. 'Glory, why'd you bring that here?' she asked with dismay. 'I thought we agreed it was nothing but heartache in there.'

'Because it's been long enough,' Glory said. 'And because we owe it to Frances to at least look at what she gave us.'

'I'm going to need a drink if we're going to do this,' Constance said.

Glory pulled a bottle of Grant's whisky out of her oversized handbag with the Union Jack emblazoned on it.

'Anything else in that Mary Poppins bag?' Constance asked.

'Just my camera and film,' Glory replied. 'Thought I might go down to the Jokers' Council and take some shots after we've finished here. Now get us some glasses.'

Constance did as she was told. She hated blended Scotch, but once the three girls had nicked a bottle of Grant's from an off-licence and had got blind drunk on it. Glory was nothing if not nostalgic.

♥

'You ready to open this thing?' Constance asked. They were on their third shot, and Constance's tongue had gone numb halfway through the second drink, something for which she was truly grateful. 'I don't think I can drink any more of this.'

Glory nodded then pulled the brown paper packing tape off the top of the box. The smell of Frances's perfume and stale cigarettes wafted out. Glory reached in and pulled out an object wrapped in newspaper. When the paper was unwrapped, it revealed a music box. Glory gave it to Constance, who wound it up and it started playing 'The Blue Danube'.

One by one, the girls removed every item from the box. Some were wrapped, some not. Constance and Glory treated the wrapped ones like Christmas presents. There was a squat glass paperweight, a small crystal vase, and a figurine of a shepherdess holding a crook with lambs by her feet.

'I gave her that after I sold the Mick photo,' Glory said softly, touching the shepherdess. 'She said she'd love it forever.'

Constance nodded. 'I remember.'

They pulled out scarves, handkerchiefs, and a dress. Constance recognized the dress. She'd made it, after all. And at the very bottom they found a jewellery box. Glory opened it, and inside was a gold bracelet Constance recalled as one of Frances's favourites, along with a number of other pieces. Except for the bracelet, the rest were costume jewellery. They were trinkets Glory or Constance had told Frances they liked. Glory slipped the bracelet on.

A pair of oversized hoop earrings, several skinny silver rings set with a variety of stones, and a pretty brooch were inside. Constance took off her earrings and slid in the hoops.

'What do we do with all this?' Glory asked as she plucked out a ring and put it on the table. 'Do we give it back to Reg?'

'I don't think so,' Constance said. She stacked the rings up and slid them onto her index finger. 'Don't you think she would have left it to him if she wanted him to have it?'

'I suppose so,' Glory said. She reached into the box again. 'This brooch is pinned to the lining. Bugger, I can't get it off.' Suddenly, the bottom lining of the jewellery box pulled away, revealing a thin book. DIARY was embossed on the cover in gold.

'Oh dear,' Constance said as Glory slipped it out of its resting place.

Glory opened it and read a little before saying, 'This is all about when she was married to Reggie. Listen: *Reg and I moved into our new flat. Reg told me again that he wanted to get out of the Firm, but Ronnie wouldn't have it. Reg said that Ronnie likes being a gangster too much. I don't know about that. I think Reggie also likes being a gangster. But I wouldn't mind if he did get out. He always said Ronnie would never get out of the game and that's why he was still there.*'

Glory began flipping the pages. She stopped about halfway through the book. 'Oh, this is just, well,' she said, and then began reading again. '*Reggie got home late again. I asked him where he'd been and he told me to mind my own business. When I told him I was his wife and it was my business he told me to take another Seconal. Then he grabbed my arm and shook me.*'

'I don't think I want to hear this,' Constance said. She began toying nervously with a silk scarf she'd pulled out of the box. It was a bold Pucci print and must have set Frances back a ton of money. 'Let's not,' she said, reaching for the diary, but Glory pulled away and wouldn't let her have it.

'*I wish I'd never married him,*' Glory continued. '*He's already screwing other women. Some slut from the local, I think. And it's only been a month! I'd tell Glory and Constance, but they'd say leave him and I just can't. Not now. Not after waiting so long to marry him.*'

'Please stop,' Constance said. 'We *would* have told her to leave him. And it's horrible that she was too afraid to tell us how miserable she was.'

Glory's flowers drooped, and she nodded in agreement. 'We would have told her to tell him to piss off and then give him the shove.' She flipped a few pages forward and read to herself. Then she looked up at Constance.

'Oh, Constance, there's this: *I haven't told Reg, but I'm not*

*taking the Seconal any more. It was making me feel sad. Violet
keeps coming over telling me how unhappy I'm making her son.
I know I can be difficult, that's what they keep telling me. Maybe
it would be easier for everyone if I wasn't around. At least that's
what Reg keeps saying anyway. He said sometimes he wished I'd
done a better job at that thing I tried before. It's like now that he
has me, he doesn't want me any more. I feel like I'm going as mad
as Ronnie.'*

Glory flipped towards the end of the volume, then continued,
'*Last night I found out that Reggie's been keeping a flick knife
under his pillow. He says I ask too many questions about where
he's been and what he's been doing, then he pulled it out, snapped
it open, and held it against my face. He told me in this horrible
voice that he wished he'd never married me, that he is going to
kill me. And I believe he'll do it, so I'm moving back with Mum.
He used to be kind. He treated me like a queen. I don't know what
happened to make him change like that. I always thought it was
Ronnie who hated me. But Reggie is going to kill me.'*

Glory shut the diary and put it on the table. 'She never
made it back to her mum's, did she? It's the last entry and
it's dated three weeks before she died. What if we've been
wrong?'

'What do you mean?' asked Constance. 'You really don't . . .'

'Oh, think about it,' Glory replied. She reached out, grabbed
the whisky bottle and took a swig. 'It wasn't Ronnie who killed
Frances and made it look like a suicide, it was Reggie. Reggie
might have even started the rumours about Ron – to throw
the scent off him. After all, there must be people in the Firm
who know about Ronnie's power. And plenty of others who
suspect.'

'He'd never do that to Ronnie,' Constance said. '*Never*. Or
to Frances: he loved her.'

'But it's perfect!' Glory laughed a little hysterically. 'Ronnie
doesn't know what's real and what's not half the time. And
he's got that cutting power. And if he snapped and confessed,

he'd go back to the sanatorium, not prison. And then Reg would be in the clear and could run everything without having to look after his crazy wife and his crazy brother.'

'But Ronnie would know if he killed her,' Constance protested. 'Surely he'd know.'

'Not if Reg convinced him otherwise. Not if he was trying to drive him insane. Well, more insane.'

'Reg'd *never* do it,' Constance said stubbornly. 'You haven't been around them the way I have. They have this bond . . .'

Glory gave an exasperated sigh and took another swig, then shook the diary at Constance. 'This isn't the diary of someone who wants to kill herself. It's the diary of a woman who's *afraid*. Afraid of her husband. She wanted us to know even though she was afraid to tell us outright!'

'Then why not just ring us? Or ring the coppers? Or that detective who's been following them around?'

'Really?' Glory asked sarcastically. 'Really? You can't think of a *single* reason why she might not do that?'

Constance held out her hand, and Glory passed her the Grant's. She took a gulp, barely tasting the awfulness of it.

'Well, what do we do about it?' Constance asked. 'What do we do about the bastard?' It felt as if fire was bursting in her brain, and a red haze filled her vision.

Glory took the bottle back, took a long swallow, and then spoke with a dark anger that mirrored Constance's own rage. 'I don't know. But I do know we'll make him pay.' Acacias bloomed across her head, their spiky thorns a dull grey, then they changed to orange lilies and finally settled as deep purple monkshood. 'Don't matter how. Don't matter what happens to us. We've got to make him pay for Frances.'

♣

'We should just kill him,' Glory said softly. '*I'll* kill that bloody bastard.' A month had passed since Constance and Glory had read Frances's diary. And with each passing day, Glory had grown angrier and angrier until she was obsessed with killing Reggie.

'Don't go off like that,' Constance said hotly. It was early morning, and they were in the living room of Constance's flat. The latest jacket for Ronnie lay beside her, waiting for the domette to be sewn in. Her favourite shears and sewing box were on the coffee table. 'We can't just kill Reggie Kray. Until we find a way that don't put us in prison. And much as I want him dead, I'm not going to jail for it.'

Venus flytraps grew on Glory's head, their pink mouths open and glistening. 'Is he supposed to get away with it, then? Just like that? Like she was nothing at all?'

'No!' Constance said violently. 'And I hate it! I hate waiting as much as you do! Maybe more! I'm supposed to protect both of you, but I couldn't protect either. She's dead and you're constantly in danger of having something 'orrible happen to you because of me.' She started crying. Glory hugged her.

'You can't protect everyone, luv. The world doesn't work that way. I suppose we could just leave them to the coppers, but then you're still stuck here working for them for however long it takes for one of them to slip up. And that could take years.'

'I'm stuck,' Constance said miserably. 'And I can't get unstuck.'

'You stuck, are you?'

The girls started. Standing in the doorway to Constance's apartment was Ronnie.

''Ello, Glory, Constance,' he said as he eased into the room, shutting the door behind him. He wore one of the suits Constance had made for him, a sharp-looking double-breasted of fine black worsted. Even his pristine white shirt had been made by Constance. And the spectacles he wore were the silver-framed ones instead of his usual black ones. 'Seems like you forgot to lock the door. Very unsafe. You're both looking nice today.'

'Thanks, Ronnie,' Constance said.

'Yes, we were talking about Reggie,' Glory spat out before Constance could say anything else. 'That he murdered Frances and made it look like she killed herself.'

'Reg'd never do that!' Ronnie said angrily. 'He loved her. Treated her really nice.'

Constance put her hand on Glory's arm, but Glory just shook it off. 'And then he set it up to make it look like you done it if anyone got suspicious. The slit wrists, and all. You know what I'm sayin'?'

'Reggie loves me more than anything or anyone in this world. He'd never do that to me. That's just mad.' Ronnie shrugged. 'I know Reggie. He's my brother. More than a brother.' He began blinking rapidly, then stared blankly into space. Constance had seen that expression before, and it always meant Ronnie was getting out of control.

She reached out and grabbed her shears.

'He let it seem like it could be you,' Glory said. 'Cut her up so everyone would think you did it if they didn't believe she killed herself. He told you you did it though, didn't he?'

'I remember,' Ronnie said stubbornly. 'I remember killin' her.'

'Do you?' Glory asked. Her flowers turned into yellow climbing roses with sharp thorns. She took a step closer to him, then leaned towards him intently. 'You were just out of the sanatorium, after all. The rumours are Reg got you out before you were cured . . . And Reggie can be persuasive. Think about it, Ronnie.' Glory tapped a finger on her temple. 'You didn't like her, but why would you kill her? You love Reggie. You'd never hurt him that way. But Frances, she was afraid of Reg there at the end . . . We have her diary.'

'Frances was unwell,' Ronnie replied. He was shaking his head like a dog shaking off water. 'She was going to leave Reg. He loved her.' He was flexing his fingers now. Glory stepped back. 'He loved her. I couldn't let her leave. You stop saying that.'

He made a sudden lunge towards Glory, slicing through the flowers on the right side of her head. Glory screamed and fell to her knees, blood sluicing down her face. He reached out to cut her again. Constance dropped her shears, then jumped in front of him, raising her arms. His hand slid off her jacket.

'Did ya think that dress was the only thing I'd made for myself? My dad taught me a girl has to take care of 'erself.'

Ronnie laughed and shoved Constance away. She tumbled over Glory and fell backwards, landing hard. It knocked the breath out of her and for a moment she lay there, gasping for air like a beached fish.

Glory wiped the blood from her face. Then she howled as she got to her knees and punched Ronnie in the goolies. He gave an '*oomph*' and doubled over. Glory staggered to her feet and kicked him in the face.

'I'll kill you just to see the look on Reg's face, you fucker,' she said, kicking him again. 'And this is for Constance because you locked her up here. And this—' she kicked him again. 'This one is for Frances, just because.'

Ronnie pushed himself up, then grabbed her foot, yanking her down to the floor. He ripped through her blouse, leaving four cuts across her stomach. And then he sliced off the rest of her flowers, laughing as he did so.

Constance saw her shears a few feet away. She crawled to them, picked them up, and then struggled to her feet, breathing heavily.

Glory was losing the fight. She whimpered, her arms over her face.

Fuck, Constance thought. *Fuck. Fuck. Fuck.*

Constance wasn't big enough to stop him despite the protection of her jacket, and he was going to kill Glory if she didn't do something fast.

Ronnie stopped for a moment, then straightened his jacket as if he wanted to be neat and tidy when he killed Glory. He leaned over her again, hands reaching for her throat.

Rage consumed Constance. She ran up behind Ronnie and grabbed his jacket by the collar with one hand, pulling it down to his elbows, trapping his arms so he couldn't get his hands out. He wasn't going to hurt Glory any more. Constance hadn't saved Frances from one Kray brother, but she was going to save Glory from another.

She lifted the arm holding her shears into the air and then plunged them into Ronnie's back. He screamed. She stabbed him over and over again, until her hand grew numb and he fell to the floor.

He rolled on the ground, blood sliding off his jacket and shirt. Constance stood over him.

'You was supposed to make us clothes so we can't be hurt,' he gasped. 'You tricked us.'

'No,' Constance told him, breathing hard, her heart pounding, his blood spattered on her clothes everywhere except her jacket. 'No one else can hurt you. No one 'cept me if I want.'

Ronnie tried to get to his feet, but they slid uselessly against the blood-slicked floor. He gave a wet wheeze, then stopped moving.

Constance ran to Glory and crouched beside her. 'We can't stay here,' she said. 'Who knows when Reg or someone in the Firm might show up.'

Glory nodded, but didn't move.

'Did you hear me, Glory? We got to go.'

Tears began rolling down Glory's cheeks leaving trails in the blood that was drying there. 'It wasn't Reggie. It wasn't Reggie. We didn't kill him! We didn't kill Reggie! Just Ronnie.' Then she put trembling hands up to her head. 'My flowers.'

'I know, Glory. But we need to go.'

Constance dragged Glory to her feet and pushed her into the loo. She ran warm water in the sink, wet a flannel, and proceeded to wipe as much of the blood off Glory's face as she could. Glory's head had already begun to stop bleeding, sap sealing over the open wounds. Constance ran to the kitchen, grabbed a tea towel, and then grabbed a hat off a peg on the wall as she ran back to the loo. She wrapped Glory's head in the towel, then settled the hat on top. Glory winced and went pale.

'Wipe that blood off your belly before you change into my blouse.' Constance yanked off her jacket and dropped it on the floor. Then she unbuttoned her blouse and tossed it to Glory.

She ran to her own wardrobe, grabbed a jumper and pulled it on. When Constance went back into the main room, she saw Glory holding the jacket out to her.

'Not leaving this jacket behind, Constance,' Glory said with a wild laugh. 'It saved our lives. What are we going to do about Reggie? I want him dead.'

'Glory, there's a dead Kray on the floor!' Constance exclaimed as she took the jacket and yanked it on. 'We killed him, and even though the coppers will be happy, we'll go to prison for it.'

'Self-defence,' Glory said. 'Look at my flowers.' She laughed hysterically.

'Even if that worked at trial,' Constance said, 'there would be Reggie coming after us. He might have been happy with Ronnie in the asylum, but he wouldn't want him dead.' She was trying to be calm. One of them had to be. It was clear Glory was in no fit state.

'Then what do we do?'

Constance looked at Ronnie's body and discovered she was completely indifferent to what she had done to him. It scared her that she didn't care. Ronnie hadn't killed Frances, but his death would wound Reggie horribly. And that was a start. 'I have a notion,' she said. Her eyes narrowed. 'But I need you to ring someone, Glory.'

◆

The black cab screamed around the corner and raced across the tarmac towards the plane. Constance held on to the handle with all her might. They'd given a hundred quid to the driver and told him there was a hundred more if he got them to the airport fast.

He had.

The taxi came to a screeching halt in front of the stairs leading up to the plane.

Glory opened the door and staggered out of the cab. Constance dug into her wallet and pulled out two hundred quid.

'The extra is to forget you ever saw us.'

'Miss, I am only too happy to oblige.'

Constance nodded and slid out. Glory took a few wobbly steps. Constance rushed to her side and supported her, and they limped to the stairway. The black cab sped away.

'What happened to you?' Mick asked, running down the stairs towards them. He grabbed Glory's left arm and helped support her as the three of them wobbled to the base of the stairway. Painted on the tail of the jet was the iconic Rolling Stones red lips and tongue. Fangs peeped out on either side of the tongue.

'Ronnie Kray is what happened,' Constance replied.

'He's dead,' Glory said with venom in her voice. 'And we're fugitives. Or we will be once they find the body. I guess the coppers might want us, too. But it was self-defence.'

Mick looked back and forth between the girls then finally said, 'So, you're asking me to fly the two of you out of the country on our tour plane to get away from the police and Reggie Kray?'

Glory sagged in their arms. 'I told you Ronnie killed Frances, but it wasn't him, it was Reggie.' There were only a few steps left to go to the door.

'Nice girl, Frances was,' Constance said. Things were beginning to feel utterly surreal now. 'We went to school with her, you know. The three of us.'

Mick nodded. 'Glory told me.' They reached the top of the aircraft steps. 'We've smuggled worse things into the States,' Mick said. 'Is that blood on her neck?'

'Yes,' Constance replied. 'Things got messy. You're being awfully calm about this.'

'I love her,' he said.

'So do I,' Constance replied. 'She's my best friend. But I need to stay and make sure my mum and dad are safe, and hers too. Not sure how I'm going to do that.'

'You can't stay here!' Glory said. Then her knees gave out. Together, Constance and Mick carried her into the plane and settled her into a seat. 'You can't.'

'*You're* going to be okay,' Constance said. 'That's all that matters.'

'Mick, tell her she's being ridiculous!'

Mick looked at Constance, then said, 'Give me a moment. I think I might be able to help you.'

♠

'Mr Jagger tells us you need our assistance,' the man said. Constance had been waiting for him at the bottom of the stairs to the jet. He wore a tidy navy-blue suit. Constance didn't much like his tie or the knot he'd chosen for it. 'He's explained the . . . unfortunate incident. He seems to be under the impression that this is the sort of thing Silver Helix deals with. He's mistaken. This is a Scotland Yard matter.'

Constance considered him for a moment. 'Then why are you here?' she asked.

'We'd very much like Mr Jagger to join us. We've asked him before. It's one favour for another. We stoop to serve.'

'I think you might find *me* more useful in the long run than Mr Jagger,' Constance said. Mick was being heroic, no doubt for Glory's sake, but Constance wasn't going to let him join Silver Helix after he'd already turned them down. She stood and zipped her jacket closed. She pulled her flick knife out of the hidden pocket, snapped it open, and then stabbed at her heart. The leather barely dimpled.

She smiled at the man. 'Would you like to try?' she asked, holding the knife out handle first.

He grinned and nodded. Then he grabbed the knife and tried to gut her; when that was fruitless, handed the knife back. 'Wild card?' he asked.

'Clothing that's impervious to harm,' Constance replied.

'Interesting. I think we may be able to accommodate you,' he said. 'I'm Alan Turing. Enigma. What should we call you?'

'I'm the Seamstress.'

♥

Constance sat in her flat watching the telly. A cup of tea and a plate of biscuits were on the low table at her elbow. Black-and-white film of a man surrounded by photographers and policemen escorting him out of the Old Bailey came on and the voice-over said, 'Reggie Kray being led out of the Central Criminal Court after being convicted of murdering his twin brother, Ronnie Kray. Despite protesting his innocence during the entire trial, he was sentenced to life in prison.

'An anonymous tip led Scotland Yard to the grisly crime scene where they found irrefutable evidence of Reggie's guilt.

'The notorious Kray criminal empire has fallen apart in the last year according to Scotland Yard. The Krays made their life of crime seem glamorous and their clubs were frequented by all manner of people, from celebrities to politicians, to under-ground criminal types.' The announcer droned on about the Krays and their history, but Constance got up and turned the telly off. She went back to her chair, sat down with a satisfied smile and drank some tea. It was perfect. The phone rang and she went to pick it up.

'Hello,' she answered, knowing full well who it must be.

'Yes, Mum, I saw it. Yes, it was a shame. No, I have no idea what happened. Mum, all I did was make clothes for them. Yeah, I'm peachy, Mum, go back to watching the telly. I'll come round later today.'

She hung up, went back to her chair, picked up her sewing and then began to whistle. Later in the evening, when she had finished this jacket for Redcoat, she would continue working on her own designs.

Her agreement with Silver Helix had been mutually beneficial. They gave her what she wanted, and she gave them what they wanted. And what she wanted was her own design shop. Glory had suggested calling it 'Needles and Pins' in one of her many letters from the States, and Constance decided that suited her just fine. She'd hired some fine tailors, all of them women, to execute the clothes that she didn't always have time to make.

She stabbed the red satin fabric with her needle and smiled as she began to sew the hem with neat, precise stiches.

♣ ♦ ♠ ♥

Night
Orders

by Paul Cornell

London, October 1973

CHARLIE SOPER KNOWS THAT front is everything. When the going gets tough, all our boy has is an expression. He's no good at the rough stuff, he just looks like he might be. Plus, he's staring right into you, as if he knows all your secrets. And everyone's secret is that they're not as hard as they want to make out. It's not that he practises in the mirror, but he knows when he's got that look on his face; he can see it in how people react to him. 'Like the devil's got into you,' that's what his old mum used to say.

He's made a bit of a career of it now. Technically, he's still only a junior analyst working over the files, learning the crafts of memory and connection that are at the heart of what 'Box 500', as it's called in the trade, does. Whatever Joe Public thinks about Roger Moore, they're actually kept safe from the KGB by dear old Mavis Clewer with her nicknames and stack of personal quirks for every single comrade in London. But Charlie feels he's on the way up, though his prospects were advanced in a most peculiar way. One day there was a rustle in the file room at Curzon Street, a whisper went round, and in walked the DG himself, and over he went to Charlie's desk.

Charlie was straight up on his feet of course, and was ready to be all yes, sir, no, sir, hope you didn't hear about Linda down the King's Arms, sir, pretty sure she's not one of them, sir, I asked nicely. But the DG just crooked a finger in his direction and beckoned 'come with', and off Charlie went, into the creaky old lift and up to the higher echelons.

He's made that trip several times since, though on subsequent occasions he's been summoned by phone call. He gives Mavis a wink over his shoulder as he goes, and, bless her heart, she doesn't mark him absent. He could probably use that trick now to knock off early and go down the pub, but he doesn't. In his heart of hearts, Charlie Soper has certain loyalties, notably to the DG, who brought him in as part of a new intake of redbrick university boys. Just as good with the modern languages as anyone from Eton, the thinking must have gone, and a sight less chance of having been buggered by a Bolshevik.

So that's where he's going now, getting out of that creaky lift, brushing the dust of the files off his Marks & Sparks suit. He smiles at Barbara at the desk in the front office. She thinks that's an affront, as always, just raises a palm to permit him to go through and dismiss him in the same gesture.

He walks into the DG's office and immediately feels a bit of the Roger Moores coming on, because here's not just the DG but a group of the great and the good from the upper reaches of Box. Charlie's been to enough of these meetings now to know that doesn't mean this lot are all on the same side. The DG is beset by the sort of intriguers who feel that the Cambridge Five couldn't have really ended with Anthony Blunt, that maybe Harold Wilson's a KGB agent, that maybe the DG is. They're the sort who could sit here drinking his brandy of an evening and still be building their dossiers and hiding their memoirs in safe deposit boxes. *Et tu, Brute*, and you, and you, and all.

'Glad you could join us, Charlie.' The DG always uses his

first name in company, but never when they're alone. Meaning he wants this lot to know they're on a first name basis.

'Always happy to help, sir.' Charlie takes up his usual spot, a seat the DG has kept for him, at an angle to the others, at a slight remove, by the window. He could look down at the shoppers in Mayfair, but he has standing orders to pay attention to the meeting at all times. On that first occasion, the DG had him arrive first, and had taken considerable care with his location and his instructions. He's to take no notes, indeed, to pay no particular heed to what's being said, but to watch faces, looking from one to the other of the DG's guests, and only every now and then to the DG himself.

He notes, as he makes himself comfortable, the slight shifting of the others in their seats, the clearings of the throat, the hostile glances in his direction. Charlie thinks he knows why the DG places him here, though he's never asked. Since the arrival of the wild card virus, twenty-seven years ago, British intelligence has been characteristically slow to adapt. There is, of course, the Silver Helix, but the less said about that bunch of amateurs the better. Everyone in their business is looking out for an ace who can read minds. Everyone's paranoid that the other lot, across the waters or across the road, has just that. Charlie reckons the DG has decided, as intelligence officers often do, to sell a pantomime, a con, as the genuine article. Charlie's got an intense expression, he's signed the Official Secrets Act, and this lot wouldn't be able to think of another reason a junior like him is in this office. He'll do. Charlie rather likes his unique position.

So he lets himself grin at the uneasy senior officers.

'The matter on the table is this,' the DG begins, without ceremony as always. 'Last night, around 11p.m., one of the dogs, a chap named Alex Ruskin, a petty criminal by trade, was conducting a burglary on orders, at a house in Kensington. He was discovered, and the owner of the place, a captain in the Household Cavalry, one Peter Faulkner, took matters into his own hands. It turns out Faulkner is . . . well, this is, in itself, delicate.' Charlie pricks up his ears. He's pretty sure he knows what's coming. He keeps his expression steady, knowing how he's likely to look at all this pussyfooting around this subject. 'It seems his regiment may not have known that Captain Faulkner is what the Americans call an ace.' That caused a little ruffle of feathers in the room. 'He produced some sort of . . . electrical discharge which injured Ruskin considerably. Ruskin is currently comatose, and under guard.'

'Is Faulkner under arrest?' asks one of the more rotund senior officers.

'He was, called it in himself, claiming self-defence, not that that cuts much ice with the courts these days, especially with him being of . . . the *special* persuasion. However, and here's the rub, a judge was woken up and he was out on bail before resumption of play this morning.'

Charlie looks around the faces. There is, perhaps, not as much surprise on one or two of them as there might have been, but he has no special skills in this area. Most of them seem taken aback.

'Almost as if he's in the Firm,' said someone Charlie thinks is probably with surveillance. The master of the kennel, who you might think would be in on this meeting, is conspicuously absent. Maybe that's because he's always treated like an NCO, coarsened by his association with the rough boys. Or maybe there's another reason. Charlie only knows who that person is from the gist of previous meetings like this. Introductions are never made while he's in the room. Perhaps that adds to the impression that he's been briefed about the others. Perhaps the DG wants to prevent him learning as much as is possible, given the circumstances.

'My thoughts exactly,' says the DG, 'but I've put out feelers to the funny people and the cousins, and he doesn't seem to be anyone's. Other than the regiment's, and I don't fancy calling up his colonel and getting the military gossiping that

Ruskin was our man. We'll get Ruskin back quietly in the usual way, assuming he ever wakes up.'

'What was he doing in there?' That was an emaciated-looking, rather ascetic sort, the kind that gets by on gin and sunflower seeds and was, in Charlie's opinion, far too often seen on Russian postage stamps.

'Need to know, I'm afraid.' They shift in their chairs again. Charlie doesn't need mind-reading to know that the DG's now made it plain that this meeting is *only* so Charlie can get a look at this lot. 'But of course I like to keep you informed of all my doings.' Charlie has to suppress a grin. He's really rubbing it in now.

'So who was the handler?' This voice was as upper class as all the rest, but with just a trace of his original Eastern European accent. Charlie has a soft spot for the ideological ones. This would be one of those poor bastards who had his family torn apart by Stalin and came over to go through who knew how much vetting.

'Foxton,' says the DG, as if carefully placing a piece on the board.

They're not pleased to hear that, and if anyone already knew they're pretending really well that they didn't. They aren't surprised to hear that name, and they're worried that they might be here by association. *Spot on about that I should think, dear chaps.*

'And what does *he* say?'

'That Ruskin was inside the building far too long. Foxton was watching the break-in from across the road, as per standard procedure. The search required was of a specific desk inside the house, and Ruskin had been given leave to break it open if necessary. Even a negative would have taken five minutes, but Ruskin was in that room for forty-five. Foxton had actually gone to the phone box on the corner and called it in when he saw the flash of lightning behind the curtains. He waited to see the emergency services arrive, then walked away. Unless he gave Ruskin a very odd steer on the way over, he can hardly be faulted in this.'

'Did Ruskin perhaps go off-piste and fill his pockets?'

'Nothing was found on him.'

'So . . .' That was Thin-and-Hungry again. 'What happened in that room?'

'That,' says the DG, placing his finger on his desk, 'is the question.'

There's a bit more chat after that. Charlie stays put when the DG gives the others leave to go, waits as he always does until the padded door has huffed close, waits some more as the DG paces, thinking. Then the DG looks up, as if realizing he's there and nods that he can trot along too. It's not as if he actually has anything real to contribute. He is but the catalyst for the DG's thoughts as to which man raised an eyebrow, which tutted at the wrong moment.

But it plays on Charlie as he takes the rickety lift down once again. He's a bright lad, and he can't help but consider the question. He knows how burglaries on assignment go. For the more involved ones, the dog is sometimes accompanied by an officer, who knows more exactly what to look for, inside the target itself. The public school chaps just love that, put up their hands and go 'me, sir' to get to climb in over windowsills and jemmy open drawers. So this one, unaccompanied, was meant to be straightforward. Here was a puzzle he knew about but was not involved in. And puzzles were his business. Provided he trod carefully perhaps here was an opportunity to show the DG that he was not just an ugly face.

Who would know more about this, off the books?

♣

Which is how he finds himself on a date with Stella Loughbridge from the typing pool. They go to a Wimpy in town, which she raises an enormous eyebrow at as if he promised her the Ritz.

She's put on eye make-up as if she's about to parachute into occupied Europe, if Europe was occupied by Mungo Jerry. The Wimpy is full of smokers. The telly's on, a dusty old set behind the counter, because some masochist asked to see the news. It's a bonus of Charlie's work that what he does rarely features among the catalogue of strikes and queues for coal and ancient arseholes talking about bringing back rationing and national service. Charlie would not do well in national service. People were saying that in the next few months, unless things turned around, the electricity would be switched off for a couple of nights a week. Box was meant to have its own generator, but so much for anonymity, eh, if the building was the only one in Mayfair lit up like a Christmas tree?

'We'll go dancing later,' he promises. Because he does know a club, a place where his short back and sides should get him laughed at, but doesn't.

'Don't count your chickens,' she says, holding the menu at arm's length and fumbling for a fag. At last she orders a salad and Charlie opts for egg and chips. The girls in the typing pool 'went out on dates' in a vaguely American way. They didn't necessarily mean anything by it. Charlie knew he needn't feel he was in here. But that gave him leave to use the occasion for purposes other than romance. He was not, in any sense, a breaker of hearts.

Charlie knows how to listen. He's been on courses about it. He asks some everyday questions as they eat, and he nods a lot, and Stella, not used to being listened to, because it's amazing, he's found, how few women *are* used to being listened to, tells him a lot about how her day went, how her week went, what everyone else in the typing pool is up to. It's brilliant, the sort of fine detail of life Charlie suddenly feels he's missing, a bit, living in his bedsit. She's warming to him too, pleased to be so listened to, but that's a bit awkward now, because he's led her into this under false pretences. He keeps nodding and listening, though, and finally she gets to the bit he's after, about how someone's boyfriend was the one tasked to sit at Ruskin's hospital bed early on, and how the comatose man had whispered something to him, very dramatically.

'What did he say?' asks Charlie, letting his genuine interest show.

'He said he's worried that he let his country down. That he has to tell someone . . .'

'What?'

'That's it. He stopped there and went under again. Very dramatic. Must be driving the top floor up the wall, that.'

'Must be.' Charlie becomes aware of noises around him. This lot are cheering something. Is it good news for once? He looks round and sees that the Prime Minister is on the telly. Which must have been why some arse wanted it on. Churchill's got his best 'fight them on the beaches' face on. A couple of the older blokes have stood up, anticipating that the old bugger's going to announce that they're going to war again or something. Who with? It's not as if they're going to fight the Ruskies on their own. A couple of minutes into the familiar drone, though, and it's clear the PM's just taken up BBC time to bash the strikers, who he says are part of the Soviet threat to the free people of the West. He still says every sentence as if it's going to be engraved in stone one day, but this is not one of his finest hours. Charlie turns back to Stella, who's still hanging on every word. 'Bloody Churchill.'

Stella looks shocked. 'Shh! Everyone will hear you!' She looks around, and it becomes clear that's not true. There are lots of frowns and sighs among the straight backs and attentive faces. Not that it would matter. It's not as if this is Stalingrad. Not yet. She looks back to the screen. 'He's doing so well for his age.'

'He must have a picture in the attic.' Charlie doesn't even try to keep the sarcasm out of his voice. The British turning aside from the matter of just how the Prime Minister can keep on being an active political presence at the age of bloody one hundred is extraordinary to him. Of course, everyone's guessed what must have happened. You get *Private Eye* referring to it sidelong every now and then, when they talk about the PM's 'unfortunate condition'. But nobody wants to say it out loud. It wouldn't be cricket, old chap, to say that the most respected figure in British public life has got a bit of the ace to him now. That he himself has been made a bit *special*. If the old bastard *did* say it out loud he'd be doing a service to the whole culture of aces and especially bloody jokers, the poor sods. But no, it's still the superpower that dare not speak its name. How very bloody British. 'They say he's going to have a big parade for his hundredth birthday.'

'That'll be lovely.'

'Nice for him. As long as he stays in the posh areas.' Charlie's sure she's heard the same gossip he has, that the DG is often the recipient of orders in the dead of night straight from the PM's office. One of them recently, it's said, was asking for a full-on intelligence group to be set up, tasked with electronic surveillance of the coalminers. The DG is supposed to have batted that one back, asking next morning if it was a mistake. That's all anyone's heard and nothing's happened. Everyone in the Civil Service has heard of old Winston's infamous night orders, which come straight out of a bottle. The chiefs of various branches of the establishment therefore keep having to make individual judgement calls on whether or not the leader of the nation is actually, officially, asking them to do something terrible. Because it always is something terrible. The fact that, in those moments, those blokes and Winston's cognac are, completely unaccountably, running the country between them, that one of those blokes might one night decide one of those orders sounded like a good idea, chills Charlie to the bone.

Stella stubs out her cigarette. 'Actually, I don't feel much like dancing.'

Charlie knows it's his own fault. He's let his face fall. It's

for the best. 'Let's find your bus then. I've got somewhere to
go on to.'

She looks him up and down, unimpressed. 'Have you?'

◆

In Charlie's experience, Shad Thames is always wet. That's his
memory of it, even in the height of summer. The tall edifices
of the giant warehouses are always dripping down onto the
narrow streets below. Some of those streets are still cobbled.
Down here it could be 1874. The warehouses haven't been used
as such for years, and now most of them are derelict. Some
of them are official housing, slums more like, some of them
squats. There are washing lines with clothes on them, hanging
between the buildings, silhouetted against the moon. Some of
the clothes are too big for normal people. There's graffiti all
over the wet old brick. A lot of it incomprehensible, some of
it artistic. It reminds Charlie of West Berlin. Graffiti as a badge
of pride. Of what you can't get away with in the dictatorship
next door. There are rough, locally made posters for bands and
comedy nights. There isn't a lot of rubbish. Probably because
it doesn't get taken away. So the smell of refuse fires hangs in
these wet old streets. Charlie can hear distant music, a baby
crying somewhere high up in the warehouses, where lights
show in gaps and in the few places where windows have been
put in. That cry doesn't quite sound as if it's coming from a
throat built in the usual way. The buildings are too high for
the sound to echo downwards, so it always feels quiet on the
ground here, which contributes to the sense of threat. How
do they get up there? Nobody's going to be paying electricity
bills, are they? And nobody's going to risk those old grain
elevators. These are the people who take the stairs.

There was once talk of doing up this area, making it fashionable, even. But that would require money. And even if
anyone had any, it wouldn't happen here, not now. Because

here is where the opposite of money lives. Here's the hatred that dare not speak its name.

Docklands is jokertown.

Charlie went to Australia, once. Everywhere he went, he expected to meet an aborigine, but he never did. Even in tourist places which they were meant to own. Still a white bloke at the desk. He never asked where they were. You just weren't ever going to meet such a person. It was as if they were fairies.

As he's got older, he's made the connection to places like this. There have always been jokertowns, and there always will be. All of Docklands and the Isle of Dogs is unofficially where *they* live. And if they come into town it causes a bit of a commotion. And nobody ever talks about it. So to get to Woolwich or Canning Town, or anywhere south of West Ham, really, you can't get a cab, you have to take a series of obscure bus routes. Obscure, that is, unless you read specialist publications like an intelligence analyst with an interest in this facet of human nature tends to. It's as if there's a grey area around the Thames, where industry and commerce have failed, and been replaced by infection. Until you get down to Greenwich, and then, bingo, all is empire and sea power and did you know we invented time?

It's not just jokers down here, of course. It never is. Those specialist publications leave you certain about that. Those bus routes are known to other communities too. As Charlie walks along the street in his nice new mac, he can hear his footsteps echo. Maybe they were sitting out on their steps before he turned the corner. He doesn't know enough to give whatever signs the other visitors give. He knows he's in danger, but he's pretty sure he's not in as much danger as he's meant to be. And if he gets as far as being able to have a conversation, he knows the lingo.

Still, he doesn't quite know why he's here. He thinks it through. He realized he knew a bit more about Foxton, Ruskin's handler, than most people did. He was aware of his interest in a rather obscure musician, for a start. Again, he's letting himself be led by that little bit of knowledge, hoping for advancement through cleverness, that's what he's doing. Is that pride going before a fall? Bit late to think about that now, Charlie-boy.

There's a particular pub, the Prospect of Norway, which lies out on an actual dock, jutting out into the Thames. It used to be for dockworkers and seafarers, but it's had to move with the times. Charlie's been there on a couple of occasions, and it still looks the same: blacked-out windows; lamps outside making it shine closer against the distant lights along the opposite shore; no board outside announcing chicken in a basket, nothing to draw too much attention, even here. From inside is coming the sound of very loud rock music. That's why Charlie is wondering if Foxton will be here tonight, because the Prospect brings together this evening at least two of his favourite things.

Charlie enters, and immediately finds himself looking up at an enormous joker bouncer, something like a beetle with a big moustache on its twisted face under several big black eyes. It's wearing a T-shirt with the name of the pub on it. Charlie gives it a cheery grin, and after a moment, it slaps him on the arse with a mandible or something and tells him to go on in, then.

The downstairs bar is reasonably empty. Black brick, posters all over, a message board with desperate scrawls and adverts, some of them for things which really could scare the horses. Charlie has to shout over the din from upstairs to get a pint of mild. But as the joker barman, or Charlie assumes he's a joker, because he's wearing sunglasses in this murk, is pulling it, the noise reaches a crescendo of applause and then stops. It turns into the trundle of lots of shifting feet, and Charlie's glad he's got his beer in, because down the big wooden stairs comes a rush of people, mostly jokers, almost no women, a couple of transvestites. Charlie gets to a table and puts his foot up on the rail, watching. And it turns out he was right, because there's Foxton. The man's got a receding hairline, and a nervous, bureaucrat's face, so it's odd to see him in a casual sweater and very clean tight jeans. He's talking to a couple of other blokes, and they look rougher, probably locals. Still, he looks as if he fits in.

Foxton glances over and clocks Charlie. He freezes, a look on his face as if he's thinking of making a run for it. His companions look over too, angry or worried. Charlie raises his glass. Foxton obviously realizes there's no point in leaving. Instead, he tells his friends it's fine, heads on over. 'I come here for the music,' he says, before any greeting.

'Obviously,' says Charlie, trying to sound sincere. Foxton is one of a handful of Box officers who've pretty obviously taken to avoiding him in the corridors. They're the ones, Charlie thinks, who really have got something to hide, the ones who've bought the DG's bluff that Charlie can see into their souls. But, and it's pretty lucky for those lads that Charlie thinks this, he reckons anyone working for Moscow would know better than to be so obvious about it. He'd very much like to be able to tell Foxton that he really can't see through him. Well, not in any special way. Charlie isn't one of those lads who enjoy people squirming at the sight of them. But that'd compromise his value to the DG. That'd be letting the old man down. 'You like these Anthony Newley types.'

'He's changed his sound.' And suddenly, which is a relief, Foxton feels he's talking to a fellow enthusiast. 'And his band—'

'The Spiders?' Charlie has seen the name on the posters. 'Delightful.'

'Jokers, most of them.' That's slightly more dodgy ground. Box employees are tested for the virus, which had been the subject of some Civil Service consternation a few years back, so it's no longer a question of aces and jokers being subjects for vetting. But they're still the cause of raised eyebrows. Everyone is happy with them being contained in the Silver

Helix. Nobody talks about it. Charlie suddenly realizes that his date tonight would have heard the gossip about him, and was giving him the benefit of the doubt, which makes him think kindly of her. Foxton being seen here would raise eyebrows further, on a couple of counts. Charlie thinks Foxton might now be wondering if Charlie *is* actually here on business, or if this is now a secret they both share. If Charlie is admitting to something.

'Good for him.' That's sincere as well. He hopes Foxton hears that sincerity. Maybe now would be a good time to ask his questions, but Foxton is looking back up the stairs.

'Oh. Here they come.'

Down the stairs, to the growing applause and the occasional whoop of the crowd in the bar, is striding an extraordinary group of people. Their leader, holding up a palm to acknowledge the crowd, is incredibly thin, in a stage costume and make-up that he could only get away with in here. Behind him is a writhing bunch of tentacles above a loping body, wearing some sort of glittering tabard, a literally skeletal figure with what looks like transparent skin over his bones, in something more like their leader's jumpsuit, and a tree-like mass of wood in vaguely human form with, seemingly, no modesty to preserve. Their leader accepts a beer from an acolyte and heads over to their table, grinning at Foxton. 'Hello, Seb. Who's your friend?' The accent isn't quite East End. It isn't quite anywhere.

'This is Mr White,' says Foxton, using an offhand Box pseudonym to indicate to Charlie that real names aren't on the cards here.

'Client of yours?'

Foxton looks awkwardly at Charlie. 'Just a friend. I only represent a handful of artistes.'

Charlie finds himself breaking into the most enormous smile. *You old rogue, Sebastian.* And, bless him, he's playing it largely by the book in terms of the job. Though they're really supposed to say they're just a pen-pusher in the Civil Service, not an agent who could make you a star, kid. He shakes the man's hand. 'Charlie.'

'David.' The wooden joker taps David on the shoulder and he raises a very rehearsed hand. 'No, give us a second, this is important. Come over to my table, yeah?'

He means just Foxton, but Charlie goes too, and the band-leader accepts this immediately. He's right about this being his table. A space is cleared for him, drinks brought as they sit down, the patrons nearby stand just close enough to feel they're being included in the conversation. 'I've really turned things around,' he begins. 'You were right about cutting out the space shit. That's why my band are just The Spiders now. Nobody's ready for science fiction again, not after the wild card. You saw that audience. We're ready for the big time.'

Foxton considers. He may not be what he claims to be, but he's still a fan, and he can at least bring to bear the skills of a case officer. 'You're big in this community. But . . . how do I put this . . .?' Charlie sees David's eyes narrow just a little; he feels much the same way.

'They're jokers, you mean?'

Foxton just spreads his hands, sorry. Charlie wants to say something, but his own issues here really have nothing to do with this horrible little panto. He's gained, he supposes, a measure of fellow feeling for those with the wild card virus since everyone started to think he was one of them.

'That's it, then.' Suddenly, David is smiling, broad and empty. He stands and sticks out a hand towards Foxton, stiff and meaningless. 'Take care of yourself, Sebastian.' Suddenly, he himself is playing a part.

Foxton looks panicked, but, especially with Charlie present, feels he can't say anything. He watches David go back to his band, slapping their shoulders and bursting out laughing. 'It's . . . for the best,' he concludes at last.

'I'd say so. You couldn't take them to Hollywood, could you? You have been having adventures down here.'

'I'm a supporter of the jokers, you can't come down here and—' He suddenly stops himself, takes a drink. 'Oh, what's the bloody point?'

'If it's any consolation,' Charlie says, 'he doesn't seem the type to support any cause after it stops suiting him.'

'Still, he felt he could afford more compassion than I think he can.' Foxton looks grimly at Charlie. 'Why are you here? Really?' The hangers-on no longer want to be near their table, but have given them the respect of a certain distance now, as friends of David's. They can talk freely.

'Ruskin.'

'Oh. And I thought I could get away from the office for one night. Are you here on orders?'

Charlie just raises an eyebrow.

Foxton sighs. 'What do you want to know?'

Charlie wants to ask why they were breaking into a cavalry captain's house in the first place, but the DG would already know that, and would have briefed him. 'Go over it again for me. What happened inside the flat?'

'I was watching from the park across the road. We had no idea the owner was home: the place was dark. Not that it mattered, Ruskin's good at his job. He should have been able to get in, do it, and get out without waking anyone. Two minutes into the operation, I saw the bastard enter the front room. Ruskin had left the curtains open, on orders. There he is, framed in the door, suddenly, right behind Ruskin, who's still rifling through the desk. He hadn't even switched the light on, and Ruskin hadn't heard him enter. I gave the bird call for "get out". But like a shot, the man grabs Ruskin, puts him in an arm lock.'

'And then he zapped him?'

'That's the strange thing. I'm about to get out of there and call it in, but then the target lets Ruskin go. Ruskin is talking to him, saying something, maybe trying to distract him long enough to get out of the window, so I stay: I have to be ready with the car. Only then the target starts talking at some length himself. He looks desperate, it looks like he's trying to persuade Ruskin of something. He's marching around the room, making big gestures. Ruskin could have got out of the window, but he doesn't, he's just standing there, listening, and he looks amazed.'

'Does Ruskin know why he's there? I mean, the case background?'

'Of course not. He's just a dog. What sort of amateur do you think I am? Anyhow, this insane conversation continues, until suddenly the target seems to realize something. He starts to shout and point at Ruskin, as if only now is he angry at him. Ruskin jumps for the window and . . . pow.' Foxton shivers visibly at the memory. 'The thunder shattered the window. The light . . . it was like I was looking into an arc lamp. I was stumbling about. I thought I'd been blinded. But slowly some vision returned, and I could see what had happened. Ruskin was lying half in and half out of the window. He was burned all over. There was smoke coming off him. I went and called it in. That's it.'

Charlie believes him. He finishes his drink, and watches as the tension drains from Foxton, as he feels absolved. Charlie isn't sure how he feels about that. He gets up and looks back to see that David is surrounded by his joker friends. Foxton is looking over at them as if he's aching to say something that he now can't, that he never will.

Charlie leaves them to it. He salutes the bouncer at the door, and the joker wishes him a good night.

♠

He's got a long walk ahead of him, maybe even as far as Bank Station if he can't find a stray cab. The night bus, the stop for which is a mile away upriver, isn't due for another hour. So he uses the little compass in his wallet to find north and starts idly picking his way through the streets, considering that conversation. What would a petty criminal and a cavalry officer find to talk about, particularly in those circumstances?

But here, what was this, approaching down the middle of the high-sided street, its engine echoing loud enough to wake the kiddies? There actually is a night bus that comes down here, one he hasn't heard about. And there's a stop for it too. It's a welcome sight. Charlie heads for the stop and hails the bus.

The stop somehow turns towards him and suddenly Charlie has a knife at his throat. Then there's a bag over his head. He can hear a bunch of people around him now, as if they appeared out of nowhere. Did they get off the bus? 'Hoi!' he shouts. 'I'm not fighting you! Leave it out!'

He's lifted off his feet, and a second later is winded by landing on a cold metal surface. Did nobody in the bus see all this? Did he just get ambushed by a . . . pirate bus? But the floor of a bus would be smooth, wouldn't it? This is more like a van. And the engine sound has altered too. Yeah, suddenly he's in a van. He tries to sit up, and strong hands help him with that. He's shifted to sit straight against the side. He lets them do it. He appreciates the lack of punching.

The journey takes about half an hour. He tries to strike up a conversation, but whoever's in here with him doesn't respond. He's pretty sure that if this were someone playing for the other side, he'd have been drugged already. Also, all this would be an enormous risk to take for a small fish like him. He's been briefed on how to resist torture. For a couple of days at most. He pushes that thought aside. The sounds outside indicate they're heading back to Central London. Then the sounds change, as if they've gone underground, maybe into a garage. An embassy? No, don't leap to conclusions that make your stomach lurch, Charlie. The van stops, he's pulled out and marched along, his hands held in one firm grip. They get into a lift, then get out and he's dropped, with reasonable gentleness, into a plush armchair. He hears the door close and a moment later the bag is pulled from his head.

Charlie finds himself looking into the literally stony face of Brigadier Sir Kenneth Foxworthy, commonly known as Captain Flint. The brigadier does not look best pleased. Charlie isn't all that pleased himself. 'Begging your pardon, sir,' he says, allowing a tinge of sarcasm to be audible, 'but I'm with Box. I know exactly where we are.' Which is in Foxworthy's office in the MI7 building near Regent's Park. 'So, can I ask, sir, was the bag really necessary?'

'It's not about where you are, Soper. It's about who brought you here and how.' Foxworthy's voice, so often heard on radio and TV, and so well imitated by Peter Cook, always made Charlie think of the sound from a stylus on a record before the music started playing. As if he hadn't seen the briefs on all the members of the Silver Helix as they were updated. As if his lot didn't keep a close eye on their lot.

'I've signed the Act, sir.'

'Silver Helix operations are UK eyes ultra, and well you know it, lad. Drink?'

'Glass of milk, please, sir.'

'You'll take a brandy and like it.'

Foxworthy shoves an appropriate glass into his hand and when Charlie sees the label on the bottle a moment later he decides this is probably the best idea after all. He tries and fails to stop his hand shaking. He finds a line from Roger Moore. 'I take it you wanted to see me, sir?' Being in a small room with the bulk of this man is quite unnerving. It's like sharing a loo with a bit of Stonehenge. And the man's reputation adds another level of nervousness. Stonehenge isn't about to rip your ears off for looking at it in a funny way.

'Obviously. What were you doing at the Prospect of Norway?'

'I went for the music, sir.'

'The music was over by the time you got there.'

'Unlike yourself, sir, I was misinformed.' So they were

watching Foxton that closely? Why? What did the Silver Helix have to do with all of this?

Foxworthy puts a large granite hand on Charlie's shoulder. *'Let's get straight to the point, shall we? You are a meaningless little apparatchik. What is your interest in Foxton?'*

Charlie throws back his brandy. He's decided that he's going to need every bit of Dutch courage he can get. Because this bloke has now irked him. 'You first, chum.'

Foxworthy stares at him. He can't have been talked to like that, Charlie thinks, in a very long time. *'You will call me—'*

'You just said I was an apparatchik, like we're already living like that lot in Eastern Europe. I didn't appreciate that. I'm a duly appointed civil servant, answerable to my guvnor, who's answerable to Her Majesty's government. I do my best to act like a professional, within what's allowed in a free country. I don't go about abducting people. If you think that increases your authority rather than diminishes it, mate, we're on the way to a dictatorship.'

'What the hell are you talking about?' Foxworthy seems suddenly amused. At least he's interested to hear the answer. Charlie thinks he's got his measure now. Here's one of these blokes who has to be above it all, who can't lower himself to sustained anger at Charlie. He's thinking he'll hear him out, then surprise him with some considered, civilized violence. So right now is a bit of a test of how right Charlie is about the way the country's going, and, like a witch underwater, if he's correct that he's right up the creek.

'We all hear the mutterings about old colonels having conferences with skinheads and Blackshirts and the press barons. They're starting to feel they've got Winston's nod about "taking back control". And depending on the time of night and how much he's been at the –' Charlie mimes throwing a drink back from a bottle, 'they might get it and all. I'd say it's time for those of us who move in professional circles to remain strictly within the rule of law. What do you reckon? Sir.'

As he looks into the face of the White Cliffs of Dover, Charlie reckons his time might be up. '*We have ways of making you talk, you know.*'

'Watch a lot of old war movies, do we, sir?' Which is when Foxworthy finally snaps, and throws back an arm, ready to knock his block off. So Charlie says something else. Very quickly. 'Trouble is, I don't bleeding know anything. Not yet.'

Foxworthy visibly restrains himself. He lowers his arm. He gives Charlie the slightest of nods. They understand each other now. Foxworthy has received an assurance from Charlie that he'll also learn what Charlie learns. Which, thank Christ, turns out to have been the point of this kidnapping. Foxworthy turns to talk to a lampshade standing nearby. 'Get rid of him.'

Charlie has a good idea of just who all these obedient inanimate objects are, but that doesn't mean he can spot them. He grabs for the brandy but misses as something is on him from behind, and the bag goes over his head again. He just hopes that this lot have an implicit understanding with their boss about precisely what 'get rid of' means.

One very speedy and uncomfortable trip downstairs later, Charlie finds himself thrown bodily outside into the cold air of the freezing hours. He lands on the pavement. The door slams behind him.

He takes off the bag and looks around, wondering if there is any clue to the presence of the tail he'll presumably have from now on.

He turns to look back up at the nondescript official building, where no lights are now on. They're showing a wonderful commitment to saving energy. What does this all add up to? He hopes it's worth the bruises.

Charlie decides it's too late to head home to the suburbs, and elects to walk back to work, where at least he'll get a few hours' kip under his desk.

♥

In the end, he gets only a couple of hours of blissful blankness before the noise of the cleaners disturbs him. Down here in the registers, the Hoovers make a fearful row. He hauls himself up and feels his bruises. Light is streaming through the high, dusty windows. It occurs to him that here is, of course, one further source of information about this whole business, and he just happens to be in the perfect place to find out about him.

He heads to the night office, where Tom Pullman is just standing up and looking at his watch, ready to pass over guardianship of the red and black phones to the day officer as soon as you like, thanks very much. He looks up as Charlie approaches and smirks. 'Look what the cat dragged in. One can only hope there actually was pussy involved.'

'Meow,' replies Charlie, bitchily. 'Is Mavis in yet?'

''Course she is. Doesn't sleep much at her age.' Pullman indicates the door behind which the senior analyst keeps her office.

Charlie knocks and obeys the call to enter. Mavis is at her desk, empty teacups stacked around her, possibly, given the size of her habit, only this morning's. She's got her head down over a red folder, a magnifying glass in her hand. One hand rises as if of its own accord, flaps to indicate that Charlie should sit. Charlie does her a small service in clearing a space to do so.

At last she looks up. 'I should make the time to get myself glasses,' she sighs. 'Left eye is short-sighted, right's long. Fine for walking. But present me with dense text, and it is rare that I am not so presented, and I become an owl. Now. You're in early. You've been out late. You've been up to mischief, dear heart. Speak.'

'I'm interested in Captain Peter Faulkner of the Household Cavalry.'

'Ah, Captain Lightning.'

'Does he use an ace name?'

'No, that's my little noodle nickname for him. I have one for every ace we know of.' And probably not one for me, thinks Charlie, because she'll have realized exactly how the DG is making use of me. 'He is at the centre of many people's thoughts as we speak. Why yours?'

Charlie decides to push his luck. If we're in a climate now where the Silver Helix feel they can kidnap British citizens, why shouldn't the DG be employing his own little fixer, above and beyond the terms which Mavis will have heard about? 'I'm doing a bit of looking into, Mavis. You know.' And he casts his eyes upwards in a gesture he can entirely deny the import of if push comes to shove.

'Perhaps.' And perhaps not. But she decides to be kind to him. Mavis has always had a soft spot for Charlie. Charlie thinks he might know where that is and all. 'What do you wish to discover?'

'What his habits are when he's outside of barracks. His home life and all that.'

'We keep a file. As we do on all aces and knaves and jokers of note. You'll have been into the stacks already?'

'Actually, Mavis, I gave in to my baser nature and came to you first.'

She breaks into a smile, allows it to stay on her face. Mavis may have a feeling for him, but she's not the sort to let that influence her. She's just enjoying him now, in the moment. In another moment, she might well call the DG and ask under just whose authority Charlie is working. 'A most kind affirmation, dear heart. And it has saved you a journey. Because Captain Lightning is not in the stacks. His file has been placed in the Special Pile.'

The Special Pile was Mavis's withering term for a locked cabinet at the end of the personnel section in which were kept files that had been deemed too sensitive for anyone with a security clearance of any kind to look at. The only person with a key was the DG, this being a system he himself had put in place. It was designed, he had said, to assist in mole hunts from above and at the same time shut down internecine investigations. It was a matter of legend that included in the SP were files the mere existence of which would be a matter of amazement to journalists. Box weren't above keeping tabs on anyone, but did they really have suspicious information concerning, say, Churchill himself? There'd definitely be a file on Harold Wilson in there. But this system allowed the DG to meet with both the PM and the Leader of the Opposition and say of course Box didn't involve itself in party politics. 'Ah. Out of bounds, then.'

''Fraid so.'

Charlie gives her a look he's practised in front of the mirror, heaves a sigh, and leaves, pausing at the threshold for maximum dramatic effect. But no, there's nothing left he can say. The Special Pile is a dead end, but one that's indicative. A sensible fellow would step away now, before he's done anything incriminating. Is Charlie a sensible fellow?

He spends the day at work, keeping his head down, thinking it over. At the end of the day he pops down the Dog and Duck, not a service pub, which is why he likes it, and spends a few pounds on the fruit machine while chatting up Ferdinanda, the barmaid with the unlikely name. She knows nothing of relevance, and he talks to her as if he is a sublimely free office clerk who's looking forward to his holidays. With a few pints of Watney's Red Barrel, it's a sublime palate cleanser.

Which is why, perhaps, Charlie finds himself across the road from a certain house in Kensington. It shows no sign of burglary. Box only hires the best. What's he hoping to achieve here? He's not entirely sure, until he sees the door open. Charlie has taken the course the Watchers run on basic surveillance. He doesn't look away, just lazily steps forward as if he'd been walking along and had happened to look in that direction. It's not late enough that the presence of a person on this pavement would be notable. His face remains a mask.

The target, and this must be Captain Peter Faulkner, is too worried to pay any notice to his surroundings. He hasn't taken the same course. He's still pulling on a heavy mac, leather gloves on his hands, blond hair cut as short as you like, just a hint of sideburn in the military way. Then he's off down the street, clop-clop-clop on those shiny shoes. He hasn't taken a cab, so he's going somewhere local. No riding the bus for this sort of man. Charlie lets his training move him and follows lazily, looking around normally then looking back. In the role he is now playing in his head, he is wandering home from the pub (which is not so far from the truth), dawdling to make sure the wife's in bed when he gets there (which is).

What is he looking for in the shape of the man's back? What does he want from this whole business? Advancement? Yes, obviously. But under that, yes, let's lift up that stone and have a butcher's, shall we? Under that is a need for recognition. For a pat on the back. For sir to say he's been a good boy. Charlie knows that. He knows himself. It doesn't make what he's doing wrong, but it does make it . . . more frightening. In a world of wrongs being done, he's the one with worries pinging back and forth somewhere deep inside him about how what he's doing is hubris. Or is that just class again, that he's worried that by flying too high, he's also stepping out of line?

Faulkner makes a couple of turns, but not like someone trying to lose a tail, more like someone who's memorized a map. Charlie sees him hesitate at one of them, put a finger in the air, and then turn to the right. It's not hard to find a small square of green in Kensington, and eventually he does. He then hangs about awkwardly, loitering by a tree in the pool of light under a lamp, with flats in the square all around looking down on him. He really hasn't done that course. It's easy for Charlie to find a dark corner and watch. It occurs to him that it'd be really dreary if all this turned out to be about what English civilization has been about since it was invented: posh boys bumming each other. Would he be able to recognize that sort of assignation from this distance? Yeah, probably.

It's only ten minutes before someone turns up. This one is a lot more professional, at first glance. He has, at the very least, thought about this. But no, it looks as if that's all he's done. He loops around the square, carrying shopping, for all the world as if he's going to stop at one of these houses and go in, but Charlie just has a feeling about him, a feeling he probably wouldn't have if this bloke was genuine, and just as well, because the bag man looks in on Charlie's corner before completing his loop . . . and now Charlie is crouched behind some trees so he doesn't get to see that bit . . . and when he looks again, the man has approached Faulkner, and, no, he doesn't give him the bags or take anything from them or get given anything to put in them, that was just for the cover, so this isn't a drop off, they're here to talk. The conversation is brief, and looks angry. Faulkner is demanding something from the bag man, who is . . . getting emotional himself. These two don't look like cogs in the machine, they look like . . . comrades? Maybe. Maybe with a capital C.

Except that Faulkner has a certain disdain for Bag Man. He's being abrupt, trying to give orders, and Bag Man doesn't like it. Now Bag Man isn't looking so professional either. This level of intensity, in the street . . . this is *showy*. This doesn't fit with anything these two could be. The Soviets don't berate their agents in public. You're their hero of the Revolution until suddenly you find yourself on the front end of a speeding car. Slightly easier to believe in these two as student sympathizers, making up their own rules, hungry for the cause, arguing all the time, seeking seniority. But these are two grown men. And no, they do not quite seem to be on the same side.

And now Bag Man *is* giving Faulkner something. Reluctantly, as if, okay, he supposes he can have it. Charlie wishes he'd prepared for this, had brought his opera glasses, which he's used three times for cricket, several times in the field, and never for opera. It's small, whatever it is, slipped into that mac pocket. An envelope? Yeah. Then Bag Man is off. Charlie takes a moment to watch him go, is fairly certain he'd recognize that gait, that shoulder slope, that slick of thinning hair.

But why settle for fairly? It's not as if he's on a mission here. It's not as if Bag Man recognizing him later would mean anything.

Charlie doesn't care if Faulkner sees him emerge from cover, which is unlikely anyway, given how he'll have ruined his night vision in that lamplight. He runs a few steps, gets to the edge of the square, sees Bag Man still marching off, in the distance. Now *this* man might well be the kind to head for the bus stop.

Charlie makes his gait faster, catches up, then deliberately stumbles, falls into the man, sending them both sprawling.

Bag Man leaps up as if he might be about to die. He's staring at Charlie with an intensity that really helps with imprinting every detail of his features onto Charlie's retinas, click-click-click.

And Charlie is pretty sure, having seen him close up, what sort of accent he's going to need here to be most reassuring. 'Mate . . .' he slurs, letting the beer have its say, 'give us a hand, eh?' He reaches out a wobbly hand. Bless him, the man hesitates only for a moment and takes it, helps him to his feet. Given that he's still shaken up, he actually takes a second to make sure Charlie's okay. 'I'm fine, I'm fine, 'bliged,' he says.

'You're all right to get to the bus or the Tube?'

Charlie feels a bit rotten now. 'I'm fine. You're a good bloke. Cheers.'

With a little nod, the man is on his way.

Charlie wanders slowly after him, keeping up the part, lets him get away. Then he reaches his own bus stop, sits down in the shelter, finds his notepad and makes a quick first sketch. But there's no way he's going to forget that face. Some faces have Britain in them. You could display them like archaeologists display tree rings to indicate changes in climate, but in the case of the faces it's the political climate. There's a game he played in training, in which he was asked to match faces drawn on cards with those secretly drawn by an opponent, only they weren't able to use physical descriptions. 'Open University lecturer', 'confirmed bachelor', 'nudist', that sort of thing. Charlie was very good at it. Bag Man feels like a victim of whatever's churning underneath the body politic at the moment, not the cause of it. He might well be a comrade – that would have been one of the words out of Charlie's mouth during the face game – but he wasn't one of those filthy Soviet apparatchiks, and he wasn't a naive believer: he was someone who . . . who wanted something better.

Now there is a dangerous thought, Charlie-boy.

Charlie slips the finished drawing into his pocket. He catches his late bus home, collapses into bed and sleeps so hard that the alarm going off feels like seconds later.

♣

That morning is another hungover slog through the usual reports of embassy comings and goings, all of which now seem as mundane as spuds. Charlie's got a taste of the action, the action that nobody in real life quite has, and it's making him itch.

At first tea break, he pops down a flight in the clanking lift to see Maudie in Ops. Maudie is the girl who's had pictures in the Royal Academy's summer exhibition. Charlie got a look at them once, and couldn't get his head round what went where. But for Box, she's strictly representational, though today he notes she is wearing a maxi dress in a design that swings more towards her hobby than her employment. He bets there's a big floppy hat somewhere, glances towards the coat peg and there it is. 'How can I help you?' she says, in mascara which says to Charlie that her bosses down here are aware of her worth and don't mention dress codes too much.

'Could you give me a quick sketch?'

'What's the operation line?' She's wanting a name to write on the piece of paper poised before her.

'Nothing like that. Just for fun. This is a man I met in a dream. I was thinking of writing a novel about him.'

She gives him an 'oh, come on' look.

'Seriously. I've got a book in me. I can feel the edges when I sit down.'

Which gets him a full-throated chuckle despite herself. 'I'm on my break.'

'So am I, but I've got five minutes.'

So she condescends to help, and he quickly describes Bag Man. He doesn't show her the sketch he made. He wants to let her skills express themselves to their fullest. She sketches swiftly, asks him for opinions on each part, makes notes beside those parts, crosses out, throws the paper away, starts again. Charlie has an urge to pick up those discarded papers and pocket them, but that way lies questions. She nails it on version four. Charlie can see no difference between the man looking out at him from the paper and the man he met. Now all he has to do is take this picture back to his own section and do some comparing with the usual suspects.

Maudie stands up and takes a look at her work from a slight distance. She cocks her head to one side, charmingly. 'You dream about Ray Boulton?'

Which makes Charlie realize. What he'd taken to be fellow feeling, or his skills at work, was actually just, in the back of his head, recognizing this bloke. 'The National Union of Journalists Ray Boulton?' She taps the side of her head, she was one step ahead there, boy. Or . . . no, she means she's worried about what he's got going on up top. If only she knew. 'It does look like him, yeah. Too much red cheese before bedtime.'

'I'm starting to wonder if you're trying a bit too hard to fit in with the public school boys.' She flaps a limp hand like Larry Grayson.

'If I was,' says Charlie, taking his sketch and leaving with a jolly wave, 'I'd pick someone else to find under my bed.'

◆

In his breaks that day, Charlie reads up on Ray Boulton. Not the most ferocious of union officials, nor the most left wing. Castigated by some of his peers in the TUC for insufficient fervour, in fact. Must be awkward around the revolutionary dinner table, with so many of Ray's members working for newspapers that would want them all hanged.

But Ray hasn't been a working journalist for a long time. So what was he doing meeting Faulkner as if he was an amateur spy? Now, this is where Charlie might hit a bit of a wall, because if he had any authority behind his . . . whatever this is . . . he could go and have a word with Boulton, scare him a bit. Just like Sergeant Rock or whatever he calls himself did to him. Yeah, thank you, conscience. All right then, Charlie thinks, how about the opposite to that? And that's how, right after work, he finds himself in the reception area of Congress House on Great Russell Street, where, the books of the day have told him, Ray Boulton has been in conference with the faithful. He's about two rungs down from the top flight of the NUJ, from what Charlie can make out from the byzantine organizational diagrams Box have for the unions, but his recent appearances in the media, attempting to be a voice of recon-ciliation between the PM and the workers, have got him noticed.

Charlie hangs around the foyer, as a lot of folk are doing, taking care to pop out to admire *The Spirit of Brotherhood* statue every now and then, to give the impression, unless that receptionist is really paying attention, that he's a new arrival every time. To help with that, sometimes he's wearing his coat, sometimes it's flung casually over his shoulder.

He's starting to think *sod this for a game of soldiers* when, coming out of the lifts, there he is. Charlie happens to be dressed completely differently to the previous night, so he suspects that, if he does this entirely confidently, as if he's never met Boulton before, the union man might not make the connection. He's decided to do the only thing he can do, the most basic move in tradecraft. He's going to insert himself in the middle of the meaning without knowing what the meaning is. It's like at university, when he very much enjoyed not having read the set text but going to the tutorial about it anyway. He falls in beside the man as he heads for the door, and mutters to him. 'Got a moment? Faulkner sent me.'

Boulton stops just outside the building. He takes Charlie a couple of steps away from where his colleagues might hear, but still, he's not scared or intimidated. His expression says that this is tiresome and a bit puzzling. 'What does he want now?'

Charlie drops his accent to the same social level as this East End grammar school boy. 'He wants more.'

'*More?* What does that mean?'

'You know what he's like.'

'Can't say I do. I'm not going to vote for him for General Secretary, if that's what he means.'

Charlie has no idea what that means. He's never tried poker. The services discourage an interest in gambling. He suspects it might be a bit too attractive. 'So what do I tell him?'

'Tell him I'm fed up with him playing silly buggers. I was willing to indulge his need for secrecy, because I thought he could be about to tell the British public something they might need to know. But there's no reason for him to be sending vague and mysterious messages to me.'

'Oh no.' Charlie is suddenly the embarrassed friend, and has made his accent leap up into the stratosphere where Faulkner's own speech patterns probably live. 'I'm terribly sorry. He just told me to come to you and say that. You mustn't let on. He'd had a couple of stiff ones. What's he gone and done?'

'Your friend has joined the National Union of Journalists.

Yes, shocking and extraordinary, I know, something that must be done in the dead of night. He approached me directly, and, as I said, insisted on such secrecy that I thought he must be about to write some enormous exposé of the upper crust and needed membership to get it into a paper as his own work. So I made sure it was processed quickly and brought it to him myself, in a meeting that was as ridiculous as it was clandestine. He should know, by the way, when the newsletter comes out next month, he'll be listed as part of the membership on the public record like anyone else. If it's more secrecy he wants, I can't give it. And you should tell him this is not something he should feel ashamed of. If his conscience is getting the better of him about speaking out about those around him, that's between him and his editor.'

'I'll have a quiet word. My apologies again. I shall make sure this doesn't become any more ridiculous, and if I may rely on your own discretion—'

'You may. If I can rely on this being an end to all this tomfoolery.'

'Indeed. Many thanks. I'm sorry to have taken up so much of your time.' And Charlie is off, pleased to have got away without having to invent a name.

♠

So where does Charlie go from here? He's sure this all means something, but he has no idea what. So much of his job is about being one of those blind sods who's feeling out the shape of an elephant, usually while the elephant is about to fuck you. Charlie does not want to end up being fucked by an elephant, especially because he's on his own with this one.

That thought has just about resolved itself into action by the time he gets back home and starts to make himself egg and chips for tea. Maybe now is the time for him to arrange a meeting with the DG, put all this on the table, cash in his brownie points and leave it to those who can see more of the elephant.

Which is when his phone rings. He answers it, and hears the familiar click of a secure line being put in place. Then it's Barbara, the DG's secretary. 'Good evening, Mr Soper. There's a problem in production, I'm afraid. Could you pop back to the office, please?'

Charlie uses his free hand to switch the gas off. Those eggs will be wasted. A problem in production means he's going to have to take a taxi. 'On my way.'

♥

This time, Barbara is pointing towards the inner door as soon as he leaves the lift, as if she'd started pointing before the doors opened. Charlie is dead nervous about this. He has only ever been summoned like this once before, one night when it was all hands on deck for an embassy shooting. But this time round he hasn't seen the great influx he saw that evening, all the grey men heading for the same building, like a herd of bureaucrats migrating. This time he has a terrible feeling it's just him.

He enters the DG's office, and here it's just him, too. The DG doesn't do all that pretending to be working on something, keeping him waiting a bit, like they do in the movies. He doesn't have that much wankery in him. Indeed, his eyes are fixed on Charlie as soon as he closes the door behind him. 'Well,' he says, 'this is delicate.'

Charlie's stomach lurches. 'I have been looking into something, sir. I was about to bring it to you—'

'Let me do the talking, please.' Oh fuck. 'You'd better sit down.' Oh fuck me sideways. Charlie sits. The DG looks like a stern but kindly headmaster, which, honestly, is just about what he's always been in Charlie's head. All those books full of posh boys at boarding schools having adventures, you read them even if you're from Charlie's street. Even if you don't recognize anything in them, they leave their mark. Only he doesn't have, he suddenly realizes, the native responses of the real posh boys who work here. He's only ever been used to the kindly part of this relationship. He does not know how to react in the face of the . . . metaphorical, at least let's bloody hope so . . . cane on the backside. Not from someone who's where the DG is in his head. This, thinks Charlie, is why you should never let yourself trust these posh bastards.

'My previous visitor,' the DG begins, 'made a very strong case for taking you off for a stay in the country.' There's a country house owned by Box, somewhere down the Thames. It's where training sessions take place, above Charlie's pay grade. It's also, it's said, where the rough stuff happens. Where, if you're a British national who's not willing to reveal who the rest of your network of comrades is . . . well, the stories say that's somewhere the rule of law bypasses.

Charlie now wants to throw up. But come on, mate, look to your skills. Compose yourself. Quickly. What would a traitor say at this point? What's the opposite? 'I can see why, sir.'

'Can you really? Walk me through it.'

Charlie almost bursts out laughing, because he's so startled that he's managed to grab a fingerhold on the way down. 'Well, sir, I've been looking into what happened between Captain Faulkner and our hired hand Ruskin in that front room. I've been doing it in my own time, without telling the firm. That might look like the sort of thing a very stupid comrade would get up to.'

'Why "very stupid"?'

'Because I've been doing it pretty much openly.'

'Indeed? I'm told you used a range of covers and Box resources.'

'Not openly to those I was looking into, sir. That would have been foolish. I mean openly as far as Box goes. I told no lies in-house. If asked, I would have shared what I'd learned.'

'But nobody asked you. So you didn't tell.'

'As I said, I was about to.'

'And on whose authority were you doing this?'

'As I've said, sir—'

'That was a bloody rhetorical question!' Suddenly, the DG is furious in a way Charlie has never seen before. It must have been building up in him, completely beyond even Charlie's notice, which is shocking in itself. He supposes he deserves it. He was scrabbling around for excuses, like a child. He keeps his silence now.

The DG gets up, paces back and forth, sits down again, once more in control of himself. He has now shown Charlie the context he is within. '*Why* did you do this?'

Charlie pauses a moment, acknowledging that he now has to decide whether or not this is a rhetorical question too. *The real answer is, you ancient arsehole, I did it to please you. Because I have something inside that is cringing now, and was cringing before, and took action to prevent cringing in future. I hate myself for that as much as I hate you right now, and yet I am still cringing.* He wants to say, like a caught schoolboy, *Dunno, sir.* He will not do that, at least. 'I suppose I was . . . hoping to demonstrate initiative, sir.'

The DG is silent for a long time. Charlie is pretty sure that if he was going to be sent off to the opposite of a health farm, this interview would have been conducted there, in a room with a soil floor. But . . . his insides are not so sure. 'That is not what you have demonstrated,' he says, finally. 'You are to cease all such investigations immediately. You are to burn any notes you have made. Your pay grade will be reviewed. Dismissed.'

Is that it? Charlie stays seated. He wants to say *I deserve answers.* He wants to protest undying fealty to the man in front of him as if he's being dragged off by the guards in a banana republic. He isn't bothering to try to hide whatever emotions are now dangerously close to the surface.

The DG has met his gaze. There is nothing in his expression

to suggest boys will be boys, or that this little rebellion was in any way secretly approved by his authority. 'Do you *want* to be hurt?' he says.

Charlie silently gets to his feet and walks to the door, unsure of where his feet are. He doesn't look back. He doesn't look at Barbara on the way out.

♣

So that's how our boy ends up at the Queen's Tap, which is a Box pub, because he wants to have a few, and he doesn't mind who sees it. Indeed, he's quite keen on them seeing it. If his manner of advancement has been cut off, he thinks, he might as well do it in style. But tonight there are only a few in, and of his own only Tom Fotherington. Tom's so public school that he even still wears the tie, but he's a decent sort, so Charlie plonks himself down next to him. He knows better than to share anything about his conversation with the DG, or about his career prospects, because he didn't come here seeking actual career *suicide* . . . probably. And Tom might even be here to . . . no, of course not. Charlie's not that important. He really bloody hopes.

'So . . .' he begins, over his second pint, still in two, three, four minds about what he feels about bloody anything. 'How was *your* day?'

'Utter panic. Right as we were about to go out of the door. They kept my shift on an extra hour, called the next shift in early.'

Charlie pricks his ears up. He just missed that. The shift on each department keeps different hours. The margin is meant to allow quicker briefing when something major's going on. Tom's in supplies. 'What's the flap?'

'Something big is impending. No idea what. I should think we'll see it on the *Nine O'Clock News*. It feels like when the Provos have an active service unit in town.'

'You think it's a bomb?'

'Or an assassination. Quiet as the grave in the Irish section, mind you. So it's not the boyos this time. Something must have come in from an informant, but that's the odd thing . . .'

'What?'

'Nobody *with* informants in the field seems to be joining in with the buzz. It's as if information pertaining has suddenly appeared from . . .' Tom gestures skywards.

'From the DG?'

'Which means he's heard it from someone in Whitehall, which is not the way this is supposed to work. *We're* meant to be looking out for *them*. Heads will roll, I should think, after we've rushed around, beating all the bushes they've pointed at.'

'Which bushes?' Charlie wishes all interrogations were as easy as the ones between colleagues in the pub. But he has a horrible feeling about this, that he might not actually be as far away from the heart of things now as he thought he was.

'Well, all the military service records were out and being gone through. The union busters were in and out as well, all getting their pockets shaken out, one after the other.' Charlie hates it that that's automatically what the officers running operations inside British trade unions get called. But right now his head is suddenly busy with connections. And one big central worry. Did the DG follow *all* his investigations before he got called in and carpeted? Was the old man aware that Charlie has been meddling with both a military officer, of whom the DG is certainly aware, and a union official, of whom he may well not be? 'And,' Tom continues, 'the weird squad were in as well. The Silver Helix, diplomatic relations established, red carpet extended, though they were virtually marched from the doorway to the DG, not allowed to look left or right. Not that their sort need to gut our files like we're chicken in a basket.'

And the boss knave himself. So all the aspects Charlie had discovered were in place. But if this *was* all about Charlie, if the DG had known he'd stumbled onto something big, or been unwittingly fooling around with some carefully arranged plan, then he wouldn't have been let loose like this. He'd at the very least have been regarded as an asset, and thus kept in a corridor somewhere, doing a crossword. What his current freedom says to Charlie is that the DG does *not* in fact know everything he's found out. He has been seen approaching the edges of some sensitive issue, not pirouetting into the middle of it.

Which gives our boy a little moment of pleasure. That he's ahead of his boss. And it gives him a few burning questions to ask himself. Which he does, over three more pints, during which he tells Tom they'd best shut up about work, and tries to talk cricket instead.

Turns out Tom is a footie man. Ironically.

Which is how, after a period the length of which feels somewhat uncertain, Charlie finds himself, in the early hours, on a familiar street once again. He is brandishing his weapon of choice in his gloved hands: a coathanger borrowed from Cassie at the pub, which he has bent into a particular shape that he recalls from another of those courses he attended on his own initiative. It does not take too long to get new locks fitted. One goes to Yellow Pages, and lets one's fingers do the walking. New, secure, windows, however . . . He is now in Faulkner's empty, untended little patch of soil where a garden should be and having, he hopes, already made sure nobody's about, he is repeating what the previous burglar did, slipping the wire in through the gap in the wood, and working it round to . . . There, the small window is open just enough for him to push his pen through and flick up the catch. Then he spins the wire in his hand, and uses the loop he's made on the other end to drop through the small window, and pull open the catch on the big one below it.

So easy a drunk could do it.

He hauls himself over the windowsill and into the front room, then closes the window behind him, draws the curtains again. He pauses for a moment. The house is silent. All is dark. But after a moment, the streetlight outside gives him enough light to work by. He's in a nice little parlour. There are family photos, flowers in vases, a desk, some commemorative plates. Faulkner is clearly a prissy young man, civilized before his time.

Why is Charlie here?

To make a connection. A connection he's pretty sure the DG doesn't know about. A connection the finding of which might save his career. He pieced it together in the pub, and he's kept repeating it to himself to get it straight. The DG must have been told, by those above him, that there's about to be a high-profile assassination attempt. He knows a serving military officer is involved. He knows someone known to the Silver Helix is involved. Which puts Faulkner, recently part of a mystery, right in the frame. But the DG doesn't yet know that Faulkner also fits the third part of his puzzle, that Faulkner has a surprising union connection, because only Charlie knows that. It might take days for the DG to track that down. And, if this is about an assassination, they don't have that long. Now, were Charlie sober, he might well have just called it in, allowed himself to take small credit like that. But no, our boy is grandiosely sozzled, and being influenced by powers greater than himself that he's been soaked in for so long it almost feels like they're part of his character. Almost. He is doing something rash, just as men with guns and bombs in similar situations have often done something rash. But, oh dear, Charlie only has a coathanger.

His plan, such as it is, is to find the union membership documents that Faulkner was given, photograph them, and take those to the DG. Solid proof. So me showing initiative wasn't so ridiculous, was it, sir? What it all adds up to, he has no idea. He'll breathe a sigh of relief and leave that to the greater powers to sort out.

He tries a couple of drawers in the desk and finds the papers. He's just about to get his camera out when the light comes on.

Charlie turns slowly, one hand still, unfortunately, in the pocket of his mac. In the doorway, in his dressing gown, with lightning flickering between his hands and a pair of piercing eyes under his blond short back and sides, stands the galloping captain. 'Another one!' he says. He sounds exasperated. Which is not quite the emotion Charlie expected. 'Why?'

'Complicated,' says Charlie. 'Mate, it's been a long day, can I sit down?'

'Throw your gun on the floor.'

Charlie slowly withdraws his hand from his mac, and throws his camera on the floor.

'Don't tell me you're not armed?'

'Search me if you want.'

Faulkner instead takes a step closer, the intensity of the lightning increasing. 'No false moves,' he says.

'I have always thought,' says Charlie, 'that was a very strange expression.'

'Who do you work for?'

'By now I'm probably between jobs.'

'Who did the first one work for? Why didn't he *know*?'

Charlie wonders what they were both supposed to know. 'Listen. I'm going to tell you the truth. I think you were burgled on orders, just on the basis of you being an ace in the military who was . . . d'you reckon you've been behaving oddly lately? It would have been very obvious, you're no bloody good at tradecraft.' He burps. 'Sorry. I'm a bit pissed. Anyhow, that odd behaviour got you looked into, and you zapped the poor sod who'd been employed to do that, and then word came from on high that you weren't to be troubled. So now a whisper has come down again that no, you're definitely dodgy, but that other word from on high is still protecting you from the consequences . . . except it probably won't when they've put all the pieces together.'

'It won't matter after tomorrow morning.'

'Oh. Shit. Don't go telling me stuff like that. I'm still hoping to get out of here.'

But Faulkner has a fanatic's gleam in his eye now. This one, thinks Charlie, has been acted upon by greater powers even more than he himself has. He was born with a silver spoon in his mouth and in that spoon there was some serious shit. 'The previous one tried to tell me he didn't know anything, that he wasn't there to kill me. I didn't want to hurt him. I told him I was acting on the highest authority, that whoever he reported to must have got it wrong, that someone there must have been informed about what I've been ordered to do.'

Ruskin would have played along with that too, thinks Charlie, kept that conversation going until he could try to get out. Hence the long conversation. 'Surely,' he says, 'you know by now that the establishment isn't one big thing, but a bunch of warring cliques that couldn't coordinate a piss-up in a brewery? Why do you think everyone was informed of whatever this mission of yours was?'

'Because of who it came from! From the very top! And I've been proven right, haven't I? He's ordered you to let me proceed! And yet here you are!'

The whole thing comes together at once in Charlie's head. And he's sure he didn't manage to keep up his usual poker face. Because in that second he also knows he's dead. 'Oh,' he sighs. 'Oh, sod this for a game of soldiers.'

He leaps for the window. As Ruskin did.

The window explodes with light.

Charlie wasn't as fast as Ruskin, and that's saved him. He staggers back towards Faulkner, who's quickly slamming his palms together, over and over, building up a bigger and bigger charge between them. Charlie notes, absently, that the sofa is on fire. Faulkner is looking at him with bulging eyeballs, as if, should Charlie go for the window again, he'll use whatever charge he's got, and that might well be enough for Charlie to go down and for Faulkner to follow up with his hands and whatever else he's got handy.

'You poor bastard,' says Charlie. And he means it.

'Your . . . sympathy is misplaced!' yells Faulkner, building up to his big moment.

Charlie wishes he had a Roger Moore line. He has a moment to decide on the freshest looking flowers. He grabs the vase and throws the contents over Faulkner's hands.

Faulker goes up like Guy Fawkes. And for similar reasons.

Charlie lands on the carpet, and watches the man stagger, screaming, for just a few moments, thank God . . . before he crumples into a blazing heap.

Charlie is breathing so hard he feels as if he's going to throw up. The room is starting to fill with smoke. And there goes the fire alarm upstairs. Charlie has one thing he has to do before he gets out.

He goes to the desk, gets those union membership papers, and throws them on top of the burning Faulkner, watching until every detail of them is ash. He just hopes Boulton hasn't finalized the content of next month's newsletter.

◆

The rest of the evening's a bit of a blur. Charlie stumbles out of a burning house as the fire crew is rushing in. The next thing he knows, he's in the back of an ambulance, with an oxygen mask on his face. After that, he's in a hospital bed, and the ward is completely dark, and all he can hear are the sounds of snoring, but there is a very awake man standing beside his bed, looking in astonishment at him.

Charlie realizes it's the DG. 'You,' he says, 'have friends in high places. I don't know how accidental what happened tonight was. You should give some thought to what story you're going to tell. But that's just for form's sake. Because blundering into the middle of all that suited everybody. It turns out.' It appears as if there are questions he wants to ask Charlie, because he's still looking as if he's witnessing a miracle. But before Charlie can start to cough out an answer, the DG is marching off. Charlie goes back to sleep.

♠

A couple of weeks later, once Charlie's back at work and has taken the hint and told his story of having been working covertly for the DG the whole time, to much applause in the corridors, he's invited to visit 10 Downing Street.

This makes him worried all over again. He hasn't seen the DG since that deniable hospital visit. He gets the feeling he's not going to be called upon again. In his best suit, he waits in a corridor, then is called in to the office of the Prime Minister.

There he is, enormous, standing at the window, everything in this stuffy museum of an office looking too small for his big hands. He turns, as if in the middle of an important thought, and has just realized Charlie's here. 'Ah,' he says. 'Mr Soper. You have done both me and your country a great and solemn service.'

Charlie has thought about what he's going to say. He's got away with it. He should just accept that. But that would be letting down other people. Or maybe he just can't resist biting the hand that hasn't slapped him. 'By saving your life? Because Captain Faulkner was planning an assassination?'

'Indeed. And he had the access to do it. Without having to sneak in some weapon. Though . . .' Churchill finally makes bleary, red eye contact with Charlie. 'His motives remain a mystery.'

Yeah. Because Charlie burned those papers. 'There are those who say, sir, that after a certain time of night, after dinner, after drinks, after the black dog of depression is given its hours, orders are issued from this office which are, as a matter of policy, ignored. I've often wondered what might happen if one of those accidentally got through and was acted upon.'

'I do not see what—'

'I've often wondered. But I think I just found out. What happens is that everyone falls over themselves trying to hint and obfuscate and they end up blundering into each other trying to both obey and not obey what they know to be an entirely undemocratic instruction.' Churchill is silent. Reddened. Furious. But he knows. He knows Charlie has him. And, thank God, he does not feel able to threaten Charlie with anything. He knows there are others who'd jump to take advantage of what Charlie's worked out. And he has no idea what evidence Charlie's picked up along the way. 'I gather you thought, late one night, that you might end your premiership with a certain degree of spectacle. Make one last heroic sacrifice for the beloved country. Take down with you the bastards you see as a threat to it.'

Churchill pauses. Considers. 'Your country does owe you . . . advancement. And I personally owe you a debt which—'

Charlie didn't think he was going to get angry in the moment of doing what he'd already decided to do, but now he is. 'Oh no. No, sir. No, sir, I won't hear those words in this office in that voice after all the much better words you've said from here before. There's only one thing I'm after. And then we're even. There is one more sacrifice you can make for your country. Then we all get to stand up and applaud. And you get to take a bow knowing we mean it.'

Charlie sits there, more pent up than he has ever been in his life, an iron filing that is fighting against the current acting upon it from all directions. The great face he is looking at finally loses its frown and becomes . . . relieved. There is, incredibly, a lifting of the chin, direct eye contact, a pleased new appraisal of Charlie. Of someone who kept something safe after the one doing the looking had misplaced it one night.

There is just a slight nod. Then Churchill turns back to the window. After a moment, a secretary knocks and enters, and Charlie realizes he's been dismissed. He's not sure what that means or how he feels. He looks back and sees that Churchill is swaying slightly on his feet, and thinks suddenly how he'll never get to tell people about this moment.

♥

A few months later, Charlie is in the pub after work, celebrating a promotion that he's been assured came about because of the recommendation of his immediate superiors, and not because of word from on high. Anyway, word is that the DG's on the way out.

The crowd around him goes silent as they realize what the television newscaster's just said, that the Prime Minister has announced his retirement.

Charlie carefully and giddily takes to his feet, and joins in the raising of glasses. He means it too. Mostly.

♣ ♦ ♠ ♥

Police On
My Back

by Charles Stross

London, 1981

A HOT JUNE EVENING IN the East End, and Allen
Crippen was ready to crash.

His first week in London – the week just past – felt
like half his life, and it was turning out to be a complete shit-
show. Forget the bright lights and big city hustle. The London
he'd found stank of overcooked cabbage, consisted of squalid
rows of terraced houses and cheap sixties prefab estates adja-
cent to rubble-strewn wasteground and chain-link fences.
Vacancy/For Sale signs on every street, some of them so old
they'd bleached in the harsh summer sunlight. Graffiti on
crumbling walls: NEVER MIND THE BOMB WHO'S GOT THE
BIGGER COCK. It felt just like the other half of his life, back
home in Birmingham. Why had he even bothered coming here?

Sweating profusely under his balaclava and biker jacket,
Allen rubbed his right arm and winced. His ribs and arm still
ached from the shoeing he'd taken from Brum's finest last
week, when they'd thrown him out of the cells at Steelhouse
Lane with the admonition, 'fuck off to Jokertown or hang
yersel', we don't need your kind here'. Not that he'd done
anything to deserve it besides assaulting their knuckles with

his face, or maybe waking up in the isolation ward at Birmingham General. On top of the bruises – it had been a *friendly* police interview, they hadn't broken anything or fitted him up for a robbery charge, at least not yet – he was badly sunburned, his skin peeling and itching furiously from the half an hour of overcast daylight he'd copped before the penny dropped.

Still, he was a tenner richer for nine hours of hauling boxes between lock-ups under a railway viaduct. Mal at the shelter had pointed him at the opportunity. A row of viaduct arches fronting a pile of rubble that dated to the Blitz had been boarded up and turned into garages or storage spaces. When he got there he'd found a hard-faced guy called Gary who needed a lorry emptying into one of the dank spaces. No questions asked or answered. If he went back tomorrow – if he was up to it – there might be another one. The pay was shit, but it wasn't like he could sign on the dole. Not with the police probably looking for him . . .

'Not fucking worth it,' he muttered to himself as he turned the corner onto East Ferry Road, towards the chimneys of the power station. Another few days of this and he'd have the dosh to rent a bedsit of his own. Maybe. But he couldn't get his head around the idea of living here. Except—

As he passed the edge of the park and turned towards Millwall, the pavements became busier. The shops were closed and shuttered but here and there a haze of smoke and noise overflowed from a pub doorway. The sunset warmth had winkled the locals out of their brick-and-mortar shells, skinny kids with scabbed kneecaps kicking a ball around, a gaggle of pensioners chilling on a street corner. A bus farted slowly past, its bored conductor catching the breeze on the open rear platform. And here and there, the obvious signs of a jokertown. A beggar with one too many eyes sitting cross-legged behind an up-turned hat. A West Indian woman of about Allen's age making her way along the other side of the street, outwardly normal but for a giveaway bulge below the left sleeve of her cardigan. And, of course, the fucking tourists.

'Get it out for the lads!' shouted the middle one of the three guys blocking the pavement in front of her. His mate paused for a swig from his can of Special Brew, belched cacophonously, and sidestepped into her path as Tourist Number Three darted past and stopped behind her. 'Whatcher got under yer arm? Been out shoplifting?'

Oh, for fuck's sake. It was the third incident Allen had seen in as many days. Essex lads tanked up on cheap lager, West End girls on a hen night, drunken posh kid students from the colleges in town – they liked to come and get some joker action, collect the mutants like a pack of Top Trumps, and maybe throw in a bit of casual street harassment if they wouldn't strip off to order.

The joker lass wasn't interested. 'I'd rather not,' she said, her icy cut-glass intonation like someone off the news. 'Why don't you go pick on someone your own size?' She didn't say *please*, Allen noted. No victim here, just blunt assertiveness. But the tourists didn't seem to get the message, and the one with the can was taller and wider than Allen. His mate reached out to grab the back of her top—'

There was a long gap in the traffic. Later, that was all Allen could think of to explain what happened next. The woman recoiled as Tourist Number Three grabbed the woman's cardigan and yanked it off her left shoulder, buttons tearing to reveal her extra arm. The beginning of a triumphant shout from Tourist Number Two as she stumbled sideways, face crumpling in humiliation. 'Hey!' Allen shouted. 'Leave her alone!'

Everyone stared at him. 'Izzat another geek?' Tourist Number One hissed, eyes narrowing. *Oh fuck, I'm done for now.* 'C'mon, get yer kit off for the team!' Number Two was already in the street, heading for Allen's side of the road. 'Get 'im, lads!'

Allen closed his eyes and did *it* again. The thing the police had hauled him in for, the thing there wasn't an actual law against *as such* but if *I ever set eyes on you again, my son*, the thing with the bricks baking in the summer sun and the hot pavement stinking of dog shit and the sense that *if he willed it* all that was solid could turn into air. And he could *feel* their boots on the ground like they were pounding his tender skin. Only it wasn't his skin he was sensing them with, it was the dirty grey tarmac of the road that quivered and softened like quicksand. Tourist Number Two shouted, dismayed, 'Hey, what-thefuck—' as he stumbled. Then Tourist Number Three was in it up to his left ankle, flailing at the air.

Allen opened his eyes and glared at them. 'Give her back her cardigan!' he shouted.

The tourists weren't paying any attention to the geek in the balaclava. The woman was another matter, staring wide-eyed, feet frozen in situ as if she feared the ground would liquefy beneath her as well. 'Come on!' he waved as Tourist Number One finally went down, belly-flopping on the watery black slurry that had replaced the road. 'Over here – while they're distracted.'

'Give that. To me.' She bent down and grabbed her top as she crossed the road delicately as a gazelle, staring at the surface as she came to Allen's side. Stepping onto the pavement, she asked, 'Did *you* do that?' One eyebrow arched in near disbelief.

'S'pose so.' Turning to face the road had brought his face into direct sunlight and Allen hunched over, unconsciously avoiding the prickly heat. 'You going to be okay?'

'Oh, I was always—' Tourist Number Three tore his foot loose from the liquid road and bellowed rage, then took a plunging step towards Allen. A van skidded to a stop just short of the quagmire with a blare of horns. 'You'd better come with me,' said the woman, sparing the traffic an assessing glance. 'Unless you want to hang around and explain yourself to the Old Bill?'

Allen did a double-take. *Come with me?* The three-armed woman was right: he didn't want to stick around. And besides, she wasn't afraid. It wasn't like he had anywhere else to be, or knew anyone. 'Lead on,' he said, and as he turned his back the road solidified behind him.

♣

Jenny led the guy hastily away from the scene of the crime, thinking hard. 'You're new around here, ain'tcha?' she prompted, taking stock of him with rushed sidelong glances. (*Height/weight*: five ten, about ten stone; *hair colour*: unknown; *eye colour*: ditto – that damned balaclava. Also black jeans, black biker jacket, black leather gloves.) 'To Jokertown, I mean? Where are you from?' (*Age*: indeterminate but probably young. He had the kind of inarticulacy that age eroded. *Accent*: Midlands.)

'Brum.' He cleared his throat. 'Birmingham.' He paused. 'Where are you from?' A sudden double-take. 'Wait, I didn't mean it like that—'

'I was born in Greenwich.' (She smiled without showing her teeth. At least he didn't mean anything by it, not like the arseholes she'd been stuck in classes with at college in Hendon.) 'I'm Jenny. You are . . .?'

'Allen. I, uh, I only got here this week—'

She held up a hand, diverted them both around a street corner. Kept an ear open for sounds of shouting or pursuit. (That was the trouble with tourist incidents. You could never be certain how the cards would fall. Or whether the uniforms would bother to follow it up. And the last thing she needed was to be picked up with Allen.) 'This way. So what's your story?' *What's under the mask?*

'I, uh, I woke up in an isolation ward last week. Dunno why, neither of my parents are carriers – the doctors said I was fine and kicked me out but I'm an albino now – I got sunburned on my way home even though it was raining – then, then—' he was breathing too fast and hunching over.

Panic attack? Jenny wondered. 'Stop,' she said. 'Deep breaths.' *He's only had a week to get used to it*, she realized, feeling a twinge of sympathy. She'd got sick aged eleven, three-fifths of a lifetime ago. 'So . . . you burn really easily and you can liquefy roads? Am I getting this right?' She wished she could take notes: this *never* happened.

'I, uh, two cops visited me at home. Took me down the nick then told me to fuck the hell off and not come back.' Jenny suppressed a wince. 'My parents . . . Mum hung up the phone.' Some winces weren't worth suppressing. 'So I came here.'

'Well . . .' *Fuck*, Jenny thought, *he's telling the truth.* 'Is it just tarmac you can melt?' she asked, leaning against the chain-link fence. *Please tell me it's just a little tarmac, nothing more.*

'Oh *no*.' Was he smiling behind his balaclava? The sun was below the buildings but if he burned that easily – *damn that mask.* 'I can do stuff like this.' The fence rattled and she jumped slightly, turning just in time to see the overgrown heap of bricks in the wasteground rattle and slump. Her heart sank. No question he was a knave – ace talent, but damaged by the virus. So new they hadn't cut the price tags off him, painfully honest, and it was totally just her luck that he'd run away to the Big Smoke and landed on her patch.

'You made the bricks crumble,' she said, trying to control the tremor in her voice.

'Not just bricks. It's stone, concrete, tarmac, you know?' He made a funny sound, almost a hiccup. After a moment she realized he was close to tears. 'I melted a coffee mug in the isolation ward, that's how it started. I was studying to be a civil engineer.' (*Occupation*: student, the recording angel in the back of her head ticked off.) 'Now I'll be lucky if anyone lets me on a building site—'

'C'mon,' she said, holding her hand out to him. *Catch 'em while they're still fresh*, the script wrote itself. 'When did you last eat?'

'Yesterday I, uh, I had a KFC, but I'm saving to rent a bedsit—'

'And tonight you're crashing in a hostel, right? Which is it? The one round the back of the Samuda Estate, or the Sally Army hall—' She tugged him into motion and he followed sluggishly, too hungry and tired to realize how painlessly she was hoovering up the contents of his head. 'Listen, I'll make supper for you, it's the least I can do, we look after our own here—' *liar* '—and you saved me from having to deal with those arseholes—' *true* '—so why don't you come with me and tell me all about yourself? I was going to cook a chicken curry, it's always easier with more people—' *food always works.*

'Yes, thanks,' he said, 'But you don't have to—'

'Yes. I do,' Jenny insisted. 'It's my job!' And she made herself smile at him, even as she thought, *just don't ask what it is or who's paying me to do it.*

◆

Jenny Scott lived in a council maisonette on a drab concrete estate, one of the prefab blocks that had been rolled out in the fifties and sixties to fill the gaps left by a Luftwaffe bombing campaign that had reduced large chunks of the East End to rubble. Ageing gracelessly, the window frames had rusted and the concrete stairwells smelled of piss. Half the ground floor windows were boarded up. But Jenny's flat was well-maintained. Allen sat gingerly on the edge of a brown corduroy sofa that smelled faintly of ancient cigarettes. Jenny bustled around the kitchen, keeping up a continuous stream of chatter about the neighbours, local news, anecdotes about a drop-in social centre she had something to do with, the weather . . . all the usual, all utterly mundane, and all utterly unexpected. *She's not afraid,* he realized, wondering if he should be nervous about her apparent lack of concern over having invited a masked stranger into her living room. *Why isn't—'*

It was getting dark, he realized, the north-facing window not admitting enough light to hurt. He tugged his mask up, wincing as the wool scraped his cheeks and the bridge of his nose like a wire scouring pad.

'Huh. You *are* white,' she said, coming back into the living room with a couple of plates. 'Were you an albino before the virus? Let me see you. Ow, that's got to hurt! Have you put anything on it?'

'Just this?' He held up the woollen balaclava.

'You won't want to be wearing that around London, man, they'll think you're a Provo.' She smiled faintly. 'You need sun-block, but I can't help you there.'

'Can I help? I mean, is there anything I can do to help?' he asked.

'Yes.' She thought for a moment. 'Glasses are in the sink – pour us both a beer?'

They sat at either end of the sofa and watched the shadows lengthen as the sun set and the rice steamed. After finishing her Double Diamond Jenny dived back into the kitchen and began briskly throwing together a curry, adding fresh plantains to a casserole of goat she'd stewed the day before. Allen crossed to the music centre and knelt, rummaging through the shelf of LPs beneath the deck. Lots of stuff he hadn't heard of, jazz by the look of it – but also more familiar stuff: Pistols, Banshees, Clash. 'Mind if I put some music on as well?'

'Sure!'

They ate goat curry by the light of a sixty-watt bulb and the sound of *Sandinista!*: 'The Crooked Beat' fading into 'Somebody Got Murdered'. Allen noticed Jenny watching him curiously. She ate normally, not using her second left arm. He was about to ask about that, but bit his lip and held his tongue in time. Not wanting to spoil this astonishingly unexpected moment. In Allen's experience strange women, even strange women with three arms who he'd rescued from a bunch of tossers, didn't invite him back to their home and feed him. Somehow he didn't think it was because of the way he oozed sex appeal right through the weave of his woolly headgear. But on the other hand – *the third hand, ha ha* – he wasn't ready to look the gift horse in the mouth just yet. There'd be plenty of time to swallow his boot all the way past his tonsils and slope off back to the hostel later.

Jenny put her plate down on the cluttered coffee table and reached for a tobacco tin. 'Smoke?' she asked.

'I—' Allen shook his head. 'I don't.'

'Oh, too bad.' Unapologetic, she opened the tin and began to assemble a roll-up. The tobacco went in first, then a thin crumbling of what looked like brown shoe polish on top. 'There's not much good stuff around right now but I've got a bit of slate.'

'Slate?'

She raised an eyebrow in his direction: 'Small town, huh?'

'I, uh, I'd like to try it? If you don't mind, that is . . .'

Jenny gave him a small smile. 'I wouldn't be offering if I minded, would I?'

How Allen had got to be twenty and a student in Birmingham without smoking a joint was one of those imponderable questions that used to perplex him when he lay awake in the small hours of the night, much like worrying if he'd ever lose his virginity (scratch that, as of last year – Freshers' Week had claimed a lot of scalps) before more urgent concerns took over. Like worrying about the police coming after him, or about having somewhere to sleep tomorrow night. As had happened with his virginity, he got his first toke on a sofa with a strange woman to whom he was very grateful, but gained absolutely no insight whatsoever into how he'd ended up in this position, or how to repeat it. However, it took the edge off his free-floating anxiety. 'You're single?' he asked as she lit a second spliff. Clumsy but direct.

'Welcome to Jokertown.' She drew in a slow lungful. 'I get

by, like everyone else.' The record side ended. 'You want to change that?'

Allen stood, slightly dizzy, and stared his feet into submission before stamping over to the turntable and very carefully swapping side two for side three, lowering the needle on 'Lightning Strikes'. He turned to face the sofa. 'Why—' inarticulate, he waved a hand at himself. 'Why me? I don't get this. Not that I'm not grateful, but—'

'But what? What's to get?'

'What do you want with me?' He persisted. 'I'm nobody!'

'No, you're not. I can tell.' She gave him a lazy smile. 'You've just had a bad time lately.' She patted the sofa beside her. 'C'mon and sit down. You can crash here tonight, on the sofa, s'better than the hostel. Tomorrow I'll introduce you round the community centre. Get you set up. 'S what friends are for, innit?'

'Whose friends?' he asked, abruptly certain that she wanted him for something.

'I don't know, Allen. *Are* we friends?' She looked up at him, a flicker of apparent anxiety crossing her face. 'Come on, sit down. You want to make new friends, don't you?'

♠

Over the next few weeks, Allen kept resisting the urge to pinch himself to see if he was dreaming. *This kind of thing never happens*, he kept telling himself. Except that it had, and not even the aches and blisters of moving stacks of boxes between white vans and lock-ups for cash in hand could make it feel real to him.

He went back to the hostel just once, the evening after he met Jenny, to grab his bag from the locker and return the key. He'd paid for another three nights but didn't argue when the guy on the desk told him he was keeping the money. For a horrible moment as he waited on Jenny's front doorstep he worried that he'd dreamed the night before, but then the door opened and her face lit up when she saw him. He'd followed her inside, still balanced on a knife-edge of disbelief.

She'd invited him to move in with her. They hadn't had sex, but had stayed up into the early hours, listening to music, talking, smoking – his throat felt as if it had been sanded – and she had a spare bedroom and if he could pay a share of the rent and help out about the house he was welcome to it. And if they hadn't had sex she'd barely looked away from him, her eyes huge and expressive and liquidly brown, and if she had three arms (one of them withered) who was he to throw stones, his skin was as dead-fish-belly white as hers was dark brown, and . . . he pinched himself again.

There'd been more work hauling boxes for Gary, although he'd grumbled when Allen turned up late – Jenny had insisted on dragging him round to the community centre first. The centre wasn't much to look at, a former church hall with chipped Formica tables and folding chairs, staffed by volunteers who seemed to have nowhere else to go. There were posters taped to the walls. Propaganda from the plod pompously declared that the Twisted Fists were mad, bad and dangerous to even think about, and please phone the local community constable at the number scribbled in biro below if you know anything about them. (*Fat chance.*) Another poster earnestly explained the evils of cannabis in terms of how it corrupted youth and funded street gangs in the Jamaican immigrant community: Allen tuned it out once he realized it was talking about his new roommate. 'The decor's a bit shit but they mean well,' Jenny had apologized, with a nod at the front desk. 'They run socials every Tuesday and Thursday night and they help people like us when we're down on our luck.' No pointed hints there. He offered to volunteer for a few hours, once he found his feet, and that seemed to satisfy her.

On the fourth night they smoked too much, got giggly, and she finally invited him into her bed, where they grappled clumsily until he discovered a broken mattress spring the hard way. But the next morning she sang quietly to herself over breakfast, and he walked on air all the way to work.

Everything seemed to be going fine until, a couple of weeks in, Gary pulled him aside one morning and said, 'The boss wants ta see ya.'

Allen did a double-take. Right up until this moment he'd had no inkling that Gary even had a boss. 'What about?' he asked.

'Dunno: 'e's the boss.'

The boss in question was visiting that morning. Gary's office was a garden hut wedged incongruously at the back of one of the dank lock-up arches under the railway viaduct. It was dark enough inside the tunnel for Allen to remove his hood safely as he followed Gary through a maze of second-hand furniture, orphaned bicycles, and the spoils of a thousand house clearance sales. 'Who is he?' he asked nervously. Gary ignored him.

'Boss? Gotcher new fish 'ere. Allen, this is Mr McAndrews, the boss.'

McAndrews loomed out of the office chair in the hut, towering over a desk piled high with scribbled invoices and ancient-looking ledgers. 'Eh. Leave us,' he grunted, a Scottish burr underlying his raspy voice. Gary scarpered. 'So.' He stared at Allen, who shivered slightly.

Gary was a yard rat, but McAndrews' vertically slit pupils and cleft lip lent him the unnerving appearance of a thuggish tomcat in human skin. And his suit fitted too well to have come off the peg at Burton's.

Allen tried to fill the silence. 'You asked for me?'

'Aye, that I did.' The inspection continued. Eventually McAndrews nodded minutely, then spoke again: 'What brung ya to the Big Smoke, my man?'

'I—' Allen shivered in spite of the heat. 'I came down with the virus. When I recovered, the police told me to get out of town. Why—' he caught himself before he said too much.

Asking McAndrews questions felt like a bad idea. There was something predatory about him, sharp suit or no.

'A's good. So whit can ye dae fer me?'

Allen blinked. 'Excuse—'

'I *said*, what is it that you can do?' McAndrews abruptly shifted to cut-glass BBC English, polished with just the faintest sheen of menace. 'The other night, on East Ferry. What did you do?'

'There were these three lads hassling Jenny Three-Arms, and I, I . . .' Casting around, Allen noticed for the first time that even though they were surrounded by crumbling Victorian brickwork he was standing inside a wooden hut, beneath a plywood roof. 'There's this thing I can do to brick and stone. Tarmac, too. I can show you?'

McAndrews nodded. 'Not in here. Outside.' Mask back in place, heart beating too fast, Allen followed the boss out into the yard that fronted the viaduct. 'There,' McAndrews said, pointing at the brickwork with a claw-tipped finger.

'Are you sure—'

'Aye.'

Allen reached out and touched the viaduct abutment. Mortar crumbled to powder first, then the red clay bricks, baked in an oven some time when the railways were young, began to disintegrate. He dug his fingers into the crumbling wall, gouged out a fistful of dust, then shoved his hand in as far as his wrist and twisted it around. 'Probably a bad idea to go any deeper.' He glanced up nervously as a commuter train rumbled slowly overhead, shaking the ground.

'Aye.' Not a man of many words, McAndrews shoved his hands in his coat pockets and looked unimpressed. Then he glanced aside at the yard. 'Stand over there. How deep can ye dig? How much can ye move?'

'What? You want me to . . .?'

McAndrews smiled, baring needle-sharp canines. 'Yer a mole-man: I want ta see yer tunnel. Give it all you've got, aye?'

Allen narrowed his eyes. *A challenge, is it?* He reached out with the odd new sense he'd acquired, like touch only so much more. There was a buried cable not far away, loaded with malignant power, and if he went down too far a pipe, probably a sewer. *So avoid.* Flexing imaginary muscles he established a six-foot circle and told the tarmac to liquefy. Then he began to dig as he'd never dug before, not even in the cells below the police station. (What he'd told Jenny had been a lie by omission – the West Midlands Joker Squad hadn't exactly *let him go*.) The tarmac began to bubble, then climb up in a crater rim around the growing pit. Fire spewed out, tumbling over the edge. 'I could go faster if I had something to shift it out of the way,' he told McAndrews. 'I mean, I can move it around after I tell it to disintegrate, but it's very slow. A fan, maybe a leaf blower, something like that.'

'Huh.' McAndrews walked around the crater, peering over the rim. After only a minute it was already waist-deep. 'How long can ye keep it up?'

'I—' Allen blinked. 'I've never tried.'

'Keep going, then.'

After five minutes he was sweating hard and took a break. McAndrews stopped him after his third session. He'd dug a trench nine feet deep right across the yard and filled it in again, fusing the earth solid – twice over. 'Stop, lad.' McAndrews stepped onto the newly re-formed tarmac and stamped on it experimentally. 'Huh.' He glanced sidelong at Allen, who was breathing hard and shaking slightly, then reached into an inside pocket for a wallet so plump it disturbed the hang of his jacket. Opening it, he extracted a wad of banknotes. 'Take the rest of the day off, lad.' Allen wasn't sure that graduating from *my man* to *lad* was a good thing, but 'Summun'll pick you up here tomorrow at ten. If Gary gives you any lip tell 'im Pussyface wants you special.'

McAndrews turned and stalked away towards the Daimler Double-Six parked in one corner of the yard, leaving Allen clutching a bundle of cash. Startled, he turned and hunched towards the wall before he counted it. *Two hundred quid?* He boggled and pocketed it hastily, lest it vanish like fairy gold in the glare of sunlight. A good week's pay, cash in hand, for thirty minutes' work? *I could get used to that*, Allen decided, watching as Pussyface held a telephone handset to his face with one hand, backed the big Jaguar limousine out of the gate and roared away. *I wonder what he wants.*

♥

Thursday morning was Jenny's regular trip into town. If anybody asked, it was her appointed time to sign on down the dole office (not than anybody ever did). She caught the bus as usual, changed twice, doubling back on herself and checking for a tail. Then, once she was certain nobody was shadowing her through the busy streets, she headed for Victoria Embankment and an office building with cramped interview rooms, wired glass in the door windows, and an omnipresent smell of stale tobacco and instant coffee.

New Scotland Yard.

Sergeant Rutherford was away from the desk when she sat down at the keyboard, so she spooled paper into the typewriter and began pecking out her report on the week so far without interruption. She'd run into Allen the day after her last session and he didn't make the criteria for an emergency that would justify breaking her routine – although he came close – so she wrote it up as she saw it. *Homeless knave fresh off the bus from Brum, vital figures such-and-so, doing casual labour for one of the Fish's fences, hospitality offered and taken.* In other words, a promising contact, likely to get the target's attention and spill everything he learned in her ear. *Exactly* the sort of informant Rutherford had demanded from her last week. So why did she feel so ambivalent?

Tarmac, melting. Feel of beetle-legs skittering down her spine.

His eyes, wide in adoration. Maybe it was because he was an open book? She was sure he was holding back *some* secrets, but they were the secrets of a twenty-year-old civil engineering student. Ex-girlfriends, trouble with the police back home, guilt-tripping himself because he hadn't phoned Mum and Dad since he'd run away to town. That sort of thing. Maybe he was hiding an angle on his ace talent, but she'd already seen it in action, knew there was more to it than just squishy roadstone. Meanwhile he was just so *truthful* with her. She could *feel* his honesty, just as she could sniff out lies whenever she heard them, and trying to turn him to the dark side just felt *wrong*. She stared at the paper and sighed.

'Penny for your thoughts, Constable?'

Rutherford loomed over her from behind, one beefy hand leaning on the desk in front. 'Developed a new contact the day after my last report, sir. New boy in town, landed a job with one of the Fish's back doors – nothing obviously illegal yet – and he's crashing in my spare room.'

'*Well* now.' Rutherford smirked. 'A likely lad? You pumping him yet?'

Jenny kept her face still. 'Purely in a professional capacity, sir.' Rutherford was old school but canny: he'd made detective sergeant, after all. But he had entrenched views, to put it mildly, when it came to women, immigrants, and virus survivors. Which made three strikes against Jenny, and she'd have been right out of the door before she got her feet under the desk if he hadn't read her reports before he first clapped eyes on her face. As it was, what she got from him was patronizing tolerance alternating with irritable demands, rather than the professional respect an undercover officer ought to expect. 'He's working for Gary's Scrap and Salvage right now. Had some kind of run-in with West Midlands. I want to check if he's a nominal.' A subject with a record on the Police National Computer system.

Rutherford grunted. 'Do the paperwork, I'll sign off on it. Anything else?'

'You should know he's a knave, sir. Power over concrete, brick, stone. And he manifested in public last Friday. So I'm guessing the Fish will get wind of him soon enough.'

'Right.' The sergeant grunted, mollified for the moment. 'When you're done with that you can run off a couple of photostats before you piss off: the inspector will want to know. Oh, and fetch me a coffee while you're about it?'

♣

On Thursday evening Allen took Jenny out for dinner at a local Italian restaurant whose proprietor had six fingers on each hand. She didn't ask where he'd got the money for the meal, or the new sports jacket he wore. Afterwards, when the summer rain started, he wrapped it over her shoulders and they walked home together, laughing, with their fingers entwined.

Early the next week one of Pussyface's blokes turned up, driving a battered white Ford Transit pick-up. 'You Crippen?' he said, and jabbed a thumb at the truck. 'You're riding with me today.'

They drove to some rubble-strewn wasteground in the wilds of north London where he met a new gang boss. 'Dig us a tunnel,' he was told. 'Make it about six feet in diameter. Go down so it's ten feet under, and make it a hundred feet long. A dead end will do, 's'long as it ends over on the far side of the fence and you don't break any pipes or sewers.'

'Okay,' said Allen, and the ground began to soften under his boots.

''E's a fucken' joker JCB,' he heard one of the goons say when he clambered out across the top of the debris heap for a break. 'Eh, right?'

'More like a fookin' mole-man,' said another. 'I don't wanna know what he's got under that mask.'

'Will the roof support its weight if he drives over it?' asked the new boss, pointing at Transit Bloke's wheels.

Allen grimaced. 'You should have asked for that when I was starting out.'

Sorting this out took an extra hour: fusing clay and rubble and brick dust into something like breezeblock was wearying after the fact. By the time he had finished, the gang boss was on the phone and a couple of lorries were pulling into the site. But the tunnel was dug. 'What's it for?' he asked.

The gang boss turned a flat stare on him. 'Never you mind, son,' he said. Then he pulled out his wallet and began counting tenners. 'Pussyface said you could do it and 'e was right.' *Two hundred pounds, like winning the virus-laden lottery every afternoon.* As he headed for the Tube station, the men behind him began unloading wooden crates from the trucks and carrying them towards the mouth of the tunnel. *Easy money, no complications.*

On Saturday, Allen and Jenny slept in. Later he helped her shop for food and she helped him buy new clothes. And on Sunday they didn't get out of bed before noon.

Monday dawned overcast and humid, pregnant with a threat of thunderstorms before nightfall. Allen found Transit Bloke, whom he now knew was called Ron, waiting for him at Gary's yard again. Back up north they went, back to the wasteland with the pick-up heaped with debris. 'Boss says you're to fill this in and pack it as tight as you can,' said Ron.

'What—' Allen stared.

'Go on, get to work.'

Allen closed his eyes and sent fingers of perception into the ground. 'There's something down there,' he said after a moment. 'Crates of stuff.'

'Ignore them. Fill around them. Boss wants 'em buried deep.'

'Around—' He opened his eyes. Ron's expression was closed, and he held his fists tightly by his side. 'What *is* this?'

'It's what the Fish is payin' yer to do, dig 'oles and fill 'em in again.'

Holes. There was something in one of the crates, the one

nearest the end of the tunnel (beneath the lot on the other side of the fence). It felt stonelike-but-not, calciferous, once living but now reverting into the state of matter over which Allen held dominion. He shuddered, full of grim surmise. The other boxes were full of crap – broken crockery, rubbish, cans of used engine oil and detritus – but the one at the end was deathly. He opened his mouth to object, then stopped. Speaking out could cost him much more than just a day's wages. *I don't even know what this street's called*, he realized dismally. Nor was he able to go and squeal to the police, or even write them an anonymous note.

So he filled in the anonymous grave, and told himself never again.

When he finished, instead of forking out his pay packet Ron ordered him up into the cab and drove clockwise around the North Circular for half an hour. 'Boss said to bring you in for a chat at the end of the day.' A sidelong glance. 'Reckon you'd do well to listen to 'im.' He turned off the main road and drove out east, heading into suburbs Allen barely knew the names of, where the houses held themselves aloof behind hedges as stiff as hairsprayed up-dos, garages the width of their frontage with doors proudly open to display gleaming Porsches and Rollers to the passengers on the upper decks of passing buses. At last they pulled up outside a wall, where another of Pussyface's blokes eyeballed them from behind his mirrorshades and nattered briefly on a walkie-talkie before sliding the barred gate open. 'Go on in. I'll wait with the wheels.'

Bone-tired, sweaty, and wondering what the hell he had got himself into – it was clearly too late to get out of it – Allen shuffled past a windowless garage to the portico fronting the McAndrews mansion. Before he could ring the doorbell the gleaming slab of oak swung inwards. 'Come in, sir, you are expected.' Allen blinked at the dimness. He'd never met a real butler before, assuming that's what the tailcoat and black tie denoted. 'Please follow me, sir.'

The boss's digs were posh beyond any reasonable middle-class aspirations. Chequerboard marble floor, oak-panelled walls, paintings of nobs in nineteenth-century dress. The sole discordant note in the hall's ambiance was the dial telephone screwed to the wall beside the sweeping staircase: GPO engineers had no respect for cultural heritage. Pussyface had a study (or rather, a Victorian gent's smoking den) beside the drawing room. It was crammed full of oak furniture with oxblood leather padding and brass trim, shelves on three walls crammed with gilt-edged books bought by the yard, all presided over by a rather naff painting of the Battle of Culloden. The desk had probably seen battle at Trafalgar. It supported three telephones, a whisky decanter, an ornate silver salt-shaker, and a drably functional automatic pistol.

'Allen Crippen, welcome to my manor.' Pussyface neither stood nor smiled, but waved vaguely at the spindly rococo visitors' seats before his desk. 'Siddown, lad. So what you fink of the work?' Today Pussyface was channelling Bob Hoskins in *The Long Good Friday*, if Hoskins had been born to a man-eating tiger.

Allen sat obediently, pulse hammering. 'I—' He paused. 'There were bones in one of the boxes,' he said quietly.

Pussyface stared at him unblinking. 'How d'you work that out?'

'Bones are . . . they're like stone, you know? I can feel them, a bit. Not much inside me or you or anyone else alive, but once they're dead – it's really weird, I just *know*.' He watched his boss, wanting to lose his rag and shout *I'm not your fucking gravedigger*, but aware it would be futile. 'The other boxes were fine, I mean, I couldn't tell anything about them, but the one at the end—'

Pussyface blinked and looked away. 'He tried to grass us up, laddie. Don't you forget that. I'm very forgiving. If you owe me money you can't pay me back if you're dead, know what I mean? And dead bodies draw the filth like flies on a fuckin' stoater, so it means grief all round. I don't hold with murder: if anyone murders someone on my turf I'll fucking kill them and no mistake. If you cross me I'll batter you but leave you alive – unless you're a squealer.' In the twilight of his den, Pussyface's slit pupils were dilated, huge dark circles focused on his prey. 'Like the waste of space you just buried. Do you understand?'

'I—' Allen swallowed. 'I just wanted a job, nothing illegal.'

'Tough. You've got one now and you're on the inside whether you want it or not because I got a use for you.' Pussyface blinked and glanced down at his desk, then pulled a drawer open. 'But I tell you what, let's do a deal. Ask me no questions and I'll not burden your conscience, lad. It's best for both of us if you don't see nothing irregular. Just you remember to look away when I tell you to and we'll be fine.' He pulled out an envelope. 'And there'll be more of these. 'Ere. Take it.'

Allen caught the envelope between nerveless fingers.

'That's a retainer,' Pussyface added. 'Same every month. Plus a commission every time I've got a call-out for you. Dig a hole, fill it in, no names, no pack drill, ask me no questions, I'll tell you no lies. There'll be no more bodies, I got that. In the meantime, you'll work for Gary, humping boxes whenever you feel like it, aye?'

Allen swallowed again, and nodded.

'Get out,' Pussyface said genially. 'Ron will take you home. You're crashing with Jenny Three-Arms, huh?' He shook his head. 'Odd bird, no accounting for taste. Get out. Wait,' he added before Allen made it to the door: 'Ron'll pick you up from the yard tomorrow. Got a little job for you, your chance to start earning your keep.' He grinned broadly. 'You're on commission now. Welcome to the big time, lad.'

Allen fled, nerves in tatters, and didn't think to open the envelope and count the contents until he sat down at Jenny's kitchen table that evening.

Two thousand pounds in an envelope a month, and all he

had to do was dig holes and fill them in. What could possibly go wrong?

◆

By the prickling in her thumbs and the easing of her lodger's shoulders, Jennifer Scott recognized that she'd lucked into a big break. The evening after her meeting with the sergeant she had got home to be met by Allen with an expensive bottle of Scotch and a bouquet of flowers. After the inevitable enthusiastic tumble – the lad was still as eager as a puppy, hadn't quite worked out that she wouldn't kick him out of bed if he didn't hurry – he unwound enough to tell her that Pussyface had bunged him a fat retainer. But as she toasted his success and they worked their way down the bottle he unwound even further, becoming morose. 'That guy scares me,' he confided, flicking ash from a post-coital spliff into a guttering tea light. 'He had me dig a tunnel under someone else's yard then bury a load of boxes down there.' The reflection of the candle flame flickered nervously in his eyes. 'And his bloke Ron has a sawn-off shotgun taped under the driver's seat of his Transit. I don't care if he paid for the community centre, there was something *not right* about it.'

Clever lad, Jenny thinks sarcastically, then regrets it a moment later. She's got four hard years on him, it's not his fault he's still wet behind the ears. 'What sort of "not right" do you mean?' she coaxed, digging for details.

But she'd pushed too far, too fast: 'I've never met a real gangster before,' Allen said, then sighed unhappily and changed the subject.

She was at the centre the next morning, keeping her ear to the ground as usual, and Allen evidently had an uneventful day hauling boxes in and out of Gary's lock-up. Whatever was in the boxes – colour TVs, VCRs, crates of booze that fell off the back of a lorry, mate, honest – Gary sold it cheap, or at least below cost. Gary worked for Pussyface, and Pussyface worked for Edgar 'the Fish' Morton, and the Fish needed legit businesses to launder the cash proceeds from his various criminal enterprises.

Legend had it that the Fish had held his own against the Kray gang. Rumour had it that the Met couldn't get anything on his operation. Informers didn't turn up dead, they just vanished into an unmarked grave. Rumour had it he'd nicked a leaf from one of the barmier Palestinian terror groups' book, buried informers alive and dropped food and water into their coffin through a pipe until he had finished interrogating them, at which point he substituted a bullet – or if he was *really* mad, just pulled out the tube. 'Pillars of the community' was all anyone would ever say about the Fish and his Glaswegian enforcer with the vertical pupils and retractable claws, and they didn't mean it in a nice way, flash donations to local charities notwithstanding. They meant something more like a gibbet than a kindly support.

On Sunday, Jenny wheedled Allen into helping her at the centre again, making up care packages and then stepping out to deliver them to some of the elderlies who were housebound. A lot of them had ended up in grim concrete prefabs like the Barkantine Estate tower blocks. There'd been an unofficial council policy of shoving cripples, nutters, and jokers into a housing ghetto back in the sixties. Out of sight, they remained conveniently out of mind, and while these days they were *officially* the disabled and special needs cases, a lot of the old prejudice remained. Many of them were too timid and vulnerable to go out on their own or in daylight.

As for Allen, he wasn't enthusiastic about helping at first, but the way he sat up and paid attention when she smiled at him would have been hilarious if it wasn't so predictable. And he got the point eventually. 'They're our people and if we don't look after them, who will?' she guilt-tripped him, after he got the willies from meeting Mrs Halcyon. *I'll turn you into a fine upstanding public service employee yet, see if I don't*, she resolved. And anyway, Mrs Halcyon freaked out *most* people on first acquaintance. (A lonely seventy-seven-year-old widow who didn't bother locking her front door because she craved company, yet the local wide boys and thugs were too frightened by her appearance even to burgle her.)

Allen sighed. 'I don't know what the fuck I'm doing here,' he said, waving one gloved hand at the window at the end of the lift lobby on the twelfth floor.

'Here as in Barkantine Court, or here as in London?'

'Both. Neither.' The lift arrived, smelling of stale cigarettes and piss as usual. 'I ran away, didn't I? And I'm not sure it was the right thing to do.'

Jenny took his hand as he pushed the button for the thirteenth floor. (Next stop, Albert Parsons. No legs, just a mass of tentacles from the waist down. Easy on the eyes after Mrs Halcyon.) 'I'm happy you're with me,' she said, studiously artless.

'Yeah, but apart from that . . .'

Another house call, then back to the lift, sixteenth and final floor. (Next stop, Sybil 'Fawlty' Knox. A bad case of scleroderma, her soft tissues turning to living leather. Barely able to move unaided.)

'. . . there's *too much money*, Jenn, know what I mean?' His expression was almost pleading. 'It's, like, there's got to be some kind of catch, right?'

Damn right there's a catch, she thought grimly. 'You could always go home,' she prompted. 'Let 'em forget about you?'

On the way back down he was breathing too fast. 'Can't go back.' He looked desperate. 'They said they'd kill me—' He shut up, but clung to her hand like a child afraid of drowning in the paddling pool. Which, in a manner of speaking, he was. *He's telling the truth*, she realized dismally. That was the worst thing about her second-rate talent: it made turning a blind eye to some of her colleagues' less salubrious activities impossible. But her deuce was half the reason she'd drawn this duty, of course.

'Then it sounds like you're better off here,' she said, hating herself a little for leading him deeper into the maze. 'With me, right? You worry too much about the job. But, tell you what, if you think something stinks, let me know and I'll give you a sanity check, all right? Why don't you tell me about what you got up to last Thursday that put the wind up you? Wasn't it something about burying boxes?'

♠

Thursday rolled round again and this time things got interesting. Jenny's first indication that she'd rattled the higher branches of the org tree came when Sergeant Rutherford met her outside the briefing room. 'Skipper wants a word, luv,' he said, taking her elbow and steering her towards the corner office. 'It's about your nominal from last week.'

'What? Allen? He's got prior?' She started slightly.

'No conviction as such, but not for want of trying.' Rutherford paused, one hand on the inspector's office doorknob. 'Go on in.'

'Damnit,' she muttered under her breath. Opened the door: 'Sir? You wanted to see me?'

'Come in, Constable. Take a seat.'

Inspector Matthews was younger and sharper than Rutherford and a whole lot chillier. 'Your lodger is Allen Crippen, yes? Formerly of—' he rattled off an address in Solihull. 'Correct?'

Jenny cleared her throat. 'Can't say, sir. He hasn't been terribly forthcoming about his background. Hence the, er, nominal request.' For a trawl of the Police National Computer system. 'But the age and accent fit. Did we find anything? The sergeant hasn't briefed me yet.'

'Yes, we found something.' Matthews gave her an odd look. 'Did you enjoy playing with matches when you were a kid?

Read this.' He slid a printout across his desk. Jenny picked it up and frowned intently as she read.

'Infected three months ago, university field trip to a municipal sewage works . . . six weeks in a coma? Then—' her frown intensified. 'Sir, this isn't right.' She put the music-ruled printout down again. 'Assuming there's only one Allen Crippen with XTA from Brum, I can't see him doing any of the stuff on the charge sheet. I mean, GBH, assaulting a police officer, escaping from custody, destruction of Crown property?' She remembered his bruises, their barely faded echoes. 'He's a knave, sure, but he's also wet behind the ears. This is West Midlands' MO, you know what they're like?' She stopped, suddenly aware that it might sound like special pleading.

Matthews' stare was piercing. 'Yet here he is, in on the ground floor with the Fish, Constable. Doesn't look terribly innocent, does it? I appreciate that you've done well to take him in and lend him a sympathetic ear, but some actual operational intelligence would be gratefully received. If his intel checks out, and *if* you think it necessary to supply additional motivation, I will ask if our colleagues up north might be willing to reconsider the minor stuff, but tunnelling through a custody suite wall? He's going to have to cough up something *really* good to get out of that.'

'Well, let me give you his down payment.' *Now* Jenny knew she was on solid ground. It had taken a while to get it out of him. 'Last Thursday Pussyface tested him – had him bury a cache of some kind, possibly including a body, then pulled him in for a job interview. The cache was dug in via a tunnel under wasteground in Winchmore Hill—'

♥

Pussyface's 'jobs' didn't amount to much at first. Excavating rubble sites, shoring up cellars, checking houses for subsidence and fixing it. He spent three whole days at Pussyface's mansion, expanding the wine cellar under the back garden, packing and lining three new rooms and a corridor with compressed clay and fusing it in place before a regular construction crew showed up to finish it off. It was mildly tedious but at least he was doing something useful, and the envelopes full of cash were nice (even if Pussyface was getting him on the cheap compared to a real firm of structural engineers). His fears persistently failed to materialize, until he began to wonder if McAndrews had been yanking his chain: had there ever been a body in the first place?

A few weeks after Jenny discussed his work history with her superiors, Allen found himself sitting in a greasy spoon, frowning mildly as Ron the driver introduced him to his new teammates.

'Guys, this is Allen. Allen is our construction specialist, a real live human JCB. Allen, this is Mick. And this is Nigel. Don't ask their surnames or where they live, right?'

'New fish!' Mick chortled quietly.

Allen nodded. He felt adrift and out of place, nervous every time the waitress sent him a jaundiced look. She was probably just afraid he was putting off the regular punters, with his hat, dark glasses, and a scarf tugged over the bridge of his nose. Mick, whose own nose resembled a dropped cauliflower, was otherwise boringly human to all outward appearances. Nigel was also human enough, apart from the greenish pallor of his skin and the elf-like points of his ears. 'Pleased ta meetcha,' Nigel announced, his throat swelling as if he'd swallowed a frog.

'Got it,' Allen agreed. *I think.* 'What are we here for?'

Ron spooned sugar into his coffee. 'Some light civil engineering, the boss called it. We're renting a shop front in Hatton Garden. Tomorrow you're going to dig a tunnel from the basement. We're renovating the shop and there'll be skips coming in to take away the debris. Be sure you don't cut through any sewers or drop the road down on yer head. *Or go too deep and hit the Tube.*'

'A tunnel—'

'A tunnel. Under the street, beneath the pavement, around a lift shaft, and into the cellar of the building opposite. The walls are reinforced concrete eighteen inches thick and wired with alarms, but you can drill between them, right?'

Allen froze. 'You're talking about breaking into—'

'No names, no pack drill,' Ron growled. 'You already dug one tunnel. What's another between friends, eh?'

'But that was—' Allen stopped.

'I think you'll find it ain't so different in the eyes of the law.' Ron's eyes glinted malevolently. 'You're just a pickaxe. Leave yer conscience to the handle, aye?'

Hatton Garden was a very upmarket business district. Every other shop window seemed to be a jeweller's. Half the offices belonged to advertising agencies populated by posh young things with braying accents and expensive spectacle frames. Discarded Porsches were strewn along the kerb as thickly as the bin bags around Jenny's flat. A discreet brass sign by a door around the corner read *De Beers*. The shop that the Fish's people had rented was unaccountably empty, sandwiched between the greasy spoon and another damned jeweller with a window display of wedding rings, each worth more than Allen could dream of earning in a year. Nigel and Mick already had a load of tools set up inside the front window, sawhorses and plasterboard and other stage trappings suitable for builders intent on refurbishing a retail unit. Ron led Allen into the back, past a stockroom and a cramped office, to a warren of narrow passages floored with worn lino. They went through the break room to a staircase leading down into a darkness that smelled faintly of sewage.

'Yer going to need to take care as you dig,' Ron warned him. 'There's lots of tunnels down here, an' not just the Tube and sewers: them jewellers like ter move stock below ground to stay out o' sight of the likes of us.' He cracked his knuckles then opened a door onto a whitewashed cellar illuminated by a single dangling yellowish bulb. Someone with a spray can had scrawled measurements and angles across the middle of the far wall, like a maths lesson gone wrong. 'We're gonna need a crawlway at least two feet wide and high, starting right here. The bigger the better. The lift shaft at the target is a hundred and thirty-six feet in that direction. There's probably a cross-tunnel between the De Beers vault and the target – you don't wanna breach it by accident. The road starts twenty-eight feet past the wall and is forty-six feet wide, and you'll need to shore up the ceiling, it's a bus route and gets armoured car deliveries . . .'

'That's going to take time,' Allen warned him. 'Also, there's going to be a lot of loose debris.' He glanced around the cellar. 'More than enough to fill this room to the ceiling.'

'You turn stuff to powder, right? Start by stacking it here and then look for a sewer we can dump it down. The boys'll run you a hose from the water mains and you can flush all you like. Anyway, you won't know 'til you get started, will you?' It was a pointed hint.

Allen huffed. 'Going to need lights, too. And a tarp and a shovel.'

'So? Get started! It's a bank holiday the Monday after next. We need to be through the lift shaft and at the vault wall by Friday 22nd if we're going to have a clear weekend for the job.'

♣

Sunday morning, and the early mist had dissipated beneath the merciless August sun. Police cars and vans filled the waste-ground, lights out, as a white van bearing Metropolitan Police badges bumped across the potholes and loosely packed gravel. A big white pavilion was going up, thanks to the efforts of a squad of uniforms drafted in for the heavy lifting. A couple of armed officers with bolt cutters forced their way into the hut at the entrance to the neighbouring piece of wasteground, followed by a pair of uniformed detective constables with gloves and cameras. 'This it?' asked one, as his sergeant approached from behind.

'It'd better be.' The sergeant was clearly tense. 'It's where we're supposed to be per the warrant.'

The rumbling of a heavy diesel approaching along the street drowned out any further words as a low-loader pulled up alongside the entrance. A dusty yellow JCB sat on top of it, spare excavator blades and a pneumatic drill waiting and ready. The engine stopped. Workmen in donkey jackets and hard hats began unloading the excavator from the low-loader. A smaller police van pulled past – with some difficulty – and stopped next to the checkpoint. Its occupants, one human and the other not, approached the sergeant. 'Where do you want us to start?' asked the driver as his teammate cast around, tail wagging furiously.

'Should be about ten yards that way.' The sergeant checked his notepad. 'They tunnelled in from that side of the fence, not breaking the surface here. What we're looking for should be just over here . . .' He paced out the steps to a quiet patch of ground, undisturbed by the team. 'They did it a week ago. Can you find it?'

'We'll see.' The van driver looked doubtful. 'Kate's good, but that's hard-packed ground and if they didn't dig down we may have to start from the other end.' He glanced at the JCB and its bucket scoop hopefully. 'Or cut a couple of layers off the surface first.' Beside him, Kate snorfled quietly then raised her liquid brown eyes towards him. 'Good girl, let's see what you can find . . .'

The dog took no urging. Bored from incarceration in the back of a van, the bloodhound trotted around the yard as her handler coaxed her towards the area against the fence that the sergeant had indicated. Nose down, she cast about for a couple of minutes before settling on a patch of ground six feet inside the perimeter. Clearly pleased with herself, she looked at her handler and barked briefly.

'Good girl! All right, if you start digging here—' the dog handler pulled out a spray can and drew a circle around Kate's position, '—I'll bring her back when you've got the top couple of feet off.' He frowned pensively. 'She's pretty positive. I've got to warn you, it might be a false lead – she sometimes comes up with dead animals – but if there was intelligence leading to this site . . .'

The sergeant grumped lugubriously. 'Okay, lads, let the nice men with the digger through. Looks like we've got a scene after all.' He tugged on his gloves and turned to the hut: 'Let's see what we've got 'ere in the way of papers while they're excavating. Bag it and tag it and take it away.'

The van's doors opened and forensic service bodies in white overalls began climbing out and filing towards the tent like ants towards a spilled scoop of ice cream. Game on.

◆

The evening of the second day of the Hatton Garden dig, Allen got home late and dog-tired, brick dust in his hair and smears of London clay on the knees of his jeans and the elbows of his shirt. 'Shower,' said Jenny, tugging him towards the bathroom. Her nostrils wrinkled: 'What have you been *doing?*'

'Digging.' He tugged his hood off, then began unbuttoning his shirt in the cramped confines of the corridor. 'It's hot down there and there was a broken waste pipe leaking next door.'

'You're washing *that* yourself,' she warned, kicking his shirt into a pile and refusing to pick it up. 'What is it this time? Did they show you the planning forms?' It was only half in jest. She'd been winding him up with it for the past week, knowing full well that the Fish's people didn't bother with the expense of filing for planning consent on anything. It wasn't needling, exactly, just trying to ensure he stayed within sight of what was legal and what wasn't. The odd spliff was one thing, but undermining buildings to get tenants out so the

Fish could redevelop them . . . she wanted to keep Allen sensitive to it, for her own selfish reasons.

'No forms on this one, not ever,' he said, kicking off his jeans. He sighed, looking despondent. 'Bastards.'

'What has he got you doing now?' she demanded, ears pricking up as he climbed into the cubicle.

'Digging a tunnel under a road in Camden,' he called indistinctly as he turned on the power shower. 'For a gang of bloody jewel thieves.'

Whoa. Jenny stepped inside the bathroom, keeping her face still. *Crisis of conscience, already?* Allen wasn't exactly *happy* about working for Pussyface, but this level of resentment was new. 'You're sure that's what they are?' she asked over the flowing water.

'Hell, yes. They've got me tunnelling into a fucking vault so they can clean it out over the weekend and I don't know how to—' His next words were lost as the phone rang.

'I'll get that,' she said automatically. The number was ex-directory and not many people had it. 'Jenn speaking,' she said. 'Who is this?'

'It's the benefits office.' Her employer's prepared cover for calls, in case she wasn't alone. 'Something's up with your latest claim and we'd like to go over it with you. Can you come in tomorrow afternoon?' Sergeant Rutherford sounded strained.

'My latest—' *Oh fuck.* She glanced back at the laundry on the landing outside the bathroom. 'Yeah, I'll do that. What time? Two thirty? Okay, I'll be there. Yeah, bye.'

She hung up as the shower turned off. 'Who was that?' Allen called.

'Dole office. Fuck, they're probably looking for fraud. I've got to go in tomorrow morning.'

'I could come with—'

'No, that'd be a bad idea,' she said hastily. 'I've dealt with these arseholes, they'll think we're conspiring or something.

POLICE ON MY BACK

Shit.' Make it sound good, she told herself. 'I thought they knew I was square with them. After last time.'

'Last time—'

'They're used to jokers,' she said sharply. Discrimination was a fact of life, employment included. 'How about you?'

He stepped out of the bathroom, a towel around his waist. His skin was so pale she could see a tracery of veins through it. Was it a case of opposites attracting, or something else? she wondered. 'It's a living, not a job,' he said, and clammed up.

'Listen, are you *sure* they're thieves . . .?'

'*Yes*, I'm fucking certain!' Frustration raised his voice. 'Sorry. I don't like it but I don't know what to do. If they empty the deposit vaults that's robbery, innit? And I'll be part of it? Complicity. Aiding and abetting.' He sounded upset.

'You could go to the police,' she said, as if it was just a random thought. 'I know a guy who'd give you a fair hearing—' She stopped. He was shaking his head.

'They'll arrest me,' he told her. "S why I left home.'

'Oh.' She took his arm and led him back downstairs, thinking furiously. 'Are you sure about that?' she asked. 'If they're not after you for something big they might agree to drop it if you turn evidence against Puss—'

'*Fuck*.' He growled in frustration. Eyes screwed up against the daylight filtering through the blinds, hands fisted at his sides. 'Like that's going to happen?' he asked rhetorically.

Now or never. She steeled herself for a little white lie. 'Allen, I trained as a cop. Did my apprenticeship, know a few people. I could ask on behalf of a friend—' Every word was true, every phrase calculated to mislead. She felt like a shit. But he was still shaking his head. 'At least think about it?' she pleaded.

He looked at her, and it felt as if she'd been slapped. 'And you still think you're Little Miss Law and Order? Or just another XTA survivor signing on the dole because they loved you anyway? I don't think so.' He slouched onto the futon in the living room. 'Anyway, Pussyface will kill us both if he thinks

I've told you anything.' He laughed, an atonal, despairing bark that was nothing to do with mirth. 'He knows where I live, remember?'

♠

Jenny was on edge until Allen left for work the following day. He was twitchy, but said no more about her suggestion. They ate together, then made love until they fell asleep, entangled. The next morning all he said about their discussion was a mumbled, 'take care' before he slipped out. But they hadn't fought: just . . . disagreed. Still, she felt a certain foreboding as she stepped out of the front door at lunchtime to head for her meeting.

"Ello, luv. Going somewhere?'

Shit. Jenny tried to step backwards and slam the door in his face, but a thug in a cheap landlord's suit shoulder-barged her inside and punched her in the gut while his wingman followed. They looked like bouncers from the wrong kind of nightclub, only bouncers didn't walk around armed and especially not – in the second one's case – with a crackle of blue-white sparks sizzling between finger and thumb.

'Where is it?' demanded Thug Number One.

'What?' She shook her head, sick with dread as she doubled over.

'Yer warrant card, luv, we're not fucking stupid, we know yer with the filth.'

'I don't know what you're talking about—'

Thug Number Two reached for her, fingers arcing. The next thing she knew she was lying on the floor, retching and shivering from shock.

'Cuff her, Sparks, then find her stuff,' Thug Number One instructed his mate. 'It'll be where she can lay her hands on it in a hurry. You'll probably find it with notes on informers an' such.'

'Sure thing.' Sparks, his charge temporarily earthed, dragged her arms backwards and handcuffed her. Then he yanked her right sleeve up and stabbed her, repeatedly and clumsily, with a syringe. Things got confusing and foggy. She retained scattered impressions: being frog-marched to the lifts, then out into the car park. Being shoved into the back seat of a white Rover with Q-plates and low-profile blue lights behind the windscreen, just like a real unmarked police car. Being bounced around by the rough ride as they drove her away.

Not a real *police car*, she realized fuzzily, *no radio*, but they'd taken out the latches on the rear doors just the same. Keeping her head down and trying not to puke prevented her from tracking where they were going, and then a meaty hand shoved her head down behind the driver's seat. Finally she dozed off on a warm quinalbarbitone tide.

The next thing Jenny was aware of was a wooden chair.

She was sitting on the chair, of course. The room was windowless, lit by a dim bulb hanging from a low ceiling – *a cellar?* She was confused, her thoughts sluggish, and it took her some time to realize that her arms were behind her – *well, of course.* She couldn't move her legs, either. *Not* a real *police car.* (She hadn't *quite* ruled out friendly fire until now, but this was *so* not a custody cell.) Her belly ached and all her shoulders were sore – they'd cuffed both her left wrists together before they'd tied her to the chair. As her mind came back together her thoughts kept circling around Allen's warning the night before. If Pussyface and the Fish knew the truth about her they'd either kill her or leave her alone – nothing in between. *But I'm still alive. So what's going on? Does anyone know I'm missing?*

Sparks opened the door then stepped aside to admit her host. ''Ello, Constable,' said Pussyface, his pupils huge and circular in the dim light. 'It's past time you and me 'ad a little chat, like. You've been spending a lot of time with someone 'oo rightly belongs to me, and I want to make sure we have an understanding, aye? Just to clear the air.' He held up his right hand, and gleaming, well-buffed claws slid out of their sheaths. 'Because *misunderstandings* might be *regrettable*, and certain events over the weekend lead me to believe that you might have *misunderstood* 'ow I like to run things on my patch . . .'

♥

The tunnelling went slowly that morning.

It wasn't Allen's fault: after the first ten feet it had all been fine detail work, painstaking and precise. The ground under Hatton Garden was cluttered and crammed with weird debris and odd intrusions. Traffic rumbled overhead almost constantly, shaking dirt and dust free from the roof of the three-foot-diameter tube he was excavating. It wasn't loose-packed this time, but compacted brick and gravel and stone, with a mix-in of old London clay if he went too deep. It was too moist to disintegrate into fine dust and disperse, and was even harder to re-form into an aggregate, tending to crumble and slump rather than compressing into a solid. Worse, there were buried pipes. Not just gas and electricity mains, but a century-old network of cast-iron pneumatic power tubes, immune to his power and invisible to his perceptions. He could sense them only as odd shadows in the misty ground, and if he dug too far in any direction without stopping to feel for obstructions he risked clotheslining himself. He found it exhausting, and the need to strengthen and reinforce the roof of the tunnel as he dug under the street (and to flush the resulting waste down the sewer) was costing him.

Around noon, having made an extra sixteen feet of tunnel (then filled in eight feet and dug another five in a slightly different direction, to circumvent an obstacle), Allen surfaced at the back of the shop, sweaty and dusty. 'Need to get some lunch,' he grunted as he shuffled past Mick, who was babysitting the dig this morning.

'Don't be late, Mole! Got a way to go by sunset,' Mick called as he slouched outside, blinking at the overcast daylight.

A full understanding of what he was doing had taken some time to sink in, but the mechanical activities of the morning had given him time to mull over what Jenny had told him the night before. And to think. Digging tunnels for cash in hand was one thing. Being wanted for breaking out of cells was yet another. But robbing a safe deposit vault or a jeweller's or a bank was something else again, as was burying bodies for gangsters. If Jenny knew somebody who could get him off the hook, maybe that wasn't such a bad thing after all. If Pussyface wasn't in the picture any more, if he went down, maybe he and Jenn could disappear. *Or maybe she's been lying to me*, he thought, an unwanted realization creeping in. *I trained as a cop.* Then what was she doing in Jokertown? Did they train her up and then boot her out? Or something else?

Almost without noticing, he found his feet leading him to the phone booth on the corner. One hand counting his change, 2p and 10p pieces sticking to his fingers as he mentally rehearsed what he needed to say: *We need to talk.*

Ring-ring, ring-ring. 'Hello, Spindrift Centre, who is this . . .? You want Jenny? I'm sorry, she hasn't been in this morning.'

Allen dialled another number from memory, their (it felt odd, just thinking that) home phone. *Ring-ring, ring-ring . . .* and it kept ringing. Jenny had said something about wanting to rent an answering machine, but they were expensive and there was a three-week wait to get the Post Office engineer out to wire one in. He'd asked her why she needed it and she'd thrown up two hands. It had seemed like a pointless extravagance at the time, but now, as he waited for her to pick up the receiver, he found himself sweating. *If he thinks I've told you anything . . .* Jenny wouldn't blab, would she? *I trained as a copper.* He walked away fast, not pausing long enough to hang up.

It took almost an hour to get home. Allen tried to hail a cab but the drivers took one look at him and drove on. Only one kid yelled at him on the Tube, for which he counted himself lucky: the passengers on the bus glared but left a bench seat clear for him and his imaginary friends who sat to either side. He managed to hold himself back from running all the way from the bus stop to the entrance to the estate, but by the time he got to the walkway leading to the front door his heart was pounding with dread.

The door was shut but not locked. It opened into chaos. Drawers open, contents strewn across the floor, cupboards ransacked. In the living room, the stereo had been yanked away from the wall and the record collection pulled out and smashed. In their bedroom the sheets had been torn off and the mattress half pulled off the bed, disembowelled and searched ruthlessly.

Not a burglary, Allen realized, around the time he found the phone had been yanked out of the wall, leaving bare wires dangling. They'd taken everything on paper but left Jenny's stash tin behind. *Not the coppers*. His hands were shaking as he frantically searched the rest of the flat. There was no sign of Jenny, no blood, *thank fuck*. It had happened after she left, or—

On his way back out, thinking frantic thoughts of finding a phone booth and dialling 999, something crunched under his heel. Bending down, he saw a broken plastic tube capped with a needle. The syringe had been emptied before it rolled under the table. *Jenny doesn't inject*, he thought dismally.

He was breathless and anxious by the time he got to the community centre. Recognizing one of the volunteers on the front desk, he gasped out, 'Has anyone seen Jenny?'

'Sorry, luv,' she apologized. 'Maybe this afternoon?'

'No, you don't—' He bit back panic. 'Is anyone in the office?'

'It's Lauren's shift, but I think she's on her lunch break—'

Allen diffidently stormed the community centre office. 'Are you Lauren? Jenny's missing and I think she's been taken.'

'What? Who are—'

Lauren, middle-aged with a snakeskin complexion and wide red eyes, was visibly alarmed at Allen's appearance. He tugged his balaclava off. 'I live with her,' he said baldly. 'I know the centre gets by with donations from Mr McAndrews. I think there's been a misunderstanding and I'd like to sort things out but I don't have his address—'

'You can't do that! Why don't you call the police?'

He wanted to shout, *Jenn is the police*, but he could be signing her death warrant. 'It'll take too long, listen, I won't tell them where I got the address, I just need to know where you send the paperwork, receipts and such, no, the landlord's address in the rent book—'

Ten minutes later he was on the high street again, trying to flag down a taxi. He glanced up nervously. The clouds weren't thick enough to block out the sun, but he'd have to risk it. He pulled off his balaclava and stuffed it in a pocket then stuck his hand out again, hoping he'd get a lift before his skin melted. He'd had a bike back in Brum, a sweet little Honda 125, perfect for nipping through traffic. It was just another of the things he'd had to leave behind. Eventually a taxi pulled over. 'Where to, guv?'

Allen had enough money in his wallet to cover a ride through the East End and out to the suburbs beyond. It was a side-effect of being paid cash and too scared to open a new bank account. The address in the rent book was unfamiliar, but the council rates listed the owner as a Mr McAndrews and gave a familiar street. In retrospect it wasn't surprising that Pussyface kept his fingers in plenty of properties in London, awaiting the inevitable slum redevelopment boom.

Sitting in the back of the black cab Allen had plenty of time to stew in his own hopes and fears as the driver fought his way through the London afternoon traffic. What if he was wrong, and someone else had her? What if Pussyface had taken her somewhere else? He'd had no idea what the new cellars

were for at the time, but he was under no illusions now. At
least the syringe gave him some hope. It meant whoever had
her wanted her alive, for now.

'Okay, if you could drop me just round the next corner . . .'
Allen climbed out of the cab and scuttled for cover under the
row of scrawny trees punctuating the strip of grass between
road and pavement. His face was prickling already, and he
wished he'd thought to bring dark glasses and a hat. Anything
less conspicuous than his balaclava. Backtracking, he made a
swift pass along the residential street, eyeing the hedge fronting
Pussyface's pad. The gate was shut and it looked closed – nobody
home. But he knew better than to tackle it directly. The neighbour's garden – separated by a high brick wall – adjoined the
McAndrews manse and had a thicket of apple trees at the back.
Allen nerved himself up and leaned against their back wall,
closed his eyes, and fell forward through dust and choking
darkness.

Down under the back garden he fell, into the darkness and
musty night where the small things burrowed and coiled. Down
below a ceiling of tangled tree roots, wading through clay and
mud that swirled around him and vanished, Allen walked with
eyes closed, feeling his way forward with a bubble of air wrapped
around his face. Listening, feeling, his imaginary vibrissae
bending to feel the solid intrusions in the almost gaseous soil,
he shoved himself forward. Earth liquefied and flowed around
him, solidifying behind as he felt his way towards the cellar
wall, a clearly delineated rectangle under the lawn ahead of
him. *This is so cool*, the part of his mind in the opposite corner
to the lump of cold fright congealing in his gut observed.

Allen paused close to the halfway point beneath the lawn,
reclining in soil. He risked a molehill, pushing up a mound
of dirt to conceal an airway. When he stopped moving, he
found his air bubble stagnated, but pushing his tunnelling
ability too hard felt strange, like straining a muscle he wasn't
normally aware of. After a few minutes he began to move

again, pushing onwards until he came up against the cellar's outer wall and realized that he hadn't thought beyond this point. He had no plan beyond finding Jenny. Assuming she was even here—

He extended his awareness slowly through the voids and cavities beyond the wall. It was very strange, trying to sense the absence of rock and soil. Wood and lath and carpet and doors were all but invisible; plaster dust and stone and brick showed. Bone . . . he had an indistinct sense of bones, pulpy and warm and difficult to feel. *Living* bones with meat and blood wrapped around them. A bag of bone in the next void over, hunched around itself, and two thin stacks of bone stretched menacingly tall to either side of it, scaffoldings of malign intent. Above his head he could feel the rectangular bubbles of other rooms – the building was largely built of brick – the hallway, the morning room, Pussyface's unoccupied office.

Can I . . .? The beginnings of a plan congealed in his mind. Allen swallowed, frightened. Then he leaned close to the bricks, dug his fingers into the crumbling powder and mortar, and climbed up through the floor of the gang boss's den.

♣

Jenny tried to open her eyes. She didn't get very far: her left one was swollen shut, the side of her face throbbing with molten heat, and her right eye was gummy, the view red and blurry. No matter how much it watered the tears couldn't quite wash the blood out of it fast enough.

Pussyface tutted. 'I said ter make it *look* good,' he said mildly from behind her. 'What part of *look* do ye no' get, Sparks?'

'It's jes' cosmetic, guv, nothing permanent, like.'

'So ye're gonnae stitch her head up yerself? Idjit.'

McAndrews' Glaswegian diction came out to play when he wasn't acting the nob in public, Jenny noted absent-mindedly. Her wrists were screaming in agony and she'd wrenched one of her shoulders flinching away from Sparks, who in turn was flinching away from Pussyface's displeasure.

'But I thought you wis planning ter fridge her, boss?'

Pussyface swore horribly. 'Jesus fookin' Christ, yer numpty, did yer mam drop you on yer heid as a bairn? Dinnae mention the fridge in front o' the roast!' He cleared his throat and switched on his Scottish BBC accent – cut-glass English with rolled Rs, posher than the Queen. 'Anyway, it isn't going to happen. She's listening, isn't she? And it's her lucky day, isn't it, WPC Scott?'

Well, fuck, there goes six months' cover . . . 'I'm not a cop,' she mumbled past a stab of pain from her upper jaw, where some of the teeth felt disturbingly loose.

'Of course not, Detective Constable,' Pussyface said soothingly, as if calming a delirious patient. A hand landed on her right shoulder then lifted briefly at her sharp hiss of pain. 'It's just a little misunderstanding, isn't it? You being discharged by the Met for, what was it, oh, insubordination – or was it just that you couldn't meet the uniform requirements what with your extra arm? – and moving onto my patch? See, I do my homework. I'm a businessman, me, a *smart* businessman. And I'm nae stupid – not like Sparks, here – *not* stupid enough to murder a police officer, know what I'm saying? This is just a little misunderstanding and I'm certain we can come to an arrangement.' He stepped in front of her, smiling. 'Go see if the Mole's finished for the day, Sparks,' he said softly. 'Then bring him in.' Sparks made himself scarce. 'See, I don't rightly 'ave a problem with you running my community centre,' he added softly, focusing on Jenny, 'just as long as ye ken that yer boyfriend belongs to me.'

'Wha-what do you mean?'

Pussyface shrugged. 'Can't be doing with ye telling stories to old friends. If I send the Mole to bury something I can't be 'aving the Yard dig it up again, instead of the blokes it's in escrow for. Who were *most* disappointed,' he added. 'You cost me a pretty penny, lass. But I can be generous: your man's doin' a braw job of diggin' for me, and in case 'e as any second thoughts I'm gonnae let you 'ave free bed and board here until it's done, an' done right so 'e's going down for aiding and abetting burglary if it comes to it. And then I'm gonnae let you out and you're gonnae keep him in line for me and stop tellin' tales out of school, 'cept when I *tell* you to drop a jobbie in the inspector's lap. You want your community centre to keep on going: be a shame if anyone sold the building out from under you, wouldn't it?'

Jenny closed her eyes again. Her head was spinning with the mixture of threats, lies, and half-truths. Pussyface was a master bullshitter, she could see, having fed her just enough hope to keep her docile – hope that he wanted her for leverage and as an informer – even though she knew better than to believe him. *What the fuck was in those boxes Allen had buried the other week?* Heroin, explosives, stolen computer chips? *Escrow arrangements?* Informers' bones.

'I'll do it,' she lied, guessing that he knew it for a lie but would pretend anyway, until it was time either to get his claws in deeper or dispose of her entirely. 'But what makes you think Allen will cooperate?'

'He'll cave when he sees you here. Folks talk tough 'til they're in a corner, but your boy disnae have the guts to do anything.' He spoke with complete assurance.

The door to the cellar crashed into the room behind him in a pile of brick dust and splinters.

'The fuck–'

'–her go!' Allen shouted as he waved a pistol around. His eyes were pink and furious, his face smeared with mud and crumbled brick dust. Jenny flinched: the way he had his finger on the trigger she really hoped it wasn't loaded. 'Get back! I'll shoot!' The gun barrel wobbled towards Pussyface, who took a step backwards – he clearly had the same thought as Jenny.

'Calm down, laddie, you don't wanna do that.' Pussyface

kept his voice level as he sidled behind Jenny's chair and knelt, resting his hands on her shoulders. Pure fright stabbed at her as she felt the pricking of his claws unsheathing inches from her jugular. 'Let's nae do anything hasty, like? It's all fun an' games until some cunt loses an eye.'

Allen blinked, suddenly realizing he'd been outmanoeuvred. 'Get away from her!' he demanded uncertainly.

'An' why would I do something *that* stupid?' Pussyface chuckled.

'Step away . . .' Allen trailed off, then changed gear. 'You fucking hurt her and I'll hurt *you*.'

'No ye won't, laddie. Ye ken I've done this kind of thing before? An' by the way, you left the safety catch on. Seems ter me you dinnae take the job seriously, and that could be inconvenient, know what I mean? Yer an asset an' I've got plans for you but I can't be doing with you or your piece here grassing. You'll get her back in one piece *if* you cooperate—'

The earth floor of the cellar trembled. Jenny tensed. Allen took a step forward, death in his blood-red eyes as he stared at Pussyface. 'You can run, *now*.'

'I'll fuckin' *kill* her if you try anything, laddie—'

'Then I'll bury you alive. I dug this cellar: I can swim through earth. Think you can learn in time?' The floor trembled, a slow gelatinous rolling. 'Go on, fuck off upstairs and leave us.'

Pussyface slowly straightened, but kept his claws on Jenny's neck. 'Yer an idiot,' he warned. 'You dinnae get to walk away from this.'

She could feel his muscles tensing as if he was preparing to jump Allen. Allen stared intently, head cocked to one side, as if he was listening for some cue. She cleared her throat. 'Time out?' she husked. 'Let's not be hasty? Mr McAndrews can wait upstairs while I talk to, to—' Her head was spinning. 'Five minutes,' she concluded woozily. *In five minutes he can untie me, we can get away and worry about where later* – and *fuck, Pussyface nails us some time after that—*

'Give me the gun, son,' Pussyface growled. 'Ye dinnae ken how tae hold it safely and ye're not gonnae use it, so why bother?' The whole cellar was shaking now, vibrating in time to her speeding inhalations.

'But—'

'Throw it out of the door and I'll go an' wait upstairs like the lassie wants.' Like a cat staking out a mousehole, patiently waiting. 'I'm not gonnae stay an' let you drop the roof on me.'

Allen waited, frozen, for a while, then blinked. 'You first,' he said. Dust was puffing in tiny clouds from between the corners of the doorway. A rattle of gravel cascaded down upon Jenny's head and she whimpered faintly. Being buried alive wasn't a phobia, but it wasn't something she was enthusiastic about, either.

He lowered the gun barrel and Jenny shouted 'No!' as Pussyface began to make his move. Kicking, she threw herself sideways, tensing in anticipation of the shock of landing on her shoulder as the chair overbalanced. But instead of a jarring impact with the ground Jenny fell against Pussyface, who stumbled backwards as he tried to sidestep her fall.

The floor shuddered and somewhere above the cellar there was a crash of breaking glass.

Pussyface picked himself up, stepped out from behind her, and punched Allen. Allen doubled over and let go of the gun as Pussyface grabbed it. For a sick moment, Jenny stared sideways as the gangster raised his pistol – but the walls were still shuddering in the grip of a pocket earthquake. He turned, cast her a black stare, and darted up the staircase. A door at the top slammed.

The floor was still shaking. 'Are you all right?' Allen gasped at her, stumbling to his knees painfully. 'We've got to move, he'll be back with his mate as soon as—'

'Idiot!' she wailed in frustration and pain. 'He'll have bolted the door upstairs! We're trapped down here!' The ceiling was still shaking. 'Make it stop!'

'If I stop shaking, he'll come back,' Allen panted. 'Let me untie you.' He pulled a utility knife out of his muddy overalls. 'I won't let it fall on you.' He moved behind the chair to work at the knots around her arms and legs. 'Are you a copper?'

She licked her lips, feeling numb. 'What if I am?'

'Then I—' The sawing at the rope around her legs paused for a moment, then started again. 'I need to report a crime or two, don't I? Let's start with, oh, a gangster kidnapping a police officer. And trying to break into the private deposit vaults under Hatton Garden.'

'Yeah, that'll do it.' She swallowed. 'Where did the gun come from?'

'Pussyface's desk upstairs.' Her left leg loosened, swung down until her heel banged on the floor. 'Listen, it's *a very good thing* you didn't hold it at any point, for *any* purpose other than to hand it to the nearest police officer, that being me, at my request: understood? Because possession without a licence is good for a five-year stretch, so you didn't do that. Right?'

Her other leg came loose. 'Understood.' She felt his hands under her armpits, lifting, and then the chair back slid out from behind her. Free of it, she rolled painfully onto her knees. The shaking had subsided. 'Shit. What's wrong?'

'Can't keep it up.' His face was drawn, eyebrows furrowed with effort. ''Sides, I really *will* bring the roof down if I do it for much longer. Here.' He slid the knife blade across the ropes tying her wrists.

'He'll be back. Or he'll send Sparks. We've got to get out of here!' She looked round frantically as Allen worked.

'I've got it covered.' Allen kept at the ropes. Another minute and her arms, burning and sore, fell limp to her sides. She held her hands up and tried to chafe some life back into her wrists. 'Can you block the—' He fell silent, regarding the warped doorframe and the fallen door. 'Shit.'

'I thought you said you could swim through soil?' she asked thinly.

'Yeah. Yeah, I can—' he took a deep breath '—when I'm not shagged? That's how I got in. Tunnelled under the garden from next door.'

'I need a phone,' she said, thinking aloud to keep herself within hailing distance of calm. 'If I had a phone I could call in support. But while we're trapped down here Pussyface is upstairs and you bet *he's* calling in support.' She cast around, looking for another way out. 'Once his men arrive they'll come down here mob-handed and that'll be it.'

'We can avoid that.' He suddenly sounded confident.

'How?'

'Follow me.' Beyond the doorway there was a low-ceilinged passageway, doors leading to either side. At the far end, a staircase led upwards. Debris released by Allen's display of power had fallen free, mounding up beside warped doorframes. 'In here, I think.'

'What's—'

'I dug these.' She could hear a note of pride in his voice. 'Storage cellars.' The door scraped on stone as he shoved it open. 'Come on in.' He flicked a switch tacked to the bare wall and an overhead bulb flickered to life, lighting up a long, low tunnel of a room. 'Go on,' he waved her ahead. 'I'm going to barricade us in.' Allen shoved the door back into its frame then reached out to either side and touched the walls. Plaster and then clay began to peel away in an arch just inside the doorway. 'That's not going to open without a battering ram.' He leaned against it tiredly. 'I reckon that'll buy us a few minutes.'

'But they'll—' Jenny bit her tongue. *Get a grip*, she told herself. 'What do you mean to do now?' she asked.

Allen didn't say anything for a minute. At last, as she was about to repeat herself, more forcefully, he pushed himself away from the door and paced to the centre of the room, counting silently. 'Here,' he said. His eyes were screwed shut.

'Here?' she echoed.

'Here.' He pointed at the ceiling. 'We're under the garage, I think.'

'That's no way out, he'll have guards upstairs and in the garden—'

'You want a phone, don't you?' Allen opened his eyes. 'I'm pretty sure there's one in the garage, will that do?'

'Who the hell keeps a phone in their garage?' Jenny boggled. 'If you're sure—'

'Oh, I'm sure enough.' Allen grinned. Then he reached up and touched the ceiling and the plaster began to crumble.

◆

Allen got Jenny into the garage just in time.

The first crash came from the door just as he boosted her up through the mole-hole he'd made. The door shuddered. If he hadn't reinforced it the impact would have broken the latch through its flimsy frame for sure.

'I'm in,' Jenny called quietly. 'Need a hand?'

'Yeah.' Allen glanced at the door. His head was sore and spinning from too much tunnelling, too fast. It felt as if he'd sprained something, some imaginary part of his mind. Much more and he'd be throwing up – exactly what he didn't need, with Pussyface's goon hammering the other side of the plywood door.

'Open the fuck up, we know yer in there!'

Jenny reached an arm down through the hole and waved about for him. Allen took a deep breath then glanced at the doorway. 'Stand back,' he called up to her. Then he let the walls of the cellar slump inwards. The floor rose up beneath his feet like the waters of an incoming tsunami, and by the time Jenny grabbed his hand he was almost at the point of throwing up. 'Over here, are you okay—'

'Not okay.' Allen panted for breath as she led him across the width of a garage as big as her flat. It was blessedly dark and it stank of engine oil and damp. A band of pain tightened around his temple. He leaned back against the cold metal curve of a big Daimler, the high-end Jaguar limousine being the garage's only occupant. 'Give me a minute.'

'We don't have one, they'll be round here as soon as they work out we're not down there any more. Where's this phone?'

He swallowed back bile. 'In the Jag.'

'You're kidding me!' He caught Jenny glaring at him in the wan light filtering in through the skylight. 'Wait, there's a phone in his *car*?'

'Yeah, I saw him using it back at the yard. I mean, either that or he was playing with a kid's toy, and I don't think he's the sort to do that, yeah?' He slumped sideways. 'Saw it between the front seats . . .' He worked the door handle, discovered it was locked. 'Shit.'

'Let me get this. I mean, fuck, what kind of flash bastard has a radiophone in his car, anyway?' Jenny cast about. There was a workbench at one side of the garage, cluttered with tools. She rummaged for a minute, retrieved a steel ruler and a length of stiff wire.

'The kind of flash bastard who runs a gang?' Allen suggested wearily.

'Make yourself useful, luv, see if you can find a shovel or a crowbar or something and stand next to the door?' Jenny hurried over to the driver's door and used the ruler to peel back the rubber seal alongside the window, then began fishing around with the loop of wire.

'Wait, you want me to whack whoever—'

She shrugged as eloquently as only a woman with three shoulders can. 'They've got a gun: do you have any better ideas?' With a click, the Jaguar's door unlatched. She pulled it open and peered at the radiophone. 'I wonder how this works—' She lifted the handset and listened for a few seconds as Allen, increasingly nervous, grabbed a lawn edger and slouched around to the side of the garage door. 'Uh, hello, operator? Emergency services, Police. This is Detective Constable Jennifer Scott reporting a firearms incident in progress, I need back-up—'

The door handle rattled. Allen backed up a pace, wincing. His head was throbbing, otherwise he'd be working on the concrete floor of the garage. But he was in luck: the door was evidently locked, and the hand withdrew. He glanced over at Jenny just as she climbed out of the car and gestured frantically at something below her feet, then beckoned.

'What's—' he caught up with her as she said, 'Inspection trench!'

'Inspection—'

The concrete apron gave way to wooden boards across a trench between the luxury car's wheels. Jenny bent and tugged at a handle. 'Help me with this. Now!'

'But we—'

'They'll be back with the keys any moment now. Armed back-up will take at least five minutes to arrive, maybe seven or eight this far out.' Allen put his back into it, and between them they raised the hatch. 'Go on, get down.'

'But I—' Allen stared down the steps, into the darkness beyond the bounding box of the cellars under Pussyface's mansion. The pain in his head intensified, almost unbearably. 'I'm out of juice: if I go down there I'll be trapped—'

'Do you trust me?' she asked. He looked at her and realized he had no choice. At some point in the past few days or weeks he'd surrendered. 'Listen. Go down there. Nobody's going to arrest you but Pussyface has been burying bodies since long before you came along.'

Allen scrambled down into the pit and crouched. A couple of seconds later Jenny joined him, lowering the lid. It was a narrow space, only deep enough for a mechanic lying on his back to work on the floor panel of a car, and she lay on her back beside him. It felt disturbingly as if they were sharing a shallow grave.

A click from the space above them, and daylight filtered through the cracks in the boards. 'Ain't nobody 'ere,' called Sparks.

'Keep looking.' Pussyface sounded pissed off. ''E's gotta come up for air somewhere and there's no sign of 'im out front. Find the hole, find the Mole.'

The garage door closed, but after a moment someone switched on the overhead lights. Allen heard nothing but indistinct footsteps for a while, felt nothing but fear as Jenny shivered and leaned against him like a fox hiding in its hole from the hounds. Then Sparks' voice: 'Found it!' Followed by two percussive shots that felt like hammers driven into his eardrums in the confined space. Jenny jerked against him and for a horrified moment Allen thought the bullets had hit her, but after a second he realized Sparks was shooting somewhere else.

'Stop shootin', ye moron!' Allen heard Pussyface roar despite his pounding head and ringing ears.

'But I found a hole—' Sparks whined.

'Ye'll wake the neighbours and bring the polis down on us!'

Jenny tensed again and Allen realized she was unhurt, but trying to move - whether to get comfortable, or to hide, he didn't know. He closed his eyes and reached out to feel for the comfort of soil and stone around him, but the concrete was painfully hard and a spike of pain between his eyes warned him to desist. He tightened his grip on the crowbar instead and tried to work out where Sparks and Pussyface might be.

'Someone's been at my motor,' Pussyface remarked. Something in his tone made Allen shudder. 'I locked it when I parked. An' there's a scratch by the door handle.' Quietly, almost reflectively, he added, 'Ye shouldna' ha' done that.' A quiet chuckle. 'Of course it didnae start fer you – I allus pop the distributor out.'

A click as he eased the car door open, and a faint creak as

it settled on its springs. Then a pop as Pussyface tripped the bonnet release.

'Now I ain't got all day, kid, so I'll tell you this now: I know yer hidin' in here. And you an' yer bird can come out and talk an' I'll hold no grudges and we'll settle this like civilized people, right? You've got two minutes.' More creaking, and a clattering from above the inspection trench over Allen's feet, in the vicinity of the big V6 block. 'Reet, that's the distributor arm back in place.' A clank as the car's bonnet closed over the engine. "'Course it's not *going* anywhere with the gearshift locked in place, right? So let's suppose ye dinnae want to come up an' talk: then ye won't mind if I leave you in 'ere with this.' A couple more clicks, and then the hoarse bellow of a starter motor gave way to the burbling rumble of an idling 5.3-litre V12 engine.

The inspection trench filled instantly with the stench of unburned petrol and exhaust fumes, and Jenny spasmed for a moment then coughed. Evidently the noise of the engine drowned out the sound of her distress, for the next thing Allen heard was the clunk of a car door latching shut, followed by hastily retreating footsteps and a slamming door.

'Fuck—' Jenny spasmed again. Allen tried to take shallow breaths, but the choking engine exhaust drove him close to panic. *They used to gas moles, didn't they?* He could see it in his mind's eye: Sparks waiting outside the door with a gun, the two of them trapped in here with a locked car spewing out carbon monoxide. Jenny could break into it again and turn off the engine, but that'd just tell Pussyface they'd come up for air—

Somewhere above his head, Allen thought he heard a telephone begin to ring. It was hard to tell with his ears still numb from the gunshots. Jenny raised her arms and pushed at the trapdoor at the end of the hatch, but couldn't lift it. 'Help me!' she told him. Allen took a deep breath as he tried to sit up and promptly choked, the cloying fumes rasping his throat.

Isn't carbon monoxide denser than air, so it sinks? he wondered dizzily. His arms seemed a very long way away as he pushed at the wooden coffin lid in front of his face, wheezing and coughing, and Jenny slithered drunkenly past him.

The ringing stopped or changed, somehow, from the distinctive double-ring of a British telephone to a rising and falling siren tone. Allen rolled onto his hands and knees and forced himself to crawl up the steps at the end of the trench. The hatch lay beside it, where Jenny had dragged it. She was leaning against the idling car, pawing at the driver's door window. He remembered that he had to do something, something with the crowbar lying by his feet, but standing up was hard work and thinking was even harder.

If the engine stopped something bad would happen. If the engine didn't stop something bad would happen. Jenny was waving at the window. Allen hit it with the steel bar as she flinched back out of the way, and it shattered, crystal fragments across the green leather of the seats. He dropped the bar and lurched back a step as Jenny reached inside and did something and the engine died.

In the distance, the sound of sirens. In the corner of the garage, the sound of a key turning in a lock. Allen shook his head, trying to dislodge the deafening ringing in his ears. 'Fuck,' Jenny said succinctly as the side door opened.

Numb and groggy with petrol fumes, Allen watched Pussyface's fixer step inside, warily pointing a pistol at him across the car. To his gas-addled eyes it seemed more like a prop from a kid's game of cops and robbers than a real threat: normal people didn't own guns in Allen's world. 'Get on the ground! On your face now!' he shouted.

Behind him, Jenny slumped against the car. Allen began to giggle.

Sparks didn't take it well. 'Get down! Down or I'll shoot her!'

Allen only laughed louder, until he had to lean against the

car for support. The situation seemed hilarious to him, especially the way the guy was getting angrier and angrier, pink-cheeked and waving his prop around. So angry, in fact, that a moment later he squeezed the trigger. Evidently he was aiming for Jenny, but had scant chance of hitting her with the muzzle pointed at the ceiling. But this didn't strike Allen as funny any more. It was probably a real gun and Sparks was trying to shoot Jenny and his head felt like a balloon and it wasn't funny *at all*.

Allen glared at Sparks as he struggled to aim the pistol, and he noticed that it didn't hurt when he tried to listen to the concrete garage floor, even though he could distantly feel his head throbbing in time to the wailing of the police sirens in the middle distance. 'Do something,' he heard Jenny say through ringing ears, and so he did, crumbling the topmost inches of floor beneath Sparks' feet more finely than he'd tried for before and fluidizing it as Sparks fell, flailing desperately for support that wasn't there, billowing choking clouds, clogging his lungs.

The screams took quite a while to stop.

♠

'So, Constable.'

She was back in uniform for this visit to Inspector Matthews' office, her first since being discharged from hospital, where she'd spent a couple of days recovering from a beating compounded by a potentially dangerous case of carbon monoxide poisoning. *Not* looking good. Matthews' expression was as forbidding as a glacier, chilly at best. 'I've reviewed your report. The CPS will be following it up, so at least we've salvaged that much.'

'Yes, sir.'

Matthews remained seated while she stood before his desk. 'At ease.' He paused for a few seconds, clearly considering his next words carefully. 'The CPS will not be pursuing a charge of manslaughter against Mr Crippen. They concluded it was a clear case of self-defence and it was not in the public interest to prosecute.'

Jenny was good: she managed not to slump, exhale, or otherwise demonstrate undue emotional relief under Matthews' baleful inspection.

'Sets a very bad precedent to burn informants. I've had a word with Superintendent Rogers at Steelhouse Lane and he's agreed to lose the charges against him – unless we need them later. I leave it to you to impress on Mr Crippen that we own his arse from now on.' One eyebrow creaked slowly towards his receding hairline. 'Can you do that?'

She could do that. 'Yes, sir. I'll make sure he understands.'

'Good. You're to stay on as his handler, for what it's worth.' *Now* the inspector's chilly exterior thawed a couple of degrees. 'He delivered on the deposit caper, maybe he'll be good for something else besides putting McAndrews and his gang away.'

'I think he wants to go back to university, sir. He was study-ing to be a civil engineer before he caught the virus.' With the charges dropped there was nothing but prejudice stopping him from enrolling at Imperial or UCL in the autumn. They'd discussed it that first night back home after he was discharged from hospital, both of them nervous and unsure if they had a future together. *Please don't ask for details*, she thought. The argument had been intense: the make-up sex even more so.

'A civil engineer. From Jokertown.' Matthews focused on her. 'Wonders never cease. I suppose as long as he keeps his nose out of any more bank vaults there should be no objection from this quarter.'

Jenny shrugged, eloquently. 'He says if he goes back to uni this year he'll graduate in time to get a job on the Channel Tunnel project.' A pause. 'Boy's going to go far . . .'

♣ ♦ ♠ ♥

Probationary

---

by Marko Kloos

Phase I: *Hermes*

South Atlantic, April 30th, 1982

THE SEA WAS AS grey as battleship steel, and it looked angry, white foam caps topping ten-foot swells. Sub-Lieutenant Rory Campbell knew that the large American aircraft carriers were so immense that you couldn't feel you were at sea unless you drove through the middle of a hurricane. But HMS *Hermes*, the largest carrier of the Royal Navy, was only a third the size of one of those Yank monstrosities, and she bobbed up and down in the wave troughs as she made her way south into ever more atrocious weather. But to Rory, the frigid air and the salt spray out here on the weather passageway were preferable to the smells of jet fuel and engine exhaust on the busy flight deck above.

'What dreadful weather to go to war in,' he grumbled and flicked his cigarette over the steel cables of the safety railing.

'On the contrary,' said the man standing next to him. He was a full foot taller than Rory, and the turban he wore made him even more imposing. Major Ranjit Singh, the Lion, would have looked out of place on a Royal Navy ship even without the camouflage-pattern Army uniform he was wearing, or the large curved *kirpan* knife on his web belt.

'It's perfect weather to go to war in,' Major Singh continued. His voice was deep and sonorous, and Rory suspected that his Silver Helix minder could probably sing very well. Not that this environment or the occasion called for any singing.

'This? Glasgow in December is a tropical paradise compared to this shite.'

'It keeps the enemy sentries under their ponchos and close to their warm gear,' Major Singh said. 'In the Army, we call that "recon weather".'

Rory had been with the Lion for three weeks now, and the man never had anything but a calm and mildly pleased expression on his face. There were droplets of seawater spray in his bushy, chest-length beard, and his turban looked damp, but he looked out over the churning waters in *Hermes'* wake with unperturbed serenity, taller than Rory even as he stood bent over a little, with his wrists resting on the safety rail and his palms pressed together. An iron bangle hung from one of his wrists and swayed softly with the movements of the ship.

'Well, I hope it clears up by the time we get to where we're going,' Rory said.

'I hope it doesn't.' Singh looked up at the gloomy sky. 'I hope it gets worse. It will keep the Argentinian air force on the ground.'

Rory gazed back at the dirty-looking silvery wake of the carrier. In that direction was England, seven or eight thousand miles away. And they were steadily steaming on towards the Falkland Islands, now only a few hundred miles to their south, and whatever the Argentinian military had waiting for them there. It had taken the task force most of a month to sail this far from Portsmouth, and that was a long time for the Argies to prepare their positions.

'We're really going to do this, aren't we?'

'Go to war?' Singh flexed his hands and looked at the bangle on his wrist. 'They know we are on the way. If diplomacy hasn't got them off those islands yet, I don't think it will end without bloodshed. A foolish thing, this whole affair. All over a load of wind-blown rocks in the cold sea.'

'I talked to a lad who served in garrison there once. Says it's a lot like the Highlands. In parts, anyway. I suppose we've fought over less before, we Scots.'

Rory and Major Singh didn't have much in common physically, but they shared a Scottish background. Rory had been pleased to find out that his mentor was also from Glasgow. Ranjit Singh was almost ten years older, but they had frequented some of the same stamping grounds back home in their youth, and it was always an easy bond when your histories shared landmarks and geography. Rory was from East Kilbride, Singh from Hillhead, and while these neighbourhoods were on opposite sides of the river, both men were Partick Thistle fans, and favouring the same football team was practically as good as sharing a religion. Rory liked the big, muscular Sikh, and he felt safer and calmer in his presence. He still didn't really think of himself as an ace – he couldn't fly, or bend steel bars, or shoot lightning from his hands – but the Lion was one without a doubt, and being teamed up with him made Rory feel legitimate.

'That's just my bloody luck,' he said. 'My first time out for the Silver Helix, and it has to turn into a shooting war.'

The Lion chuckled softly. 'That is what we *do*. They don't call on us unless things get ugly, my friend. But you are an officer in the Royal Navy. You would be here anyway, I think.'

'Yeah.' Rory tried not to sound defeated. When you sign up for military service, you have to expect the risk of having to go to war, but it's all very abstract when you are just out of secondary school and looking for a way out of East Kilbride. The recruiters emphasized travel, adventure, and pay cheques.

They didn't talk about month-long journeys into frigid waters and enemy air forces looking to put anti-ship missiles into your conveyance. When you are seventeen, you think yourself immortal anyway. But the Lion was right, of course – if Rory's card hadn't turned a year and a half ago he would probably be on a ship in this task force anyway, sitting in front of a radar console on one of the frigates or destroyers steaming along with *Hermes* in the distance.

There were other sailors taking fag-breaks on the weather passageway, but they all kept a respectful distance from Rory and Major Singh. They were both aces and Silver Helix agents, but Singh was also an Army major, and to a professional sailor, staff officers were just a rank or two below the Almighty, even the ones from a different service. Rory appreciated the privacy perks his probationary Silver Helix status afforded him, because even on a warship as large as *Hermes*, space was a precious commodity.

The speakers up on the flight deck blared their announcement tone.

'*Now hear this: we are now entering the Total Exclusion Zone around the Falkland Islands declared by Her Majesty's government. From this point on, there will be no drills. If you hear the action stations alert, it will be the real thing. Stand fast and do your duty. Announcement ends.*'

Rory and Major Singh exchanged glances. Singh sighed and put his hand on the hilt of his kirpan.

Above, a pair of Harrier jump jets took off from the flight deck with their engines at ear-splitting full throttle. They came into view when they cleared the front of the flight deck ramp and turned west, then started the ascent to begin their combat air patrol, position lights blinking. Rory saw that both jets had missiles under their wings, white-painted war shots instead of the blue exercise missiles he usually saw on the Royal Navy's Harriers. The sight of the live missiles increased the feeling of dread he had been nursing for a while. They were a wartime navy now.

'So it begins,' Major Singh said. 'Let us hope it ends quickly. For their sake and ours.'

♣

As the flagship of the task force, *Hermes* had a flag bridge. This was where the task force commander and his staff had their duty stations as they directed the dozens of Royal Navy and auxiliary vessels in the fleet headed for the Falklands, and Rory was the most junior officer in the room by age as well as rank. There were consoles and plotting tables and lots of ratings busy at all of them. Rory felt like the third wheel on a bicycle in this room, and only the fact that he and Major Singh had been ordered here specifically by the task force commander put him at ease. He still wasn't used to being a command asset instead of a simple console jockey, and he doubted he would ever think of himself that way.

'*Hermes* is on station, and we shall remain at spear length from the islands,' Admiral Woodward told the assembled officers. The plotting table in the centre of the flag bridge had a map of the theatre under a sheet of Plexiglas, and the admiral tapped a spot to the northeast of the Falklands with a grease pencil. 'It is my intent to send on the frigates and destroyers to provide an anti-aircraft and anti-submarine screen for *Hermes* and the invasion transports, and prepare the landings as we make progress against the opposition. Winter weather is coming, and our timetable is accordingly strict. If we do not have air superiority by mid-May or troops on the ground by the end of the month, conditions will not favour any further military operations.'

Rory looked out of the porthole on the hatch behind him. Outside, the rain had slacked off a little, but it still looked like the worst weather Scotland had to offer. If this wasn't winter weather yet, they were in for trouble. He couldn't quite understand how anyone would live in a climate like this, much less fight over it.

'At no point will *Hermes* conduct operations closer than two hundred miles from the Falklands. I realize that this greatly limits the combat range of our Harriers, but this ship is too valuable to risk. There's not a pilot in the Argentinian air force who wouldn't love to put a few Exocets into her and win the war with the press of a button.'

There were murmurs of agreement, but clearly not every officer in the room seemed to concur with the admiral's assessment. The naval airmen in particular looked less than happy. 'The Harriers have short legs as it is, sir,' one of the squadron commanders said. 'The lads will have very little loitering time over the battlefield.'

'Then we had best hurry and take the runway at Port Stanley. But this ship will be kept well away from the islands. If the Argentine air force sinks her they win the war, and we lose half of the Royal Navy's force projection capabilities.' Admiral Woodward turned and looked at Rory. 'And that's where you come in, Sub-Lieutenant.'

'Sir?' Rory felt intensely uncomfortable with the sudden undivided attention of so many staff officers.

'Your job on this deployment is to do whatever you have to do to make sure that no enemy plane or missile gets close to *Hermes*.' The admiral looked at Major Singh and back at Rory. Then he sighed and shook his head. 'Admiral Fieldhouse asked the Silver Helix for force multipliers,' he said. 'He emphasized the critical nature of this operation for our national interest and prestige. I believe he even badgered the Prime Minister. Repeatedly. And they send *two* men. One of them an acting sub-lieutenant on probationary status with the Silver Helix. Hardly the war-changing arsenal of special abilities I had hoped for.'

Rory had only met the admiral in person once, at the end of a briefing back in Northwood naval headquarters before the task force sailed. He had decided on the spot that he didn't like the man. He was abrasive and didn't seem to care one bit whether he gave offence, and emphasizing the *acting* in Rory's rank meant he was patronizing both Rory's Silver Helix membership status and his military rank in one sentence.

'Well, it is what it is, I suppose,' Admiral Woodward continued before Rory or Major Singh could reply. 'Major Singh will be going with the Royal Marines once the landings begin. We will be needing your abilities sooner, Sub-Lieutenant. Where do you need to be when action stations sound?'

'I need to see the target, sir,' Rory replied. 'Line of sight, the longer the better. A line to the radar room so they can point me towards incoming threats. And a few sailors with binoculars to share the watch with me. In case I miss something.'

'If we're under attack, they will come in low and fast to avoid our radar. Intelligence says they mainly have Skyhawks armed with general purpose bombs, so they will have to do a terminal climb before they drop. Those we can handle with the Harriers and the Seacats. But they also have a few French Super Etendards with those blasted sea-skimming Exocet missiles. If the frigates and the destroyer picket don't get those, you'll be the last line of defence other than our Seacat launchers.'

'Yes, sir.'

'Let me make one thing clear about your rules of engagement, Sub-Lieutenant.' Admiral Woodward tapped his fingers on the hard surface of the plotting table. 'Disable or destroy whatever comes our way, whether the Seacats launch at it or not. Bloody things are too slow for Exocets anyway. If it comes down to it, you are to use area-of-effect EMP. I don't care if all the lights and radios on this ship go out as long as we don't have a few hundred pounds of high explosive warhead going through our hull and lighting up thousands of gallons of aviation fuel. Is that understood?'

'Yes, sir,' Rory replied. He knew that if he let loose an unfocused electromagnetic pulse burst with all his might, he would disrupt more than just lights and radios. Part of him almost wanted to have an excuse to do that, just to see what it would do to the superior expression of the admiral to find himself on an aircraft carrier with every single electronics circuit shut down.

'Very well,' Admiral Woodward said. 'I'll see to it that you get all the personnel and binoculars you need. Place yourself wherever you see fit. But don't get in the way on the flight deck.' He rapped the plotting table with his knuckles. 'Five days ago, we took South Georgia back from the enemy. The Royal Marines got off to a good start on this one. Now we will do our part. Let's get on with it, gentlemen.'

◆

Rory's first day at war was far less exciting and eventful than he had anticipated. They were two hundred miles from the Falklands and far out of reach of the Argentinian air force bases on the mainland, so the odds of an air raid were low. The Harriers flew regular combat patrols towards the islands, and the destroyers and frigates in the task force had started their screening deployment, interposing themselves between the valuable carriers and the likely directions of attack. Rory took up his post on top of *Hermes*' island superstructure, high above the flight deck, to get a feel for his new action station. He could move from one side of the island to the other in short order to get a full 360-degree view of the ocean surrounding *Hermes*, but the top of the island was also the highest point of the carrier other than her radar masts and funnel tops, and the South Atlantic wind up here was like an ice-cold hand pushing him around. The sailors assigned to the watch with him had been excited at first, but two hours of scanning the austere grey seascape with binoculars in the cold wind had dampened their excitement somewhat. Rory didn't know what Major Singh was doing right now, but he knew that the major would go with the marines of the invasion force when the time came. Whatever he was up to, he was down in the dry, warm ship somewhere instead of wiping freezing spray off binocular lenses.

The flight deck was packed from bow to stern with aircraft and equipment. *Hermes* had taken on more helicopters than she was designed to carry in her regular complement, in anticipation of Argentine submarines. With all the men and equipment on the deck below him, Rory didn't think they'd be able to conduct any offensive operations before unloading some of the extra stuff. But around noon of their first full day in the exclusion zone, the ship's Harriers started taking off one by one. They were laden heavily with bombs and missiles under their wings, so they had to use the ski ramp at the bow of the carrier to get airborne instead of taking off vertically. He watched them roaring down the deck and leaping into the sky, engines bellowing, their wingtips clearing the noses and folded rotor blades of the parked helicopters lined up alongside the take-off strip by what looked like just a few feet. The ground crews smartly saluted every Harrier pilot before each take-off run. Rory had been an enlisted radar technician before he became an ace and a minor Royal Navy celebrity, so tactical flight operations were out of his realm of expertise, but it didn't take a master strategist to know that the Harriers were setting out for Port Stanley, the capital of the Falklands, currently under Argentinian management. The sailors on the carrier's command island with him watched the small squadron struggle into the sky with their heavy ordnance loads and head southwest, disappearing in the low cloud cover after a few minutes.

'I don't really want to go to war, sir,' the sailor next to Rory said without taking his eyes off the leaden sky.

'I don't either,' Rory replied. 'But the public have been paying our salaries. I suppose we can't take the money and then complain when our number finally comes up.'

'Yes, sir. I was just hoping mine wouldn't come up while I was in.'

'Everyone was hoping that,' Rory said.

♠

The Harriers returned a few hours later. Free of their bomb loads, they descended onto the flight deck vertically, hovering over their designated landing spots gracefully before settling down. Rory counted them and was relieved to find they were still the same number of planes that had taken off earlier. There was no cheer or jubilation among the deck hands as they chocked the Harriers' wheels and helped the pilots out of their cockpits. It was just an efficient businesslike atmosphere, professionals at work, just like any other day in the service. Rory wondered what the bombs from those planes had hit, and whether it had made a dent in the Argie defences. Part of him still hoped that the Argentinians would back down after the first show of force from the Royal Navy, that they would see reason once they saw modern warplanes with live bombs overhead. They were the *Royal Navy*, not some third-rate corvette navy from a backwater nation. But after the return of the Harriers, an hour passed, then two, and by the time he ended his watch and went down to the officer wardroom for dinner, there had been no announcement from the commander that everything was over, that Argentina had decided they had lost the game of chicken. Still, it looked as if both sides had decided they weren't bluffing after all.

♥

Rory was in the middle of his meal when the commander finally did make an announcement, and everyone paused their conversations at once.

'This is the commander. I am glad to announce we had a very good day today. We have started to soften up the defences at Stanley with no losses of our own. And earlier today, the Argentine cruiser General Belgrano was torpedoed by one of our submarines on station south of the Total Exclusion Zone. That removes the threat posed by the Argentinian navy to our southern flank. That is all. Commander out.'

This time there was some cheering going on in the ward-room, and the conversations that picked up again had a decidedly more excited note to them.

'The *Belgrano*,' the lieutenant across the table from Rory said. 'That's their biggest surface ship. She's an ex-Yank cruiser. USS *Phoenix*, I think. Served in World War Two. Shame, really.'

'Wonder if they sank her,' Rory replied.

'As long as she's out of the picture and not pointing her guns at us. So what exactly is it you can do?' the lieutenant asked. 'I mean, if that's not a state secret.'

'It's not,' Rory said. He was a recent addition to the crew, a newcomer in a group of officers who had been working together for many months or even years, and he was glad whenever he had a chance to socialize with someone other than his Silver Helix minder. His story was well known in the Royal Navy – he was one of only a handful of aces who were on active military duty – but he also knew there were a lot of embellished versions of that tale out there, and he rarely had an opportunity to correct the rumour mill.

'I make directional EMPs,' he said. 'I can turn off any electric system. Slag it, too, if I want.'

'Anything? So, could you shut down this ship?'

'Most of it, I suppose,' Rory said. 'Whatever I can see, anyway.'

'That is bloody brilliant,' the lieutenant said.

'Small bits too,' Rory continued. He pointed at the lieutenant's wristwatch with his fork. It was one of the new digital quartz models, the ones that showed the time on a little display window. 'I could focus and just pop the circuit board in that watch of yours.'

'Please don't,' the lieutenant smiled. He put a protective hand over the face of his watch. 'My wife gave that to me before we left Portsmouth. When did you find out you could do that EMP thing?'

'I was on HMS *Juno* the year before last. I was an engineering tech. One day, we were working up on the dish for the anti-aircraft system. It was supposed to be de-energized, but it turned on while we had three lads in front of it. I could feel it somehow. Can't explain it, but I knew how to shut it down, and I did. Just by thinking hard about it.'

'Bloody brilliant,' the other lieutenant repeated.

There were other officers at the table with them, and one of them looked rather sceptical at this pronouncement. 'So when the Argie ships come into sight, you can turn their lights off. That will be useful. Right after they fire their Exocets at us.'

'If I can see the missile, I can blow its guidance systems up,' Rory replied.

'Right,' the other man said. He wore the flight suit of a Fleet Air Arm officer, which meant that he flew a Harrier or a helicopter. 'I suppose we don't have anything to worry about, then.'

'I'll do what I can,' Rory said.

'As will we all. It's just some of us are going to go out to drop GP bombs on the Argies instead of sitting on a carrier two hundred miles away. Different risk factor. And my lads don't get special perks for doing their jobs.'

'Knock it off,' the lieutenant across the table said. 'The aces get their own berth because they're bloody *aces*, mate. They hadn't come along, you'd be whinging about them not sending any with us.'

'The other guy's all right. The Army major. He'll be handy on the ground. I've seen him bench press five hundred pounds in the gym with the marines.' The pilot turned his attention back to Rory. 'But you're going to be bored. With the Harriers, there's no Argie plane getting close enough to this ship to launch anything. We'll be getting it done the old-fashioned way. Guns and missiles.'

'I do hope you're right about that,' Rory replied. The other man's eyes narrowed, and Rory could tell he was looking for signs that Rory was being clever with him.

'You'll see,' the flight officer said. 'The Royal Navy hasn't lost a ship in combat since World War Two. And that was before we had anti-air missiles and fighter jets.'

Their side has those too, Rory thought. But instead of voicing it, he just nodded and focused on his dinner again. He loathed conflict, whether it was a shooting war with Argentina or an argument over fish and chips in the wardroom.

'Don't mind that tosser,' the other lieutenant said after the flight officer had left the table a little while later. 'Those fighter pilots all think they're special. Jealousy's a terrible thing.'

'I still hope he's right,' Rory replied. '*And if we do lose a ship, I hope it won't be my fault*, he didn't add.

Phase II: *Sheffield*
Inside the Total Exclusion Zone, May 3rd, 1982

The crew mess and wardroom had television sets mounted on the bulkheads, and they all watched the news during the next few days whenever they could. It was odd to catch up on events that had happened just a little over a hundred miles away, sent to the ships of the task force via satellite relay from BBC stations eight thousand miles to their north with a day-long delay.

ARA *General Belgrano*, the Argentinian cruiser, had been severely damaged by the torpedo attack, with substantial loss of life. Even as the BBC report was finishing, some of the officers in the room said they heard that *Belgrano* had been sunk, not just damaged. In the military, there was no communications system faster than the wardroom rumour mill, but Rory knew that some of the officers had their posts in *Hermes'* Action Information Centre or on the bridge, and were privy to information the rest of the crew didn't have. He didn't know the exact complement of a cruiser like the *Belgrano*, but his lads in the wardroom had mentioned she had served in World War Two, and old ships like that needed a lot of manpower, many hundreds of sailors. Even if most of them got out of the ship and onto life rafts, the South Atlantic was freezing. If someone had to get sunk, he'd rather it be the *Belgrano* than *Hermes* or one of the other Royal Navy ships, but it was still not pleasant to think about sailors drowning or freezing to death, even if they were the enemy right now.

At the end of the news, the BBC reporter used the phrase 'Falklands crisis', and the lieutenant commander in the chair next to Rory's huffed a little.

'"Crisis",' he repeated. 'We've dropped bombs on a town and sunk a cruiser. They shot down two Argie planes yesterday, too. If this is a crisis, I want to know what qualifies as a war.'

♣

War came to *Hermes* the next morning for the first time.

Rory was on watch again on the command island. Several radar contacts had been spotted by the picket ships the fleet commander had sent out to screen the carrier from air attack, and Rory was the last-ditch insurance. It was a precaution because the contacts were too far away from *Hermes* to pose an imminent threat, so when the action stations alarm sounded, Rory jumped a little at the unwelcome surprise of it.

'*Action stations, action stations.*' The alarm blared, and all around him things got busy as crew members ran up and down stairs and gangways and slammed shut watertight hatches.

*'Silver Helix personnel to the flag bridge. I repeat, Silver Helix
personnel to the flag bridge at once.'*

Rory was already on the command island, so he didn't have
far to go to reach the flag bridge, where Admiral Woodward
and his support staff were already waiting along with the ship's
captain. Rory's mind raced as he stepped across the threshold
of the watertight door and reported in. Major Singh, the Lion,
had to come from much further below decks than Rory, but
only twenty or thirty seconds after Rory stepped onto the flag
bridge, a door on the opposite side of the compartment opened,
and the big Sikh stepped through it. He didn't even look
particularly out of breath.

The admiral and several of his staff officers were still in the
middle of a discussion at the plotting table, so Rory made sure
he stayed out of the way of the sailors hurrying around and
console operators delivering reports from the nearby Action
Information Centre.

'*Glasgow* announced "handbrake" at 1104 hours,' one of the
officers told the admiral. '*Sheffield* was in contact with *Coventry*
at the time and signalled they were hit just two minutes later.
No further details from *Sheffield*. Their UHF is silent.'

'Send out *Arrow* and *Yarmouth* to *Sheffield's* last known
position,' Admiral Woodward ordered. 'And launch one of the
ready helicopters to verify what the blazes is going on.' He
looked across the flag bridge and only now seemed to notice
Rory and Major Singh. 'Gentlemen,' he said, and waved them
closer. Rory approached the plotting table, still unused to the
sensation of senior officers making space for him in the
confines of the small compartment. 'We dispatched our three
Type 42 destroyers as anti-submarine pickets between our
position and the southeastern Falklands. A few minutes ago,
we got a signal that indicates HMS *Sheffield* took a hit. We
don't know what exactly happened or the extent of the damage.
It looks like it may become a busy day for you, Sub-Lieutenant.
HMS *Glasgow* indicated that the attack came from Argentine

Super Etendards. That means they have started using their Exocet arsenal.'

'Do we know how many Exocets they have?' Major Singh asked.

'Not a terrific amount, but enough to make us lose this war by the end of the week if they use them well, Major.'

Admiral Woodward turned and looked at Rory.

'Tell me how far out you can spot a sea-skimming missile moving at seven hundred miles per hour, Sub-Lieutenant Campbell.'

'If I know the bearing from a radar fix, and if the seas aren't too choppy, two miles, maybe more, sir.'

'That's a damned thin safety margin,' *Hermes*' captain said with a frown. 'That gives you, what, ten seconds to bring it down? And that's if you spot it as soon as the radar does.'

'It beats relying on just the Seacats,' the admiral replied. 'Those can only get head-on kills. If we get an air radar contact within fifty miles of this ship, you are to be on your perch, Sub-Lieutenant, with a live comms link to the radar operator. Of course, plan number one is to not let the buggers that close to begin with.'

'Radar contact bearing two-one-five, distance five-seven miles, sir,' the radar operator called out, as if on cue. 'IFF says it's one of our Lynx helicopters.'

'Get them on radio, then. Sub-Lieutenant Campbell, head to your action station right away.'

'Aye, sir,' Rory replied and left the compartment in a hurry.

◆

The Lynx helicopter that had appeared on the radar screen touched down on *Hermes*' flight deck half an hour later. Rory had a perfect vantage point from the command island to see them unload two officers and then several obviously wounded personnel. Some had parts of their overalls cut away, others had thick bandages on their faces or hands. The medical personnel of *Hermes* met them almost as soon as they set foot on the carrier deck and helped them to nearby stretchers. The officers engaged in some brief but heated conversation with the *Hermes* personnel who had met them and then went over to the command island. Rory picked up his radio.

'Archimedes to radar ops. What's the airspace look like?' This was the first time he had used his official ace moniker. If he was to be a semi-permanent living weapons mount on this ship, he reckoned he ought to go by his ace name instead of his military rank, which didn't have much clout on a ship with an admiral and dozens of staff officers anyway.

'Airspace is clear of contacts, sir. We have a flight of Harriers out on combat air patrol eighty miles out at two-seven-zero degrees. You have a clean board for the moment.'

Rory went back down to the flag level, where the newly arrived officers were talking to the admiral and the rest of the ship's senior officers. At first, he had felt like an interloper, going wherever he wanted on the ship if he wasn't specifically ordered to be in a certain spot, but that was another perk of Silver Helix membership. If he deemed it necessary to be somewhere to accomplish his assignment, his ace status overrode even his military rank.

'*Sheffield*'s a mission kill,' one of the new officers reported. 'We took an Exocet amidships. It knocked out our electric system and the water main. We have nothing to fight the fire. The way she's burning, she'll be gone by morning.'

'What's the casualty count?'

'At least a dozen men, probably more. The missile hit the ratings galley and the computer room.'

'Bloody hell,' the *Hermes*' captain cursed. 'What about the Seacats?'

'None were fired, sir. I think ops thought it was a false alarm again. They didn't even have the gun ready.'

'What a monumental cock-up. Get *Arrow* and *Yarmouth* out

there on the flank to help put those fires out and get *Sheffield* under tow. I will not be the first task force commander to lose a ship in action since they signed the bloody armistice in Tokyo Bay,' Admiral Woodward said.

He focused on the plotting table and pointed a finger at the point on the map marked with the icon for HMS *Sheffield*. 'Shift *Glasgow*'s patrol pattern northeast so she can close the hole and give *Arrow* and *Yarmouth* air defence support. I want two more flights of Harriers going that way as well. One from us, one from *Invincible*.'

Rory cleared his throat. 'Sir, I should go out there on a Lynx. Put me on *Coventry* or *Glasgow*. I can do a lot more good closer to the line than back here on *Hermes*.'

The admiral looked at Rory in unconcealed disbelief, then shook his head. 'Out of the question, Sub-Lieutenant. You are one third of this ship's air defence arsenal.'

'This ship is over a hundred miles from the action, sir. I could be a much better picket against enemy aircraft if you put me in a spot where they are likely to be. *Hermes* has Harriers. They can intercept what comes past the destroyer screen.'

'The destroyers are spaced out too far. If I put you on *Glasgow* and they engage *Coventry* next instead, there won't be anything you can do about it because you'll be thirty miles away. And then you'll be useless to *Hermes* as well.' He made a dismissive hand gesture. '*Hermes* carries half the task force's air power, and she's the most essential ship we have. I will not risk the Royal Navy's biggest carrier to maybe keep an Exocet away from a Type 42. They can take care of their own air defence without you. If they're not sitting on their bloody arses while other ships are broadcasting air-raid warnings. And lest you think me callous, I'll have you know that I used to be *Sheffield*'s commanding officer. Now someone get me a strong coffee and some aspirin, please.'

♠

There was nothing more dispiriting to Rory than having to witness the casualties from *Sheffield* being brought onto *Hermes'* deck and not being able to do anything to help. A lot of the injured *Sheffield* sailors had obvious burn injuries. The helicopters came in intervals, in between take-off and landing operations for the Harriers. The fighter aircraft were out for blood, now that one of the task force ships had been hit, with British sailors killed and wounded. But hour after hour, the Harriers came back, trading spaces with newly rearmed and refuelled ones leaping off the ski ramp at *Hermes'* bow, and Rory heard no reports of any air victories. The Argentine air force had got their bite out of them for the day, it seemed.

♥

A few long, demoralizing days of monotonous watch-standing later, the commander made an announcement that didn't do anything to lift Rory's mood.

'*This is the commander. I regret to inform you that HMS* Sheffield *foundered today on the way to South Georgia while under tow by HMS* Yarmouth. *That is all. Commander out.*'

Rory let the news sink in for a few moments. As Admiral Woodward had reminded him, the Royal Navy hadn't lost a ship in action since the end of World War Two, thirty-seven years ago. Almost ten enlistment cycles had passed without one of Her Majesty's warships getting so much as fired upon, and now one was sitting at the bottom of the North Atlantic. And not just an old, outdated ship like the *Belgrano*, but a modern state-of-the-art Type 42 destroyer, fitted with some of the best weapon systems in the Royal Navy.

If they can sink Sheffield, *they can sink any other ship in the fleet*, Rory thought. And here he stood, standing watch on the command deck of *Hermes*, a hundred miles from where the frigates and destroyers of the task force were shelling Argentine positions in preparation for the invasion, and he hadn't seen so much as the contrail from an enemy plane this whole time.

Rory was at the end of his patience. He was still a Royal Navy officer, albeit only an acting sub-lieutenant and therefore at the very bottom of the commissioned pecking order, but he was an ace and a member of the Silver Helix. It was disrespectful to treat him like a stationary weapons mount out here when the real war was going on a hundred miles to their west. He hated confrontation, but nothing was worse than standing around in the cold on this carrier doing nothing.

He handed his binoculars to the sailor next to him. 'You have the watch for a few minutes, Petty Officer. I am going to the flag bridge.'

♣

The admiral wasn't on the flag bridge when Rory stepped through the door, but Commodore Clapp and Major General Moore were there, discussing something in low voices while consulting a map. The Commodore was the commander of the landing fleet that would ferry the troops to the beaches when the ground invasion started, and Major General Moore was in command of the land forces, Royal Marines and Army alike.

'Something on your mind, Sub-Lieutenant?' Commodore Clapp asked when Rory stepped up to them.

'Yes, sir. I was looking for the admiral, actually.'

'He's out on a Sea King headed for *Invincible*,' the commodore replied. 'Anything of concern we need to know about?'

'No, sir,' Rory said. 'But that's just the problem, see. I've been up there for a week with binoculars glued to my eyes while the lads on the frigates get bombs chucked at them. There has got to be something else I can do. I don't think the admiral quite understands what I can bring to the field.'

'So you want to be on the line,' Major General Moore said in a tone that sounded almost appreciative to Rory. 'And what is it that you can do that I can't do with a squad of my Royal Marines commandos?'

'Your commandos have to get close to the enemy. Close enough for rifle fire or anti-tank rockets. I just need to be close enough to *see* a plane. Even if it's just through binoculars. And I can slag its radar and electronics in five seconds.'

The major general and the commodore exchanged a glance that looked meaningful.

'Really now,' the major general said. 'That's from several miles out. In any weather.'

'As long as I can lay eyes on it,' Rory said.

The commodore and major general exchanged another look, this one more poignant than the last, and Rory could have sworn that the Royal Marines general smiled a little.

'Tell you what, Sub-Lieutenant. We will have a chat with the admiral and see where we can slot you in. There may be an upcoming opportunity for you to demonstrate your skill set. No promises, though.'

'Yes, sir. Thank you, sir. I really don't want the Silver Helix to think the armed forces are not using their special assets to best effect.'

Rory sketched a salute and walked back to the starboard door of the flag bridge.

'Is that cheeky little bugger blackmailing us?' Commodore Clapp asked the major general, who chuckled.

'I believe so,' Major General Moore replied. 'Enough pluck for a Royal Marine, that one.'

Outside, the driving frigid Antarctic wind doused Rory with a fresh shower of seawater, but he found that his mood had improved just a little bit.

◆

Just a few hours later Rory found himself in an air group briefing room filled to the last chair with some of the toughest-looking troops he had ever seen. Most were wearing the Army and Royal Marines DPM-pattern camouflage uniforms instead of Navy dress, and all of them radiated a mood that felt rather like what Rory sensed in his regular hometown pub when a particularly critical Partick Thistle match was about to start on the telly. Major Singh was in the room too, but he sat on the other side when Rory came in, and there was no way to make it across the compartment full of seated troops to join his Silver Helix colleague. At the head of the room, Major General Moore stood behind a briefing lectern.

When the general spotted Rory taking his seat, he nodded grimly. 'You got your wish, Sub-Lieutenant. I rather hope you don't come to regret it.'

Rory took his seat, one of the last two remaining ones. Behind the general a projector screen was set up at an angle, showing the white square of a blank slide. General Moore pressed a button on his wired remote, and the first slide whirred into position with a click. It showed an overhead reconnaissance photo of a grass airfield. Several aircraft of different types were parked to either side of the airstrip.

'Our two Silver Helix guests were not present at the original mission briefing, so I will repeat the main details for their benefit.' He extended a small pointer stick and tapped the projection. 'This is a small Argentinian airbase on Pebble Island, on the northern tip of West Falkland Island. The Argentines set it up right after they moved in. It's just a short grass strip, but it's in a rather inconvenient spot for us.'

He moved the pointer to the Argentinian planes lined up on the grass above and below the runway. 'The Argentine air force have about a dozen planes there. They are mostly Pucarás. Twin-engine turboprops, used for light attack and recon duties. The light attack capabilities don't worry us too much because our Harriers can run rings around them if they try to make runs on the fleet. What's more of a concern is their reconnaissance function. We are in full preparation for the landings, and reconnaissance by these aircraft will compromise our planned manoeuvres and give the enemy advance warning of our intended landing sites. Therefore, we have tasked D Squadron, 22 SAS Regiment, with the destruction of these aircraft and their support facilities.'

The general changed slides. The projection on the screen changed to a wider shot of the airfield. Several small structures were circled in various colours. 'D Squadron will ingress by helicopter to a point five miles from the objective. The Boat Troop scouted the target last night. Due to the strong headwinds coming from the southwest, the range of our helicopters will be reduced, so we had to cut the window for offensive operations on the ground from ninety to thirty minutes. Therefore, the aircraft on the ground are top priority targets. The fuel and ammo dumps and the support personnel are secondary concerns. Take out targets of opportunity, but your primary objective is those aircraft. HMS *Glamorgan* will provide artillery support from offshore once the aircraft are destroyed or disabled.' He looked over at Rory, who started feeling very out of place in a briefing room full of hardened commandos. 'The original plan had Mountain Troop infiltrating the facility to lay explosive charges on the aircraft while the other troops provide overwatch. That is a risky endeavour because the Argies undoubtedly expect a raid and will have sentries out. Sub-Lieutenant Campbell over here will ingress with D Squadron and take up overwatch position with the covering team. If you can disable or destroy their planes from that position, infiltration won't be needed, and the risk to D Squadron will be greatly reduced. I probably need not tell you that the lads would greatly appreciate it if they could remain out of small arms range.'

Some of the SAS men laughed. Most of them had shifted in their seats to look over at Rory. He saw the appraising glances from the commandos and wondered briefly if he should have kept his mouth shut on the flag bridge after all.

'If Sub-Lieutenant Campbell – Archimedes – cannot disable the Pucarás from the overwatch position, we will go to Plan B, and things will get considerably noisier. But keep the timing in mind, because the window of operations is a small one. Do stick to the timetable if you want to get off that rock and back to *Hermes*, unless you have a desire to sample the quality of the cooking in an Argentine POW camp.'

There was more laughter from the troops. Rory smiled weakly at the joke. He was Navy, not SAS, but even he understood very well that having to spend time in a POW camp was not the worst possible outcome for anyone on this mission.

Major General Moore ran them through the timeline of the raid once more — undoubtedly for the benefit of Rory and Major Singh, the last-minute additions – and concluded the briefing a few minutes later. Rory didn't feel any more prepared than before he had walked into the room.

'A word, Sub-Lieutenant,' the general said when everyone started filing out of the compartment, and Rory stayed behind. 'I got Admiral Woodward to agree to this because it's a night-time raid, and there won't be any air threat to *Hermes* while it's dark. But we are taking a risk sending you out like that. Major Singh will come along and make sure that you come back in one piece. And please make it worth that risk. Don't make me regret convincing the admiral to let you come along.'

'Understood, sir,' Rory said. 'I'll do my very best.'

Outside in the passageway, Major Singh walked up behind him and patted his shoulder. The Silver Helix agent was in his camouflage Army uniform, but tonight he had web gear on top of his jacket, and he had exchanged his blue turban for a black one.

'Congratulations,' he said. 'You are a commando now. Let's get you to equipment issue and dressed for the part. The mission starts at 2200 hours.'

Phase III: Pebble Island
West Falkland Island, May 14th, 1982

After three years in the Royal Navy, Rory didn't get seasick often any more, but riding in the back of a Sea King helicopter into forty-knot headwinds charted some brand-new territory for nausea in his brain. It didn't help that the cargo compartment was crowded with battle-ready commandos and their equipment. The SAS lads looked calm and collected, but Rory could tell that everyone was tense, except maybe for Major Singh. The Lion sat in the jump seat next to Rory, his backpack and rifle upright between his legs, the fingers of his left hand lightly touching the pommel of the dagger on his web belt while the big Sikh looked at the helicopter's bulkhead absent-mindedly. Rory would have liked a calming chat before the start of the action, but the interior of the Sea King was noisy, and conversations had to be held at near-shouting volume. Whatever space inside the helicopter that wasn't taken up by a geared-up soldier was filled with ammunition and equipment. The Sea King had windows, but it was pitch dark outside, and the total lack of visual references combined with the buffeting from the winds made Rory queasy.

They flew through the darkness for what seemed like hours until the helicopter finally started a series of banking and descending manoeuvres.

'Thirty seconds,' the pilot called out towards the back.

All around Rory, the SAS troopers started readying their gear with practised movements. Rory tried to emulate them, fumbling with the straps of his assault pack and untangling the Sterling submachine gun they had issued him back on *Hermes*.

'Relax,' the Lion said next to him and reached down to free Rory's gun sling from the support strut of his seat. 'We are not doing a parachute drop. We are just getting off the normal way.'

'In the dark. Onto enemy territory,' Rory added, and Major

Singh grinned. His teeth looked very white in the semi-darkness of the Sea King's cargo hold.

'That is how war works,' he said. 'Especially when the SAS is involved.'

The helicopter settled on the ground, and the troops opened the sliding doors to either side of the Sea King. The SAS men filed out of the cargo hold quickly and smoothly, and it was evident they had done this a thousand times. Rory tried not to hold up the egress too much and followed Major Singh as fast as he could. A few dozen yards away another Sea King landed, this one carrying the other half of D Squadron.

Outside, the SAS charged their L1A1 rifles, and some of them set up a security perimeter. Rory hadn't realized just how much extra ordnance they had brought with them until the other troops and the Navy airmen had unloaded the helicopters completely.

'Everyone check their loads,' the officers announced. 'Everybody will carry at least two rounds for the mortars in addition to their combat load.'

The SAS added the green plastic containers with the mortar bombs to their rucksacks and secured them with straps. Rory did the same. When he looked over to Major Singh, he saw that the Lion had lashed three double containers to his pack.

'Mountain Troop, take point with the lads from Boat Troop. Keep your intervals. And don't get distracted admiring the scenery. Once we get there, we have thirty minutes,' the SAS major in command ordered.

They all synchronized their watches, and the SAS squadron marched off into the darkness. Rory wasn't an infantryman, and the last time he had marched with a pack and a rifle had been during basic training. But these men were the best at this particular sort of thing, so he decided to stick close to Major Singh and do everything the SAS men did.

♠

There wasn't much scenery to admire on Pebble Island. Rory remembered the assessment of his Navy friend that the Falklands looked a lot like the remote parts of Scotland, and he had to agree. It was all rock-strewn and hilly, with very little vegetation other than grass. Doing everything the SAS men did turned out to be easier in intent than practice because even with all their heavy gear they were the fastest marchers he had ever seen. Rory puffed along behind Major Singh and the supremely fit commandos.

'It's just like Scotland,' he said to the major as they were ascending a little hill, the wind whipping into their faces, making everyone pull the cords on their parka hoods tighter. 'There's even bloody sheep. Look.' He pointed over to a herd of them, barely visible in the darkness a few hundred yards off their path on the slope of the hill.

'Ten thousand sheep on this island,' Major Singh informed him. 'Been a sheep farm for a hundred and fifty years. I doubt the sheep care whether they get shorn by Argentines or British.'

They reached the summit of the little hill a few minutes later. On the plains ahead of them, maybe a mile or so in the distance, Rory could barely make out some structures, a few low buildings rising from the sparse grass. When he checked with his binoculars, he could make out the silhouettes of aeroplanes backlit by the moonlight reflecting from the nearby ocean.

'Send a signal to *Glamorgan* and let them know we have the objective in sight,' the SAS major ordered. 'Mountain Troop, let's get to work. Air and Boat troops, move out to the blocking and reserve positions. Ten minutes until go time, gentlemen.'

♥

Rory and Major Singh went ahead with the Mountain Troop, whose task it had been to sneak into the Argentine installation and place demolition charges on the aircraft before Rory volunteered his talents. The SAS men moved silently and professionally, using hand signals to coordinate their movements. Major Singh stayed close by Rory's side and directed him silently whenever Rory didn't see or understand a hand signal. As a Navy sailor, he had only received minimal weapons instruction years ago, and he had forgotten almost all of his knowledge about infantry formation tactics from basic training. He had never been afraid of the dark, but this place was unsettling, especially given the knowledge that hundreds of armed men were camped out in that installation just a mile and a half away, ready and willing to kill them if they made their presence known.

Mountain Troop was five hundred yards from the edge of the airfield when the captain in charge ordered everyone to spread out and take up firing positions. He made his way back to Rory and Major Singh. 'Can you do your thing from here?' the captain asked Rory. 'Any closer and we have to keep an eye out for their sentries.'

Rory checked his surroundings with the binoculars again. 'I see three I can get for sure. But that low building there – I can't see what's next to that, or behind it. Too bloody dark.'

'Try these.' The captain opened a pouch on his web gear and handed Rory a set of goggles on a head strap. Rory put them on, and the captain reached out and turned a knob on the goggles. Rory's field of view instantly turned from various shades of black to a grainy green, but everything further than fifty feet away instantly became visible as if it was merely the beginning of dusk.

'Latest generation image intensifier,' the captain said.

'You SAS boys get all the expensive toys,' Rory replied. He looked around at the men in their fighting positions, then back at the airfield. A few small lights were burning over at the installation, and even though they looked like little glowing pinpricks to his naked eye from this distance, they flared bright as stars through the night vision goggles. What had been largely a featureless expanse before now looked perfectly defined to Rory. 'There's the runway,' he said. 'And four . . . five . . . make that six Pucarás. There's some sort of transport as well. And four more I don't recognize.'

'Let me see for a moment.'

Rory handed the night vision gear back to the SAS captain. 'Looks like Turbo-Mentors,' he said after looking at the field for a few moments. 'Training craft. But they can still report back our positions once the invasion fleet starts moving.' He returned the night vision goggles to Rory. 'Question is, can you fry the bastards from this far away?'

'Absolutely,' Rory said. The captain grinned at the conviction in his voice.

'That's what I wanted to hear. Wait for my go. Confirm?'

'Waiting for your go, sir.'

'Good man.' The captain got out his radio and spoke into it in a low voice. 'We have positive ID on the primary assets. Our man is ready to turn them into lawn decorations. Lock and load, and prepare for a response from the garrison force.'

The troop leader radioed back their acknowledgements. For a moment, it was dead silent on their little hillock apart from the ever-present South Atlantic wind.

'*Glamorgan* is standing by for bombardment,' the SAS captain said. 'You are cleared to engage, Sub-Lieutenant.'

'Do your thing, Archimedes,' Major Singh said next to him.

Rory took a deep breath. Then he scanned the line of ground attack craft parked five hundred yards away and focused his attention on the leftmost one, the plane closest to the end of the runway and therefore the one likely to take off first in the event of an alert.

Whenever anyone asked – and plenty of people had since his card turned – he never quite knew how to explain his ability. The closest he had ever come was to liken it to secondary school, to his biology classes. They'd had a human anatomy model in the classroom, a plastic dummy that had removable parts. You could strip all the layers away – first the pectoral and abdominal muscles, then the rib cage, then the internal organs. Heart, lungs, intestines, until you had the shell of half a body with nothing but the spinal column and the strands of the nervous system. Whenever he looked at a machine with electronics in it, he felt as if he was back in that classroom looking at the anatomical mannequin with its layers peeled away and the nerves sitting out in the open. He could feel the energy in the batteries and capacitors, sense the silica and copper pathways of the electrical systems. The Pucarás were over a third of a mile away, but he could still focus on each node in their artificial nervous systems in turn. They were simple machines compared to the Royal Navy's Harriers, but they still had basic computers, gyroscopes, radios, inertial navigation devices, all sorts of things that required circuit boards and capacitors.

Rory concentrated on the plane in the centre of his night vision goggles' field of vision. As always, he got just a little dizzy when the electromagnetic energy built up between him and his target. He directed it towards the nose of the plane and swept the electronics with a sharply focused pulse. Even from five hundred yards away, he could feel the pathways of the wiring and the circuit boards start to glow as he pumped a voltage into them they were never designed to withstand. It was silent and invisible to the commandos, and he reckoned they'd want tangible evidence that he was doing what he said he'd be able to do, so Rory focused again and doubled his effort. The second sweep had rather more dramatic results than the first. The overheated circuits were already damaged beyond repair, but now the wiring in the plane burst into flames. Rory gave it a third EMP pulse just to make sure the plane was thoroughly slagged.

'Well?' the SAS captain asked.

In the distance, flames started licking out of the crack between the Pucará's avionics access panel and the fuselage.

In the near-complete darkness, they were visible even without night vision goggles. Rory nodded towards the plane in response. 'That one's flown its last sortie,' he said.

The captain trained a set of binoculars on the distant aircraft. Then he grinned and slapped Rory's shoulder. 'Bloody brilliant. Now do the rest, if you wouldn't mind.'

'Not at all,' Rory said, feeling a little smug. He wished the admiral had come along for the mission, even though he knew that flag officers *ordered* commando raids, they didn't join them. He turned his attention to the next plane and repeated the process, focusing a tight beam of electromagnetic energy and then sweeping it over the next Pucará in line, then the one next to that. The other two were lined up on the other side of the runway, so he got up and shifted his position a little to get a better viewing angle. Major Singh and the SAS captain moved with him and took up positions on either side of him again when he settled on the grass and adjusted his night vision goggles once more.

'Movement,' someone behind them called out in a low voice. 'Sentry, single mover. Two o'clock, coming out from behind that low Quonset.'

Rory looked in the direction the other SAS trooper indicated. There was a lone Argentine soldier out there, walking from one of the few buildings on the airfield over to the fuel pumps, which blocked his view of the plane that had started to burn. In a few moments, he'd either see or smell the fire coming from underneath the Pucará's hood.

'Look lively, lads,' the SAS captain said. 'Things are about to get interesting. Do hurry up, Sub-Lieutenant.'

Rory swept the remaining two Pucarás. They were small, graceful aircraft, and they looked as if they would be a blast to go for a ride in. It seemed a waste to destroy them, but he remembered the burn victims from the *Sheffield* being offloaded on the *Hermes*, and what little regret he felt dissipated at once.

He had just disabled the sixth and last Pucará when the first one on the other side of the line exploded with a dull thunderclap that rolled across the dark glen. The fire he had set just moments earlier had probably spread to the fuel tank or loaded ammunition. The orange-red bloom of the explosion roiled into the night sky and lit up the airstrip. The sudden brightness washed out the display of Rory's night vision goggles. When his vision returned, the Argentine sentry was no longer in sight.

'They'll be looking for us any second now,' the SAS captain said. 'Do the rest. Corporal Park, signal *Glamorgan* to commence bombardment.'

Rory's heart pounded as he returned his attention to the rest of the parked aircraft. The four Turbo-Mentors were next. He swept them one by one, as hard and tightly focused as he could, and three of them caught fire almost instantly, one of them belching a tall jet of flames from its portside wing before disappearing in a bright orange fireball. The boom that followed was so loud that it felt as if it made the ground shake a little even at this distance.

Somewhere out over the ocean Rory saw what looked like lightning flashes. A few seconds later, another explosion threw up a geyser of earth and rocks near the fuel dump. This one looked a lot bigger than the one caused by the aircraft blowing up. After a few seconds more, another explosion followed, then a third. That one hit something unseen but volatile. Even the disciplined SAS men couldn't hold back their astonished excitement at the fireworks display in front of them. It looked like New Year's Eve over the Thames. Glowing bits of debris flew outwards from the explosion in a huge shower of sparks and smoke trails. The destroyer HMS *Glamorgan*, waiting several miles offshore, had started her planned bombardment with her 4.5-inch main battery guns. A second or two later, the heat from the explosion washed over them. It smelled like hot metal and gunpowder.

'They hit the ammo dump,' Major Singh said with satisfaction in his voice. 'On the third shot. Good show.'

'Are the planes all slagged?' the SAS captain asked Rory.

'All done for,' Rory confirmed.

Glamorgan's high-explosive shells came in with clockwork-like regularity, a round hitting the airbase every five or six seconds. It seemed extremely foolhardy to lie prone only a few hundred yards from an airfield that was being worked over by artillery from miles away, but the gunnery officer on *Glamorgan* knew his job. The destroyer's big guns walked their fire all over the area of the base, but none of the rounds fell close to Rory and the SAS. After a few minutes, the bombardment ceased. The silence that followed was almost total. Only the crackling sounds from the fires on the airbase reached their ears.

'Right, then,' the SAS captain said into the silence. 'Scratch one airfield. Everybody grab your gear and fall back for assembly. Mountain Troop, keep overwatch. And radio the mortar crews to leave their tubes. Ditch the bombs, too. We'll go light and fast on the way back.'

Rory got up from his prone position with a little groan. Using his ace ability always tired him out. It usually felt as if he had just washed down a dose of sedatives with a dram of cask-strength Scotch. He pulled the night vision goggles off his head and held them out to the SAS captain.

'Here's your toy back, sir,' he said. 'I wouldn't mind a set of those myself.'

'Tell you what,' the captain said. 'I'll give you that set when we get back to *Hermes* and report them lost. You saved us a lot of blood and sweat just now.'

The captain reached for the goggles and started stowing them in their pouch again.

A few yards to their right, the Lion looked back at the airfield in the distance and sniffed the air. Then he held up a hand and froze. 'Something's not right.'

Rory followed his gaze. There was no movement he could make out with his naked eyes despite the illumination from the fires. 'What—' he began. Then a fusillade of gunfire from the direction of the airfield cut him off. Rory could hear the supersonic crack of bullets screaming past them in the darkness. A machine gun opened up, green tracers reaching out to them like laser beams from a science fiction film.

'*Down!*' Major Singh shouted. He whirled around and dived for Rory. The SAS captain was closer to him, though, and just a little bit faster than the Lion. He grabbed Rory by his web gear and yanked him down onto the ground. Rory saw some of the tracer rounds skip on the rocky soil nearby at a shallow angle and bounce off in various directions. The SAS captain let out a strained little grunt and tumbled to the grass with Rory. Next to them, the SAS men dropped prone again and started returning fire. The reports from their rifle shots were deafeningly loud. Rory groped for his submachine gun, but found that he had dropped it, and the rounds snapping past his head made him disinclined to look around for it right now.

'I'm hit,' the SAS captain said in an almost conversational tone. Rory looked over to the man to see the expression on his face. He didn't looked panicked or in pain, but surprised.

Major Singh appeared next to them. He grabbed Rory by the belt with one hand and the SAS captain's web gear with the other. Then he hauled them both off the ground and dashed away from the incoming fire. Rory didn't even have time to yelp in surprise. Even with four hundred pounds to carry, Major Singh was twenty-five yards behind the line of SAS men in a matter of seconds. There was a little depression in the terrain, and the Lion deposited Rory and the SAS captain in it carefully. 'Medic to my position,' he shouted, a deep and sonorous roar that momentarily cut through the cacophony of the gunfire.

Two SAS soldiers came out of the darkness and dropped next to Rory and the captain. 'You hurt, sir?'

'I don't think so.' Rory patted himself down to check for bullet holes, but came up clean. 'But the captain's hit.'

'The enemy has a concealed trench line parallel to the

northern runway edge,' Major Singh said. 'A very well concealed trench. I didn't see it until they moved their GPMG up into position, right before they opened fire. Contact *Glamorgan* and have them send a barrage. Tell them to shift their fire a hundred yards north from the last volley.'

'Yes, sir,' the SAS soldier said and dashed off. The other SAS man had taken off his pack and was already working on the captain, whose surprised expression had at last shifted to one of extreme discomfort.

For a little while when he had rendered the Argentine aircraft inert from a distance, Rory had felt as if he had his thumb on the scale, that he was making a difference. Right now, that feeling had dissipated completely. He tried to stay as low to the ground as he could. All around him, the SAS were shooting at the Argentinian defenders. The troop with them was made up of only a dozen commandos, and one of them was wounded on the ground in front of him, but it seemed implausible that eleven rifles could produce such world-ending noise. Rory felt as if he had been dropped into the middle of World War Three. He had no idea what to do or where to be.

Major Singh didn't have any problem working out his role on the battlefield. With the captain out of commission and the major with another troop on a hill several hundred yards away, the remaining SAS men deferred to the Silver Helix agent without hesitation.

'Fall back to Boat Troop's position by squads, bounding overwatch. And what is that blasted destroyer waiting for?'

As if on cue, the first shells from *Glamorgan*'s renewed barrage exploded at the edge of the airstrip, and this time Rory felt the tremors of the detonations travelling through the ground below him. They were like hammer blows from a very pissed-off deity – the short, sharp whistling of an incoming shell followed by the concussion of the high-explosive frag-mentation warhead. The small arms fire from the Argentinian defenders instantly slackened off and then faded into silence.

'They're getting back under cover,' Major Singh said. 'All squads, disengage and rally at the exfiltration assembly point. We have forty-five minutes to reach the aircraft.'

'Come on, Archimedes.' The big Sikh walked up to Rory and pulled him to his feet. 'You made this a victory. Let's not have the enemy turn it into a defeat.'

The SAS captain in charge of Mountain Troop had been shot in the lower back. He was unable to stand or walk, and they had brought no stretchers to carry out the wounded.

'You lads get back to the helicopters and leave me here with a few flares,' the captain said, his face a grimace of suppressed agony. 'I'll make sure the Argies find me. I'll see you all in England when this bloody war is over.'

'That is a load of noble nonsense, Captain,' Major Singh said. 'Corporal, give the man his second morphine dose. I will carry him back with us. And there will be no discussion about this. Now get a move on, everyone. There isn't any time for St Crispin's Day speeches right now.'

♣

They speed-marched across the dark landscape faster than Rory had ever marched before. The SAS squads took turns guarding the rear of the spread-out column, and every five minutes they switched places. That meant they had to cover four times the distance Rory did, but he was still close to the limits of his physical endurance. Next to him, Major Singh strode along without any signs of fatigue, even though he was carrying the wounded SAS captain. They had left their mortars and all their heavy ammunition behind, and every other man just carried a weapon and a light assault pack. Nobody knew exactly how large the Argentine garrison was, or whether they had the fortitude to chase a squadron of elite SAS commandos across the island in the dark, but the SAS men all went by the book as though they had a thousand angry enemy marines on their heels.

They reached the helicopters with just ten minutes left in their exfiltration window. The major in charge held brief tactical counsel with the troop leaders and Major Singh, but everyone decided to proceed with the exfiltration rather than return to the airstrip to attack the defenders again and attempt to claim the field entirely. Rory had never been so relieved in his life as when they boarded the Sea Kings and took off for the relative safety of HMS *Hermes*.

The mood on the flight back to the carrier was very different from the ingress. The men were laughing and joking as if they hadn't just exchanged live fire with the enemy in actual battle. The wounded SAS captain was doped up on morphine, but conscious, and he gave Rory a weak thumbs-up when he saw him looking.

'You're a bloody hero, sir,' one of the SAS sergeants sitting across the troop compartment shouted to Rory. 'You won't have to buy a pint for yourself again until we're back in Portsmouth. The Special Air Service will make sure of that.'

Rory smiled and returned the commando's grin. He was glad to have played the role he had. It had felt good and right, exactly the sort of thing he had hoped to do when he had joined the Silver Helix. He had saved lives and used his ace power without hurting or killing anyone. But when he looked at the SAS captain who had taken a round to the back to keep him safe, his satisfaction was considerably tempered.

Phase IV: Bomb Alley
North Falkland Sound, May 21st, 1982

During the days after the Pebble Beach raid, Rory was treated like a celebrity in the fleet, and for a little while he came close to believing that he deserved at least some of the applause.

The Pebble Beach mission had been a resounding success. Rory had destroyed all six light attack aircraft and four reconnaissance planes. The shelling from HMS *Glamorgan* had taken out the ammo and fuel dumps. There were still Argentine troops on the ground at the airfield, but those were of little concern to Admiral Woodward and his staff, now that the Argentinian air threat from that part of the islands was completely neutralized. And thanks to Rory – Archimedes, as everyone now called him without hesitation – the operation had gone down with no British casualties except the wounded SAS captain, who had been flown out to the hospital ship to be airlifted back to the UK.

'The Black Buck raids tore up the runway at Stanley, and our lads are flying combat air patrol around the clock between us and there,' the admiral told the assembled staff officers at the invasion briefing. 'Thanks to Archimedes, the enemy will have no use of landing strips on the islands any more. Whatever airpower they bring to bear will have to come from the mainland, and they will be at the very limits of their operational range. Therefore, we are accelerating the invasion schedule to beat the winter weather. Operation Sutton begins tomorrow at 2300 hours. We will land 3 Commando Brigade as planned at San Carlos and work our way south from there once we have established a beachhead.'

He turned his attention to Rory, who was starting to get used to being the centre of attention. 'Archimedes is going to land with the Royal Marines commandos on Fanning Head at San Carlos and take a position on the high ground overlooking Falkland Sound and the inlet of Port San Carlos,' he said and indicated the places on the projected wall map. 'They expect us to land at Stanley, on the other side of the island. It will take them until daybreak to realize that we're coming from the opposite side. But once they do, they'll send the rest of their planes from the mainland bases to bomb the landing craft. They will throw everything they have left at that beachhead. Your job is to make sure they don't succeed. Our ships will have little space to manoeuvre in that narrow sound. You have demonstrated that you can disable those aircraft faster and more reliably than the Seacat missiles from the surface ships. Drop their planes out of the sky before they can release their bombs.'

This was on a different scale from Pebble Beach. That raid had been a squadron of SAS, only forty-five men and two helicopters. This was a full-scale amphibious landing, five thousand men plus equipment, ferried onto the landing beaches by dozens of ships. It would be a target-rich environment for the Argentines. But the admiral's esteem of Rory had risen immensely since Pebble Beach, and the rest of the officer corps on *Hermes* had treated him with far more respect and deference than before. Nobody had addressed him merely as 'Sub-Lieutenant' since that night, and Rory didn't want to give them a reason to doubt his abilities. Besides, the frigates and destroyers supporting the landing craft would have their own air defence missiles and guns, and the marines would bring shoulder-fired ones to shore when they landed, so he took comfort in the knowledge that he was far from being the only anti-air asset for the landing.

'We'll keep the lads safe,' Rory replied. 'Whatever it takes.'

'You are an asset now. I will send you out with D Squadron again. They'll be tasked with clearing your observation post and keeping you safe.'

'What about Major Singh, sir?'

'Major Singh will be needed to augment and assist 2 Para when they land at San Carlos. Have no fear, the SAS lads will take good care of you. Just make sure you make it worth the investment. We are scrapping one of the recon missions at Darwin to free up D Squadron for your use.'

'Yes, sir.' The thought of going into battle this time without the reassuring presence of the Lion nearby made Rory anxious. But Silver Helix or not, he was still a junior officer, and when the admiral told you to jump, it was best to be in the air before asking for an altitude parameter.

'This is it. If we do this right, we'll have the Union Jack flying over Stanley again within a week or two. I don't know about you, gentlemen, but I'd rather prefer to be on the way home once the bad weather sets in down here. See to your units and prepare for executing Operation Sutton in twenty-eight hours. *Dismissed.*'

◆

D Squadron, 22 SAS Regiment, seemed to have adopted Rory as their personal ace and good-luck charm. They kitted him out in the same gear they were wearing, which was considerably better than what the Paras or even the Royal Marines were issued with. The submachine gun he received was integrally suppressed, they fitted him for splinter protection armour, and – as promised – he got his own set of night vision goggles. When they boarded their helicopters for the main assault after nightfall the next day, Rory felt a little better knowing that he was protected by the best the British Armed Forces had to offer, but the memory of the brief but violent engagement at Pebble Beach kept the fear simmering in the back of his brain. The raid had been a prelude. This was full-out war, everything they could put on the board against everything the enemy had. Rory spent the last few hours before the start of the operation writing the letters he had been holding off on since they left Portsmouth. Before, he thought they'd bring bad luck and maybe cause the event for which they were contingencies. After Pebble Island, he had changed his mind. One letter to his parents, one each to his siblings, all crafted as well as he could to soften the blow of his death, should it happen, and give them something to remember him by. It was much harder than he had expected, harder even than gearing up for the battle itself, and when he had finished, he felt emotionally drained.

They took off from the darkened deck of *Hermes* an hour

after local sunset. Before Rory stepped through the door of the Sea King, he looked out over the ocean to starboard, which was full of ships, all running with dimmed position lights. *So many ships, so many lives at stake.*

The weather was better on this flight. The Sea King didn't get buffeted as it had in the raid a week earlier, and Rory kept most of his dinner in this time. He knew most of the men of D Squadron by name and sight now, but he still missed seeing Major Singh. This would be the first time out on his own as a Silver Helix operative, and naturally it would be in support of the biggest amphibious invasion the Royal Navy and Marines had staged in almost forty years.

Their target zone was a hilltop called Fanning Head. It overlooked the San Carlos estuary, where the amphibious landing ships would soon be making their way to shore, slow and vulnerable and loaded with hundreds of Royal Marines and Army paratroopers. As they approached the hilltop, their escorts, smaller and more nimble Gazelle helicopters, rushed ahead to scout the landing zone. Rory sat near the front of the Sea King's cargo bay, close to the cockpit, so he could see outside through the front canopy. Out of the darkness, tracer rounds reached up, streams of glowing fireflies, and connected with one of the Gazelles just as it crested the hill. The Gazelle banked hard to the left and dropped out of sight.

'Incoming fire!' the pilot shouted. 'Going evasive. Hang on to something, lads.'

The second Gazelle, somewhere out of sight on the port side of their Sea King, opened fire with its rocket pods. The unguided rockets streaked towards the hilltop, but Rory didn't see the results of the impacts because their pilot had initiated a sharp banking turn to starboard. The helicopter raced down the slope of the hill, away from the incoming fire.

'We'll have to abort!' the pilot shouted. 'There's Argie infantry on the hilltop.'

'You put this son of a bitch down right now!' the SAS major

in charge shouted back from his jump seat just behind the cockpit bulkhead. 'We'll take care of the infantry.'

'Ten seconds,' the pilot replied without argument.

'Lock and load!' the major shouted. All over the cargo hold, SAS soldiers cycled the bolts on their submachine guns.

'You stay between me and Corporal Park,' the burly sergeant sitting next to Rory shouted. 'Do what I say when I say it.'

The helicopter touched down hard. The corporal sitting next to the nearest sliding door was out of the craft even before all the wheels had fully settled, and the rest of the section piled out of the Sea King after him. Outside, there was immediate small-arms fire.

'Come along now, right behind me.' The burly sergeant pulled Rory along, and they left the cargo hold. As soon as they were outside, the sergeant pushed Rory into the prone position.

'Don't get up unless someone tells you to,' the sergeant said as he took up a firing position close to Rory. 'And you bloody well better hope they tell you in English and not Spanish.'

♠

The fire-fight was brief. There was only a small Argentinian team on this hilltop, and they only put up token resistance in the face of opposition from a full SAS squadron. Some fell, most of the rest ran, and a few surrendered when they saw they were outnumbered and outgunned. The SAS men secured the hilltop and stripped the Argentinian soldiers of weapons. These were the first enemy troops Rory had seen face-to-face. They looked tired and haggard in the light from the SAS field torches.

'Left us some gear,' one of the SAS troopers said. The Argentines had set up an observation post – three tents, a few trenches, a mortar pit, recoilless rifle positions, and a number of radios connected to a twenty-foot antenna that was whipping in the stiff breeze.

'Signal the naval gunfire support that we have control of

Fanning Head,' the major ordered. Everything the SAS did was efficient and businesslike, right down to collecting and stacking the discarded rifles from the surrendering Argentinians.

'Two and a half hours until daylight,' the major continued. 'Time for you to set up your stuff, Archimedes. I guarantee you that these skies will be thick with aircraft as soon as the Argies work out where the landings are.'

♥

They had brought three different sets of observation binoculars and tripods in the Sea King. The SAS unloaded the gear and helped Rory set everything up. This was equipment usually built for artillery observation, but today Rory had a different use for it. He lined one of the high-powered binocular tripods up so he could see down a large part of the length of Falkland Sound, the most likely approach route for enemy aircraft. The other two went to face to the west and northwest respectively. This way, Rory had two hundred degrees of magnified vision from this spot. The SAS manned a security perimeter, and three of them set up their own radio sets. They were ready for action just as the sky in the east started getting light. Overnight, dozens of amphibious ships had moved to the shoreline of the inlet below them, and almost as many frigates and destroyers were out in the Sound, screening the vulnerable troop carriers. The retaking of the Falklands had begun in earnest.

♣

The sunrise was almost beautiful. Rory watched the scene in the Sound below from the hilltop observation post. Most of the troops had landed by the time the sun peered over the mountaintops to the east, and now the landing ships unloaded the heavy equipment, vehicles and light armour. Out in Falkland Sound, the frigates had taken up station in a rough line that extended for several miles. Any enemy plane coming up the Sound would have to run the gauntlet of their air defences before they got to the transports, but the frigates would also have to bear the brunt of the bombing runs.

'Tea, sir,' one of the SAS men said behind him. Rory turned to see that the commandos had set up their personal folding stoves to heat water. The soldier handed him a mess tin that had steam rising from it.

'Thank you, Sergeant.' Rory took the hot tin, grateful to have something to warm himself up. The wind up here bit even through the many layers he was wearing. It was bearable if you moved around, but standing still and watching the horizon was freezing business.

It was just after ten in the morning when the first Argentine plane appeared in the sky over Falkland Sound. A single jet popped over a mountain ridge to the southwest, changed course sharply, and dropped low over the water. The roar from its jet engines reverberated from the hillsides.

'Light attack plane, bearing two-twenty, coming in right above the water,' one of the SAS observers said, already tracking the target with the super-powered binoculars mounted on one of the tripods. 'He's got underwing ordnance.'

Rory got behind the eyepiece of his own stationary binoculars. It took maddeningly long to find the plane through the high-power optics. The Argentine plane was a light jet, slender and graceful, with a pointy nose and bulbous tanks on the wingtips. It roared up the Sound at what had to be full throttle. There were cylindrical objects under the wings, but Rory couldn't tell whether they were fuel tanks, bombs, or rocket pods. He focused his attention and felt the familiar light dizziness as the electromagnetic energy between him and the distant plane built up. Just as he was about to direct an EMP blast at the nose of the aircraft, the pilot pulled up from his suicidally low approach run, and Rory lost him with the binoculars as the plane rapidly gained altitude in the middle of the Sound.

'*Fuck!*' Rory shouted. He didn't bother trying to reacquire the plane with the optics. Instead, he shielded the left side of his face with his hand against the morning sun and looked out over the Sound with just his eyes. By now, the Argentine plane was within half a mile of the southernmost ship in the screen.

'He's making a run on *Argonaut*,' someone said behind him. 'Take him down, take him down!'

The Argentine plane levelled out and dipped its nose towards the water once more to line up whatever weapon he was about to release. There was a distant pop and a whooshing sound coming from the frigate, and an anti-air missile left the launcher mounted on the side of the ship. At the same time, Rory let loose a strong blast of EMP energy in the direction of the plane. It must not have been quite as focused as he had intended, because both the plane and the missile racing to meet it went haywire at the same time. The plane spun around its longitudinal axis until it flew inverted. The missile cork-screwed wildly and splashed harmlessly into the water five hundred yards from the frigate and its intended target. Rory knew that the pilot had just lost everything in his cockpit that had an electric wire connected to it – every screen, instrument, radio. He still had his flight controls, though, and he managed to roll the plane upright just a second or two before it hit the water. At this distance, Rory didn't see the canopy blow off the plane's fuselage just before the splash of the impact, but the orange and olive-green parachute canopy that bloomed in the sky a moment later was hard to miss. The pilot had managed to eject at the last second.

'Splash one!' an SAS lad shouted, and the rest of them cheered as if someone had scored at a football match. Except that Rory was trying for the opposite – he was there to stop anyone scoring. He was the goalkeeper right now.

'*Argonaut* says they've lost their radar,' the SAS radioman reported. 'They are swapping positions with *Antelope*.'

Whoops, Rory thought. The Argentine pilot hadn't gotten any ordnance off before Rory shut him down, but part of *Argonaut* must have been caught in the slightly unfocused blast he had panic-fired at the attacking plane.

The sounds of anti-aircraft gunfire and jet engines ebbed. Far out in the middle of Falkland Sound, *Argonaut* halted her forward motion, then started steaming backwards. Another frigate, presumably *Antelope*, had changed course and was heading towards *Argonaut*. The Argentine pilot's parachute was in the water now, but the hull of *Argonaut* blocked Rory's view of it. He hoped they were fishing the pilot out of the water before he drowned.

The respite did not last very long. Maybe ten minutes later, the next Argentine plane appeared, and this one had brought company. The two-plane flight came over the ridge that bordered Falkland Sound and banked and dived at the task force at a much closer distance than the light recon plane that had come before them. These were much more lethal-looking, with triangular delta wings that had big bombs slung underneath, fighter planes obviously built for speed. This time, Rory didn't bother waiting for someone to call out a bearing or a type designation. He focused on the first plane and pushed all the energy he could muster into the pointed nose cone of the fighter jet. There was a bright flash and a muffled explosion. The sound only reached Rory a few seconds later, and by then the enemy pilot had pulled his jet into a steep climb. Presented with such an easy target, the frigates and destroyers of the screening force didn't need a special invitation. Heavy gunfire thundered across the Sound, half a dozen warships opening up with their gun mounts. Two of the frigates launched their Seacat missiles, which homed in on the stricken jet from two different directions. One shot past the plane and flew down Falkland Sound, where it splashed into the water far in the distance. The white smoke trail of the other Seacat converged with the plume of black smoke in the wake of the Argentine jet, which was still heavy with the bombs the pilot had failed to jettison. This time, Rory saw the canopy fly away from the sleek fuselage, and the pilot ejected just before the Seacat struck home and blew the plane apart in a brilliant plume of sparks and smoking parts.

The second Argentine jet had barrelled on undeterred, and it was fast, so much faster than the little plane that had made the first attack run on the *Argonaut*. It banked to the right, fired flares, then banked to the left and past *Argonaut*, which was still going in reverse. Then the pilot pulled up the nose of his plane and pointed it at the next ship in the screening line on the Sound, a destroyer. Rory focused and blasted the jet like he had the first one, but he was a fraction of a second too late. Two bombs detached from the triangular wings of the Argentine jet and tumbled through the air towards the British destroyer. One bomb skipped off the water and bounced past the destroyer's stern. The other one hit the hull in the aft quarter of the ship. Rory held his breath, expecting the huge explosion that was sure to follow. He could see the stern of the destroyer rocking from the impact of the heavy bomb, but it didn't blow up. The Argentine jet, its nose section now on fire, made a valiant attempt to line up on another British ship, maybe to fire its cannon or ram it, but the plane was too low and the pilot had too little control of his craft left. One wingtip clipped the surface of the water, and the plane cartwheeled into the sea with an enormous splash. As quickly as this latest duo of attackers had appeared, silence descended over the Sound again.

'Bomb didn't go off,' the SAS man next to Rory said in amazement. 'They released too low. Didn't give the fuse time to arm itself. Lucky buggers on that ship.'

'*Antrim* confirms they got hit by a dud,' the radioman called out. 'No word on damage yet, but it holed the hull.'

Rory sat down hard on the sandbags next to him. He felt as if he had the world's worst case of vertigo.

'Splash three,' the SAS sergeant said. 'Good job, mate. You okay?'

'I can't hold them off if they keep coming in like that,' Rory replied.

'Can't you blast them all at once?'

'Focus is too wide,' Rory replied. 'It's like a flashlight, see. The wider you make the beam, the more gets caught in it. I try to do two or three planes at once, I'll catch one of our ships in it too. They're coming in too bloody low.'

'They've got some guts, all right. Didn't think they had it in them.'

The battle had been on for fifteen minutes, and already Rory felt drained. Between him and the anti-air systems on the Navy ships, they had downed all three attacking aircraft, but two of the screening force ships were already damaged. *Antrim* had a hole in its hull, and *Argonaut*'s radar was out, probably because of his failure.

Overhead, two Royal Navy Harriers thundered past and headed down Falkland Sound. Rory and the SAS sergeant watched them climb as they flew over the formation of warships assembled on the Sound, then peel off to the southwest in search of targets.

'About time they turned up,' the SAS sergeant said.

The land battle around San Carlos was still being fought by the Royal Marines and the Army paratroopers. They could hear regular exchanges of small-arms fire from the hills on the far side of the inlet. The settlement of San Carlos wasn't even big enough to be called a town. It was just a handful of buildings that looked like a very spread-out farm. Armoured vehicles in British camouflage were advancing past the houses and into the hills beyond, and the beach was bustling with activity.

In the distance, Rory heard jet engines again. He hoped they belonged to the Harriers that had overflown them on their way south just a few minutes ago, but when the planes came over the hills to the southwest, their wings had triangle shapes, loaded with bombs. Rory saw the puffs from the cannons of the frigates on the south end of the formation as they started pumping shells towards the new attackers.

'Incoming air!' the SAS sergeant shouted. 'Two Daggers, bearing two-three-zero. Here we go again.'

Below them, Falkland Sound came alive once more with gunfire and the sound of anti-air missiles launching. Rory focused on the lead plane descending into the Sound and went back to work.

◆

For the next two hours, the Argentines came in like clockwork, a new pair of planes every ten minutes, then flights of four. Rory had never expended so much mental energy. Focusing his EMP blasts at targets several miles away took an enormous amount of concentration. He knocked down plane after plane, frying their electronics to slag and setting their wiring harnesses on fire. Most pilots ejected, but some went into the sea with their planes. And despite his best efforts, some of the Argentine jets still got close enough to strafe British ships with their guns or drop bombs. Most of the drops were misses, and almost all the rest didn't go off because the Argentinians came in low to avoid the curtain of gunfire and Seacat missiles the fleet threw at them. Rory dropped two planes from a four-plane flight into the ocean with one forceful EMP blast, but watched in horror as the other two Argentine jets lined up on a frigate and peppered her superstructure with cannon fire. Rory blasted one of the jets out of the sky just as it pulled out of its attack run and started to climb away. Then two missiles streaked in out of nowhere and connected with the remaining Argentine attack jet. It disintegrated in a thunderous explosion that echoed across the Sound. The remains of the wreck, carried by the momentum of the jet, ploughed into the hillside at the other end of the inlet. A moment later two Harriers streaked across

Rory's field of vision. They split up and banked away, one west and one east.

'*Antelope* is hit!' the radio operator in the tent behind them shouted.

'We can bloody well *see* that!' the SAS sergeant next to Rory shouted back. Out on the water, smoke came from the super-structure of the damaged frigate. The cannon shells had managed to set something on the ship on fire. But she was still in the fight, radar antenna spinning and gun turrets turning to point back towards the southwest end of the Sound.

Rory sat down on the sandbags with a groan. The SAS sergeant handed him a canteen, and he drank half of the water in one greedy gulp.

'You're doing brilliant,' the sergeant said. He picked up a stick and pointed at a row of marks he had scratched into the earth next to his binocular tripod. 'That was number thirteen out of fifteen.'

'We downed *fifteen* planes this morning?'

'*You* did. The Seacats and the Harriers got seven more. That's twenty-two down. They really want us off this beach, don't they?'

'How many bloody aircraft do they *have* in their air force?'

'I don't know for sure, sir. But I think we'll see most of them today at some point or another.'

♠

By the early afternoon, the Argentine planes had stopped coming. When an hour had passed without any attack runs, Rory allowed himself a little flash of optimism. *Maybe they did run out of planes.*

The SAS captain in charge of the troop came up to Rory's position.

'The ships are offloaded. The marines are advancing south towards Goose Green. There's a command post set up two klicks past the settlement,' he said. 'I suppose we can get off this hill now. Good work all round. You saved a lot of lives today.'

Rory thought about all the planes that had splashed into the waters of the Sound below them before the pilots had had a chance to eject. But their planes had been carrying bombs, and the British warships, for all their martial looks and intimidating weapons-bristling presence, were fragile and staffed by a lot of sailors. A few lives traded for many, but it was still a grim trade when you were the one whose thumb tipped that scale.

End Phase: Blood and Coffee
Goose Green, East Falkland Island,
May 25th, 1982

Back home in Scotland, Goose Green would barely register on a map. On the Falklands it was a town – its third-biggest settlement, in fact – but it consisted of only about two dozen buildings, clustered on a little peninsula jutting into Falkland Sound. It reminded Rory of the remote towns in the Highlands, the ones with one shop and one pub supporting populations of a hundred people and a thousand sheep. But after a whole week of camping out on wind-blown hilltops all along the shoreline as the British troops made their way south, the place looked like civilization to Rory.

While he was keeping away the Argentinian planes trying to make attacks on British ships and ground forces on their way south, the troops had prised Goose Green away from the Argentine troops that had dug in all around the town, and it had taken two bloody days and nights of hard fighting. But now the Union Jack was flying over the town hall again, there was a pile of surrendered Argentine rifles and machine guns sitting by the dock, and Rory stepped into a heated room for the first time since they had left *Hermes* to assault San Carlos.

'There's the walking weapons system,' Major General Moore greeted him when he walked into the command post set up in an old farmhouse. 'You have done fantastic work, Sub-Lieutenant.' Instead of returning Rory's salute, the general held out his hand. Rory accepted the handshake.

'Thank you, sir. I think I could sleep for a month straight now.'

The other officers and senior sergeants in the room, Army paratroopers and Royal Marines alike, looked just as tired as he felt. They were all in battle fatigues and still decked out in combat gear, and most of them were dirty and still had camouflage paint on their faces. He didn't dare ask how many they had lost in the fight, but he knew that medical evacuation flights had been leaving from the hills around Goose Green constantly since the end of the battle.

'If you are looking for your Silver Helix colleague, he's in the kitchen. You should get yourself some hot coffee while you're here. You bloody well earned it, I'd say,' the general said, but his smile looked hollow.

♥

'How is your war going?' Major Singh asked when Rory walked in. The Lion sat on a kitchen chair that looked far too rickety for the weight of the big Sikh. He looked exhausted as well. The major's boots and the hilt of his big knife were flecked with mud, and there were dark stains on the major's uniform that didn't look like sweat or spilled coffee. It seemed he'd had a very busy week with the Royal Marines.

Rory looked around for the promised coffee. There was a pot sitting on an electric heating plate on the counter nearby. The Lion pointed to a cupboard wordlessly. There were cups inside, and Rory took one out and filled it from the pot, trying hard to control himself and not just guzzle the stuff straight from the spout.

'To be honest, it has been the most boring and most terri-fying week of my life. Both at the same time, somehow, if that makes sense.'

'Yes, it does. Long periods of boredom interspersed with moments of sheer terror. That's what it's like to go to war.'

Rory took a sip and promptly burned the roof of his mouth, but the taste was so decadently delicious after a week of horrible instant coffee that he didn't care.

'Thirty-nine planes,' he told the Lion. 'They just kept coming. And I kept sending them into the water. Why did they keep coming? They had to notice that none were coming back.'

'They did their duty,' the Lion said.

'They fished out the ones that ejected. Some didn't. I saw a few of them go in, and no chute. Pilot and all.'

'And you find it bothers you.'

'Yes,' Rory said. 'It does. I killed those men. Of course it bothers me. I used my powers to *kill* people.'

'And it should,' Major Singh said. 'It will always bother you. Killing isn't a natural act. We do it because we must, not because we like it.'

Rory's gaze flickered to the kirpan on the Lion's belt. He knew that the weapon wasn't merely ceremonial, that Major Singh kept it honed to a shaving-sharp edge, and suddenly he found himself pitying the Argentine defenders who had stood between Singh and Goose Green. 'You've been to war before,' Rory said. 'You're used to it.'

'You never get used to it.' Major Singh stretched his legs with a sigh and took another sip of his own coffee. 'I was in 1 Para ten years ago,' the Lion continued. 'I was just twenty years old. It was during the Troubles, right after Bloody Sunday.'

A shiver ran down Rory's spine. Northern Ireland was still dangerous ground for British soldiers. Ten years ago it had been a free-fire war zone, car bombs and snipers and night-time assassinations.

'I went out on patrol with a few lads in a Land Rover, and

we got lost in a very bad neighbourhood. Ended up in the middle of a crowd. They turned the car over and set it on fire. That's when my card turned. I don't remember how I got out of the upturned car. I don't remember pulling everyone else out of the burning car. I don't remember how long it took me to fight my way through the crowd, or how long it took for reinforcements to find us. But I do remember the faces on the bodies of those I killed that day to save my comrades. All nine of them. I pity them, and the families that must have mourned for them. But I do not regret it.'

Major Singh turned his cup in his hands and held Rory's gaze with tired-looking but unwavering dark eyes. 'The men in those planes were brave beyond measure, and they meant to kill you. You and the people you were charged to protect. You did what you had to do. That's why you wanted to join the Silver Helix. To protect. To defend. And sometimes that means having to kill. That is something you must accept.'

The Lion got up and walked over to the counter to refill his cup. The top of his turban brushed the ceiling of the kitchen in the old farmhouse. 'Most people hear "Silver Helix", and they think of the flashy business they see on the telly. Aces flying or lifting girders off people. But most of what we do isn't flashy. It's going to ground with the lads and helping the cause. Think of all the men on those ships who *didn't* die because you were there. I know the thought doesn't help much right now, but it will. Later, after all of this is over. When you've had time to remember.'

He walked back to his chair and patted Rory on the shoulder on the way past. 'It's a good thing that you're bothered. I wouldn't like it much if you weren't. It tells me that you are right for the Silver Helix. When we get back to England, I'll tell Sir Kenneth that I endorse the removal of your probationary status.'

The news of his impending full acceptance into the Order, the professional validation he had sought ever since his card turned, would have made Rory feel proud and grateful at any other time than now, and anywhere else but this godforsaken, wind-beaten little patch of rocky ground in the North Atlantic. But after this week, his ability to feel anything but bone-deep tiredness seemed to have gone on extended leave.

'Thank you, sir,' he said to Major Singh. 'I will not disappoint you or the Order.'

Major Singh sat down again and nodded. 'You're welcome. You've earned it. But make sure that this sort of thing is what you want to do with the rest of your life. Because what you have seen here is not the worst you'll ever see. Not even close.'

♣

Outside, the newly hoisted Union Jack on the flagpole in front of the town hall whipped fiercely in the wind. In the brief time Rory had spent in the farmhouse kitchen with the Lion, the number of Royal Marines and paratroopers in the town seemed to have tripled. Overhead, Navy Harriers roared past towards the hills in the east, where the Argentinians were still holding on to Port Stanley, even though Rory knew their chances of winning this war had gone in the sea with all the planes he had splashed.

In the distance, Rory heard the distinctive whop-whop-whop rotor noise from Chinook transport helicopters, and the sound made Major Singh smile.

'It seems we will not have to walk all the way across this blasted island after all,' he said to Rory. 'Those are the transports from *Atlantic Conveyor*.'

A Royal Marines lieutenant came trotting up to them, one hand on his green beret to keep it from flying away in the wind.

'If you don't mind, sirs, General Moore is asking for you. Looks as if we're accelerating the schedule and going for Port Stanley early now that the choppers are off the boat safely.'

'We'll be right in,' Major Singh told the lieutenant, who nodded and trotted off without a salute. They were in the field, Rory reminded himself, in a shooting war. You don't salute on the battlefield because you don't want to tell the enemy marksmen who's important.

'Well then,' Major Singh said. 'Let's get this unpleasant business over with. I'm ready to go home. Until the next war.'

They walked up the muddy path to the town hall, the Union Jack on its pole flapping an urgent beat, like a tied-up animal frantically trying to shake itself free.

Until the next war, Rory thought. *Hope that one breaks out long after I'm retired.*

Twisted Logic

by Peter Newman

Part 1

London, 1984

ROGER GAVE HIS TEA a final stir as he waited for the Prime Minister's speech to begin. There were five minutes to go, which meant it would be the perfect temperature for sipping when he sat down to listen.

Though he wasn't the only one to have contributed to the speech, and though Mrs Thatcher was known to take what was written and make it her own, he felt proud. This was important work he was doing. He, Roger Barnes, was important. True, he hadn't been invited to watch the speech in person, but they were his words just the same. Words that would reach the ears of millions.

As a special treat he had bought himself a PYE Tube Cube so that he could watch the speech live in his office. The LED clock on the front displayed the time in glowing red. He frowned. It was fast. He checked his watch and wall clock to confirm.

Yes, nearly three minutes fast! Roger shook his head, disgusted. It was brand new and he'd only picked it up this morning. He'd never trusted digital. Despite the hype there was something cheap about it. Springs and cogs and craftsmanship would always be superior to plastic fads.

Still, the fact that it was wrong bothered him. He liked everything to be in its right place, performing perfectly. How else was one supposed to face the chaos of politics without a firm, ordered bedrock to stand on? He considered changing the clock but that would mean going back to his car to find the instructions and there wasn't time, and he wasn't the type to fiddle with the buttons and hope for the best. That was how accidents happened.

He glared at the clock and felt a twinge in his chest, sharp enough to make him gasp. It escalated quickly but faded equally swiftly, leaving him shocked and sweaty, but otherwise normal.

Two minutes before the speech was due to begin he turned on the television and adjusted the aerial until the lines were suitably crisp and the crackle had faded to an acceptable whisper.

Satisfied, he sat down, arranged his chair, and took a sip of his tea as Mrs Thatcher's face appeared on the screen. Even in black and white, and shrunk to fit a nine-inch square, she was impressive. There was an innate authority about her that was admirable, the sense that she knew exactly what she was doing.

'This year,' she began, 'as before in our history, we have seen men and women with brave hearts defying violence, scorning intimidation, and defending their rights to uphold our laws.'

The opening was met with applause and Roger smiled. He was pleased she'd kept the connection to history; suggesting the actions of the police and those who'd returned to work were not just right but inherently British, and that by extension, all right-thinking people would support them.

Given things had started so well, it was a surprise to Roger when the second wave of pain came. He clamped off a cry before it became a scream and gripped the table so hard the tea jumped in the cup, sloshing over the edge to fill the saucer.

'By their action, we have seen a new birth of leadership in Britain. And that is the most important thing, the most enduring thing, that is going to that come out of this coal strike.'

It felt as if his muscles were trying to peel themselves from the bone, and his skin was burning, as if he'd spent too long in the sun. His eyes went from Mrs Thatcher, who continued to talk as if everything was fine, to a picture of his family on the beach that he kept on his desk. He'd looked at it many times but never with such intensity.

Wendy's smile was awkward, lips curling up but pressed together. His wife had always been embarrassed about her teeth, said they made her look like a donkey, though he'd always thought that harsh. A rabbit perhaps but not a donkey. His children's smiles were much more genuine. Funny that he'd never appreciated that before, his attention normally taken by the ice-cream splodges on Roy and Christine's shorts.

It occurred to him that he might be about to die. Wendy had always said that if he didn't relax he'd have a heart attack. Perhaps this was it. But even as he had the thought, he realized the pain was receding.

There was a tap on the door.

'Come in.'

Alan's head appeared. Like the rest of him it looked smart, conservative, and old before its time. 'Everything all right in here?'

'Oh, yes, everything's fine.'

'Sorry, thought I heard a noise.'

'Ah, yes. Sorry. That was me. Having a little trouble with my television.'

'Portables! I can never get the bloody things to stay in tune. Seems like all I have to do is fart and mine goes on the blink.'

Roger gave a strained smile. He didn't really approve of Alan's constant toilet references. 'Mmm.'

'You watching the speech? So are we. Want to come and see it with the rest of the exiles?'

'No, thank you.'

'We have beer.'

'No. Thank you.'

'Suit yourself.'

He breathed a sigh of relief as Alan went. The man meant well but seemed to have no idea that some people might actually enjoy their own company. At least he'd learned to knock before coming in. It had taken two years to teach him that trick. It had taken the dog two months.

Berating himself for thinking about Alan while the Prime Minister was speaking, he turned back to the television.

'. . . And the national interest demands, that violence does not pay and be seen not to pay. Let violence cease. Let the law be kept. That is the spoken and unspoken hope and wish of millions of our fellow citizens.'

It sounded good, but he'd missed the middle section. Had she seeded the idea that what the miners had done was not picketing at all? It was one of the key points to victory, to change the perception of the picketers from victims defending their way of life, to thugs holding the nation to ransom. Damn Alan! He'd come at the worst time.

The third wave of pain came so suddenly, so powerfully, that Roger didn't even have time to brace himself. Several screams escaped him. The first from shock, the second from his head striking the desk, the third when he hit the floor. There may have been a fourth or even fifth, Roger wasn't sure. He'd lost count at some point.

Everything went white, then black, then white again, before fading. Was he dead? Was this the heart attack? Details began to return: an off-white ceiling in dire need of a repaint. A little patch of damp that he'd not noticed before but would now never unsee, and a small spider hurriedly trying to spin a new web before the cleaners came.

He was on his back. There was no pain any more but he felt odd, light-headed, as if he hadn't eaten enough. Someone was knocking repeatedly on his door. 'Rog? Roger? You in there? It's Alan. If you don't answer I'm coming in.'

'Give me a minute!'

Was it his imagination or did his voice sound different somehow? Perhaps it was all the screaming. A wave of shame hit him. What was he going to say to Alan? With effort, he hauled himself upright, and then sat back on the chair. The family picture had fallen over and he set it upright, relieved to find no cracks in the glass.

'Roger?'

He didn't bother turning to the door as it opened. 'I'm fine, Alan. Honestly.'

'It sounded like someone was torturing a pig in here.'

'I had a chest pain. It's passed now.'

'You should see a doctor about that.'

He sighed. 'I'm sure Wendy would agree with you.'

'Look, why don't you slip out now, take the afternoon off?'

'Absolutely not.'

'They're all at the conference anyway. Nobody would know.'

Roger spun round, appalled. 'I would know.'

Instead of replying, Alan took a step backwards in horror, one hand going to his mouth. 'Christ!'

Roger looked over his shoulder, expecting to see a rat or a spider, or worse, some terrible news story breaking on the television. But everything looked as it always did. 'What is it?'

Alan was standing in the corridor, a shaky finger pointing at Roger. 'Your face . . . it's . . . oh God . . .' He looked as if he was about to be sick, and then swallowed hard, backed off until he hit the opposite wall, and ran.

With a horrible sinking feeling, Roger tried to catch a glimpse of his reflection in the television screen. Something was definitely off, there were blotches, but it was hard to see details. He hurried to the toilets at the end of the corridor. There was a frantic conversation going on in one of the meeting rooms, but the occupants fell suddenly quiet as he went by.

At the door, he paused and looked back over his shoulder. Nobody was in sight but he could see little tufts of brown littering the carpet. He knelt down to peer at them only to discover they were clumps of hair. His hair. He reached a shaking hand up towards his scalp and a fuzzy cloud drifted down past his eyes, reminding him of dandelions shedding in a summer breeze.

'Oh God,' he whispered, and stumbled into the toilets.

Bright lights and a mirror revealed the harsh truth. Most of his hair had gone, large patches of his skin as well, peeling off to reveal something else underneath.

There was no pain. Roger told himself that had to be a good thing, though his mind was already turning over the idea of nerve damage. He leaned closer, brushing away the last flakes on his cheek. Where pasty white flesh had been, his face was rendered a rich brown, dark grained, solid. He pressed it with a finger.

There was no give there at all, and though he felt the contact, it was distanced, muted. It was as if someone had carved his likeness out of mahogany but left out the hair because it was too difficult. He made a fist, and sure enough, wooden knuckles parted the dry skin, poking through.

The next thing he knew, he was running, back down the corridor and into his office, slamming the door shut behind him. 'I'm in shock,' he mumbled to himself. 'Perfectly under-standable.' He went to his abandoned cup of tea and had a sip but immediately spat it out. It tasted disgusting! He put the cup down harder than intended and the handle snapped off in his hand.

He stared at it for a few moments, and then began to cry.

Wendy. He needed to call Wendy. She'd know what to do. He picked up the phone but there was no ring tone. That struck him as unusual. Perhaps he could use Alan's phone.

He was halfway to the door when it was opened by a man in a suit Roger had seen on the news many times before. He was six foot six even without the turban that threatened to brush the ceiling, with the kind of physique normally found in American action film stars. A long dark beard covered the buttons of his shirt, and there was a kindness to his eyes. His name was Ranjit Singh but to most of the world he was known as the Lion, one of the aces who served the Silver Helix. Though it was hardly necessary, the Lion flashed a badge. Roger failed to take in the details as he was too busy trying to hide his face.

'Don't come in!' said Roger.

The Lion waited outside. 'Mr Barnes?'

'Yes?'

'Please stay calm, I'm here to help you.'

Roger lowered his hands a fraction. 'Help me? Have you looked at me?'

'Yes. We're aware of your condition. You're a victim of the Xenovirus Takis-A.'

'The wild card virus?'

'Yes, Mr Barnes. You need to come with me.'

'I'm sorry but I have to call my wife.'

'You need to come with me, Mr Barnes.'

Roger looked at the Lion, realizing for the first time that he hadn't come alone. At least two other shadows fell across the back wall. 'Of course, I'll just pack my things.'

'Mr Barnes, that will not be necessary.'

The subtext was obvious: he wouldn't be needing them where he was going.

'Oh,' said Roger as he allowed himself to be led away.

♣

A few days passed by in a blur of shock and tests, the bad news forming a list in his mind as bland facts, too big to process:

He had turned into some kind of freak.

He was not allowed to see Wendy.

He was not allowed to see his children.

He was not allowed to call anyone.

He was not allowed to leave the room.

His world had shrunk down to four walls and a bed, the kind of chamber given to a criminal or, judging from the padding on the walls, a psychotic. Doctors came and went at odd times, peppering him with questions about how he felt while prodding him, examining him, checking reflexes and vital signs.

They couldn't find a heartbeat. That was the thing he found hardest. The stethoscopes were unable to detect anything, and so far the needles they'd tried had simply bent against his wooden skin. When he asked the doctors about the results of his chest X-ray, they paled and mumbled words like 'inconclusive' before hurrying away.

One shower had washed away the last remnants of his old self. Eyebrows, body hair, all of it gone, from legs, chest, and armpits, even the irritating ones on the inside of his nose, though that was poor consolation. His skin had gone too, replaced by living wood, hard and smooth.

The door opened and Roger sighed. Nobody had bothered to knock since he'd come here. A doctor entered with a trolley. 'Hello, Mr Barnes. How are you feeling?'

'The same.'

She nodded and picked up a clipboard. 'Has your appetite come back?'

'Not really.'

'I see. Have you experienced any light-headedness, dizziness, anything like that?'

'No.'

She made a note, then looked at him. 'I'd like to know what your health was like before your infection. We have your blood type and medical history on file, but I was wondering about exercise. Did you play any sports?'

'Not since school.'

'Did you cycle?'

'No.'

'Run?'

'Only for the bus.' He smiled but she didn't return it.

'I'll put no formal exercise.'

'Yes, that's probably for the best.'

She took a bar from the trolley and passed it to him. 'I'm going to add weights to this to see what you can lift.'

Roger sighed. He hated this sort of thing. He'd never been the tallest or strongest of men, and so had been quite relieved to reach an age at which he was judged on his brain rather than his ability to cartwheel or kick a ball.

The first weights were light and he lifted them easily. The doctor added more. She hadn't given her name, but then, none of them had. After the first two, he'd given up asking.

She added more weights. He lifted those too, straight above his head. 'How am I doing?'

'Very well, Mr Barnes. You've just lifted two hundred pounds. You've never trained before?'

'Never.'

She made another note and they went on. Every so often, she asked if he was tired. He wasn't. There was no sweat, no breathlessness. Did he even do those things now?

They had just reached five hundred pounds when the door opened to reveal the Lion.

'Is there a problem?' asked the doctor.

'No problem. Mr Barnes will be coming with me now.'

'What's going on?' asked Roger.

'You'll see, Mr Barnes.'

'Where am I going?'

'No time for questions. It doesn't do to keep *him* waiting.'

◆

An hour later, Roger found himself being shown into a small but well-furnished study that smelled of books and cigars. Two padded leather chairs faced each other, inviting. One seemed to be for him but he didn't immediately go to it as he was too busy staring at the occupant of the one opposite.

If anything, Sir Winston Churchill was more impressive up close than he was on the television. The man was big in every sense of the word. He filled the chair, he filled the room, he filled Roger's vision.

'Thank you,' Churchill rumbled, and the Lion slipped out, closing the door with a soft click.

To Roger's amazement, Churchill stood and offered his hand. 'Barnes, isn't it?'

'Yes, sir,' replied Roger, surprised at the firmness of the other man's grip. 'It's an honour, sir.'

'If things go well, Barnes, the honour will be mine. Now sit down, and try not to gape, man, you're not here to catch flies.'

Roger closed his mouth and sank into the chair.

'Brandy?'

'No, thank you, Sir Winston.'

Churchill made a huffing noise and poured one for himself before sitting down opposite Roger. 'I know you've gone through a bit of an ordeal recently but I have a favour to ask of you, Barnes, a big one. There's no dressing it up, so I'm going to come straight out and ask if you'll do it.'

Ever since he was a boy, Roger had worshipped Churchill. As a man, he still admired him. Preparing a speech for the former PM was every writer's dream, and so it was with great restraint that he answered: 'I'll certainly listen to what you have to say, sir.'

'Good. That's all one can ask. Do you know what it takes to win a war?'

'I'd imagine it would involve a number of factors. Superior tactics and intelligence, better numbers and more advanced equipment. I doubt any single element is essential but the right combination . . .' He noticed the other man's scowl and trailed off, realizing too late that the question had been rhetorical.

'Wrong,' Churchill boomed. 'It all comes down to sacrifice. Men and women willing to risk their lives in order for our cherished society, our freedom, and our liberty to endure. The question is, are you one of those men?'

Roger rather suspected that he was not. 'Excuse me, sir, but I wasn't aware we were at war any more.'

'There are many types of war. The one I refer to is a war of ideology, of the rule of law versus fear. The enemy I speak of is the Twisted Fists.'

Roger had of course heard of the Twisted Fists, a terrorist organization that killed people in retaliation for attacks on those unfortunates mutated by the wild card virus. His eyes widened as he began to realize what Churchill was asking him.

'You see our problem, don't you? To bring down these murderers we need to get someone on the inside. The trouble is that their leader, Black Dog, doesn't recruit from the unin-fected. Only survivors that have been changed, as you have been changed, are of interest to him. To use the language of the man on the street, we need a joker. Barnes, I am asking you to be that joker, to be our undercover eyes and bring down the Twisted Fists.'

He shook his head. 'I can't become a terrorist, sir. I have a family that depends on me, and besides, I don't know the first thing about . . . well, I wouldn't even know where to start.'

'If you did this for your country, I would see to it that your family were provided for. Can you say the same?'

'I'm not sure I follow, sir.'

'Do you think you will keep your position in light of your transformation?' He took a sip of brandy as Roger's face fell. 'My own encounter with Xenovirus Takis-A has given me a more enlightened view of your predicament. However, I am no longer the Prime Minister, nor am I your immediate employer.'

They were going to fire him. Of course they were. Jokers were less than popular in the press, seen at best as a problem and at worst a plague. He tried to imagine getting another job that wasn't menial and buried his face in his hands. 'Oh God.'

'I would have your answer.'

'But if I did this, I'd become a criminal.'

'Yes. As far as the public were concerned, you would be a Twisted Fist. A terrorist. A murderer.'

'Can I at least tell Wendy?'

'Certainly not. To ensure this remains secret, only you and I will know the truth.'

'She'll despise me. My children will think I'm a monster!'

'Yes, they will. But we have no one else. You are a right-thinking man, one of us. You are also a joker. Do you know how rare that makes you?'

'I'm sorry, sir. I can't do it.'

Churchill leaned forward in his chair, making it creak ominously. 'You would prefer to stand by and do nothing? The Fists kill five innocents for each joker that has suffered. When the next strike happens, how will you sleep knowing all of that blood is on your hands? That you could have been the shield that stood between them and death?'

He wanted to say that it was the killers that would be responsible, not him, but somehow, a few feet from Churchill's quivering jowls, it seemed inadequate. It occurred to him that Alan's cousin had been killed by the Twisted Fists two years ago. As an employee of the government, all of them and their immediate families were at high risk of Fist retaliation.

Had anyone else asked he would probably have refused but Churchill was more than just a man: he was a living piece of history and a national treasure.

He gave a long sigh. 'If I do this, you'll protect my family?'

'You have my word.'

'And if anything happens to me, you'll tell them the truth about what I've done?'

Churchill nodded. 'When this is over, and the Twisted Fists have been brought to justice, I will tell the world,' he smiled, 'and your wife, that you are a hero.'

'All right,' said Roger. 'I'll do it.'

'Are you sure? When you leave this room, there will be no

turning back. This is a long and dark path I am setting you upon, with only my thanks, and the knowledge that you are serving your country, to warm you in the nights ahead.'

'I understand.'

'Then let me offer you my hand once more, in friendship.'

Roger took it, clinging to Churchill the way a drowning man grasps at a lifeline. All too soon, he was dismissed. As he stepped from the room, the door closed behind him with a click, final.

♣   ♦   ♠   ♥

Twisted
Logic

Part 2

London, 1986

ONLY ONE OF THE lights still worked in the back of the van and it was struggling, cutting out for a second every time they hit a bump in the road. In some ways nothing had changed since the virus had taken his life from him. He'd gone from being a test subject in Churchill's secret facility to part of a UK cell of the Twisted Fists. Both seemed to involve a lot of time in poorly lit places, and doing what you were told.

'Any questions?' asked Blister. Even muffled by bandages, his accent was strange. Part American, part something else Roger couldn't place. The man had clearly travelled a lot, though Roger doubted it was by choice.

Bird picked her nose with the fused remains of her right hand. 'What are we having for dinner after?'

Nobody laughed. A lot of the Fists thought Bird was funny but Blister didn't. It was one of the reasons Roger liked him. He ignored her and turned to Roger. 'What about you, Green Man?'

Green Man. That was who he was to the Fists. They all took on other names, rejecting their pasts and the society that no longer served them. He had no idea who Bird or Blister used to be, and probing anyone on their personal history was discouraged. Perhaps that was why it was so difficult to make any inroads into the group.

Time had passed. Two years since he'd seen Wendy or his children and it felt more like ten. He was finding it harder and harder to remember who Roger Barnes was. Roger didn't condone violence. Roger wasn't a killer. Roger paid his taxes and obeyed the law. Green Man was a different case altogether.

There was always a justification for the things he had done. The first time he'd killed had been to prove his loyalty – nobody was truly considered a member of the Twisted Fists until they had participated in a successful strike. And after that? Roger found it didn't much matter after the first. He looked down at his hands, remembering how hard it had been to scrub the stains from the grain in his fingers. This time he was going to sully them for promotion. The Fists were looking to elevate some of their best, and he and Bird were two of the most promising candidates.

Of all of them, only Blister had actually met the Black Dog, and there was no way to take down the Fists without getting close to their elusive leader. So, to save lives in the future, Roger was going to take some tonight. The irony was not lost on him.

'You with us, Green?'

'Sorry?' Roger glanced up to find Bird grinning at him.

'Blis asked if you had anything to say. What's up? You're usually well chatty.'

'I'm just getting my thoughts together, that's all.'

It wasn't that he didn't have questions, just that they were the wrong sort. "Is there not a better way?" and "How is this going to help our cause in the long term?" was not what the Fists wanted to hear.

'We're ten minutes out,' said Blister. 'Prepare yourselves.'

Bird unzipped a long bag to reveal a chainsaw mounted on

a bespoke harness. Roger's eyes widened as she began buckling it to her arm. He'd heard rumours that Bird was bloodthirsty but he'd always thought they'd been exaggerated. Apparently not.

'What you looking at, Green?'

'You're . . . you're not actually going to use that on people, are you?'

'Yep. It's quick and painful and messy. Pretty much the opposite of how you want your sex to be.' She laughed at his disapproving face. 'No good just killing a few nats, is it? We've gotta send a message, really put the shits up them, you know?'

He was appalled at how casual she was about the whole thing. But he was British and well brought up, so he nodded and said nothing.

Soon after, the van came to a stop, and Blister took up position by the side door, his silhouette lumpy, asymmetrical, more like a toddler's scribbled impression than an actual man. 'They took one of ours. See that you take five of theirs. We'll keep the engine running.'

The door slid open with a squeak, and Roger followed Bird outside. Run-down houses could be seen lining car-packed streets, all tinted an apathetic streetlight yellow. Many of the doors lacked numbers, but Roger was able to count across from one of the few that did, identifying the target's house. He opened the front gate a few seconds after Bird had vaulted it.

Watching her run, it struck him as strange that the virus that had changed him so fundamentally had done so little to her. Only one of her arms had been affected, the forearm stretched and the fingers crushed together into a sharp cone, so that it resembled a huge bird's wing, stripped of feathers. Admittedly, the resemblance was harder to spot now that a chainsaw had been attached to the end.

Where Roger tried to hide his altered appearance out of shame, Bird wore hers proudly, having stripped the sleeve from her leather jacket to better display her mutation. Just looking at her made him want to pull his hood further forward.

Bird hit the door at full tilt, smashing the cheap lock and tumbling into the hallway with a cackle.

'There goes the element of surprise,' muttered Roger.

'Don't worry, Green,' she replied, 'our element of "what the fuck" is well strong.'

Before he could ask what that was even supposed to mean she pulled the ripcord and the chainsaw roared into life. With a wink and a shout he could barely hear, but was sure contained the word 'bastards', Bird charged up the stairs.

Roger reminded himself that the people they were about to kill were extremist thugs, and that in addition to the joker they'd beaten to death last month, they'd hospitalized half a dozen others over the years. But watching Bird, and contemplating what he was about to do, the moral high ground seemed to slip through his fingers.

A quick sweep of the downstairs area confirmed that all of the targets had gone upstairs to bed, though by the sound of things, none of them were sleeping any more. Thumps and bangs could be heard through the ceiling above his head, like a drunken drummer unable to keep the beat.

With a sigh he returned to the hall to go and see how Bird was doing.

A man in his underwear crashed into the wall at the top of the stairs. Blood, someone else's, was splashed across the side of his face. He barely noticed the collision, or Roger, his attention on something behind him.

'Oh shit oh fuck oh God,' he said, nearly falling in his haste to escape the nearby massacre.

The hallway light had been disturbed at some point and swung wildly back and forth, alternately casting each side of the man's face in shadow. Nevertheless, Roger was able to identify him by his prematurely white hair and lazy eye. His name was Jason Abbott, and he was on their list.

Abbott didn't waste any time talking, and plunged down the stairs towards Roger. He wasn't a particularly burly man but he had momentum and height, and the kind of demeanour that would make most people think twice about getting in his way.

Before the virus, Roger wouldn't have dreamed of crossing such a man, the only choice being whether to run or offer up his wallet. However, mutation and time with the Fists had changed him. He took a firm grip on the banister and braced himself.

Abbott smashed into Roger the same way an egg smashes into a wall. There were several cracks, one of which was the man's nose breaking, another probably a rib, and then he fell onto his backside with a moan.

'Sorry,' said Roger. 'It's nothing personal but you picked on the wrong people.'

Abbott started scrabbling backwards. 'I'm not being taken down by a freak!'

Roger grabbed Abbott by the throat, barely feeling the other man's punches to his stomach, and squeezed. 'I really am sorry about this,' he whispered.

Abbott gurgled, then died, and Roger stepped over him.

Upstairs looked like the set of a cheap horror movie. A jagged line ran across one side of the landing wall, and blood spatters arced on several surfaces. A body lay on its back, the hips several feet too far away from the torso. If he'd still had the capacity, Roger would have thrown up at the sight of it.

In the background, the chainsaw's buzz fluctuated as it chewed into something new, accompanied by a juddering scream.

One on the stairs, thought Roger. *One on the landing and one with Bird at the moment makes three.* He looked into the bedrooms, counted two more bodies and breathed a sigh of relief. *Five. It's done. Thank God.*

He closed his eyes for a moment and took a deep breath. A

churn of emotions was starting up inside, but he would face them later. Right now he just had to get back to the van.

A muffled sob caught him as he was mid turn. It was coming from under the bed. Roger crouched down, putting one side of his head flat on the floor. A watery pair of eyes met his.

They'd been told to expect five, not six. This man was younger, probably still in his teens. Roger took in the details in an instant: shaved head, a half-finished tattoo on one forearm, and the strong smell of cheap aftershave.

Not on the list. He gave a slight nod to the man, got up, relieved, and turned to find Bird in the doorway. She was covered in gore, nearly all red save for the gleam of eyes and teeth. The chainsaw growled idly at her side. 'What you got there, Green?'

'Nothing. It's time to go.'

She took a step towards him. 'You're hiding something.'

He raised his arm and grabbed the edge of the doorframe, blocking her entry. 'We've got our five, and the police will be here any minute. Let's go.'

'Five is good, six is even better.'

'That's . . .' he paused. She was being so ridiculous he barely knew where to start. If there was one thing Roger hated more than anything else in the world, it was arguing with stupid people. 'Look, we had files on the others, we knew the kind of people they were. Killing indiscriminately is another matter entirely.'

'He's a nat. What more do I need to know?' She put a hand on his chest. 'Now get out of my way.'

He tried to think of some way to dissuade her. Clearly there was no rationality or honour to appeal to. 'Wait. If you let him live, he'll spread the word of what happened here. A living witness will do so much more to put fear of the Twisted Fists into the minds of the people.'

Bird's face screwed up as she thought about it. 'Maybe. I'm still gonna kill him, though.'

'But why?' he asked as she pushed at him.

'Insurance. One day, this little fucker is going to come after us. Revenge. Can't do that if he's dead.'

'I'm sorry, Bird, but I will not let you do this. It's not right.'

'Blister's the boss, not you.' She raised the chainsaw. 'Last chance. If I can't go past, I'm going through.'

'That's ridiculous. You'd attack a fellow joker simply to satisf—'

The chainsaw came down, biting deep into his arm just above the biceps. Since the virus, pain had barely been able to touch Roger. When someone struck him, he was aware of it, but only distantly, as if muted. This was different.

Agony rooted him to the spot. His jaws clacked together, his body shook, his eyes fixed on the spray of woodchips and the whirring teeth of the chainsaw as it worked its way through his arm.

No blood leaked from the wound, just a thick sap, dark as the feelings slowly welling inside.

There was a soft thud as his arm landed on the carpet.

Bird nodded to herself and stepped through the cloud of sawdust towards the whimpering figure under the bed. It was her nonchalance that finally broke Roger. If she'd seemed exultant or appalled he might not have acted, but the fact that he had been maimed and it meant nothing . . . that his *life* meant nothing . . . was too much to bear.

He caught the collar of her jacket as she passed him and flung her back onto the landing.

Bird flew. Not like a bird, but like a stone cast from a sling. She sailed the length of the space and slammed into the opposite wall, denting it, nearly passing through to the other side. One part of Roger was shocked by his own strength while another was struck by the cheap building practices.

'Okay,' said Bird, spitting bits of plasterboard as she hauled herself out of the wall, 'now it's on.' There was an awkwardness to her movement – he'd obviously done some damage – but she came on nonetheless, chainsaw buzzing and ready.

Roger ran to meet her. He was stronger, much stronger. He might only have one arm, but that was more than enough to deal with the likes of her.

Bird waited for him to get in range, then swung the chainsaw in a wide arc. Roger jumped back but was unable to stop it cutting through his clothes and scoring a line across his chest. Suddenly, he didn't feel so in control. The anger that had powered him stuttered and began to teeter on the edge of becoming fear.

Bird grinned and pushed forward, jabbing at him with the chainsaw. Her mutated arm was long, giving her a much better reach. He couldn't get to her without putting himself at the mercy of her weapon.

He continued to retreat as she advanced, until he was backing into the bedroom where the fight had started. His foot stepped on something uneven and the next thing he knew, Roger was on his back, Bird far too close for comfort.

He'd managed to scrabble onto his knees before he realized she hadn't actually attacked him. Though he couldn't hear her very well over the noise, a single look confirmed the reason why. She was laughing.

'You fell over your own arm! Ha ha! If you could see your-self! Oh God, it's too much!' she declared, then threw back her head to laugh some more.

She was right. He had tripped over it. The anger returned but cold this time. He knew exactly what he was going to do, even as he started to act. He took his severed arm by the wrist and lifted it. The joints had become solid. *Not a living thing any more*, he thought. *Just a lump of wood.*

Bird was still laughing as he stood up but she stopped when she saw the look in his eye. He swung his severed arm like a club. Bird managed to get the chainsaw in the way but it didn't matter, the force was enough to send her staggering.

He went after her, bringing the arm down again, and again, tireless, furious. She kept the chainsaw up, shielding herself as she tried to find her feet and recover. Roger didn't give her the chance, hammering her with relentless power.

At some point, he caught her on the elbow, shattering it, and the chainsaw swung down, taking a chunk out of her thigh. Bird fell, screaming.

Roger kept going.

The chainsaw stopped.

He brought his limb down directly on her unprotected skull.

There was a horrible crunching noise.

Bird stopped.

Roger kept going.

By the time his cold rage had passed, there was little left to recognize.

The sound of sirens brought him to his senses. It was time to go. With an arm still dangling from his hand, Roger rushed out of the house and into the waiting van across the road.

Blister slammed the door shut behind him and the van pulled away into the night.

Roger slumped at the back. He wasn't sure how he was going to explain what had happened and survive, but he knew that he should say something. But what? However he dressed things up, the bottom line was that he'd fought a member of the Fists to save a nat. They'd kill him for sure.

A glance at Blister did little to reassure him. Normally the man seemed open, but something had changed in his demeanour. It was as if he already knew. Roger wanted to ask what was going to happen but no words came, and the silence stretched to the point where it became unsafe, tense.

It stayed like that for a long time.

♣

The cellar was small but secure, with two chairs and a working sink. It bothered Roger that the chairs didn't match, just as it bothered him that the mop and bucket they used for cleaning down here were perpetually filthy. Why bother trying to clean at all if you're just swapping new muck for old?

The stump of his right arm was tingling in an odd way and he had a strong urge to be outside in the fresh air. However, in his current predicament, what he wanted was less than relevant.

Blister followed him into the room, closing the door and gesturing for Roger to sit. He did so and tried not to stare as the joker lurched awkwardly across the room.

After some careful positioning, Blister settled his lumpy form and regarded Roger in a manner several degrees from warm.

'I imagine you'd like to know what happened.'

Blister shook his head. 'I already know what happened. You and Bird took out the targets, then you took out Bird. What I want to know is why?'

'Yes, I'll explain. Although the truth is this really isn't about Bird.'

'Come again?'

Despite himself, Roger frowned at the use of language. 'What I mean is, this is about the Twisted Fists. What they stand for and what they hope to achieve. If you'll indulge me, I'd like to talk a little about Mrs Thatcher.'

Whatever Blister had been expecting him to say, it clearly wasn't this. 'If you think it might save your life, go ahead.'

Roger swallowed. 'I'm certainly hoping it will, though I rather fear you're not going to like it, as it will involve my being somewhat critical of you.'

'Of me?'

'Well, not you personally, rather the Twisted Fists and the way they're run.'

The bandages around Blister's mouth rippled as he barked out a laugh. 'You're going to justify Bird's murder by criticizing the Black Dog?'

'In a manner of speaking, yes. Should I begin?'

'Why not? It's your funeral, Green Man.'

'When Mrs Thatcher went up against the miners two years ago, there was a lot of talk about right and wrong, and what was best for the country, but none of these things mattered in terms of why she was able to defeat them. People often think it's about ethics but it isn't. They get added later, once the fighting is over.

'The conflict between the government and the miners' unions was a war on two fronts. She knew a fight was coming and she was prepared for it. In the past, the miners' unions had been able to hold the country to ransom, but this time Mrs Thatcher had stockpiled enough coal to enable us to last well beyond any strike the miners could manage. In effect, she pulled their teeth before the fight began.

'One battle took place on a practical level – their ability to damage the economy versus hers to endure – but the real war was one of perception. You see, the miners were sympathetic figures. Closing a pit also meant breaking a community. They were victims, hard-working people that were easy to empathize with, but she managed to turn them into law-breakers, invalidating their moral position.

'As I hope I've made clear, there was never any danger of the strike itself defeating her, but if the public had sided with the miners, Mrs Thatcher would have had no choice but to make concessions.'

Blister waved a hand. 'There a point to all this?'

'Yes. The miners lost not because they were wrong but because they were outmanoeuvred.

'In many ways our predicament is even worse than that of the miners. Jokers are easy targets for the press, and we have no representatives at a higher political level. No one to speak in our defence. It doesn't matter that terrible things happen to jokers because nobody cares, at least nobody with the power to make a difference.

'For that to change, the Twisted Fists need to change.'

'Are we at the point where all this relates to Bird yet?'

'Ah, yes. Well, that's fairly simple. We'd killed our five and Bird wanted to kill another. The rule is five for one, not six for one. I tried to stop her and she,' he glanced at his stump, 'attacked me. I killed her to protect myself and the honour of the Fists.'

'You chose a nat over one of us. That goes against everything we stand for.'

'With all due respect, you're wrong.' Blister's eyes narrowed as Roger continued. 'The point of the Twisted Fists is to put people like us on equal footing with everyone else, to make clear that our lives matter too. It is not to prove that jokers are superior to nats. And can I say I dislike the terminology as it's really quite loaded.'

'You chose to kill Bird rather than let her kill the nat. You gave his life more value than hers.'

Roger raised a finger. He didn't mean to but the argument was animating him now. 'The only thing that elevates us from being the worst kind of criminals is honour. The only thing. If we lose it, we lose everything. Don't you understand? If we are known to play by certain rules then people can deal with us. If we have a code, if we really stand for something, then we have to abide by its rules.

'And yes, I did give his life more value than hers, but I would have done that regardless of any virus. She was a foul-mouthed sociopath.'

'She was one of our best agents.'

'Then you and Black Dog need to be more discerning about whom you recruit. I'd rather be alone than have her at my back.'

Blister reclined in his chair and looked at the floor. He seemed sad, though it was hard to tell if this was because of the state of the Twisted Fists or that he was about to have Roger put down.

Roger wondered if he should say something more or if he had already said too much. At least if he died, Churchill would tell Wendy and his children that he wasn't a traitor to his country. That seemed like small consolation.

The chair scraped loudly as Blister pushed it back. 'Stay here,' he said, and walked out of the room.

Roger breathed out a long sigh. Had that gone well? As he reviewed the discussion in his mind he managed alternately to convince himself that he would be all right, that it had been a disaster and he was about to be executed, that Blister hadn't made up his mind yet, and that he'd made no sense at all.

How had it come to this? He knew the steps leading to this point, could follow the logic that linked them, and yet when he tried to put it all together, he couldn't quite believe it. 'Absurd,' he murmured.

The door opened behind him, and Roger instinctively straightened, as if some fine-tuned sense could detect authority even before it had entered the room.

'I hear you have a problem with me.'

The voice was deep, a rich blend of accents, the kind that resonated in the gut as much as the ear. Roger would have sold several members of his family and all of his in-laws to have one like it.

The owner of the voice swept past him in a swish of black robes. He was tall too, and powerfully built, plunging Roger into a bottomless lake of inadequacy. Something wasn't right about the face. Rather than being concealed by the hood, part of it protruded, the muzzle and teeth of a snarling dog. A black dog.

It was then Roger understood just how bad his situation was. He'd finally managed to meet with Black Dog, but in the worst way imaginable. As the initial shock subsided, he realized that it wasn't Black Dog's face he was looking at, but a mask. Combined with the robes, it created a grotesque kind of theatre that should have been laughable but absolutely wasn't. The man was terrifying and all he was doing was standing there.

Roger had imagined this moment many times. Because he'd

never been sure of exactly when he'd get to meet Black Dog, he'd prepared three different core speeches with a number of movable points that could be bolted on where appropriate. Hours had been spent in their creation and, privately, Roger was rather proud of them.

Could he remember a single bloody word of them now?

No, he bloody well couldn't.

'Is the problem me?' asked Black Dog. 'Or is it you?'

Was that a reference to what had happened with Bird or was it deeper? Did he know that Roger was a spy? If that was the case he was about to be tortured, and if there was one thing Roger was more certain of than anything else, it was that he could not bear being tortured.

The words came out of his mouth before he'd had time to consider them. 'You're too reactive.'

Black Dog folded his arms.

'Killing five for one is simple and powerful, but what does it achieve in the long run?'

'It makes people think twice before killing our kind.'

Roger had to fight the urge to nod in agreement. The man was a natural leader, who dominated the room just as Churchill did. It was not just that Roger wanted to win him over, he wanted to impress him as well. Nevertheless he made himself say: 'And then what?'

There was a pause.

'Even if the Twisted Fists succeeded, and no more jokers were killed, we are still unemployable in all but the worst of jobs, we have no representatives in Parliament, no support in the press. In fact we play directly into their narrative of being monsters.'

'We're only as monstrous as they make us.'

'My point is that we're not aiming high enough.'

'Go on.'

This time it was Roger who paused. He certainly had ideas of how to make the Fists evolve. It was impossible to be in an organization and not see the flaws. But his mission was to take the Fists down, not make them more effective. Still, he couldn't complete his mission if he was dead, and the desire to prove himself to the Black Dog remained there, physical, like a hand at his back.

'It will be a long time before one of us gets elected. If we want to make change now, we need allies. Normal allies. Preferably ones with pull in their communities or with a platform to speak from. The Fists have funding, I know that much. There are a lot of poor and hungry people we could help. The kind being neglected by the government, like us. They're desperate and we can save them. People always remember who picked them out of the gutter. They're natural allies and they can vote. We have to stop this being about jokers and nats, them and us.

'If the Fists can become champions of the dispossessed, we can change the way we're perceived. We can be Robin Hoods rather than Sweeney Todds. I happen to know some rather troublesome journalists who love this sort of thing.

'As to sympathetic politicians with power, that's more difficult. However, I do know a few rumoured to be up to no good. If we could have them followed, perhaps find some evidence, I'm sure they'd listen to our needs with fresh ears.'

Black Dog nodded, the action exaggerated by the movement of his snout. 'You like to talk. Me, I like to see things done.' From the sleeve of his robes he produced a traditional Green Man face. It was intricately made, with carved leaves framing the eyes, nose, and mouth, before flowing down into a long beard. He placed it in Roger's hands.

'I don't understand.'

'It's your mask. From now on, this is who you are. This is who the authorities will hunt. When you need to go in public unseen, take it off.'

Roger knocked on his cheek. 'I'm sorry, but have you seen my face?'

'Cover it with make-up or prosthetics when you need anonymity. Find a way. You need to become something bigger if you are going to lead this branch of the Fists.'

'You're promoting me? But I failed the test.'

'This is the test. What you're suggesting sounds interesting, but I'm too cynical to believe it will work. Prove me wrong and you pass. Fail, and I'll come back and kill you myself.'

'What about Blister, isn't he in charge here?'

Something changed in Black Dog's eyes: perhaps he was smiling beneath the mask. 'No, he's gone, as are all the others here. I'm moving them to other cells. As you don't approve of my recruitment methods, you can find and vet your own people. Now, put on the mask.'

Roger did so without thinking.

'Good luck, Green Man. I look forward to seeing what you can do.'

'Thank you.'

Black Dog strode out, pausing at the door to add, 'You've got two years.'

The Cracks
in the City

by Peadar Ó Guilín

Belfast, Northern Ireland, 1987

FOR THREE DAYS, BADB, Goddess of War, sat in her own excrement. Bent double in a rusted cement mixer, with nothing to eat or drink but the blood and bodies of summoned crows, she hid and bided her time.

Everything hurt. She was near the end of her cycle, so her joints felt like molten rock and her skin consisted entirely of scabs. Flies and vermin swarmed over her and not even passing beggars could bear to look inside the old machine.

And still, divinely patient, she waited.

But the goddess was not idle. When she closed her eyes, the city of Belfast stretched out below her. From the ground it appeared chaotic. Taigs hated Prods. Prods murdered jokers. Brits fought the IRA and the INLA and the Twisted Fists. But from the air, it was a chess set like any other, except that this game would never end. She would see to that.

As a crow, Badb flew over a column of Saracen armoured cars, thundering down the street to quell a riot on the Falls Road. She watched masked men bundle a weeping mother into a van, never to be seen again. In Lincoln Place a boy with too many arms was being beaten by three others wielding baseball bats. Nobody played baseball in Northern Ireland, but sales of the equipment were booming.

Night fell. At last, she saw the first signs that her weeks of planning had not been in vain.

First came the SAS, all in black, their steps soft as butterflies on the roofs of the derelict two-storey buildings on either side of the road leading into Belfast's jokertown, the Island. Badb herself had supplied the intelligence that brought them here.

Seventeen years earlier, twenty-one thousand soldiers had poured onto the streets of Northern Ireland. Some of the squaddies going home in coffins today were buried next to fathers who'd met the same fate before them. Badb had done her work well. The blood of heroes – and there had been hundreds by now – fed the land so that it grew lush and green for as far as the eyes of a crow could see.

Finally, at ground level this time, three more men and one woman, all wearing balaclavas and armed with AK-47s, set themselves up on either side of the street. She had lured them here. They too thought they were about to spring an ambush, but their lives could now be measured in minutes.

Badb's heart began to beat faster. She could see, as no mortal could, that a glow surrounded one of these figures. *A true believer.* A hero . . .

And then, before all the escape routes could be closed off by the arrival of more soldiers creeping in from both ends of the street, one of the so-called elite up on the roofs knocked against a stone and sent it tumbling down two storeys.

The hero reacted before anybody else. 'Run!' he cried. 'Through the factory!' He was no giant as her uncle had been long ago. But he sprang to his feet. He picked up his closest comrade, shoving her in the direction of the nearby buildings before the first bullets from above kicked up the spot where he'd just been crouching.

He was going to get away! Or be hunted down and killed too far off for Badb to benefit from it. She had to get out of here and follow him, although every muscle in her body had shut itself down from days of immobility.

Bullets struck the cement mixer, rattling it like the loudest drum in the world. A man cried out for mercy. It was a value all sides in the conflict claimed to honour, but nobody was watching tonight and his pleas ended in a gurgle.

Badb felt the hero pause and then . . . *Glory! Glory!* A bullet took him through the brain. She sensed his blood jetting onto the parched earth, the legions of those who had passed before him stretching out bony fingers to welcome him.

Oh, the pain of his death! The murdered future, where this noble soul might have loved a wife; ploughed fields; made peace. Gone now, all gone, and Badb, the goddess, screamed for its loss. Her voice shattered windows; streetlights guttered; Saracens rolled to a stop, every battery flat, while up on the surrounding roofs, soldiers voided themselves and covered their ears as a vortex made entirely of crows spun in the pitch darkness overheard.

Like a cannonball, Badb shot out of the cement mixer.

Then she ran.

She failed to mark the passing of time, but deep in the night, laughing and crying, she stepped into an empty court-yard in the ruined shipyards. Here, as it started to rain, she completed her transformation. Always strong at the start of her cycle, she ripped away clothing and rotted bandages with her own hands. Old skin sloughed off in the downpour, giving way to youth and beauty. Her back straightened and she laughed, mouth open to taste the rain – the most delicious thing in the universe! She wept. She shivered. She danced, swirling, swirling, and then—

'You!' she cried, spinning to a halt. 'Who are *you*?'

A handsome little man, somewhere in his early twenties,

goggled at her naked body. Four empty beer cans lay at his feet, while another dangled from his fingers.

'I . . .' he said. 'Um . . . Billy, uh . . . O'Donnell. Billy O'Donnell. Are you . . . are you one o' them aces?'

Billy O'Donnell. He had the sweetest lips imaginable. The largest eyes.

'How much did you see, Billy O'Donnell?' She moved next to him, her heart beating. She loved him, she LOVED him and kissed his lips, delighting in the taste of beer, breathing deep of his scent, rubbing the stubble on his cheeks.

He wanted her too, of course. His breath matched hers as she pressed against him, but when she took two handfuls of his Stiff Little Fingers T-shirt, he jerked away from her with a cry.

'No! No! I need to keep that on.'

That was *not* how one spoke to a goddess. She would lose her great strength in a day or two, but now she tore away his clothing like tissue paper. A sweet little chest waited underneath, except that bandages covered each nipple.

'What have we here?' she asked

'Please . . . please . . . I have to go . . . I have to—'

Under the bandages, instead of a right nipple, he had a mouth. It began babbling the moment she uncovered it: 'Dirty Papist whore! Left-footed Fenian Catholic cow! Lie down, Croppy! Lie—' She laughed and laughed while Billy wept. There was a mouth on the other side too.

'Proddy bitch!' it hissed. 'You Orange snout Jaffa black Protestant, dirty—'

Both voices stilled the moment she covered the lips. 'Are you from a mixed marriage, Billy O'Donnell?'

He nodded with a sob. 'Please,' he said. 'I . . . Please . . .'

'I love it!' she cried, startling him. 'I love *you*!' She ripped off the bandages completely. She kissed the mouth on the left of his chest, licking the lips with her tongue, while feeding her fingers to the one on the right. 'And what about this?' she asked, grabbing him between the legs. What religion does this belong to?'

'Any . . .' he groaned. 'Any . . . one you want.'

♣

Later, back in her hidden, booby-trapped home, Badb read poetry. Nobody wrote about sex like Nuala Ní Dhomhnaill. The joy. The sliding of limbs. The perfume of a man's body that she called *'cumhracht'*.

Poor Billy O'Donnell. He had seen too much and would have to die. *Not yet!* Badb still loved him too much. But in a day or two, when rationality returned, she would track him down. A joker like that wouldn't be hard to find. A joker like that, however sweet, would die and never be missed.

♦

Two weeks after it happened, Billy Little, as he usually called himself, was still grinning. His stepfather would box his ears for making calls at work, but he picked up the phone anyway, dialling Armi's number. He waited . . . and waited . . . nothing. He was desperate to talk about her again. The nameless woman. But nobody less than a best friend could be trusted with such a secret.

When Billy thought about it – and he thought of nothing else! – his cheeks grew hot and his hands itched as though they remembered the feel of curves; of smooth skin.

These were hardly fitting thoughts for a funeral parlour, of course.

He sat beneath a portrait of Her Majesty, Queen Margaret. What would her highness have thought if she could read his mind? Or Granda, uniformed, staring out of a framed photograph on the desk in front of him?

Billy had only kissed two girls before and the second time,

when Rosie McMichael had slipped her hand under his jumper at the school social, he had run terrified from the hall and had spent the last two weeks of term pretending to be sick.

He could never risk a kiss again. Or so he'd thought.

But then, *she* had happened. The ace. The gorgeous woman who didn't care who he was, what he was. Who seemed – by God! – to enjoy it. To enjoy *him*. She knew all his secrets: that his card had turned; that his real da had been a Catholic named O'Donnell. It wasn't the sort of thing Ma had wanted to boast about when they'd moved home from England and she'd remarried. But Billy still remembered and when the black-haired woman had asked him his name, that ancient truth had come spilling out.

He trembled. *If only he could find her again.*

The clock ticked. Armi still wasn't answering the phone. Billy tried to fill in paperwork, but couldn't concentrate. Finally – and his stepfather would kill him for this! – he pulled the newspaper out from under the desk. It was two days old and the worst kind of tabloid, the kind with a topless model on page three.

He'd peered at her already, couldn't help himself. But the blonde's passionless smile and unnatural pose did nothing for him now. What he wanted was jet-black hair. He longed for laughter and fury and breathlessness. So he turned the page, flicking past gossip about that American Wild Cards tour. Stuff about Peregrine's pregnancy. About Fantasy – oh, God, Fantasy! – at the Royal Ballet. He turned the page one more time . . . And there, right in front of him, was an article about how the army were offering a reward for the capture of what they called the Screeching Ace.

Billy's heart beat faster. £100,000. A huge, huge sum of money.

Not that he would betray her for something like that! Life-changing though it was. He loved her, whatever her name was. He loved her. And yet, he lingered on the page.

For £100,000, he could go to New York and visit Dr Tachyon's clinic there. Jokers had been cured before, hadn't they? What if he were cured? What would his life be like then?

The phone rang and he jumped, as though guilty.

'Billy Boy!' came the drunken voice at the other end.

'Billy Boy, yerself.' Armi had the same first name, which had led to endless confusion in school.

'Come out for a drink. Bring yer snooker cue. Nobody's gonna die in the ten minutes you have left to work.'

Billy threw the paper with its poisonous temptation in the bin and ran to fetch his cue.

♠

The day after the emotions wore off, Badb sat in her office in Thiepval Barracks. She had long since learned that cutting into parts of her body that were covered by clothing meant that lesions were far less likely to break out on her face and hands. But over the next few months, she would appear to age rapidly and she'd be forced to hide it with make-up and feigned illness.

For now, she closed her eyes and flitted to the crow that sat just outside.

She watched the back of her own head. She heard the clock on the desk muffled by the glass. Then, she took off, sailing around the building to another windowsill.

'Bloody RUC Special Branch!' Tom, her boss, railed against the police. 'Bloody amateurs! They'll get us all killed—'

It was nothing Badb hadn't heard before. Besides, it wasn't Special Branch that had got his agents killed, but her. For every piece of intelligence she fed her British employers about the IRA, she passed another back in the opposite direction. She couldn't allow anybody to *win* the war after all, or who would feed the land?

She chose another crow, one she'd ordered earlier to circle

high over the city. The wind whistled past, rippled her feathers, held her aloft.

This is how it was to be a goddess – to feel nothing. To see everything. She soared for a while, watching for patterns, cracks in the city she might exploit to make each community feel threatened so that heroes must arise to defend it. Foreigners always thought the Ulster conflict a simple struggle between British Protestants and Irish Catholics, but it was so much richer than that! Layer upon layer: communists; agitators; aces; jokers. There were British regiments that hated each other more than they hated the IRA, and every year terrorist organizations killed more of 'their own' than they ever did of the opposition.

The bird she occupied was tired and would fall from the sky soon. She moved on. She listened to a conversation in an IRA safe house. She scratched a warning to one of her agents on a gate. She checked a drop in the Island, but no, not one of her joker contacts knew anything of a boy with mouths for nipples. She would keep looking. She flitted from crow to crow and—

Badb tumbled back into her own body as a hand grabbed her by the wrist.

'Anya! McNulty! By Christ, woman, get it together!'

She opened her eyes to find Tom Grayson's face less than an inch from her own, displaying all the attributes of the mood known as 'panic'. She smelled perspiration from him along with the usual Old Holborn rollies and the rotting tooth he had at the back of his mouth. She saw that he had locked the door behind him for some reason.

'I didn't know about this,' he blurted. 'I swear to you. They didn't even tell the boss they were coming. But I hope by Christ you weren't lying when you said you weren't a joker because—'

A fist punched right through the pine of the door, then fiddled unsuccessfully with the key, before ripping the whole thing off its hinges.

The brute responsible wore an eighteenth-century army

uniform, complete with a red jacket and shiny buttons. Was this the famous Redcoat? Wasn't he supposed to be dead? He flung the crumpled wood aside before puffing out his chest and standing to quivering attention.

'Sah!' he shouted. 'Door opened, sah!'

What came next was even stranger.

A man made entirely of stone ducked under the lintel and stepped into the small room. *'My apologies, Miss McNulty.'* When it – *he* looked up, Badb saw two eyes of flame looking into her own. And there was another light too, one that only she could sense. *Glory. Belief.* She was in the presence of a hero. Every part of her skin turned hot at once, while new lesions opened on her back and chest.

'You have no right!' babbled Tom. 'She's our best handler. She's worked with the Force Research Unit for—'

'You know who I am?' asked Captain Flint. He wasn't talking to Tom.

Lying would have aroused his suspicions, so Badb nodded once and received a nod in return.

'We're in the province on other business, Miss McNulty. We finally have a lead on the Screeching Ace. But since we are here, well, if you're a joker . . .' he paused to gauge her reaction. *'Your considerable talents should be employed with us instead.'*

'She's *not* a joker,' said Tom. 'I have assurances from the regimental doctor that—'

The arrival of another woman interrupted him. She was middle-aged and black with a strong Birmingham accent. She squeezed her ample frame through the broken door, out of breath and sweating slightly. 'You trying to kill me, Flinty?'

'Madam,' said Tom.

'Esmerelda,' she told him. 'Charmed.'

'Madam. Esmerelda . . . your services are not needed. Like all FRU handlers, Anya McNulty is evaluated by a telepath once a year.'

The woman smiled, still wheezing a little from climbing the

stairs. 'Oh, I don't mind doing it again. I've come all this way. And what harm could it do, anyway?'

What harm indeed? With a perfect memory and an ability to spy on anyone anywhere, Badb had gathered great power to herself. She controlled the local FRU telepath as surely as any of her agents in the IRA or the Twisted Fists. The doctor, too, turned a blind eye when she wrote her own fitness reports. But these strangers from Britain were beyond her influence.

'It's insulting,' Tom said. 'Anya couldn't be more loyal. Her father was killed by the IRA.'

Badb had arranged that murder herself. But now she was only two moves from checkmate.

She put on her professional voice. 'I've heard of this ace,' she said. 'The Screamer. Or the Screecher. How can *you* expect to find him when we cannot?'

'They have a new source,' said Tom. 'We should be handling him, not the Silver Helix!'

'*Enough. And no, Mr Grayson, we won't be sharing the identity of our source with the FRU. Too many of your agents have met an unhappy end. Now, my dear,*' Captain Flint turned to Esmerelda. '*We'll get this over with. Miss McNulty, will you sign a consent form? Miss McNulty? Are you all right? Is she asleep?*'

Badb opened her eyes. 'Thank you, Captain Flint. I am fine. I give my full consent. There is no need for a form.' She held her hand out towards Esmerelda. On the chessboard, her king tottered, but she had one move left.

'Good for you, love,' Esmeralda was saying. 'Unlike some, you won't even notice me goin' in there. Won't feel a thing. Now, let's just see . . .'

Down by the fence, a crow pulled at a particular wire that for some reason was always missed during routine sweeps.

The entire base shook. Then came sound, like a great fist, as the gatehouse turned into a fireball and shards of glass flew through the room. Several embedded themselves in Badb's back and neck just as Esmeralda caught her wrist. But the mind of the goddess was already in another crow, pulling yet another wire at the top of this very building. Now the ceiling came caving in. Tom and Captain Flint disappeared in a rain of rubble and Badb, bleeding all over her back, found herself alone and face to face with the telepath in a 'fortunate' pocket of air.

A series of moods passed over Esmeralda's face. Her mouth opened as though intending to plead for mercy, but she was still touching the goddess's skin and must have guessed the outcome. When Badb removed a shard of glass from her own back and shoved it into the telepath's neck, 'fear' and 'panic' showed on her features. But not 'surprise'. Not even a bit. *Fascinating.*

There was another ace in the room, or part of one, anyway. The brutish Redcoat must have had unnatural speed to go with his strength, because he'd almost outrun the explosion. His head and arms poked from the rubble. His eyes were closed and he hissed like a leaky balloon until the goddess blocked the airways with her hands. He was definitely dead now.

All that remained was for Badb to remove herself from suspicion in the murders. She lay down as far from the two corpses as she could get. Then, she pulled a piece of rubble onto her legs. Bones snapped, followed by a stab of pain so intense it sent her flying above the city for a whole minute. *Good. Most satisfactory.*

Captain Flint still lived too. She could feel his heroism through the wreckage.

He had come to Northern Ireland in search of an enemy ace – Badb herself, of course, although he couldn't know that yet. Still, this new information implied that somebody somewhere had talked, probably to the RUC confidential line. She had contacts there.

Billy O'Donnell was about to leave the board.

♥

Two days later, crutches dug into Badb's armpits, opening wounds that soaked the bandages under her clothing. It was still early in her cycle, but broken legs, and the extra bleeding that happened whenever she encountered a hero like Captain Flint, had weakened her. There were other kinds of power, however. When she swung into the laundrette on Mieville Street, the women working there paled and left at once.

She rested against a machine. Then, closing her eyes, she flew around the building, looking for anybody watching her.

Mieville Street lay at the intersection of three communities – Protestant, Catholic, and joker. Graffiti splattered every building in sight: crowns, fists, harps. Slogans of every kind: *No Surrender! Tiocfaidh Ár Lá! Five for one!* There were painted flags and provocations and threats. If Badb knew how to love, she would love this place. It was the very landscape where heroes were born and fattened and killed.

A furtive movement in an alleyway sent her flitting to a crow with a better view. Yes, it was the man she expected and he approached alone. The joker came into the shop. His neck was a foot long and wound like a spring, so obviously, people called him 'Bobby'. They'd be more careful if they knew what she knew about him.

'How's about ye?' he asked. And of course, he nodded. Bobby couldn't help it.

Badb didn't look up. She had covered her face with a veil and, as was traditional in all the stories, the Goddess of War appeared to her worshippers as a woman washing blood from clothing. A great deal of blood. Bobby's nodding grew more nervous the longer he watched.

Eventually, he asked, 'What ya got for me?'

'Two members of the DUP,' she said. 'You want them?'

His face twisted into hatred. 'They're tryin' to send us all back to Rathlin where they won't have to look at us. Well, we're not goin'! Bastards!'

'You want them or not?'

'Aye, I want them. But . . . but what're you lookin' for in return? Yer always after somethin'.'

'Nipples,' she said.

'Wh-what? What?'

She handed him a piece of blood-sticky paper with a name and address. 'Kill him,' she said. 'Your men must bring me his nipples.'

He was used to her strange requests. 'He's the one you had us lookin' for before? I'll do this wee job myself.'

'You will not. Nobody who knows me can be involved. Do it tonight.'

Bobby nodded. Of course he did. And then, he was gone.

♣

The CCTV cameras caught them: a trio of men, wearing masks of that American preacher fellow – what was his name? Captain Flint had no idea. But they were certainly jokers. One of them had three legs, and another tore down the door of the house in Lurgan Park by charging it with his head. Then, all three drew guns and ducked inside.

'*Why?*' Captain Flint asked a pair of terrified police officers. '*Why am I only seeing this footage now?*'

'Um . . .' said the first, a skinny man with an enthusiastic Adam's apple, 's-security? We don't want it falling into the hands of . . . of the enemy.'

'*By George, the only enemy you lot seem to care about are your colleagues in Army Intelligence.*'

'They got themselves bombed the other day, didn't they? Had to be an inside job. They can't be trusted.'

'*Oh, I know all about the bombing and you are the ones who can't be trusted.*' He glared at them, well aware of the effect his burning eyes were having. '*That boy died because you lot leak like a sieve. The jokers were even going to mutilate him before they were surprised. Now,'* another glare, *'is there anything else you're not telling me?'*

They resented him, he could see that much. But the chief constable had ordered full cooperation with the Silver Helix in this particular matter and the elder of the two sighed and nodded. 'Aye,' he said. 'We now know the Screeching Ace is a beautiful young woman with black hair. She was seen on the edges of the Island the day of the ambush. We'll get you a tape of the call the boy made to us, but that's all he was willin' to say until we got approval to award him the money.'

'Better,' said Captain Flint, *'much better.'* He felt a sudden itch between his shoulder blades, as though somebody were staring straight at him through the sight of a sniper rifle. But when he spun around, there was nothing on the windowsill but a ragged-looking crow. He sighed.

'Yes. Be so good as to get me that tape.'

He left them at once, taking an armoured car to a house on Lurgan Street to meet with the boy's distraught mother. As the public face of the Silver Helix, he was often the one to talk to the families of the fallen. He hated it. But it was part of his duty to Queen and country, and while both were much diminished these days – one through a lifetime of smoking, the other because of pernicious foreigners and a cowardly leadership – he, at least, would always be faithful. Even in the face of a mother's tears. *'I'm sorry for your loss, Mrs—'*

'Call me May, sir,' she told him. 'I know why you're here. But I don't know nothin' else. 'Cept they had knives and they were gonna cut into my wee boy's chest. Them twisty monsters! They should all be sent back to Rathlin Island, so they should. The *real* island, not them streets they took for themselves in the city.' She glared at him, as if she only now realized he was a bit of a joker too. 'My boy was never involved in nothin'. Certainly not with the Twisties. Unlike some people I might name.'

'Name them.'

She gulped. People here on all sides killed what they called 'touts' – informers. But this was different, wasn't it? 'Billy Little,' she said, at last. 'So-called best friend, but a bad, bad influence. He's been seen sneakin' into the Island to get drunk and the Lord knows what else . . .'

The Island kept coming up. That was where the SAS men had been incapacitated by the screaming that had followed their ambush. *'Madam,'* he said, *'if the boys were best friends, is it possible your son might have shared information with this other . . . Billy?'*

'Oh, aye. Thick as thieves, those two. Though the Little boy hasn't even shown his face over here since . . . since . . .'

The brigadier noted that a crow at the window suddenly shook itself and flew off, as though freed from a stupor. *'Madam,'* he said, *'I need to hurry. It might be rather urgent.'*

◆

What surprised Badb as she listened to Captain Flint's conversation were the photos on the mantelpiece of the sitting room. The wrong boy had died, she realized. She had seen Billy Little in this very house – an obvious check to make before ordering his death. But he was a frequent visitor here, after all. And now, he was about to fall into the clutches of a dangerous enemy.

Unless she could get to him first.

She did not like to use her crows to kill, because sooner or later it would get her caught. But this was an emergency. Police records indicated a Billy Little of the appropriate age, living no more than three streets away. She concentrated, hopping from crow to crow, leaving each with a simple instruction to follow one of their fellows. Soon, an entire flock of them descended on what looked like a funeral parlour, one bird landing on each windowsill, with more on the chimney pots. Then, she flicked from one body to the next, staying no more time than it took to glance inside the building, until, at last, she found him, curled up on a bed, with all the signs of 'sadness' on his handsome features. Weeping for his friend, no doubt.

Another flick showed her that Captain Flint was already on his way.

Badb was left with no choice but to take another risk. She tapped a beak against Billy's window. He looked up, wondering what was going on. *Tap, tap, tap.*

He stood up, wiping his eye – the same one she would attack as soon as he let her in. She could bring the entire flock to bear if necessary, but since his room faced the public street, it would be better to keep it to one bird. She might even be able to bring it out alive afterwards. She made preparations for other scenarios too. She set one crow to circling high over the whole area. Others were tasked with gathering a stack of thumb-sized pebbles on a nearby roof.

Billy came forward, but slowly, slowly. Even in his room, she saw, he kept his chest well covered, which might mean his family were as ignorant of his secret as the rest of the world.

Tap, tap, tap.

He was right there now. *Bewildered. Curious.*

Then, he looked past her and his eyes widened. Confusion and then horror came over his face. The Saracen – Captain Flint's transport – was already here. In a Catholic neighbourhood, there might have been a warning: women banging the footpath with dustbin lids; young men whistling or shouting out. But the residents of Lurgan Gardens regarded the army as theirs.

Billy turned his back and fled. Why, she wondered, was he running from the British army? Clearly, he hadn't been the one to call the confidential line in search of the reward. Had he put his friend up to it?

Through one set of eyes after another, Badb followed him down through the house. One room had a chessboard set up with a half-played game and she lost valuable seconds when she couldn't help working her way through to the inevitable checkmate. But she spied him again as he fled in through a room where an old woman lay on a slab surrounded by bottles of what looked like make-up. A back door led out into an alleyway. Badb was ready for him. She flicked up to the roof, where she grabbed a pebble in one claw. Then she took off, swooping around twice to gather speed before hurtling down towards the alleyway.

Billy was just coming out of the door. She never missed – it was simple mathematics. Once released, the pebble would strike him with exactly enough force to cave in the back of his skull.

But then, a voice called out. 'Halt! You're wanted for questioning!'

She veered away as Billy jumped onto the lid of a rubbish bin and scrambled over a fence into the next garden.

The soldier spoke into a radio. Others were approaching from nearby streets. Neighbours looked out of windows, any of whom would report it if they saw a crow killing the boy.

She flitted from one set of eyes to another, taking in the whole board. Soldiers were arriving from all sides. Captain Flint too had begun running – so slowly at first that a child could have overtaken him. But step by step his massively heavy frame gathered enough momentum to dent a tank. The squaddies caught the boy first. Three men knocked him over and kicked him as he lay on the ground.

'*What are you doing?*' said the captain when he arrived. '*By God, we're British! We don't torture!*' They looked at him in astonishment. '*Our own, I mean. We don't hurt our own. You're on our side, aren't you, boy?*'

Even through the senses of a bird's body Badb could feel the glory radiating from the stone man. The land longed for him; to drink down whatever passed for blood in that strange body of his. She fought against the distraction to keep her concentration.

Billy was weeping, but he nodded and said 'Aye'. He was

about to talk. In mere moments, the British would have a description of her younger self and would know that she transformed after her mourning cry. Even now, it wasn't too late to strike Billy with a pebble, but she'd never put an end to Captain Flint that way and it would have revealed to him her true power. So instead, she waited to gather as much information about the disastrous situation as she could.

'I'm sorry,' Billy said. 'I'm . . . I'm so sorry. Armi's dead 'cause of me.'

'You told him about the woman?'

'I . . . I made it up from somethin' I saw in the paper. He was always talkin' about the girls he was with, an' I just got sick of it, so I . . . so I . . . I never thought he'd call the police! The story got bigger an' bigger an' it just ran away with me.' Billy sobbed. Whatever about his story, the grief and the guilt were very real.

'Then why was he murdered?'

'Jokers like to kill nats,' one of the soldiers said. 'Especially Loyalists. Five for every one of their own that's killed.'

But Billy didn't know. He had no idea at all. About anything. And that was when Badb understood. The only reason the boy had fled the soldiers was that he had intended to keep her secret all along. He wanted to protect her. *Fascinating, truly fascinating.*

Captain Flint's sigh had a rattly sound to it.

They brought Billy back to the station for more questioning. Lots more. But not once did he tell them the truth.

♠

Some months later, out of curiosity, she walked past Billy in the street, and deliberately allowed him to see her face. He didn't recognize her. He only remembered the younger version of herself.

He should still die, of course. Like the boy in the story of

King Lowry, he knew a secret that sooner or later would have to come out. But there might be value in having her own Renfield. And Billy Little had access to Captain Flint now. All he had to do was claim he wanted to tell the truth and the hero of the Silver Helix would return to Ireland at a time of her choosing.

Imagine the glory then!

She paused at the side of the road as though uncertain.

'You need help, missus?' he asked, as she knew he would. It was what good boys did.

'Perhaps,' she told him. 'Perhaps I do.'

Twisted
Logic

Part 3

London, 1988

THE MEETINGS TOOK PLACE in another dimly lit room, this time in the back of a pub called the Green Man. Roger had already seen two people: Clarissa, an old woman who'd been attacked outside her own home and wanted revenge, and a young joker called Susan who needed to hide after smashing up a supermarket.

He'd promised help to both of them. He always did; the Green Man was known to be magnanimous. In return, Clarissa would allow them the use of her flat as a safe house, and Susan – he'd think of an appropriate name for her later – would owe the Fists a favour. If she could learn to manage her temper, he'd recruit her, if not, well, she could always be used as a distraction.

At times the work was so absorbing that Roger forgot he was only pretending. His meeting with Churchill four years ago had taken on the quality of a dream, and all he could remember of Wendy was her teeth. Little Roy would be nearly ten and Christine would be taking her O-levels or whatever they were calling them now. Did they think of him at all? Had they learned of his connection to the Fists or was he just an absent figure in their lives?

He wished he'd kept a family photo, something to anchor them in his mind. As it was, the demands of keeping two masters happy while keeping his own head was exhausting. Two years had passed in a flurry of work. In that time he'd established himself as the undisputed head of the UK Fists. There had been a few challengers, but he'd sold them out to Churchill, along with any others who didn't fit with his way of doing things. Only those with self-discipline and loyalty got to stay.

His network of contacts was growing, but gaining traction anywhere above street level was proving frustrating, and Black Dog's deadline loomed large on the horizon.

There was a knock at the door but the person on the other side waited for permission before entering. Roger smiled. If there was one thing he liked about being respected, it was that people remembered their manners. 'Come in,' he said.

A man entered, and Roger took a moment to match him with the information he'd been given in advance: Asif Manzoor, twenty-six, married with three children, had worked for British Telecom for three years before being made redundant, currently employed as a private electrician. Increasingly, the people coming to him were untouched by the wild card, but Roger didn't care. Like the others, Asif would have his uses, whether it be phone tapping, cutting a building's power at a particular time, or simply work that needed to be done off the record.

'Come in, Mr Manzoor. Are you well?'

Asif nodded nervously. 'Yes, sir. Thanks for seeing me, sir.'

'Not at all. Would you like a drink?'

'No, thank you.'

'To business then. What can I do for you?'

He already knew of course. Only those he'd already approved actually made it to a meeting, but Roger found it useful to have them explain themselves. It reminded them exactly why they needed him. As was often the case, Asif was in debt. Cash flow was difficult, the landlord charged unfair rent, the banks refused to give him a loan, and so he had turned to private individuals who took what he owed and tripled it. 'They're coming to collect on Friday and I don't have the money,' he confessed, tears threatening to break out of his bloodshot eyes.

Roger waited a few moments to let Asif's desperation simmer, then nodded. 'I understand, Mr Manzoor. It's not easy to make a life when the world's against you. Leave the matter with me. I'll have someone speak to your debtors, I'm sure they can be made to listen to reason.' Roger allowed the hope to flicker in Asif's eyes before crushing it again. 'I trust you have enough to repay the original amount?'

'I . . .' He shook his head. Now the tears started to flow.

'No need for that, Mr Manzoor. I will cover it.'

He sniffed and looked up. 'You will?'

'Yes. Consider it a gesture of friendship.'

Roger held out his hand. It had grown back over the years, along with his arm . . . but not quite as it was. Where his left hand was smoothed wood, his right was covered in a thick layer of bark, and shoots sprouted randomly on his arm no matter how often he trimmed them. The fingers were thicker too, the arm chunkier, still recognizable as a human limb but more an approximation than an exact replica.

Asif took it and shook it without hesitation, with the kind of reverence normally reserved for the Queen. 'Thank you, Green Man. Thank you.'

'Think nothing of it. I'm sure that if I needed something, you'd do the same for me.'

'I would, I would.'

Roger guided him to the door. 'I wish you and your family the best, Mr Manzoor.'

He'd not been alone long before there was another knock at the door. No further meetings were scheduled which meant trouble of one sort or another.

'Come in.'

Wayfarer stepped into the room with an early copy of tomorrow's paper. Her skirt was shorter than he would have preferred, and her penchant for wearing sunglasses at all times troubling, but in all other ways she was the product of a decent education and Roger was lucky to have found her.

'Is something wrong?' he asked.

She gave an emphatic nod as she offered him the paper.

Roger took it and saw the problem marked in inch-high letters.

TEENAGE JOKER KILLED BY OWN UNCLE!

Any joker killed by a nat demanded retaliation by the Twisted Fists. As it had happened on his turf, it would be up to him to see that five non-joker lives were taken as an example.

'This came around the same time,' added Wayfarer. 'For your eyes only.'

It was a small envelope containing a list of names. Sometimes Roger got to pick the targets for the strike himself. Sometimes not. He sighed. It was no surprise to find the joker's uncle on it, but the police would be expecting them, and he couldn't afford the attention a dead policeman would bring.

While he worried about that, a second name leapt out at him, one he'd come across in a previous life: Tristan Dove. Decorated naval officer and adviser to the government. He sighed a second time. What was Black Dog thinking? If the Fists killed a military hero they'd be vilified in the press.

Wayfarer waited until he looked up. 'Should I mobilize the crew?'

'Yes, but we're going to need some extra help on this one.' He folded the list and handed it back to her. 'I want eyes on these targets, up-to-date pictures, locations, and itineraries if you can.'

She nodded, vanishing the list in the manner of a street magician. 'Done.'

'And find the Hunter.'

'Herne? The one who did the . . .' she made a gesture with her index finger which would have made Roger blush if he were still able, '. . . movies?'

'Yes,' he snapped. 'That one.'

Wayfarer's eyebrows briefly appeared over the top of her sunglasses and then she left, leaving Roger to wonder how he was going to stop the mess he'd just been handed from blowing up in his face.

♣

They met on the cliffs under the setting sun, its last rays poking through cloud cracks. Roger paused to enjoy the feel of sunlight on his skin. The great outdoors had never held much appeal before his transformation, but being cooped up inside window-less rooms had really made him appreciate the simple joy of open space and the freedom to just walk.

It was tempting to simply pick a direction and go, but he diligently waited with Wayfarer for the other figure to join them at the top. There was too much work to do to go walking. A joker had been killed and the Twisted Fists needed to respond. This meant Roger had to organize a strike. *It was a little like being a god*, he mused, *choosing who would live and who would die.* Except that in this case Black Dog was the god and not him. A status quo Roger was less than happy with. While his usual crew dealt with the other four on the list, he was dealing with Tristan Dove, a man seen by many as a hero, which was why Roger was going to use a third party for maximum deniability.

Herne the Hunter was an impressive figure, an antlered giant, wild and muscular. Dark-red fur covered his legs, all the way from thighs to cloven hooves, matching the hair on his body and thick mane on his head. He was handsome with it, more mythical than monstrous. Roger would have hated him for that alone, but the Manchester United football shirt and shorts were additional incentive.

They'd met before, when Herne had called on the Fists to cover up a murder. He'd given his name as Dylan then. Roger was glad he knew it; Dylan was so much less impressive a moniker than Herne. It was easier to attach insults to as well. *Dylan the disaster, Dylan the desperate, Dylan the degenerate.* He was also Dylan the extremely dangerous, which was why Roger had called for the meeting in the first place.

Herne held up his hands as they approached. 'I know I'm late,' he rumbled. 'Roads are a joke.'

Roger couldn't help but look at his watch. 'Not to worry.'

'Traffic was mad.'

A genuine smile found its way onto Roger's face, and he exchanged a look with Wayfarer. The meeting had been arranged for six, sharp. He'd told Herne it was at five, banking on the other joker's unreliability. Whether they knew it or not, everyone would run on his time. 'Yes, well, shall we get down to business?'

'Yeah,' replied Herne, uncertainly. There was a nervousness to him that irritated Roger. 'You sure you want to do this?'

'Absolutely.' And this was true. He wanted to send Herne after their quarry. That way, when he failed to find Dove, Roger could blame the Hunter, and pick a new target more to his taste, satisfying the needs of the Fists and allowing a good man to enjoy his twilight years. 'We have all the details here.' He gestured to Wayfarer and she offered the file.

Herne flicked through the document, his owl-slitted eyes barely seeming to register the details. 'What's our problem with him?'

'It's in the file.'

Herne straightened a little, and Roger realized he'd misjudged how tall the knave was. Eight foot, at least, and that was before factoring in those antlers. 'Yeah, but I'm asking you. What you want me to unleash, does he deserve it?'

It was a good question, one that Roger had asked himself

many times. 'He is part of the establishment that keeps us down. An adviser to the Prime Minister in matters of security.'

'Oh, why didn't you say so? I'm happy to put down any friend of that bitch.'

Roger ground his teeth to stop himself from saying anything. How he wanted to put this animal in his place! But no, he needed Herne, and that meant he had to keep his peace. 'Do you have everything you need?'

'I need something of his. Something personal. You got it?'

'Wayfarer?'

She stepped forward and offered Herne a handkerchief, stolen from Dove by a hotel maid who owed the Green Man a favour.

Herne took it and sighed. 'You sure you want to do this? Last chance.'

'I am.'

'Right.' A battered silver horn hung from Herne's neck. He lifted it to his lips, took a deep breath, and paused. After a moment he seemed to become aware that they were staring at him expectantly. 'Right,' he said again, and blew.

The sun had slipped below the horizon as they'd talked, allowing a chill to creep in. Roger didn't feel it but he saw Wayfarer shiver, and silently chided the fashions designed to see all young women dead of exposure.

He'd only looked away from Herne for a moment but when his gaze returned to the knave, it was as if something else inhabited the man's body. The horn at his lips now glinted gold, not silver, and a green light burned within Herne's eyes in a way that was most unsettling. He seemed even taller too, if such a thing were possible.

'Let the quarry run!' roared Herne. 'Let it scurry, dart, and hide. It matters not, for the hunt has come. To me, hounds, to me, horse, to me—' He stopped, looking down at himself. 'Eh?'

An expression of confusion and disgust crossed the hunter's

face and Roger nodded approvingly as Herne ripped the football shirt from his body, casting the rags into the sea. A second
later, Roger stopped nodding, as the shorts were torn free and
sent after them, exposing Herne in all his glory.

'Sweet Jesus!' exclaimed Wayfarer.

'That's . . . unfeasible!' exclaimed Roger.

Herne blew on the horn a second time, longer, deeper than
the first, and from nowhere a mist rolled in, driven by a rising
wind. Up till now, Roger had always thought of the wild card
virus in scientific terms. There were many aspects of it he did
not understand but was able to fit into a framework of genetic
manipulation and altered physics. This, however, felt like something else entirely. This felt like myth and magic.

And perhaps it always had been. After all, his own body had
become living wood. Had he been in denial all these years? As
the mists closed about them, Roger felt his grip on a world of
logic and order become slippery.

Herne blew his horn a third time and the nearest edges of
the mist rippled and changed, giving birth to a black stallion
with eyes that burned with the same green fire as its master's.
Roger shook his head. This was too much. The sooner Herne
was on his way, and Roger could get back to normality, the
better.

Two more horses trotted out after Herne's stallion, like
ghosts, and Roger gasped as Wayfarer pulled herself onto the
nearest one.

'What are you doing?' he demanded.

'I don't know!' she replied. 'What are you doing?'

Absently, he'd reached up to the second horse's neck and
begun to pull himself onto its back. No, this wasn't part of
the plan at all. *This is not happening.* And yet here he was,
sitting astride a horse for the first time in his life as if it were
the most natural thing in the world.

Even through her sunglasses he could see a faint green glow
around Wayfarer's eyes. He wondered if his own had changed.

More shapes were coming out of the mist: hounds. Over two dozen red-eared, green-eyed monsters, padding silently to form a great pack at their back. They were smaller than the horses but not by much.

Herne threw down Dove's handkerchief and the pack rushed forward to sniff at it, tails wagging in excitement. 'Let noses lead us through the night, till sharp eyes find our mark, and sharper points let the crimson from his veins!'

The hunter leapt onto his stallion and raised a hand to the sky, and the hounds roared, and then, they were riding, flanked by the mist and the wind.

While most of Roger was on a horse, swept up in the madness of the hunt, a part of him remained untouched, and it worried him. He had not planned for this eventuality, had not even conceived it as a possibility. He did not wish the Fists to be connected to an attack on Tristan Dove . . .

Still, all was not lost. Twelve hours ago he'd sent a warning via Churchill that an attack was coming, with a strong recommendation to relocate Dove somewhere else, preferably abroad. No matter how many hounds Herne conjured, it wouldn't matter if Dove had already left.

They'd met not far from Dove's house, a large estate that enjoyed views of the Cornish sea, and it did not take long for it to come into sight. To Roger's horror, he saw lights on in the hallway and at least one upstairs.

But he'd sent word specifically to avoid this! Surely Churchill had heeded his warning? *Yes*, argued a voice in Roger's mind, *he must have done.*

This meant that either the lights were there to create the illusion of the house being occupied by people, or that a trap had been set. An ambush had always been a possibility, one that he'd been happy to entertain when it was just Herne carrying out the strike. He needed to remove Wayfarer and himself from the hunt immediately.

And yet, despite that thought being loud in his mind, he

did not slow the horse, nor did he call out to Wayfarer. In fact what he did was ride all the faster, doing his best to keep pace with Herne as he accelerated down the hill towards the house.

They came down like a force of nature, the thunder of hooves, the baying of the hounds, the howl of the wind, unstoppable. They tore past the house, close enough to see the flowers painted over the front door and the small swing in the back garden, and then it was behind them, a darkening shape soon swallowed by the mist.

'But . . .' began Roger, pointing over his shoulder, 'his house is over there!'

He wasn't sure if Herne could hear him over all the noise but the hunter replied in a voice just as loud, 'The hare runs fast but we are wise to his tricks.'

For hours they rode across fields and hills, the horses and hounds keeping a brutal pace, Roger's thoughts running wild alongside them. The experience was a lot like being drunk, except he wasn't saying horrible things to people or being sick or blacking out in the toilet.

Several villages were passed, and more than one farm, but if anyone heard their passing, none were stupid enough to let themselves be seen. At last they came to a stop on a rocky patch of beach. The moon had broken free of the clouds, casting a pale glow upon the waves. The horses panted while the hounds prowled restlessly along the water's edge.

Of course, thought Roger. They had caught Dove's trail and followed it as far as they could, but it ended here. Thank goodness he had specified the need to get Dove out of the country. It was getting easier to think clearly, the grip of the hunt weaker now that its energy was no longer focused.

'Wayfarer? Are you still with me?'

She nodded, though her nod was lacking in conviction. 'Can we go home now?'

'Yes. I think we've had more than enough excitement for one night.'

From further down the beach one of the hounds barked happily, and Roger's heart sank. The rest of the hunt trotted over, and soon the whole pack was echoing the first hound's eagerness. Roger followed their gaze. They were looking out to sea.

He couldn't make anything out at first, but there was a light just visible in the distance, a gentle winking above sea level, like a low-slung star. It was a ship but it was too far for them to reach.

Roger breathed a sigh of relief.

Herne's horse reared, kicking its front legs in the air as its rider spoke. 'No hill, no stone, no cracked earth shall stop us. No gate shall bar our way, no feint lead us astray, for blood's red path guides our feet, thick as Neptune's sea.'

Even the magic of the hunt could not stop Roger rolling his eyes at that one. He glanced over at Wayfarer but she was as rapt as the rest of the pack, staring out to the ship that he was certain Dove was on. It was more than an assumption. Roger knew it for a fact. He suspected that Wayfarer, Herne, and the pack knew it too.

Once more they surged forward, the hooves of their horses sending up a spray of foam as they raced out across the water. To Roger's amazement, he saw that they were not ploughing into the sea but skimming across the top of it.

He looked left and right to be sure, and a second time because it was so hard to credit. Yes, they were definitely riding over the surface of the water, and the hounds were still alongside them. No, he was not drunk. No, he was not dreaming, though he rather wished he was.

As they got closer, he could see that it was a patrol boat. Unarmed but fairly fast. The captain of the vessel had either heard or seen them as more lights came on, and its engines kicked into life.

Amazing as the horses and hounds were, they seemed bound to the same speeds as their natural counterparts. As the boat reached its top speed, the distance between them stopped shrinking, and then, by inches, began to grow.

Herne leaned back on his horse and reached into the mists which seemed to gather around his hand, thicken and take shape, until a spear had formed under his fingers, thick and heavy, green flames licking around its golden tip.

It flew from his hand with the speed of a missile, crossed the quarter of a mile of ocean between them in less than a second, and punched into the back of the boat. There was a groan as the engines stuttered and cut out, and then a hiss as water sloshed in through the new hole.

By the time the hunt had caught up, the boat was tilting, the front end lifting up as the back took on more and more water. Herne's horse hopped easily from the surface of the sea onto the deck of the boat. Roger's and Wayfarer's followed.

As they charged up the sloping deck, Roger saw the crew hurriedly trying to lower the lifeboats. Dove was among them but blocked from view by a number of soldiers pointing guns. There was no preamble or warning – things had gone too far for that – the soldiers simply opened fire.

The lead hounds stumbled as bullets struck them and faded bloodlessly into the mists. Whoever the soldiers were, they were well trained. Rather than baulk at the sight of the hunt, they simply discharged their weapons, reloaded, then fired again.

Roger ignored them, his eyes drawn to the lifeboat that Dove was boarding. He was so intent on his target that he didn't see the rifle swing in his direction. It was only after the bullet hit him in the chest that his rational mind was able to get him to attend to the real threat. By then he had been knocked off his horse and dumped onto his back.

Howls and gunshots filled the air, the pack taking heavy losses as it crossed the deck. While the bullet had lodged itself deep, the damage was only cosmetic, and when Roger stood up, the man who had shot him had the good grace to look shocked. Before Roger could take his revenge, however, the remains of the pack reached the soldiers.

It was hard to see what was happening in the crush of bodies but he heard the unmistakable sound of bones crunching, of jaws snapping, of men's screams, twisted, dying.

Herne was amid them all on his stallion, thrusting down into the carnage with his spear. He caught a glimpse of Wayfarer. She had one of the men by the head and was banging it repeatedly on the deck. Her face was like an angry stranger's.

Roger closed his eyes and took a deep breath. He had to take control of the situation. He had to take control of himself. He was not some animal to be driven mad by the scent of blood or the blast of a horn. He was civilized and educated. It was time to act like it.

A little calm returned. Roger wanted to believe this was because his own will was a match for the power of the hunt, but he could not deny that there was another possibility. For at that moment, he also knew that the hunt had ended. A hound had caught Tristan Dove by the ankle halfway to the lifeboat and dragged him back on deck. Mercifully, he died long before the pack finished with him.

Herne's stallion cantered sideways as the boat lurched. 'It is done! He is dead! The hunt is over and won! Come, man of green, the joys of mother night are calling, sweet wine and sweeter flesh.'

'No, thank you,' said Roger. The thought of going carousing with Herne was about as appealing as stabbing himself in the eye.

Herne turned his glowing stare to Wayfarer, pointed teeth showing as he smirked. 'And you, dark maiden?'

She was too busy wiping her hands on her skirt to answer. There was a franticness to the gesture, one that Roger knew well. This had been her first kill.

'No, Wayfarer will stay with me.'

There was a brief pout of disappointment and then Herne

shrugged it off, spurring his stallion to leap off the deck. 'Until next we meet, farewell!'

The hounds and the other horses had faded away, and when Herne rode out, it seemed he took the mist with him, leaving Roger to face reality.

Not for the first time that night, he sighed. Black Dog would be pleased but Churchill would be furious. Roger wasn't that happy either. Tristan Dove had not deserved to die this way. It served neither the national interest nor that of the Fists. *Not that the well-being of the Fists matters*, he reminded himself. No. He was just trying to pass Black Dog's test in order to gain his trust. That way he could lay a trap, cut off the head of the Fists once and for all, and get back his old life.

He took Wayfarer by the arm and guided her to the lifeboat, well aware that the sea was fast taking the deck from under them. 'Wayfarer?' He raised his voice. 'Wayfarer?'

She looked up in his direction but her attention seemed elsewhere. 'Hmm?'

'I don't suppose you know anything about sailing, do you?'

She shook her head and Roger sighed again. It was going to be a long trip home.

♣ ♦ ♠ ♥

Twisted
Logic

Part 4

Belfast, 1994

ROGER PAUSED AT THE door. It struck him that it had been a long time since he had gone to someone else's room for a meeting. It was stranger still to feel intimidated. He didn't dare pause for long though, Sir Winston Churchill was not the sort of man to be kept waiting.

As he raised his hand to knock, he saw his shirt had snagged on a shoot growing from his forearm. A careful tug of the sleeve dealt with the problem but not his irritation. He'd only had it trimmed two weeks ago. Honestly, his body was more effort to manage than his garden, and that was saying something.

Getting to Churchill was harder than ever, and if he hadn't had the old man's assistance it would have been impossible. The Silver Helix were here in force and on high alert, though for what, Roger had no idea. It made him nervous. He had no wish to meet the lumbering Captain Flint, let alone the Lion, Enigma, Redcoat, or the other aces in residence.

Normally this door would be manned, but at the prearranged time the hallway was empty. Nobody else knew he was coming, and there were to be no witnesses. Ironically, if he really were a terrorist leader of the Twisted Fists, this would be the ideal time for an assassination attempt.

But he was not, and in a few hours he wouldn't even be a spy any more. He would be free of Green Man, the Fists, the violence, all of it.

He knocked on the door.

'Come in,' said an unmistakable voice.

Churchill seemed much the same as when they'd first met. A little less hair perhaps, a little wider, but still commanding. He leaned heavily on his cane as he stood to shake Roger's hand. 'Barnes.'

'Sir Winston.'

'Drink?'

'No, thank you.'

'Cigar?'

'No, thank you.'

Churchill nodded and eased himself back into his chair. 'Are you getting taller, Barnes, or is time playing tricks on my memory?'

'I've gained a few inches over the years.' He'd had to have new suits tailored because of it. His neck had grown thicker too, enough to force him to adjust his collars. Not to mention the growths on his right arm and the persistent shoot that kept sprouting from the old gunshot wound in his chest. But it was unlikely Churchill was interested in those details, so he kept them to himself.

'If only it were a few inches in my case,' said Churchill, patting his belly for emphasis. 'Doubtless you have many questions, but given our lack of time, I will take the liberty of asking the most important one first. Do you have it?'

Roger took a piece of paper from his inside jacket pocket and passed it over. 'Black Dog is here in Belfast for a few days, alone. He's come for something big but even I don't know what it is. The top items on the list are the safe houses he'll be using while he's here, the bottom ones detail his options on his way out of Europe.'

Roger had a lot more than that of course. Apart from the Black Dog, he knew more than anyone about the assets of the Twisted Fists: the identities of every member of the UK cell, their plans, their allies, enough to bury them. The list he'd given Churchill didn't contain any of that, however. While he was sure the great statesman would keep his word, it seemed prudent to hold a few cards back in case he needed to bargain further down the line.

Churchill slapped him on the arm. 'Good man! This calls for a drink.' He was halfway through pouring his own glass when he added: 'Are you sure you won't join me in a brandy?'

'Yes, Sir Winston, but I appreciate the offer.'

A glass was raised towards him. 'Here's to the end of the Twisted Fists and another triumph for civilized society!'

Roger smiled politely and waited for Churchill to have a sip. 'When can I go home, sir?'

'Soon, Barnes. Soon.'

'With all due respect, why not now? My mission was to give you Black Dog. I've done that. It's taken nearly a decade but I've done it.'

Churchill put down his drink. 'Now hold on there, Barnes. What you've done is give me a piece of paper, nothing more. Should this paper enable us to capture the Black Dog, I will personally oversee arrangements to send you swiftly back to where you belong. However, it is not my way to uncork the champagne before the race is won. If the Black Dog manages to evade capture, as he has done many times in the past, we will need you in position, right where you are, more than ever.'

It made sense. In Churchill's position Roger would probably do the same but he didn't like the feeling of being used. 'How long?'

'I would have thought that was clear, Barnes. As long as it takes, and not a minute longer.'

'Can I ask how my family are?'

'Safe and sound.'

'I . . . how are they managing without me?'

'They're troupers, Barnes. They're fine and they want for nothing. As promised, I have seen to it that all of their financial needs are taken care of.' He began to cough, eventually taking another long sip of his brandy when the fit subsided. 'Excuse me. Now, tell me about the Black Dog.'

'Where do you want me to start?'

'What does he look like?'

'I don't know.'

Churchill coughed again, more for effect this time. 'My hearing must be going. I thought you said you didn't know what he looked like, which would be ridiculous, given that you have been taken into his confidence.'

'He's always masked. I've never seen his face. To the best of my knowledge, Sir Winston, nobody has.'

'How are we to apprehend a man when we don't know what he looks like? Even if we do apprehend someone in a dog mask, how will we know we have the right person?'

'Trust me, you'll know if you get him. He's not like other people.'

'I need specifics, man. How is he different? How?'

'I don't know how to describe it other than to say he's a leader. I've never met anyone like him.' In truth, he had, but Roger was sure Churchill wouldn't appreciate being compared to a terrorist. 'In terms of specifics: he's tall, over six foot, and well built. His accent is an odd blend. I'd say he's spent considerable time in the Middle East and the United States. I'd guess him to be in his forties but given that he's a joker, I've no idea how much the years show in his face.'

'What about his mutation? Has he shown any abilities?'

'None. I know he's had military training of some kind and I'm certain he is capable under pressure.' Roger could see the scowl on Churchill's face growing. 'But that doesn't matter. You know where he's going to be. All you have to do is watch the safe houses and you'll soon have him. There won't be many people of his stature going into those precise locations in the next few days.'

Churchill knocked back the last of his brandy. 'I suppose we will find out one way or another. Are you sure this information is reliable? I'm going to have to pull a lot of strings to be able to operate here on such short notice.'

He had been certain until Churchill had asked the question and now he wasn't sure at all. However, he was damned if he was going to lose another ten years, so he said: 'I'd stake my reputation on it.'

This got a nod from Churchill. 'So be it. Now, you need to leave here before Captain Flint comes back, and I need to get myself to the Belfast Hilton.'

The Roger of old would have left without another word, but as Green Man, he had grown unaccustomed to dismissals. 'And when you get Black Dog, what then?'

'Then you leave word in the usual manner and we will come and collect you.'

'Yes, sir. Thank you.'

They shook hands again and Roger made for the door. As he opened it, Churchill tapped his cane on the ground, making Roger turn. 'Nail your patience to the wall, Barnes, and keep an ear to the ground. It won't be long now, I assure you.'

♣

Over the next few hours Roger was glad for his mask, otherwise his face would surely have given him away. For nearly ten years, he'd lived in constant fear of being discovered as a spy by the Black Dog, but somehow he'd learned to deal with it, throwing himself deeply enough into running his cell of the Twisted Fists that he often forgot it was all pretence.

The day when he could leave the Fists had seemed so distant that he'd half suspected it would never come, and somehow that had made it easier to be Green Man. Now that he was finally on the cusp of going home, he found himself thinking about his old life with painful clarity. It was as if Roger Barnes had been hibernating through the horror and now he was waking up again.

He wondered about Wendy. He'd always pictured their reunion as a joyous thing but would it be? She was very conservative in her tastes and he was a giant tree. Quite apart from the fact he would be an embarrassment to her in public, there were various aspects of their relationship that, in biological terms, could not function as they had before. Given the choice, she'd probably rather remain a widow.

He hoped Christine and Roy would be more open-minded but the truth was he had no idea. The last time he'd seen them, they'd been children. They'd be strangers now.

They'd get through it though. No matter what they'd thought of him, he'd swoop back into their lives on the back of Churchill's glowing endorsement. Wendy loved the man almost as much as Roger did. He'd be like a hero in an adventure story, one of the ridiculous ones that his children used to like so much. He very much hoped that was still the case.

The knock at the door made him jump. He wasn't expecting anyone, and that meant something bad had happened. 'Come in.'

Wayfarer stepped inside. He knew she had to wear the sunglasses but wished that she didn't, as it made her much harder to read. 'When did you get back?'

'About half an hour ago,' he replied, not liking her tone. 'Is there a problem?'

Her jaw dropped. 'You haven't heard?'

'Clearly.'

'Where have you been? The news is everywhere!'

He placed his hands flat on the desk to keep them from shaking. This had to be it. Churchill must have used his information to bring down Black Dog. He tried to remain nonchalant. 'What's happened?'

'It's Black Dog! They're saying he's killed Churchill.'

The world seemed to spin around Roger. His fingers bored down, making the surface of the desk crack. An image of Wendy appeared in his mind, then faded. He tried to bring it back again but couldn't. When he reached for thoughts of his children, all he could conjure were pairs of shorts covered in ice cream. No smiles, no faces, nothing to hold on to.

Without Churchill there was nobody to vouch for him. Without Churchill there was nobody to explain his actions over the past decade, to transform criminality into heroism, brutal murder into patriotic service. There would be no pardon. No redemption. No reunion.

He was trapped.

The desk groaned under the pressure of his hands, threatening to splinter.

'Are you all right?' asked Wayfarer.

'Out,' replied Roger, dismissing her while he could still control himself enough to do so. He needed space to think and the privacy in which to express panic. It all made sense now: the secrecy around Black Dog's visit, the fact that he'd worked alone. Churchill had an odd status in the Fists. He was no joker but he was no nat either, and was still a hero in the minds of many. Black Dog wouldn't have been sure if the others would back him, that's why he hadn't told anybody of his true purpose.

Roger had thought it coincidence that both of his masters were in Belfast at the same time, but the truth had been far more sinister. He put aside thoughts of his own losses to consider what this meant. Had Churchill organized the strike against Black Dog before he was killed? Had anyone found the list Roger had given him? If one of Churchill's people had they might still bring the Black Dog down. If Black Dog had found it, however, then Roger was in serious trouble.

There was no way out. No way back to what he was. To survive, Roger would have to double down on everything he'd achieved for the Fists. He'd have to wear the mask of Green Man for real, forever.

He took a long hard look at what that would mean and shivered.

Another knock at the door made him jump just as much as the first. When he spoke, however, his mask was in place, his voice as calm as ever. 'Come in.'

Wayfarer did so and closed the door behind her. 'King Brian wants to see you. He says it's urgent.' She hesitated, then added, 'He doesn't seem himself.'

'What do you mean?'

'He's dressed differently and he's nervous, he didn't stop moving when I spoke to him. And . . .'

Her hesitance was playing into his own nerves. 'And?' he snapped.

'And it's the first time he's actually looked at my face when he talked to me.'

'I'd have thought that a good thing.'

'It is, but . . .'

'Out with it, Wayfarer. I cannot abide an unfinished sentence.'

The words poured out of her. 'But he's obviously scared. I think something awful is about to happen. Are you sure you want to go and see him?'

'Given that we're his guests, we can hardly say no.'

'Yes, it's just that I don't trust him.'

Nor do I, he thought, *but to run would be to invite suspicion. I need to keep my head in the lion's jaws a little longer. Perhaps King Brian suspects me, perhaps he doesn't.*

This was out of his comfort zone. Planning, preparation, minimal risk, in these things he excelled. Chaos and chance taking did not suit him. *It's a good thing I don't have to worry about blood pressure or heart attacks any more, or I wouldn't last the day.*

A few minutes later, he stepped into King Brian's room,

leaving Wayfarer instructions that if he didn't return within the hour she was to flee. The leader of the Belfast cell of the Twisted Fists had changed dramatically since they'd last met. He'd shaved off his beard and exchanged the usual fancy attire in favour of a worn tracksuit and hoodie. From a distance he'd pass as a child, so long as nobody looked at his face. A few of the Fists liked to joke about Brian, but Roger had always had respect for him. Anyone with his disadvantages who could hold on to a position of leadership had to be taken seriously.

Brian was pacing as he arrived, making quick, impulsive turns.

'Is something wrong?' asked Roger.

'Wrong? Fucked is what it is. Totally fucked.'

This is good. He seems worried about things other than me. 'Would you care to elaborate?'

Brian shot a look in Roger's direction, but over his shoulder rather than at his face. Someone was behind him. He felt it like a bolt of lightning to the spine, and knew who it was even before he turned: the Black Dog.

He realized he'd been wrong. This was not good, not good at all. Trapped between Brian and the Black Dog, he had no choice but to turn and face the muzzled mask.

Roger had wondered if Black Dog was a mantle worn by more than one man. The founder of the Fists should be old now, and yet the man before him projected a sense of physical as well as personal power. It would be practical too, allowing the Black Dog to be everywhere at once, and if nothing else, symbols were much harder to kill than people.

However, he was in no doubt that this was the Black Dog he'd met before. There was something compelling about him, and when he spoke, his voice was unmistakably rich. 'Churchill is dead. The papers are saying we did it.'

Within the mask, Black Dog's eyes were cast in shadows, unreadable. Roger had no idea what he or King Brian knew about his true agenda or what this meeting was actually about, and it was unbearable. 'Did we? Kill him, I mean.'

Brian stopped pacing to give a bitter laugh. 'Are you kidding me? They used a helicopter to do it, a fucking gunship. Do you see any helicopters around here?'

'No.'

'Right. Though I could use one about now. The Silver Helix are going absolutely mental. No telling what they're going to do but it ain't going to be pretty.'

'If we didn't move against Churchill, do we know who did?'

The Black Dog and Brian exchanged a look and Roger realized that there was a loop and he most definitely was not in it.

'Oh yes,' replied Black Dog. 'The public has no idea what is really going on, nor do the press. They're blaming us because we're easy targets, just as they always do. I know the truth, however. I have for a long time.'

Roger waited to be enlightened but nothing more was said on the matter, instead, Brian appeared at his side. 'Look, I hate asking for favours, but me and my people need a place to lie low until this has all blown over, somewhere in England. Can you help me out?'

'Surely you'd rather use your own safe houses than mine?'

'Can't.' He and Black Dog exchanged another look.

There was a pause and Roger decided to push. 'If you want my help, then at least tell me what sort of danger you're in.'

'We're compromised,' said Black Dog. 'There are spies in the Fists.'

Oh God. Here we go. This is why they brought me in. Stay calm, Roger. Stay calm. There's a chance they don't know it's you. Don't give yourself away. 'Spies?' He tried to sound surprised. 'Are you sure?'

'Certain. Information is slipping out to other organizations. There are hostile eyes in Jerusalem and Belfast, and possibly London as well. Check your people, Green Man, check them well.'

'I will.'

'I've tried to keep the other cells out of this but there are random factors beyond my control. King Brian has learned too much, and as such, is now a target.'

'I can protect him.'

'Be sure that you do. He has something important to take care of.'

'Is that why you asked for me?'

'Not entirely,' the Black Dog said. 'I won't tell you why I'm here or what I'm working on, but I will say this: when I leave for Jerusalem, it may be for the last time. Forces are in play that even I cannot predict. If things go well, you will know soon enough. If they don't, whatever happens, the Twisted Fists must endure.' He put a hand on Roger's shoulder. 'They must have a leader. And that leader must be recognized by the others and obeyed.' He looked at Brian. 'Do you understand?'

'What? Him? That's—' The Black Dog stared at Brian long enough to make the little man swallow. 'Sure, I hear you clear as day. I'll back him up. We all will.'

Black Dog's muzzled mask swung back towards Roger. 'Do you understand?'

Did he understand? The devil wanted him to take his place, to become the very thing he was supposed to bring down. The thought of it was suffocating.

And yet, if that happened he'd be able to complete Churchill's mission, even though the old man wouldn't be around to see it. He could go to one of the Silver Helix. If Churchill had shared his secrets with anyone, it would be them. And even if he hadn't, Roger could give them Brian as a gesture of goodwill, and then the rest of the Fists shortly after. They'd have to deal with him even if they didn't want to. Perhaps there was still a chance.

He met Black Dog's stare. 'Yes. I understand.'

◆

Westminster, 1994

It seemed as if the whole of England had turned out for Winston Churchill's funeral. Westminster Abbey was packed, as were the streets around it. The police were doing their best to keep order but the crowds were so large it was like trying to control the currents in the ocean.

Roger was among them, feeling alternately anonymous and exposed. He wore dark glasses to hide his wooden eyes, and a long coat, gloves, scarf, and hat to cover the rest of him. What little skin was left visible he had lightened with make-up. A serious inspection would spot something odd immediately, but everyone was swept up in the pomp and ceremony of the day.

Churchill was an icon, a symbol of British pride that harked back to an older time. He'd seemed immortal: certainly his ace had enabled him to remain proactive for over a century. Like everyone else here, Roger felt the loss keenly, and had come to pay his respects.

Ideally, he'd have watched the ceremony itself but the Silver Helix were all inside the Abbey and Roger couldn't get close. Worse, both the Helix and the authorities seemed to be on high alert. It wasn't just that they wanted to ensure the funeral went smoothly, it was as if they were expecting trouble. There was a tension in the air that transmitted to the crowd. Even the trio of mangy-looking crows on the rooftop opposite seemed to be waiting for something. He had the feeling it had something to do with the people behind Churchill's death, but knowing so little about the situation left him feeling helpless and out of his depth.

And so he found himself adrift in the crowd, trying to see as much as he could without drawing attention to himself.

A line of policemen formed a living fence on either side of the road, allowing cars to drop off important visitors. Roger was close enough to recognize various members of the royal family, foreign dignitaries, high-ranking military officers, lords, politicians, and the ex-Prime Minister, Margaret Thatcher. They were all so close and yet so far away, like images from a vivid fever dream. Even if the police weren't in the way, it would be impossible for him to enter their world again.

And then, some time after the famous guests had been escorted into the Abbey, he saw a black cab arrive, and three small figures in sombre dress get out. Two women and a young man, none of them much over five foot tall. He could catch only snatches through the lines of people, hints and flashes, gone even as his brain tried to decipher them, but he knew what he was seeing.

Wendy! It was his Wendy! That meant the smart young woman next to her had to be Christine, and that slight young man little Roy. He felt the ghost of the urge to cry, but no actual tears came, the ducts dry since his card had turned. His family were alive and well. Churchill had told him so, but until now a part of him had feared the worst.

They're still together. The thought was bittersweet. *I should be with them. I should have been with them. All these years, I should have been with them.*

The sense of loss was physical, as if someone were crushing his chest. He'd missed his children growing up, he'd missed a decade of their lives. A decade! *And for what?* For a mission that no longer had a leader. It suddenly struck him that Wendy had been forced to raise Christine and Roy alone. *What must that have been like? What must she think of me? A man who abandons his family. A traitor to his country. A monster.*

His usual reserve broke like a dam, shattering under the sudden swell of emotion. Without thinking, he pushed forward, jostling people left and right as he struggled to keep sight of them.

The black cab pulled away and the three started to walk towards the great arched entrance. He could appreciate Christine's excellent posture, and that Wendy was wearing her hair differently, but he couldn't see their faces. So he pushed forward again, making several people shake their heads at him, and one of the policeman turned in his direction.

Little Roy still had his side parting. Roger nodded in approval. A sensible haircut suggested a disciplined boy. His suit looked good, though the boy would probably grow out of it before he needed it again. Wendy wouldn't care about expense on a day like this, however. He wondered how she was surviving financially. Had she had to get a job or was Churchill's support enough? And had arrangements been made to keep the flow of money going after his death? Roger resolved to find out.

All too soon they had gone from view, joining the throng of guests inside the Abbey, leaving him bereft. He knew he should melt back into the crowd before someone noticed him, but he couldn't make his feet move. Though his tear ducts no longer worked, he found that his body could still go through the motions, and he sank to his knees, hand clamped to mouth to stop from crying out.

'Sir?' said a voice.

He looked up to find that one of the police officers had detached themselves from the line and come over to him. 'Can I help you, sir?'

Roger could feel his scrutiny like unwanted hands on his skin. It was important that he end this conversation and slip away before the officer realized who he was. 'I'm so sorry,' he said, trying to hide beneath the brim of his hat. 'I'm a bit overwhelmed by it all.'

The policeman crouched down next to him and put a friendly hand on his arm. 'You're not the only one, sir. He touched a lot of lives.'

'Yes,' Roger agreed, 'he certainly touched mine.'

'You knew Sir Winston?'

Roger smiled. 'I'm proud to say I did.'

That was his mistake. None of his preparations had covered his teeth. The policeman unconsciously leaned away, his eyes widening. 'Wait, you aren't right.'

'Please, don't be alarmed. I'm here with the best of intentions. I just wanted to pay my—'

'You're a bloody joker!'

'—respects.'

'Oh my Christ, you're him!'

'Please keep your voice down,' said Roger as he stood up. 'I'll go.'

The policeman's truncheon came up smartly, striking Roger on the side of the head. He didn't feel it, but the blow knocked the hat off his head and broke the glasses he wore so that they hung lopsided on his face.

'It's . . . it's the Green Man! Hey! I've got the Green Man!'

Heads began to whip round to see what the commotion was about and Roger realized that if he didn't act quickly things would become disastrous. 'I'm not here to cause trouble,' he said, holding up his hands to emphasize the point.

Unfortunately his words were drowned out by the shouts of nearby people, each one whipping the mood further from solemn, and closer to outrage.

'He's one of them Twisted Fists what did in Churchill!'

'Bloody terrorist!'

'*Killer!*'

'*Joker scum!*'

As Roger tried to stay calm, there was a loud click as the policeman snapped cuffs on his outstretched wrists. The one on his left locked shut, but his right wrist had grown back too bulky for the cuff and it remained open.

'Please!' he said. 'I just need to talk to—'

But he never finished his sentence. Hands were grabbing for him and the policeman was trying to force the handcuff closed on his right wrist, shouting loudly for back-up as he did so.

This was just what Roger was trying to avoid. He needed more time to gather information on the Fists before the police took him. A public arrest was the worst possible outcome; the

Fists would go to ground, rendering his information useless. He also knew that Twisted Fists did not have a good time in prison.

He grabbed the policeman and pulled him close, lifting the man off his feet as he did so. 'I'm sorry.'

The policeman moaned as Roger swung him around his head like a flail, cracking a few skulls and gaining himself some space. He then threw the officer at the crowd and charged in the opposite direction. A few brave souls grabbed at him but he knocked them aside with a sweep of his arms and they fell away like wheat at harvest time.

Other officers were trying to converge on his position but were struggling to do so quickly. Whistles were blown, and voices raised, only to be drowned out by the distant sound of screaming. It would only be a matter of time before one of the many Silver Helix aces made an appearance and then he'd be in real trouble.

But somehow, miraculously, none of them came. In fact nobody seemed to be following him any more. Then he realized the sounds of screams and gunfire were coming from the Abbey – nothing to do with him at all. For a moment he paused, shocked by the idea of automatic weapons being discharged in such a sacred place. The desire to go and check on his family was almost overwhelming, but he crushed it. If Captain Flint and the Silver Helix couldn't contain the problem, no one could. All he would do is add to the chaos.

As he continued to plough through the masses he told himself he wasn't being a coward. He told himself he was taking the only correct and prudent course of action in the circumstances. He took no satisfaction from being right.

A few minutes later he stumbled from the edge of the crowd and into the streets. Wayfarer was waiting on a motorcycle nearby. She passed him a helmet as he climbed onto the back.

Mercifully, she didn't say anything, the manner of his arrival being all the briefing necessary. The engine roared, the motorcycle leapt into action, and seconds later they were weaving through the traffic, gone.

♠

London, 1994

There had been no word from the Black Dog. Roger secretly hoped for the worst. It was the best chance for him to get his life back. If the leader of the Twisted Fists fell and he was put in charge, he could give the whole organization over to the Silver Helix in one go. If the Black Dog returned from Jerusalem, the best Roger could do was wait and hope that a chance came later. He wasn't sure how much longer he could face waiting.

What he needed more than ever was something to wait for, a guarantee that on the day he finally got free, Wendy and Christine and little Roy would still be there for him.

That was why he was sitting in the back of yet another battered old van waiting for nightfall. He was going to pay his family a visit. He'd tell Wendy the truth, or at least as much of the truth as he thought she could handle. She deserved to know the truth.

His fist clenched.

And I deserve for her to know the truth.

Finding their address hadn't been easy. They'd moved house at least once since he'd lived with them, and were no longer in the phone book. However, Roger had accrued a lot of favours over the years, and the rest of Wendy's family hadn't been so well hidden. Once he'd found her brother, it was just a case of tapping his phone and waiting. Wendy's behaviour hadn't changed: like clockwork she called on the first day of the month after dinner. Once he had the time of the call, he was able to have his 'friend' Mr Manzoor trace it via some old contacts at British Telecom.

Only Wayfarer had come with him. He hadn't told her why they were here and she hadn't asked any questions. It made him appreciate the privilege of his position. The power of it. So far, he'd used that power for the Black Dog and Sir Winston, may he rest in peace. Tonight, he would use that power to help himself.

Just this once. This one evening with my loved ones, and then I'll suffer for as long as it takes to see this through.

He stepped out into the night, telling Wayfarer to wait for him here and under no account to follow, no matter what happened.

She nodded, professional as ever. 'I'll be on the other end of the phone if you need me.'

He looked at the blocky piece of plastic in his hand and frowned. It seemed as if the world was losing all sense of style. Of course mobile phones had their uses but did they have to be so ugly? 'Good,' he replied, 'I'm not expecting trouble, but if you see anything, call me.'

He wouldn't answer, but the number of rings would tell him what he needed to know: one ring for regular police, two for riot troops or military, three for Silver Helix.

'Will do. Good luck.'

He stopped to look at her. She didn't usually wish him luck. Had he let slip how important tonight was? Or was he reading into things? He was undeniably nervous.

Better not to say anything, he thought, and strode away from the van.

The clouds were thick, blotting out the moon and stars, and a thin drizzle misted the light from the lampposts. He took a couple of turns, checking to see that he wasn't being followed, before turning into a leafy estate.

The new house was set back from the road in a nice part of Northwood. Trees and high hedges ensured the residents' privacy. Once past the leafy walls, he saw a crescent driveway dividing a well-manicured garden. On the way to the front door he stopped, arrested by the sight of a small kennel that couldn't be seen from the road.

'Could it be?' he murmured, and crept over.

The small silhouette of a sleeping terrier was just visible in the pale light coming from the house.

'Oh, William, you poor old thing.' They'd bought him as a puppy seventeen years ago and the children adored him. 'What are you doing out here, eh?' The dog had always liked company, and usually slept by one bedroom door or another. No doubt Wendy had exiled him here for some toilet-related misdemeanour. It was tempting to stroke him, but if William woke up, he might start barking. Better to come back once he'd talked to the others.

Roger had spent an embarrassing amount of time deliberating what to wear for the occasion. It had been one of the hardest choices of his life, and he'd gone back and forth between several suits before making a final decision. The Green Man mask was in his pocket. He'd partly taken it out of habit, and partly because he didn't want to give Wayfarer any cause for suspicion.

He ran his fingers over it now, enjoying the feel of familiarity. As much as Green Man had done wrong, he represented a more confident side of Roger's personality; rational, purposeful, strong.

I must be all of those things tonight and more, he thought.

There were fresh flowers in the baskets by the door, artfully arranged. Wendy's handiwork, no doubt. She had always had an eye for decor.

He allowed himself a smile, a deep breath, and then he rang the doorbell.

Footsteps.

A light in the hall came on.

He wondered who was coming. Would it be Wendy? One of the kids? What if she'd remarried? The idea hadn't even occurred to him until now but it made so much sense. It would probably be someone tall. Wendy always admired their taller male friends when she thought he wasn't looking.

But no, the hazy shape through the frosted glass panels in the door did not seem tall or male. He heard the rattle of a chain, then two keys being turned in the lock, and then the door opened.

It was Christine.

She looked up at Roger and her mouth fell open. He was delighted to see that she had inherited his teeth rather than Wendy's, though that was tempered by how tired she looked. Her face seemed too thin to be healthy.

'Christine,' he said. 'It's me. I've come back.'

She stared at him, the seconds ticking by as she fought to contain a number of expressions. Finally she said, 'Dad? Is that really you?'

'It is. Can I come in?'

She shook her head. 'I don't know.'

'I just want to talk. I know you've probably heard things and I know that I don't look exactly as you remember me. But I can explain it all if you'll give me a chance.'

She held on to the door, ready to close it if necessary. 'We've been told not to talk to you.'

'Give me ten minutes with you and your mother, five even. After that if you want me to go, I promise never to bother you again.'

The door opened fully. 'Five minutes.'

'Thank you.' He wanted to hug her but it was too soon for that. He'd have to take things slowly and carefully. They'd all be like wild animals ready to start at the slightest provo-cation.

She led him through the hall and into the front room. The house was bigger than their last one but much of the decoration remained the same, Wendy's floral stamp finding its way into the landscapes, wallpaper, and lampshades.

Christine directed him to one of the chairs. 'Are you . . . do you sit?'

'Of course.'

'Then sit down. I'll go and talk to Mum. I don't know if she'll come down. She's . . .'

'I'll leave it in your hands. Is Roy here?'

'No, he's on a school trip.'

'That's a shame. I've missed him too.'

Christine didn't say anything to that and retreated back to the hall.

Left to his own devices, Roger started examining his surroundings, hungry for any information he could glean. He recognized the two contemporary art books on the coffee table. Wendy had picked them up from a holiday in France and he would bet good money that she'd never opened either of them.

There was a display case containing various school trophies and certificates. Christine had kept up with her dancing, but he also saw her name on cups for several martial arts, horse riding, and clay pigeon shooting. Roy's efforts were harder to find but he did see some certificates for participation in chess tournaments.

This is good. My daughter is an over-achiever. My son has a good mind, and my wife's spirit remains undaunted.

He started to wander the room, finding photographs of holidays, birthdays, and significant successes. Not a single one contained Roger, his wedding photograph conspicuous by its absence.

And then he saw the silver-framed picture in pride of place over the mantelpiece. It showed his children, both younger, posing with the Lion. Christine sat in his left palm, Roy in his right, and the ace was holding them effortlessly while performing a slight shrug for the camera. William was in the photo too, his front paws resting on the Lion's leg.

They were all smiling, even the dog, each set of white teeth like a knife in his guts. His fingers creaked as he ground his fingernails into his palms.

It should be me in that picture. Me!

When Christine came back into the room, he had returned to his chair, outwardly composed.

'Mum's a bit shocked but she says she'll try and come down.'

'I'm happy to wait.'

Christine went to the furthest chair from Roger's and perched on the edge of it. She attended to her feet for a moment and then seemed to remember he was there. 'Uh, would you like a cup of tea?'

'No, thank you.'

'Oh.' She stood up, having barely sat long enough to leave an impression on the seat. 'I'm going to make a pot so it's no bother. Mum will want one when she comes down.'

'In that case, a cup of tea would be lovely.'

Christine bolted from the room, leaving Roger wondering how he would ever bridge the gap between them. The grandfather clock ticked loudly as he sat there, the only sound save for the background whistle of a kettle.

In truth, he would have loved to be able to enjoy a cup of tea, but he'd been unable to stomach it since his card turned. These days he subsisted on water and sunshine.

Five minutes later, Christine returned with a tray of cups, and a plate of digestive biscuits. Her hand shook as she poured. 'I'm sorry, I don't know how you take it.'

'Black, please.'

They sat holding their cups in silence, neither of them drinking. 'Mum might be a while. She's putting her face on.'

'That's fine. Perhaps we might talk while we're waiting for her?'

'Okay.'

'I have so many questions it's hard to know where to start.' He gestured at the cabinet. 'I see that you've graduated and that you have excelled in many different areas. It makes me proud.' She grimaced. *Was that meant to be a smile?* He pushed on, trying to keep things upbeat. 'But I'd like to know so much more. What you do for a living, what you do for fun, how the last ten years have been. All of it.'

'You said you could explain things,' she replied.

'Yes.'

'I think you should do that first.'

He glanced towards the ceiling. There was no sound or sign of Wendy coming down. 'That's fair. Well, as you know, everything changed the day my card turned. I was reported as a threat and the Silver Helix came and picked me up.'

'Why didn't you tell mum?'

'They didn't let me. I was taken away and put in a cell.'

'Like prison?'

'Worse. I wasn't even given a phone call.'

'But that doesn't make sense. Everyone has rights, jokers included.'

'That's true but . . .' he leaned forward and was relieved to see that she didn't flinch back '. . . Churchill's intervention changed all that.'

'Churchill? *The* Churchill?'

'Yes.' He told her about the meeting and how he had agreed to go undercover in order to bring down the Twisted Fists. She nodded as he spoke, hesitant at first but with growing conviction. He realized that, deep down, Christine must want to believe him. Emboldened, he kept going. It felt good, like a great weight were being lifted from his shoulders.

'And now I'm trapped,' he concluded. 'Only Sir Winston knew about me.'

'There must be someone else,' she argued. 'Like Captain Flint or the Prime Minister. Or an encoded file that was to be released on his death.'

'If there is one, I was never told about it.'

'What was it like being in the Twisted Fists?'

'You really want to know?'

'Yes.'

He was suddenly aware that he wasn't talking to a little girl any more but to a grown woman, one that was intelligent and capable. 'All right, I will. Can I just say, Christine, that it is so good to be with you again. Now, the Twisted Fists, where should I—'

He was interrupted by the horrible tinny ring of his phone. *Police?*

'So sorry,' he said, genuinely embarrassed.

It rang a second time. *Armed units?*

'You can get it if you want.'

A third ring, then silence. *The Silver Helix!*

'I'm sorry. Really I am, but I have to go.'

'What? But you've only just come back! You can't just go again.'

He stood up. 'I've already had much more than the five minutes you gave me.'

She did the same. 'That doesn't matter. You have to stay. If you leave before Mum comes down, you'll destroy her.'

'It will be worse if I stay, believe me.'

'Why?'

'Because they'll take me away and I won't ever be able to come back.'

'Tell them what you told me. Make them understand.'

He shook his head and moved towards the hall. 'I wish it were that simple.' For a moment he thought she was going to try and block him going, but she changed her mind at the last minute and let him pass.

He moved quickly to the front door, trying to decide on the best route back to the van, when he heard the sound of barking. It was William. Something had woken the old dog up. *They're already here.*

Consumed by thoughts of escape, he turned and rushed towards the back of the house. The door to the front room was still open and he caught a glimpse of Christine standing by the window. Her posture was straighter, as it had been at the funeral, and she was talking in a low voice.

'. . . leaving. Alone. Do you have visual?'

If he'd still had a heart, it would have broken in that moment. 'I've been such a fool. You called the Silver Helix, didn't you?'

'Of course I did.'

'But I thought you understood . . .'

'I do, better than you know.' She started to name names, each one familiar to him. Each one, a bullet: 'Jason Abbott, Shawn Weeks, Jenny Bell, Tristan Dove, Kay Livingston, the list goes on. All dead because of you. I've committed every one of them to memory. Oh yes, Dad, I know what you are and I know what you've done, and I'm going to make you pay.'

She'd played him and he'd fallen for it. There had never been any convincing her, he saw it now. Wendy would be the same. All these years he'd been clinging to a dream that didn't even exist. Churchill was gone. His family had turned on him. What did he have left?

Before he could complete the thought a pair of strong arms wrapped around him and a bearded chin appeared at his shoulder. It was the Lion. A turban-topped tower of muscle had walked right up behind him and he hadn't even noticed.

Roger was far stronger than most people, but he had never pitted his strength against an ace before; moreover, he was pinned, with no leverage, his arms trapped by his sides.

'You have some wire, Chrissy?' asked the Lion.

'Yes,' she replied and sprinted upstairs.

They knew each other well, he realized. The Lion was known to be good with children. Churchill had probably asked him to keep an eye on his family as a favour. Clearly, the ace had gone above and beyond in his duty. Roger knew he should be grateful, but all he felt was bitterness and rage.

He tried to shake off the Lion but the ace seemed to anticipate his efforts, shifting his grip with ease. Any moment now, the police would arrive, or more of the Silver Helix, and he'd be done. It was so unfair.

The wooden mask pressed against his wrist, as if to remind him it was there. It didn't matter that he'd done the right thing nor what he'd sacrificed. All that mattered was who was stronger. Roger Barnes was weak, a pawn to be used, but the Green Man was a different matter. He had the power to make real change. He raised people up. He brought them down. People respected the Green Man.

That was what he had left. The things he had built.

My followers.

My contacts.

My organization.

Green Man didn't need tea or biscuits or cosy chats on the sofa. Green man didn't need the world to play fair.

He lifted his legs, braced them against the wall, and then kicked back. The plan was to slam the Lion against the opposite wall, but at some point in the manoeuvre the Lion had let go and dropped to safety. There was an explosion of plaster and brick and dust, and the next thing Roger knew he was lying on his back in the kitchen.

The Lion stepped through the newly made hole to join him. From a glittering sheath, the ace drew his kirpan, nine inches of curved steel. Despite his age, the Lion looked fit and strong. Roger could see some grey in the other man's beard, but other than that, the years had been kind.

The observation only served to fuel Roger's hatred further. He swung for the Lion but was way off the mark. In return he received three slashes from the knife. They did not get much beyond the fabric of his clothes but Roger knew that each one would leave a scar of bark or give rise to some new shoot.

He met the next slice directly with his right hand and grabbed the blade. The Lion let it go without a fight, taking the opportunity to pepper Roger's body with punches. Each one rocked him, though he barely felt any pain.

It went on like that for a while. Roger would take a swing, miss, and the Lion would roar before unleashing a flurry of punches, each one making solid contact.

Christine came in through the kitchen door rather than the hole in the wall. In one hand she held a coil of wire, in the other, a handgun. She threw the wire to the Lion, and raised the gun at him.

'If you think that's going to stop me, you don't know me at all,' he snarled and ran at her, but the Lion was faster, and dived between them.

Just as he had expected.

There was a satisfying crack as Roger's fist connected with the Lion's ribs, folding the man in two. Then another crack as he struck the Lion on the back of his skull, driving the ace to the floor. The combination of hard wood and enhanced strength was brutal.

'Stop it!' yelled Christine. 'You're killing him!'

He stamped on the man a few times, just to be sure. He hadn't heard of the Lion being supernaturally tough, but he wasn't going to take any chances of him getting back up.

She unloaded the gun into his back. Six shots, six hits, and, in a way, he felt them all. Each one reinforced the point that her father, Roger Barnes, was dead to her.

He reached into his pocket, brought out his mask, and fixed it to his face. 'It didn't have to be this way, you know.'

She backed off when he turned towards her, reloading the gun with practised ease. A part of him was appalled but another was satisfied. He would never have her love, he saw that now, but at least she hadn't written him off. 'In a way,' he said, 'I should thank you. You've opened my eyes. I don't have any more illusions.' He gestured to the crumpled ace. 'Look closer. The Lion isn't dead, but if you fire a single shot at me or speak a single word, that will change.'

She lowered the gun and then her head, part nod, part submission.

As he walked out, he realized that he had no idea if Wendy was really upstairs or not. A moment later, as he stepped into the night, he realized it didn't matter any more. By the time he got back to the van he could hear the wail of sirens in the distance. 'We've finished here,' he said to Wayfarer as he climbed into the back.

The grumbling of the engine rose and the van pulled away.

'I've just got word,' said Wayfarer. There was a pause, long enough for him to know that it was something big. 'The Black Dog's gone down.'

'Is the source reliable?'

'Yes. They got him in Jerusalem. Word is, he was betrayed by his own people. Can you believe it?'

'Sadly, I can. Even the Fists can suffer from traitors and spies. I told the Black Dog years ago that he should be more discerning with who he recruited.'

In the dark, Roger smiled to himself. The way forward was clear now. Churchill was gone, the Black Dog was gone. Nobody had mastery of him any more. He was free to shape the Twisted Fists as he saw fit.

It struck him that he would have to write a speech for himself. Something to inspire the other cell leaders. He would draw upon Thatcher's words of nineteen eighty-four as a starting point. It seemed fitting somehow. He'd use the same message of righteousness, the same stance of power, but twisted. The words came easily to his mind as if summoned:

This year, as before in our history, we've seen joker men and women with brave hearts defying violence, scorning intimidation, and defending their rights to uphold our laws.

By their action, we have seen a new birth of leadership in the Fists. And that is the most important thing, the most enduring thing, that will come out of this betrayal in Jerusalem.

And we demand, that violence against jokers does not pay and be seen not to pay. Let violence against us cease or let the law of five for one be kept. That is the spoken and unspoken hope and wish of millions of our fellow citizens.

The time of the Black Dog was over. Now was the time of the Green Man.

♣　♦　♠　♥

The Ceremony
of Innocence

by Melinda M. Snodgrass

**The blood-dimmed tide is loosed,
and everywhere
The ceremony of innocence is drowned . . .**

Cambridge, 1996

'SO, YOU'VE BROUGHT US what? A mascot?'

'A boy toy?' another voice chimed in.

Noel Matthews ground his teeth and forced himself to maintain his superior, faintly bored expression. It was his roommate, Prince Siraj bin al-Hussein, who bristled at the mocking. 'This is Noel. He's my classmate, my friend, and probably smarter than the whole lot of you put together. Since I brought him and I'm a member, you can bloody well deal with it.'

The clubhouse of the Crabs, the notorious Clare College drinking society, was what one would expect from an exclusively male environment. It was cluttered with magazines and various kinds of sporting equipment, a club tie was tossed over the back of a chair, on another the accepted blazer to be worn by members. It smelled of tobacco, alcohol, microwave pizza, and male sweat.

A figure unfolded itself from the sofa and drifted over to survey Noel. The young man was very tall, forcing Noel to look up to meet the bored brown-eyed gaze. A hand gripped Noel's chin and turned his face from side to side.

'Not pretty enough to be a toy,' the stranger called over his shoulder to the young man who had made the suggestion. The hand stroked down Noel's cheek. Noel resisted the impulse to bite it. 'But definitely a baby. Not a hair on his chin. How old are you?' Like every other person who had spoken this boy had the fruity tones of a member of the British upper class.

Noel considered affecting a working-class accent, but knew he wouldn't be able to maintain it. He had no choice but to accept and affirm his kinship with these future masters of the universe. 'Sixteen,' he said.

Another boy, stocky, blond with a broken nose, approached. 'Any member has to be a student.'

'He is,' Siraj said, before Noel could answer.

'Oh, God, he's one of *those*,' the tall boy said, but there was the tremor of laughter in his voice. 'So, boy genius rather than boy toy.' He turned to Siraj. 'Are you proposing him for membership?'

'I am.'

'Well, we must think of an appropriate initiation for our boy genius. Mere alcohol poisoning seems too ordinary for such an extraordinary applicant. I'm James, by the way, James Nelson.'

'Noel Matthews.' They shook hands.

'That disgusting pervert,' James pointed at the young man who had suggested he might be a boy toy, 'is Ralph Sessions. Over there is Geoffrey Palance, Timothy Radcliff . . .' The introductions continued. Noel committed the faces and names to memory. 'Now give us a moment to concoct an appropriate test of your fitness for membership.'

The young men went into a huddle on the other side of the

room. Siraj went to the well-stocked bar and poured himself a brandy. 'Want something?'

'I'll take a glass of port,' Noel answered.

They sat sipping their drinks with the accompaniment of low male voices and the occasional shout of laughter. Noel studied Siraj. The neat spade beard and moustache framed a sensual, full-lipped mouth. Dark hair brushed his collar. He was on the short side. At sixteen Noel was as tall as the Jordanian. Noel knew he liked Siraj. He was also jealous of him. Siraj had wealth, charm and a certainty about his place in the world. An evil spirit urged him to betray some of those feelings.

'So not a very good Muslim, I see,' Noel said.

The insult failed to hit. Siraj just laughed, took another swallow of brandy and said, 'At home in Amman I'm a very good Muslim. Here I'm a very good Englishman.'

Noel nodded towards the cluster of boys. 'Not to them you're not.'

That did land. A frown like summer lightning flickered quickly across Siraj's face, and the smile that followed looked more like a grimace, but he didn't rise to the bait. Instead he turned it back on Noel. 'You just might be venomous enough to fit right in with us.'

At that moment Nelson returned, trailed by a handful of the members. 'We've decided. We want you to seduce and bed a woman and bring us pictures to prove it. Crotch shots and her face so we know it's not something you just pulled off the internet.'

'And no hiring some slag to do the deed. Has to be a student at one of the colleges,' Timothy said.

'We'll add her to our portfolio of loose women,' Geoffrey added.

'Fine. Challenge accepted.' Noel stood up, drained the last of his port, and set down the glass with a snap.

He and Siraj left. Once they were outside the Jordanian gave him a questioning look. 'Are you sure about this?'

'Absolutely.'

'I don't want to be accused of encouraging the delinquency of a minor. Particularly by your parents.' There was a note of real concern in Siraj's voice, and it touched Noel.

'Look, it gives me access I wouldn't otherwise have. They—' Noel jerked a thumb back at the door, '—will step into positions in law, government, and finance because of their connections. I need that if I'm going to get ahead.'

'You're not exactly a member of an oppressed minority,' Siraj said.

You have no idea, Noel thought, but instead he said, 'that's pretty rich coming from an *actual* Arabian *prince*.'

'Please, I am a Hashemite and a Jordanian. Not a dirty Saudi.'

'A family that claims descent from Hashim, the great-grand-father of Mohammed. Mohammed who was born in Mecca, which is in Saudi Arabia, so I guess you are a dirty Saudi.'

Siraj dropped an arm over Noel's shoulders and laughed. 'And you, my friend, are in danger of becoming one of those desert-loving Englishmen. Shall we find dinner and a pint?'

Noel gave a regretful head shake. 'I promised my dad I'd go over tonight and have dinner at home.'

♣

'We live so close. I just don't understand why you wanted to live at the college instead of staying at home,' his father was saying as he set the table. Jasper Matthews was thin with greying brown hair and deep lines etched his face, courtesy of the wasting disease that had left him an invalid for most of Noel's young life.

Because I'm enough of a bloody oddity, being a sixteen-year-old fresher and a damned hermaphrodite. I don't need to be living at home with Mummy and Daddy, Noel thought. He was spared voicing any of it by the entrance of his mother.

Amanda Matthews was a big woman in every way. Tall and heavy with a large shelf-like bosom and a protuberant belly that she made no effort to hide, instead picking dresses that accentuated her bulk. In part it was a rebuke to the patriarchy that insisted on unrealistic expectations of female beauty (Noel could repeat the words in his sleep), and Amanda's desire to embrace the Mother Goddess. Not that her attitudes weren't sincere. Technically, Amanda taught history, but her focus was on women in history, which made it almost a course in women's studies with an emphasis on politics and culture, rather than history *per se*.

Which made her decision to raise her intersex child as male all the more baffling. When at the age of twelve Noel had finally asked her why, her eyes had narrowed into slits and her jaw had tightened to the point at which her plump cheeks creased. '*Because the patriarchy still holds sway. Advancement's always going to be easier for a man than a woman, no matter how brilliant or talented.*' So while he had been given a gender fluid name at his birth, he had early on been Noel (one syllable) not Noelle (two syllables). It was Amanda who had insisted that Noel move into campus housing.

Because she was a professor at Lucy Cavendish College, one of the few women-only colleges, Noel had been given a place in the Old Court at Clare College, which had large, spacious rooms and views across the gardens and the river. It was there he had met Siraj, who had the room next door. Despite the age difference they found themselves to be kindred spirits. Siraj might be a prince, but to many of the well-born students he was still just a sand-wallah. Noel was an oddity because of his youth . . . and the communal bathroom on their floor meant that several students had got a look at his small, misshapen penis. Hormonal treatments from a young age had accentuated his maleness and mercifully the stunted vagina that rested behind his scrotum had never developed enough to lead to menstruation. That was one indignity he had been spared.

Siraj knew of his gender malleability. But what he didn't know was that Noel was an ace.

As Amanda walked past, she bestowed a hearty buffet to his shoulder. Noel knew his mother loved him from the fierce way she fought to give him every advantage, but sometimes during his childhood he had wished she would just give him a hug. There was a reason his father had become his dearest companion, adviser, and comforter.

'How was your day, dear?' his mother asked as she took her chair at the head of the table. 'Oh good, Lancashire hotpot. I'm starving,' she said as Jasper set her plate in front of her.

'Good. Practised my German with Franz down the hall. Went to the magic shop to pick up an item I'd ordered. Luckily for me Oliver, the owner, was in and he gave me a tip on misdirection when you're doing close magic. He also said he thinks he can get me backstage at Sebastian Crewe's London performance.' Noel didn't mention his application to the drinking society. It would upset Jasper. He would tell Amanda later. He knew she would be delighted.

'It's fine to have a hobby, but don't neglect your studies,' Amanda said as she tucked into the food. 'Being a magician doesn't strike me as a career with much of a future.'

Jasper patted Noel's hand. 'You keep up with your magic. A good parlour trick will make you a hit at parties and delight the ladies.'

'And get my arse kicked by their large, truculent boyfriends,' Noel said.

After dinner Amanda retreated to her study to mark papers while Noel and Jasper washed the dishes. 'Actually, Dad, speaking of ladies . . .'

His father's head swivelled quickly to look at him with a delighted expression. 'Oh ho, an interesting development. Come on, spill it.'

'It's nobody in particular, but if I wanted to . . . attract a girl . . . what should I do?'

'There is someone.'

'Possibly. Maybe. Come on, help me out.'

The gnarled hands disappeared back into the water and foaming suds and began scrubbing a plate. 'Well, you should always be a gentleman. Be kind. Listen more than you talk. Try to think of something exciting or unusual to do with them so you're not just the run of the mill bloke who only thinks in terms of the pub or the pictures.' He rinsed the plate and handed it to Noel to dry. 'Just be yourself, son.'

'Yeah. Okay.' *But who and what is that?*

◆

Why, Noel wondered as he watched his target take her bicycle off the rack, *did he always have to over-perform?*

He spotted the security that discreetly surrounded Princess Gloriana Eleanor Catherine Mountbatten-Windsor. She was a pretty brown-haired girl of eighteen with blue eyes, a rather lush figure, and a round face more reminiscent of her great-grandmother than her grandmother, Queen Margaret. Noel found the name Gloriana to be a bit much, but since she was unlikely ever to become queen it probably didn't matter, and of course she could always change it. Her great-grandfather had gone from Albert to George, and his brother from David to Edward. The honour and confinement of the throne would go first to her father, Henry, and then to her older brother. For the first time since the nineteen fifties Britain would have a king again.

Noel knew from his research (stalking, if he was entirely honest) that the princess was heading to the library after her seminar. He had decided that today he would make his move. It was going to be tricky, because he could woo her only during the daylight hours, but he had prepared the excuse of a night job to explain why.

He gathered up his book bag that contained a change of

clothing as well as books, and went to a nearby public toilet where he could make his transformation. In a stall he dressed in much larger clothing, closed his eyes, and willed his body to shift. Bones moved beneath his skin, muscles stretched and nerves tingled as he assumed his new form. As he tucked in the shirt and fastened his belt, Noel reflected that if his mother knew what he was attempting she would view it as a deeply misogynistic act and be furious. This was Queen Margaret's granddaughter, and Amanda respected the queen. His father would be equally horrified. His dad was a staunch royalist, following the ins and outs of every royal down to the most distant cousins.

Which begged the question: why *was* Noel doing this? There were plenty of other girls at Cambridge. Was it because of the disdain in the eyes of those boys at Crabs? The implication that the only way this skinny teenager could bed a girl was to buy one? So he would pick not just any girl, but *the* girl. A royal princess.

Stuffing his own clothes into the book bag, Noel left the stall and caught his reflection in one of the mirrors over the sink. A boy had entered the loo, a young man was leaving. Even after three years Noel still found this stranger in his skin to be arresting. He paused to study the red/gold hair, the deep golden eyes, tanned skin, and muscular build. It was said that the wild card virus took an individual's psychology into account when it rewrote their DNA. Noel was the textbook case that proved the theory.

He had contracted the virus when he was thirteen, during a family holiday to Ephesus. While exploring an old beached freighter, he had come down with what his parents thought was the flu. One morning six months later, in the throes of a particularly vivid wet dream, Noel had been awakened by his father's shout of alarm to find himself inhabiting the body of a stranger, and his hand gripping a cock far larger than his own.

His father hadn't wanted Noel enrolled in the British wild card registry, but any routine blood test would reveal the presence of the virus, so in due course Noel had been listed.

What the government didn't know was his actual power. And it went beyond the ability to become every woman's fantasy lover. At night Noel could summon the sultry and beautiful female, his Queen of the Night, who was every man's fantasy fuck. He hadn't yet had the nerve to actually *do it*, but he had tested the effect the two avatars had on people. They were virtually irresistible.

So while Noel might not cheat by using money to satisfy the Crabs' demand, he was going to cheat nonetheless; his avatars were the Ur woman and the Ur man. Sex rolled off them in waves and few people could resist their allure. The princess didn't have a chance once—

Noel's thoughts stuttered to a stop. He needed a name. Something authentic that would reassure her he was 'of her set'. Something with a hyphen. *Simon Grenville-Lacey.* That would work. He headed for the library.

♠

The library was at the western edge of the Cambridge city centre near the Memorial Court of Clare College. It was an imposing, almost industrial stone building dating from the nineteen thirties. The library tower was like an upraised and castigating finger against a surprisingly bright blue sky. It was said that at the opening of the building Neville Chamberlain had referred to it as *this magnificent erection*. Given Noel's current goal the thought made him chuckle nervously.

Clutching a piece of paper with a catalogue entry and the title of a book that resided in the stack where Gloriana tended to sit, Noel moved down the centre aisle pretending to search for the correct bookcase. The tall windows that marched like glass soldiers down the length of the room threw puddles of sunlight on the polished floor. A pair of discreet security officers were tucked away among the books, also pretending to study the titles. Noel could feel their scrutiny as an actual weight between his shoulder blades as they checked him out, but neither of them did anything beyond giving him a serious once-over.

He slipped past Gloriana with a murmured apology. She looked up from her note taking and began to say, 'Quite all right,' but the words died as she took in the splendour that was Noel's male avatar. She seemed a bit glassy-eyed.

Noel smiled at her, pretended to scan the shelves then looked back with an apologetic shrug. 'And after I disturb you the damn book isn't even here.'

'Oh, bad luck,' Gloriana said. She had a pleasant voice with a hint of a lisp.

'So sorry.'

'No need to apologize. I'm Glory.'

Noel noted that she offered no last name. 'Simon. Simon Grenville-Lacey.' He made as if to leave, and right on cue she began talking to hold him in place.

'Are you a student here?'

'As it happens I am.'

She studied him from beneath her lashes. The tip of her tongue briefly touched her upper lip. 'Are you . . .'

'A wild card? Yes, 'fraid so. But don't be alarmed.'

'Oh, I'm not. Are you an ace?'

'No.' Noel gestured at his eyes. 'I suppose these would technically make me a joker.'

'Oh no, no one would think that. You look normal apart from your eyes. One of my mum's favourite charities is the Queen Mary Hospital at the Isle of Dogs. I've been there frequently. The patients show such patience and optimism despite their afflictions.'

Noel really wished she had displayed even a tremor of disgust against the less fortunate victims of the wild card, but no, she had to be understanding. He felt a tremor of doubt over his plans, but pushed it aside. 'Look, I'm starving and you were so nice about me interrupting you. May I buy you lunch?' he asked.

She hesitated, smiled and then nodded. 'That would be very nice. Thank you.'

♥

London
The file, edges flapping like the wings of a dying bird, fell onto his desk. Captain Flint met the gaze of the agent who stood in front of his desk. *'From your method of delivery I take it I'm not going to like the contents.'* They were in Flint's office at the headquarters of MI7, the Order of the Silver Helix.

Alan Turing shook his head. 'Probably not.'

Flint's thick stone fingers struggled to lift the file. Turing picked it up and placed it in his hands. *'Thank you. But shouldn't you have brought this to Lord Dalton? Redcoat is, after all, in charge now.'*

'I have a very real concern that he would use this as an excuse to toddle off to the Palace and inform the Queen rather than deal with the situation.'

'A valid worry. The man does seem to be inordinately fond of rubbing shoulders with royalty.' Flint returned his attention to the file. As he opened the cover he asked, *'The boyfriend?'*

'Doesn't exist. There is no record of a Simon Grenville-Lacey, and he is not on the registry, though he is clearly a wild card.'

'I believe we need to have a conversation with this young man.' Flint heaved his bulk out of his stone chair.

'On your own authority?'

'It's just reconnaissance, Alan. Merely reconnaissance.'

'You know you are quite unable to look innocent, Flint.'

♣

Cambridge

Noel took his time with the pursuit. They had three lunches and a breakfast together before he made his move. Partly it was to allow Simon's overwhelming sexuality to increase her desire until it had reached the point of being unbearable. Mainly it was his own nerves and doubts. He had never actually *done it*.

He hated confessing that to Siraj, but he needed advice and guidance. The Jordanian had suggested a prostitute for practice. Noel had rejected that idea; afraid of catching something, and lacking the funds to hire a high-class call-girl to make sure that wasn't a risk. The prince offered to pay, but that felt wrong. They had settled on Siraj talking about his own sexual adventures and watching porn. Noel was surprised by how arousing that experience actually was. Despite his gender dysphoria it seemed he responded in a very male way to visual stimulation.

But today was to be *the day*. In preparation he had purchased a tiny camera at an electronics store. It made him feel a bit like a secret agent. He tried not to think about how he intended to use it. Noel had a room reserved at the Arundel House. He had also purchased a package of condoms. She would expect him to wear one and while he had a suspicion that Simon's sperm was as feeble as his own, he didn't want to test the theory.

It was a pleasant summer day and their table was at a window and offered a lovely view of the River Cam. On the opposite side punts nuzzled the bank like piglets in search of the teat. Occasionally, one went past. Most of the small boats held a couple, laughing girls reclining in the bow while a boy wielded the punt pole.

Over lunch Noel continually reached out to touch Glory's hand, run a finger down her bare arm. Each time he touched her her breath caught and she shivered. The waiter delivered their dessert and they shared the banoffee pie. The taste of bananas and toffee and cream were cloying on the back of Noel's tongue and added to his feeling of nausea.

Glory finished her coffee quickly. 'Let's get out of here.' She glanced over to the table where her security tried to look inconspicuous.

Noel left his chair, threw down money to cover the bill, and moved over to her. He leaned down and kissed her. Her mouth tasted of coffee and bananas. 'And maybe go somewhere a bit more private,' he whispered, allowing his hand to brush across her breast.

Her gasp was sharp and her arms went around his neck and she began frenziedly kissing him. 'Oh God, yes! I thought you'd never ask.'

He pulled her to her feet. 'Let's go.'

'My minders . . . what do we do about them?' she whispered in his ear.

'I'll show you.'

They left the restaurant. The two security officers followed at a discreet distance. They walked down Granta Place while Glory pressed herself against him. Fire coiled in his groin. Noel wrapped an arm around her waist and pulled her even closer. The river seemed to be winking knowingly at them as the sunlight glinted and danced off the water. At Little St Mary's Lane he turned quickly around the corner, gathered Glory in both arms, and teleported to the hotel room.

She gave a squeak of alarm as they landed in the room, and her weight caused him to lose his balance. They tumbled to the floor. 'What did you . . . how did you? *You're an ace!*' Her tone was a mix of confusion, excitement, and alarm.

'I thought it was the best way to lose your minders,' he said as he helped her to her feet. She flung herself against his chest and kissed him, caressing his shoulders. Heat came off her in waves, her face was flushed, and the way her breasts pressed against his chest drew an answering reaction from his groin. Noel's body might be confused, but Simon's knew exactly what was expected. His erection pressed painfully against his zip.

He eased her over to the bed and down onto the bedspread. 'Ow. This mattress is terrible.' She began unbuttoning her blouse with clumsy fingers. Noel helped her while she giggled uncontrollably and tried to pull his T-shirt over his head. It was thrown aside and she stroked her fingers down his chest, tracing his pectoral muscles . . . which on his male avatar were impressive. 'Oooh, nice.'

The rasp of her nails against his skin sent another electric jolt into his groin. He toed off his tennis shoes and began desperately pulling off his trousers. She got her skirt unzipped and wriggled free. Her underwear was lacy and lavender and even that was arousing. Soon they were both naked, bodies hot and sweat-slicked.

'Condom?' he gasped.

She shook her head. 'On the pill.'

She was trying to guide him into her, but he was awkward and nervous and kept sliding off. He growled in frustration.

'Relax,' she whispered into his ear.

And the door crashed open.

◆

'*Well, young man, you are in a great deal of trouble.*'

The boy seated with his hands cuffed to a metal bar welded to the table was scared. It shone in his strange gold eyes and trembling lower lip.

Good. Flint knew he was an imposing, even terrifying, figure with his flickering red eyes and seven-foot-nine stony bulk. '*So, who are you . . . really?*' The young man remained silent, eyes flicking to the narrow window high up in the wall. '*All right, let's try this one. Who do you work for?*'

That elicited a response. 'What? What are you talking about? And . . . and I want a barrister.'

'*A perfectly logical request. Unfortunately for you I'm not the* police. *I can bury you so deep that no one will ever find you.*' The young man's strange golden eyes were hard to read, but the muscles in the handsome face betrayed his fear.

Then, surprisingly, the square jaw tightened and Flint was treated to a stare as cold as an asp's gaze. There was another glance towards the window. 'You can try. What exactly am I accused of doing? Deflowering the cream of British woman-hood? Debauching a royal?'

'*Evading security – which one could argue was an attempt to kidnap a member of the royal family. It also seems that you possess some special power to arouse. A clever solicitor could make the argument that use of this power removes consent.*' He paused for a long moment. '*Which moves us into the realm of rape.*' The boy blanched at that. '*There's also the little matter of the camera we found among your possessions. So which are you? A member of the paparazzi, a blackmailer, or a rapist?*'

'I'm not any of those things. It was just a bit of a lark. A bet with some mates. God, you people.'

Flint leaned down and gripped the boy's wrist. The sharp edges of his fingers cut into the boy's flesh, drawing blood. 'Ow! Bloody hell!' the boy squeaked.

Flint released him and headed to the door of the interroga-tion room. Turing was waiting in the observation room with a slide and a sterile envelope. Flint smeared the blood from his fingers onto the slide. Turing carefully topped it with another slide, placed the pair in the envelope, and handed it to an aide.

As the door closed behind him, Turing said, 'I told the lab to rush it through the system. We'll find out who he is soon enough.'

Before Flint could respond the door opened again. Lord Dalton Carruthers, fourth and current holder of the *nom de guerre* Redcoat, strode in. Flint gave an inward groan. After Winston Churchill's assassination in Belfast and the bloody farce of his funeral at Westminster, Her Majesty's government had needed a scapegoat, and Sir Kenneth Foxworthy had loyally fallen on his sword and tended his resignation as the head of the Order of the Silver Helix. The noble Redcoat had taken his place. Carruthers was in his mid-forties, distinguished and photogenic, and possessed of an adequate degree of telekinesis to impress the public and tempt him into rash actions. Between his noble title, ace powers, and good looks Carruthers was the sort of entitled git who gave entitled gits a bad name.

'Where is he?' his lordship demanded. 'Who is he? I hope you haven't mucked things up by interviewing him without me.'

'We just sent off the blood sample. We'll have his identity soon enough,' Turing said.

'*I believe the technician is cueing up the CCTV footage,*' Flint said, in an attempt to distract the ace.

'Excellent. I want to know how this happened . . . and whether we need to flay the princess's security detail alive for losing track of her.'

Flint and Enigma exchanged glances and followed Carruthers into another room filled with computer equipment. A young man with acne scars and a few fresh pustules was sucking on a lollipop while his fingers flew across the keyboard. Images flickered past on the screen. The viewpoint was that of a camera opposite the Riverside Restaurant.

As he watched Gloriana attempting to climb the prisoner as if he were a tree, Flint found himself striking sparks from his fingers as they closed into fists.

'Hope to hell the paparazzi don't get hold of these pictures. Won't look good to have the princess behaving like a tart,' Carruthers said.

Flint glanced over to the security feed from the inside of the interrogation room just in time to see the prisoner unlock the cuffs with a thin lock-pick. '*Bloody hell!*'

'Oh, look, the bastard can teleport.' The computer tech was gazing at his computer screen as a new CCTV image appeared.

Flint's head swung from screen to computer and back to the screen just in time to see the young ace flip the bird at the camera and vanish.

'Well,' Turing said. 'That was . . . unexpected.'

'Oh, well done, Flint,' Redcoat said. 'Another cock-up.'

♠

Noel desperately wanted to go home. He wanted the comfort of his old bedroom and his father making toast smeared with Nutella for tea and playing one of his operas on the record player and preparing a casserole for dinner. But that made him feel like a stupid little kid, and his father had a way of getting Noel to talk. Instead he had returned to his room at Clare and tried to calm himself with a glass of brandy.

He had a paper to prepare before his next seminar, but he couldn't focus. His thoughts ricocheted between *oh God, what if they find me?* and *there is no way they can find me.* And the mockery he would face from the Crabs over his failure to obtain the necessary photos. He didn't want to admit that he had failed.

For a brief moment Noel wondered why he was upset about the cock-up with his initiation into the Crabs compared to his arrest . . . and that terrifying knave Flint. Unconsciously he rubbed at the scabbed cuts on his wrist. He wished he could have seen the faces of those fools when he made his escape. But none of that would get him into the Crabs.

So, what should he do about the drinking society? Noel hated to admit that he had failed, but the thought of trying again make him feel rather queasy. He would tell Siraj that he was going to take his advice and not go through with this. Thus face could be saved and pride salvaged, though he had a feeling he would constantly wonder what they would say about him within the walls of the society.

The fact that he'd made a decision turned incipient nausea

into real hunger. He didn't want to face a lot of people. He'd go pick and up an Indian takeaway and return to his room.

The sun had set by the time he headed out. A damp chill caused him to hunch his shoulders and dig his hands into the pockets of his jacket. Fog was twisting off the surface of the Cam like the white hair of river sprites playing hide and seek with the moon.

As he passed a recessed doorway he became aware of two points of glowing red in the darkness some two feet over his head. Panic slammed into Noel's chest. For an instant he froze, a rabbit in a snake's thrall. He started to run, the soles of his loafers slipping on the damp pavement. He reached for his other avatar, his Queen of the Night.

This transition was actually more painful and took longer than the switch into his sun god. The sensation of the bones shifting in his pelvis was especially uncomfortable. He was only partway through the change when a heavy stone hand descended on his shoulder. '*Don't do it, lad. If you run again my next stop will be at your parents' house.*'

Noel froze. 'Please don't tell my parents.' He was furious that his voice trembled, thick with fear. 'Are you going to put me in prison?'

'*It wouldn't be my first choice. Why don't we have a sit-down and discuss this? I have need of people with talents and yours are intriguing.*' The stone hand lifted a strand of the waist-length black hair that Noel now possessed. '*So there's a female version of the chap whose skin you wore earlier. Interesting. But perhaps you could shift back or finish what you were doing because right now you look a bit . . . disconcerting.*'

Noel considered completing the transformation, but had a feeling the stone man might have a stone prick and not be susceptible to his queen's allure. He shifted back to his normal form.

'*Where were you headed?*'

'To get some takeaway at Taj—'

'*Good, let's go. I'll buy you dinner.*'

There was no argument he could present. The threat of his parents had him falling into step with the stone giant. Noel had to take two steps to one of the knave's just to keep up. 'How did you find me?' he asked.

'*DNA.*'

'That's why you cut me.'

Flint nodded. '*We matched you through the registry. The NHS keeps a list of all wild cards active or latent.*'

'But I got sick in Turkey, how could the National Health—' Noel broke off, remembering he'd had blood drawn when he'd had strep throat the year before. 'Damned doctor violated my privacy.'

'*And obeyed the law.*'

They walked on in silence for a moment. The stone man seemed in no hurry to break it. Noel couldn't stand it and he asked, 'You're Captain Flint, aren't you? That guy from the *Queen Mary* . . . you're really old.'

'*My actual name is Brigadier Sir Kenneth Foxworthy and yes, I am really old.*'

'So what do I call you?' Noel asked.

'*Sir will suffice.*'

The condescending tone made Noel long to call him Kenny or Foxy, but he lacked the nerve. They reached the restaurant. Flint pulled out a wallet. '*Order what you fancy. I'll wait for you on that bench.*' He pointed at a stone bench across the street. '*I doubt the furnishings in there can hold my weight.*' The notes were pressed into Noel's hands. '*Oh, and don't think about ducking out the back. I have agents stationed all around us.*'

Noel felt himself blush . . . because of course that was precisely what he had been considering. He went in, ordered and came out with his food. Sat down next to Flint, opened the container, and started to eat his butter chicken and samosas. It was hard to force the food past the lump that had taken up residence in his throat. 'So, what did you want to discuss?'

'What do you know about MI7? The Order of the Silver Helix?'

'I know it exists. Some sort of police thing.'

'Yes, it is that. Unlike MI5 and MI6 we use wild cards as field agents. Your talents would be of particular interest to the organization. It would give you an opportunity to serve your country and your Queen.' The whispering voice faded away.

'Or I can go to jail?' Noel said.

'I'd prefer not to be that crude . . . but yes.'

The samosa suddenly tasted of ashes. Noel dropped it back into the container. 'I wanted to finish school.'

'You will. It's only a forty-five-minute train journey to London. Your parents and classmates will be told you are doing intense one-on-one study.' The massive stone mouth moved and Noel realized Flint was smiling. 'Which isn't actually a lie. We'll see that you are educated and graduate with a degree. Useful that your course is history and modern languages.'

Noel crumbled the samosa with nervous fingers. 'How can you ever trust me, knowing that you will have blackmailed me into working for you?'

Flint took a pipe out of his pocket, snapped his fingers to produce a flame, and puffed. The bowl glowed red to match his eyes. The smell of tobacco and spices tickled Noel's nose. The knave gave a chuckle like the whisper of the wind blowing fallen leaves. 'Enigma has evaluated your background, and I believe we know you better than you know yourself. Your father tried to enlist but due to his health he was rejected. Your mother's writings on the Queen have been quite favourable. I would be surprised to find you're a republican who advocates an end to the monarchy. I expect that at heart you are a patriot and a loyal subject. With your talents you could help keep this nation safe against threats both foreign and domestic.' His sigh carried a weight of regret beyond anything Noel could imagine. 'I'm an old man, Noel. I've seen horrible things – on the battlefields of Europe, aboard the

Queen Mary, in the ruins of Jerusalem, and right here at home. Help me prevent the next atrocity.'

♥

London
'Well. I'm queer and I admit to being tempted.'

Flint glanced down at Turing who stood at his side. Where other men might have had a shaving nick and a forgotten scrap of tissue beneath an ear, on the ace it was a place where he had failed to cover his silver skin with make-up effectively. The patch of silver glinted under the lights. *'Then I take it the male avatar has an equally powerful effect?'*

Enigma gave him a small, tight smile. 'I think both the princess and I can attest to that.'

The two of them were watching through a one-way mirror as the boy's body completed its transformation into a woman. And such a woman. Midnight-black hair hung to her waist, her eyes were pools of swirling silver, her face a perfect oval with pearly white skin, her body every man's fantasy. Even Flint felt the tug of forgotten passion.

On the other side of the mirror, Alfred Spraggs, the male half of the husband-and-wife team Banger and Mash, cleared his throat. 'Well . . . that's a bloody sight,' he said in his pronounced East London accent. 'Let's start . . . uh . . . women have a different centre of gravity.' Banger's eyes were oscillating between Noel's bosom and hips. 'You will have to . . . ah . . . compensate for . . . that.'

Flint keyed the intercom. *'Alfred, perhaps under the circumstances it would be better to have Jiniri and Petula tutor Noel in hand-to-hand when he is in his female form.'*

Banger saluted. 'Right, sir. I'll go fetch 'em.'

Noel turned to face the mirror, arms folded across the amazing bosom, and smirked. 'Too distracting.'

'Rather. Noel—'

Turing interrupted. 'That really won't do, Kenneth. One simply can't call *that* Noel.'

'*Noelle?*' Flint suggested.

'Far too chaste. Let me suggest . . . Lilith.'

♣

Noel's life fell into a routine. Two days a week he travelled to London for 'tutoring' at the headquarters of the Silver Helix in a nondescript Victorian building near the Thames. His male form was bigger and stronger than either his actual self or Lilith, but Jiniri, the Iranian-born ace whose real name was Maryam Shahidi, had taught him how to use an opponent's body weight and momentum against them when he was in his female form or his own.

In this she was aided by Petula Spraggs. While Mash lacked any formal martial arts training, she made up for it in sheer brute strength and general truculence. Her spouse was just as surly and just as violent. They mocked Noel's accent, his education, his sexual dysmorphia. Their sessions often slipped from 'training' into thuggery as they delivered their beatings.

Noel began to hate and dread the hand-to-hand sessions, in which he was continuously being told how he needed to learn to take the punch as his tutors delivered said punch. After one particularly brutal session with all three aces taking turns to punch him, Noel touched his bleeding lip, the cut beneath his eye, and held up his bloodstained fingers. 'Stop! Are you all just sadists?'

'Oh boohoo, is Little Lord Fauntleroy going to cry now?' Petula said. Then she slapped him.

Noel's head snapped to the side and he tasted blood as his teeth cut the inside of his cheek. With a yell of fury he turned on his tormentor and delivered a spinning kick to her stomach.

The door to the training room crashed open, and Redcoat strode in. 'Enough!' he bellowed as Banger and Mash jumped

Noel and bore him to the floor. They backed off reluctantly. 'Enough,' Redcoat repeated. 'Alfred, Petula, I think we can dispense with your services for the moment.' They left grumbling, shooting Noel looks that promised revenge.

Carruthers handed him a towel. Wincing, Noel wiped away the blood. 'Better?' Carruthers asked.

Noel knew he ought to be polite to the chief of the Silver Helix, but he wasn't feeling particularly tactful at the moment. 'No! It's bloody well not better! Is there a fucking point to all this?'

The lights in the basement gym flickered and dimmed as Jiniri accessed her power and grew until she stood fifteen feet tall. She had to hunch so as to not bump her head. She twisted a massive fist in the material at the front of Noel's sweat-soaked T-shirt and yanked him into the air until he dangled at face level. 'At some point your luck will run out. You will fall into enemy hands. They will hurt you. We are teaching you how to push down pain—'

'And fear,' Carruthers added. 'I'll take him now, Maryam.'

Jiniri released him, but before Noel hit the floor he was seized by an invisible force that began to tighten inexorably around his chest.

Carruthers' hand was raised and he was slowly making a fist. 'You need to keep thinking, so maybe you can plan, escape and live!' he said.

Jiniri nodded. 'The world is filled with monsters who would hurt our families, our friends, our country. We are the invisible line.'

Carruthers picked up the theme. 'The unsung heroes working in the shadows. You'll never get a medal, or the grateful thanks of the Queen, but your comrades will know . . . and if you fall they will honour you.'

Hanging ten feet up in the air, Noel gasped for breath against Redcoat's teke power. 'Oh bravo, do you two rehearse this rubbish to use on recruits?'

Anger flitted across Lord Dalton's face and he closed his fist tight. Black spots danced before Noel's eyes and he felt his ribs creak under the pressure. Noel reached for his power and transformed. He pictured a spot on Tower Bridge and went there. He wasn't sure what would happen. He had thought it would break Carruthers' grip, but instead he felt a dragging weight that interfered with his aim and he found himself materializing a few feet off the bridge and falling fast toward the water, Carruthers trailing him like the tail on a kite. The sudden plummet broke the ace's concentration and he released his telekinetic grip. Arms windmilling, he fell towards the water some twenty feet below. Noel fought back panic, pictured the gym, and with a snap returned to find Jiniri looking shocked.

'Um, can Lord Dalton swim?' Noel asked.

'What have you done? Where is the chief?'

'In the Thames, just off Tower Bridge.'

'Allah preserve us.' She hurried from the room.

◆

Newmarket

'These new tutors have really got it in for you . . . and your face,' Prince Siraj said as they strolled towards the paddock area at Newmarket. 'Which makes me wonder what the hell you are studying?'

It was a blustery October day. Noel dug his chin into his scarf and wished he'd ordered a hot buttered rum rather than a pint of bitter. They had made the short drive over in Siraj's Ferrari to cheer on a horse owned by one of the prince's uncles. It was that family connection that allowed them behind the scenes where the horses were being readied for their race.

Noel reckoned he'd place a bet on the nag in solidarity with his friend. But right now he had to craft his response. There was a part of him that loved having this big secret and another part that longed to brag about it and share it with Siraj, but he could almost hear Flint's whispered words of caution and see the disapproval and disappointment in Turing's eyes if he broke protocol.

'I told you, I joined a rugby team down in London, something to do when I'm not in class, and yeah, the profs are working me hard but it's all right. It's a good opportunity.'

'You study too hard.'

'I'm not the decaying scion of what passes for royalty among camel herders,' Noel said. He threw his hip into Siraj's side, causing the older boy to stumble and spill some of his champagne. 'I'm going to have to work for a living.'

Siraj licked the champagne off his knuckles and then laughed. 'Point taken. You *are* just a little prole. I wonder why I waste my time on you?'

'Because when you're with me, people actually think you're handsome?'

They reached the saddling paddock and found the horse, a silver-grey among a lot of bays, chestnuts, and black horses. A young man with shaggy red hair was cinching the girth while a bandy-legged jockey listened intently to an older man in a cloth cap giving him instructions. 'We've drawn a slot in the middle of the pack so break fast to get out of the jumble then hold just behind the leaders. Make your move in the final quarter of a mile.'

'You got it, mate.' The jockey touched the brim of his helmet. His jaunty silks were silver and metallic blue.

Noel studied the deep brown eyes of the horse, watched the mobile ears twitch backwards and forwards to every sound. The big body seemed to quiver with excitement. Noel found the scent of crushed grass beneath the hooves, hay, and horse oddly pleasant. He laid a hand on the horse's neck. Its coat was like silk and warmth radiated against his palm.

The trainer turned to Siraj. 'Prince, I think your uncle's going to be pleased today.'

'I hope so. This is my friend, Noel Matthews. Noel, Davy

Reynolds, one of the best trainers in Europe.'

They shook hands. 'Nice to meet you. Going to place a bet? You won't regret it.'

A bell sounded and Noel and Siraj were forgotten. Reynolds made a final check of the equipment and tossed the jockey into the saddle. Siraj beckoned and they left the area, heading towards the betting windows.

'Do you know how to ride?' Noel asked.

'Of course. I'm an Arab.'

'Could you teach me?'

Siraj gave him an odd look. 'I wouldn't have thought it'd be your thing.'

Noel gave a casual shrug. 'Never hurts to learn new skills. Never know when they might come in handy.'

'All right. We'll find a stable. Now let's get our bets on.'

♠

London

Noel had been a bit nervous to return to the Silver Helix after his dust-up with Redcoat. He had taken the early train to London and tried to slip in but found Enigma waiting for him.

'I've something to show you.'

Turing walked away without looking to see if Noel was following. He hurried to catch up. Turing took him to a room he had never visited before. There were benches, a stone table where two candles burned on either side of nine red crystal poppies. It had a very church-like feel.

'The CIA have their memorial wall to honour fallen agents. This is our version.' He jerked his chin towards the table. 'Three of those belong to former Redcoats. The first was lost forty years ago during the Suez Crisis. The second died during the Aden Emergency in 1965, the third in the Troubles in the seventies. Carruthers is the fourth man to hold the name. That's the reason we work you so hard. We don't want to see your poppy up there, Noel. Now come along. You'll be late for your session with Ranjit.'

♥

While Noel might not love the hand-to-hand training, he adored shooting, and he proved to have a good eye and sure hands, whether he was using a pistol or a sniper rifle. He revelled in the power of a gun and the fact it could solve a problem without ever having to get close to an opponent. There was no *taking a punch* when you had a gun in your hand.

Maryam had looked disappointed when Noel had said that, but his firearms instructor Ranjit Singh, an enormous Sikh whose turban made him seem even taller, had said, 'Sensible attitude.' Singh, whose code name was the Lion, drilled Noel in his alternate forms as well, and took to setting up targets outside the firing range, requiring that Noel as either Lilith or Simon teleport to the location and take the shot the second he arrived.

At first he was hopeless, but eventually he honed the skill. After one such session out on the bleak expanse of Dartmoor Noel remarked, 'Doesn't seem very sporting to just pop in and shoot someone.'

'This isn't the playing fields of Eton, Noel. One day your life may depend upon this.'

'I get it. I get it. Turing showed me the poppies.'

'Then perhaps you should take heed. Now let's return to headquarters.' So Noel had wrapped his arms around Singh and they had made the jump before the setting sun had trapped them on the moor.

In addition to the physical and firearms training Noel studied coding and computer hacking with Turing. He practised French, Italian, German, and Russian, and added Persian and Arabic, with Maryam as his teacher. Eleanor Breslin, whose code name was Primrose, walked him through deportment lessons. He learned his way around the bewildering array of cutlery that would be present at a formal dinner, and she taught him how to dance. Captain Flint took Noel to his London tailor to be fitted for his first bespoke suit; but instead of the fussy man he had expected he was instead taken to a couture house, all modern chandeliers made of steel and crystal and steel-grey curtains. Beaded and embroidered evening gowns and suits of shimmering silk were draped on abstract and faceless human forms. These were just three-dimensional hangers, nothing that would detract from the beauty of the clothing.

A graceful, softly spoken young woman offered Noel a glass of champagne. Then an elegant older woman with long, straight brown hair with a dramatic streak of grey hair on the left side emerged from the inner office. She exchanged air kisses with Flint and sent away her staff. Only when they were alone did Flint explain what he needed. 'Constance, I'll need a suit, and leave room for alteration. The boy will no doubt grow. He also has two friends who will need fitting. A large chap, and a young woman.'

'You know it takes a while, Kenneth. Which do you want first?' Constance asked.

'The suit for the boy.'

And with that she removed the tape measure from around her neck and took Noel's measurements. Afterwards she helped him to select the colour and fabric for his new suit, pick shirts, and showed him how to use a pocket handkerchief to complement rather than merely match the colours of the tie and shirt.

It was a very heady experience. A glimpse into a new world of wealth and privilege.

Flint and Turing were men of another time. Occasionally Noel was privy to their conversations as they reminisced about the war. Turing talked of his work at Bletchley Park and the breaking of the Enigma code. Flint spoke of the Battle of Britain, the fire watch at St Paul's, and the advance across Europe in

'45. It was a different lens through which to view his country; as a nation that had stood against the tide of barbarism. Like many people of his generation, Noel had a cool kid's cynical attitude towards patriotism and the corny idea embodied in the lyrics of 'There'll Always Be an England'. Noel began to suspect that the two childless old men had made him into a surrogate son. With his usual calculation for how to maximize a situation he let them have their fantasy, while knowing they could never match or replace his own father.

He liked most of his fellow aces in the Silver Helix well enough, though his relationship with Carruthers had soured after the director's dunk in the river. It seemed his lordship wasn't happy about being humiliated or taken off guard by a boy ace. But the worst part of his training was his sessions with the agency's psychiatrist, Dr Lee Teitelbaum.

The psychiatrist was in his late thirties, dark-haired, a little stoop-shouldered. He had kind but knowing blue eyes that saw too much. At their first meeting Teitelbaum had waved his pipe vaguely in the air and asked, 'So the two alternate personalities—'

Noel's lip twisted with contempt as he interrupted. 'Let's see, born a hermaphrodite with a domineering mother and a fragile invalid father, subject creates male and female ideals to make up for his/her/its emotional and psychological deficiencies.'

Lee nodded agreeably. 'Nicely done . . . but I was just wondering what might have triggered this particular manifestation? What happened the day you were infected?'

It took him off guard. Noel hadn't really thought much about that day three and a half years ago. 'Not much. We were staying in Selçuk . . . that's in Turkey. We'd spent the day at Ephesus touring the ruins. On the way back we stopped at a beach so Mum could snap some pics. There was a wrecked old freighter. I went exploring. Docs thought I'd probably disturbed a spore. Apparently the wreck dated from the forties.'

A memory surfaced. Sitting on the hard stone bench of the Ephesus amphitheatre the night before watching a performance of Mozart's opera *The Magic Flute*. Suddenly he understood why Lilith was the Queen of the Night and Simon the high priest of the sun.

Teitelbaum reached out and touched him lightly between the eyebrows. 'That right there. What did you see?'

'It was stupid. If it is actually the reason.'

'You're not going to tell me.'

'I'd rather not.'

'All right. Let's turn to the practical problem that concerns the Captain – your inability to teleport in your own form. Do you think of the avatars as people separate from yourself? Is that why they can teleport and you can't?'

'No. I know they're me. My attitude, the way I view the world and the people in it, remains the same. It's as if I get into a different car. The body may change, but I'm still me.'

'And you're certain you can't transform into Lilith during the day or Simon at night?'

'Very sure.'

The psychiatrist sighed and shut his notebook. 'Well, we'll keep trying to overcome this psychological block that keeps you from teleporting when you're you. And it would be nice not to have the avatars tied to this daylight and night quirk.'

'Why is this such a big thing?'

'It might save your life one day.'

'Once again with that—'

Noel was interrupted when the door almost bulged under what passed for a light knock. Neither of them had to guess who was outside. 'Come in, sir,' Teitelbaum called.

The door opened, and Captain Flint ducked to pass beneath the lintel. *'I've come to borrow Noel.'*

'We were just finishing anyway.'

Noel stood up and left with the big joker. *'So how are you finding this so far?'* Flint asked as they walked.

Noel shrugged. 'Good. Interesting. I'm looking forward to the defensive driving class. It's brilliant that I can learn a year early.'

Flint looked down at him. '*You still won't have your licence until you're seventeen.*' The stone face shifted into what passed for a smile. '*So don't go swanning about joy riding.*' He paused and added, '*Though you'll certainly have no trouble with the driving test once we've finished with you.*'

'So what did you want to talk to me about?'

'*I want to introduce you to a new tutor.*' He correctly interpreted Noel's expression and the smile became a rictus grin. '*I think you'll like this one.*'

They had reached the door to Flint's office. The director waved him in. A man seated in one of the high-backed chairs rose and turned to face them. Noel's breath caught at the sight of Sebastian Crewe, Britain's foremost magician. He had made the *Queen Mary* disappear on live television, had been dropped in the middle of the Channel locked in a safe and managed to appear on the press boat standing behind the reporters with their cameras all trained on the choppy waters. Crewe was equally good at close-up magic.

'*Sebastian, here's the young man I told you about. I think he has quite a knack.*'

Crewe walked over, hand outstretched. Noel felt dizzy for a moment, then clasped his hand. 'It's . . . it's an honour, sir.' He looked up at Flint. 'Why? I mean, not that I mind, but—'

'*You'll need a cover. I thought "touring magician" would work out quite nicely. If that suits?*'

'Oh yes. Very much. Beats going to work for Barclays.'

Crewe laughed. 'It does that.' They chatted for a few minutes, and set a schedule for Noel to meet Crewe at his home near Ipswich.

After the magician left Noel sought out Flint in his office and found him seated in his throne-like chair lighting his pipe. 'Thank you, sir. But how did you know?'

'*That little trick you pulled with the handcuffs was a clue. And of course we researched you once we had your identity. Your purchases at the Magic Box were easy to discover.*'

'Do you work with Crewe often?'

'*He's advised us on several operations, and helped out on one.*'

'Why would he do that? He's rich. He's world-famous—'

'*Come, come, Noel, surely you can answer that yourself.*'

♣

Turing entered Flint's office. His brow was furrowed which caused his make-up to crease, revealing faint silver lines. 'Are we setting up a honeypot I don't know about? I was going over the accounts and spotted payments to Juliana and Travis. Both? At the same time?'

Flint shifted in his chair with the rasp of stone on rock and felt a spark against his buttocks. He gave a mental sigh. Clearly the material of his trousers was wearing through again. '*I hired them to tutor Noel. The allure of those avatars shouldn't be wasted, but it would help if he knew his way around the sex act.*' Flint felt his jaw crack as he smiled. '*Actually I'd like to have him be as much of a savant when it comes to rogering as he is at almost everything else.*'

'Are you planning on having him versed in every type of sex act?' Turing asked.

'*Well, it doesn't do us much good if it's only hetero in the missionary position, Alan.*' It came out sharper than he intended.

'Kenneth, he's a child.'

'*Nonsense, he's sixteen. Old enough to give consent.*'

'So old enough for us to pimp him out?'

That brought Flint out of his chair. His hands cracked against the top of the desk and struck flames that quickly ignited the papers. There was a frenzied few seconds in which both he and Turing worked to save the reports. It allowed Flint time to master his anger. It became a cold lump like grease in the pit of his stomach.

'Alan, we haven't had a talent like this in decades. Teleportation and transformation? It's a dangerous world, becoming more dangerous by the moment. Two years ago I failed. Churchill killed, that debacle at the funeral. Never again. My duty – our duty is to protect this nation. I'll use any tool available to accomplish that goal.'

'How much of this is you trying to expiate your sins and failures through Noel?' He paused, then asked, 'Does Lord Dalton know about this?'

'I'm sure he has more important matters to attend to. Like tea at the Palace or another ribbon cutting.'

'So, no.' Turing sighed. 'All right, Kenneth. I'll go along with this. I just worry that we're taking steps that compromise not only Noel but . . . ourselves.'

◆

Cambridge

The murmurs of appreciation from the group of young men all avidly studying the photo filled Noel with bitter satisfaction. Juliana had been patient with the fumbling of an inexperienced lover, and even more so when he'd shyly asked her if he could take a photo. She had agreed without asking him why, which made him decide to explain his predicament with the drinking society and his initiation. Amused, she had entered into the spirit of the thing. She had washed away her make-up, recombed her long red hair into a more youthful style, and pulled on a pair of striped thigh-high stockings that were popular with younger women . . . and nothing else.

When she assumed a bashful expression she no longer looked like a nearly thirty-year-old woman. She could easily have passed for twenty. 'Tell them I'm a student at the London Hair Academy,' she had instructed.

'Lucky dog,' Geoffrey said, bringing Noel back to his surroundings.

'I'm heading down to London at the weekend. Care to give me her number?' Timothy asked.

'Not a chance,' Noel said. 'So what's the verdict? Is she worthy to be added to your book o' babes, and am I worthy of membership?'

The young men exchanged glances. There were nods all round. 'Get the man a drink,' James ordered.

Siraj had remained silent during the discussion. He clapped a hand on Noel's shoulder as he walked past. 'Well, we seem to have managed to corrupt you completely. Well done. And these forays of yours to London are becoming more and more interesting. You must take me along sometime.'

♠

London

A cold wind off the Thames rustled the pages of the *Sun* in its stand. The headline screamed **ROYAL ENGAGEMENT!** above a picture of Princess Gloriana looking appropriately demure in her hat and gloves. Next to her was a picture of a dark-haired young man looking dashing as he sat on a polo pony.

Noel bought a copy and quickly scanned the article. It seemed that Gloriana was to wed the heir to the Norwegian throne upon completing her undergraduate studies at Cambridge. He wondered if she would remember her interrupted tryst with a certain golden-eyed ace . . . and if that tryst were the reason for the sudden engagement. Laughing, he shoved the paper into a nearby rubbish bin and continued on his way.

Noel came bouncing into headquarters but his steps slowed to a stop at the sight of the guard's face at the front desk. 'The guv wants to see you right away.'

'Lord Dalton?'

'No, the Captain.'

'Has something happened?'

'Yeah. You should get upstairs, mate.'

He didn't wait for the ancient lift but took the stairs two at a time. On the top floor the pall he'd sensed below was even more evident. Maryam walked past. Before he could say anything he saw the tears on her cheeks and the words died. He charged into Flint's office only to find it empty, the stone chair and the knick-knacks gone.

Confused, he went back into the hall and ran into Petula. 'I was supposed to report to Flint—'

'He's moved upstairs. Into the chief's office.'

'Why? What's happened to Lord Dalton?'

The answer arrived and shock drove the air from his lungs. 'Dead. Flint's back in charge. Best get along upstairs.'

Noel ran up to the top floor and burst into the office without knocking. 'What the hell has happened?' he demanded.

The fires in Flint's eyes seemed dampened. He removed his pipe slowly. *'Lord Dalton has been killed.'*

'Petula told me.'

'I'll never get her to follow protocol.' Flint tapped the pipe against an ashtray, removing the spent tobacco. *'I believe it is time for you to put your training to good use. There was an incident in Belfast. Joker girl beaten, raped, and killed by a group of footballers from an English college. There's an active cell of the joker terrorist organization the Twisted Fists in Belfast. The director insisted on going himself to try and keep a lid on things. You know the Fists manifesto - five for one. Unfortunately Lord Dalton was one of the five.'* Flint skimmed a photo across the surface of his desk. *'We need to send a message.'*

Noel picked up the photograph. A dwarf with bright-green skin and emerald eyes stared defiantly out at him. 'Who is he?'

'The leader of the Twisted Fists in Belfast. He calls himself King Brian.'

Noel looked back at the photo. 'I could think of other things to call him. Bastard, fucker—'

'*I would prefer a more lethal response.*'

It was as if Death's cold finger had traced Noel's spine. 'You want him . . .' He hesitated. 'Killed.'

'*Yes. He's known to have a taste for the ladies. Lilith is technically a joker because of her eyes. You can make contact. He frequents a pub - Joseph Coan's in the Belfast jokertown. Make it clean, make it quick, and get out. You understand?*'

'Yes, sir.'

'*Have you ever been to Belfast?*'

'No, sir.'

'*Then we'll fly you over. Who do you want for back-up?*'

'Ranjit Singh.'

'*Very well. And, Noel, memorize a location in Belfast. Make a point of learning locations everywhere you go so you can teleport there quickly.*'

'Okay.'

Flint was silent for several long moments. The flickering red eyes were fixed on him.

'Is there anything else?'

'*No.*'

The whisper stopped him just as he touched the door handle.

'*Are you frightened?*'

Noel weighed his response. To say no would make him look like an arrogant prat, but frightened wasn't the right word. 'I'm nervous, but it's more anticipation than fear. Can I do it? I suppose we'll find out.'

♥

'I can't believe this. The Queen gives you back the Helix and this is the first action you take?'

Turing's voice was like a whip across his already-frayed nerves. '*My, my, Alan. I'm not entirely certain these robes of sainthood quite suit you.*'

Turing's jaw tightened causing make-up to flake, leaving

silver lines across his face. 'His nature is not yet set. It's hard enough to ask an adult to take such an action. What effect will it have on a boy?'

Flint paced to the window and gazed out at a grey winter's day. *'I'm worried for him too, but we use the tools at hand . . .'* His voice trailed away.

Turing came up behind him, laid a hand briefly on his shoulder. 'Kenneth, you can stop this. They haven't landed yet. Bring them home. Let someone else take care of Brian. Noel's only sixteen.' Flint didn't answer. Turing turned away. 'Is this what we've come to? Two terrible old men corrupting a boy?'

'Yes.' Flint moved to the sideboard where he kept a bottle of brandy and poured them each a glass. *'For Queen and country.'*

♣

Belfast

For such a small man King Brian was heavy. The faint gargling had died away and now Lilith was supporting the body on just the garrotte. She feared the thin wire might saw through his throat and decapitate the joker. The smell of blood was in her nostrils but not a trace of nausea. She experienced a moment of wonder that her stomach was rock solid. The only nervous tell was that her palms were sweaty.

The handles on the garrotte were threatening to slip, so she lowered the body to the floor and pulled it free. Blood leaked from the cut on Brian's throat, pooling on the battered wooden floor.

It had been easy to get the dwarf alone. All it had taken was a torn blouse, a bruised shoulder, a cut lip, and a black eye, all courtesy of the Lion bashing Noel in the car before he had transformed into Lilith. Once at the pub she had spun her tale of nat boys attacking her while Lilith's smoky charms worked their magic on the man. Brian had taken her to a private room to get her story. The barman had provided them with a bucket of ice and a napkin and when Brian had busied himself preparing a makeshift ice pack Lilith had slipped the garrotte out of the waistband of her skirt and snapped it around the joker's neck. As she had been taught by Jiniri and Banger and Mash, she twisted just so and had stayed to the side to avoid any kicks from the dying man. The thought of Redcoat had made her add even more pressure.

And now it was done.

She tottered and wondered if it was delayed reaction to the murder she had just committed. But no, it was the floor itself that was heaving and bumping beneath her feet. 'You bitch! You murderous Sassenach bitch!'

The voice seemed to be emanating from the walls, floor, and ceiling. Lilith realized with horror that the wooden floor was oozing up over her feet, threatening to trap her. She heard shouts and running feet from the common room of the pub. If they entered she was dead – assuming the grotesque living pub didn't kill her first.

She drew the pistol that was strapped to her inner thigh, and fired four times, quick double taps into the floor around her feet. There was a roar of pain from the building, and the wood's grip on her feet relaxed. It was only an instant but an instant was all she needed.

She thought of her bedroom back home and teleported.

◆

Cambridge

The soft *pop* of displaced air as she arrived did not disturb her parents sleeping down the hall. Lilith realized she had left a shoe behind. 'Bloody hell, Cinderella goes to the ball and murders the prince . . . no, the king.' Giggling uncontrollably, she sank down on the edge of her bed. After a moment, she regained control, stripped out of her clothes, closed her eyes and let her body shift.

Noel opened his eyes and realized that the adrenalin rush was gone. Exhaustion arrived in the form of a pounding headache. He stared down at his bed, longing to crawl beneath the covers. *You need to report. You need to report. You were supposed to return to Singh, then back to London.*

Reluctantly, he turned away from the lure of the warm covers on his childhood bed. Instead he slipped down the hall to the bathroom and ran a hot bath, where he washed away Lilith's rich, heavy perfume, wincing as the water hit his split lip. The water turned faintly pink. He allowed the blood-tinged water to run through his fingers.

'Tonight I killed a man,' he whispered, and waited for a reaction. None came. He sank down, allowing the water to close over his head.

When he emerged from the bathroom wrapped in a heavy robe his father was waiting. 'Dad, what are you doing up?'

'Couldn't sleep. Heard the water running.' He reached out a gnarled forefinger and gently touched Noel's black eye. 'Rugby?'

'Yeah.'

'How about some tea and toast?'

Hunger reared up to announce itself with a loud stomach rumble. 'Brilliant.'

They headed to the kitchen. Noel filled the kettle while his father dropped bread into the toaster.

'Dad, you believe in government service, right?'

'Yes. Very much so.'

'So why didn't you encourage me to enlist?'

Jasper paused, gazing into the open refrigerator. He pulled out the butter dish, sighed and finally said, 'I wasn't sure they would take you given . . .' He gestured vaguely at Noel. 'And that would have been humiliating for you. And if they did take you . . . well, I didn't want you bullied and harassed.'

'Okay.' Noel dropped teabags into their mugs. 'But if I found . . . had found a way to serve you wouldn't have objected?'

'Of course not. Your grandfather fought in World War Two. His father in the Great War. I'm the first Matthews to let down the side.'

'Not your fault. You didn't ask to get sick.' The kettle's shrill whistle cut the air. Noel jumped to turn it off. He didn't want his mother to wake up and interrupt them.

'Why these questions now, Noel? Something happen?'

'I've been doing a lot of reading about the wars of the twentieth century. It seems as if today we don't use armies, in the same way. I mean now we sometimes don't even know who we're fighting or exactly why.'

'I'll take the small wars, Noel. Anything we can do to prevent another global conflagration should be done. Because the next one might not be survivable.'

The toaster dinged and the toast popped up like soldiers to attention. Noel hugged his father tightly. 'Thanks, Dad.'

♠

London
'Where in the holy hell is he!'

'I don't know, sir.' Singh's voice over the phone sounded distant even though only some five hundred miles separated London and Belfast. 'There were shots fired. The authorities arrived, arrests were made, they carried out a body.'

'So he did it.'

'It would seem so.'

'So where the hell is he?'

The Lion remained silent. Flint could almost see his shrug. 'You want me to stay, sir?' Singh said at last.

'Yes, until we can ascertain his location.'

'This might have been too much, too soon, sir.'

Flint's answer was to hang up. He drummed his fingers on the desktop. Where could Noel have gone? He thought about calling the porter who manned the door at Clare College to see if the boy had gone back to his digs at the university. He could claim to be Noel's father. He dismissed the idea. The porter might actually have met the senior Mr Matthews. Perhaps Noel had returned home? If he were traumatized he might have sought comfort with his family. A new fear seized the old man. What if the boy talked? Revealed what he had been doing for the past few months? He stood, paced, and the hours crawled by.

It was a bit past nine when he heard the boy's voice in the hallway. 'Where's Singh?' Maryam's answer was inaudible but Noel's response made it clear. 'Well, why the hell is he still there?'

Flint threw open his office door. '*Because he was waiting for you to follow protocol and turn up as planned. Instead you abandoned your partner. Not well done, Noel. Please.*' He gestured into the office.

Noel's smile had vanished, replaced by a teen's sulky pout. 'I nearly got nabbed by that creepy pub. It's alive. I think it's a joker—'

'*I'm not interested in excuses. The fact remains you were to return to Singh and teleport both of you back to London to be debriefed.*' Noel glared at him, then dropped his head and stared at the floor. The silence stretched between them. '*I trust this won't happen again?*'

'No . . . sir.'

'*Excellent. Where did you go?*'

'I needed to . . . clean up. I went home.'

'*Why?*'

'I needed to . . . think.'

'*Because you were disturbed by what you had done?*'

The golden eyes were raised to meet Flint's gaze. Flint couldn't fully read the expression. 'You think I freaked out. I did, but not for the reason you think.'

'*Please enlighten me.*'

Noel moved over to Flint's desk and picked up and set down

a few of the items resting there. At last he said, 'I rather enjoyed it.' He turned to face Flint. 'Do you want me to run immediately to Dr Teitelbaum?' His tone was defiant.

A complex number of conflicting emotions washed through Flint. Relief and satisfaction, guilt and regret. *'No, that won't be necessary. But do keep working with him on your inability to teleport in your real form. It's quite inconvenient given your role here. Now go. I have work to do and you have a debriefing session with Turing.'*

'Yes, sir.'

'Oh, one last thing.'

Noel paused at the door and looked back.

'You have a code name now. You are Double Helix.'

'Thank you, sir. And, sir, let me know when you want me to do it again.' The door closed.

Flint stared at it for a long time. *'For Queen and country,'* he whispered. He wasn't sure if it were an affirmation or a justification. And it didn't make him feel any better.

♣ ♦ ♠ ♥

How to Turn a Girl to Stone

by Emma Newman

Cornwall, 2003

KERRY SCRABBLED OVER THE gate and ducked behind the hedge when she heard the old van chugging up the lane. She was sure it was Mandy being taken to school by her grumpy dad and she didn't want to be seen, even though she'd imagined it so many times.

In her fantasy, she'd be walking down the lane just as the van came round the corner, right next to the gate so they could pull over safely and chat to her without blocking the narrow road. Her friend would burst out of the old banger and throw her arms around her. 'I knew it was you!' Mandy would say. 'Where have you been? Everyone's been asking about you!'

Fantasy Kerry would laugh and say, 'Oh, there was a mix-up and the council said I didn't have a place at the school so I've just been teaching myself.' Sometimes, her fantasy reply was less plausible. 'They did this test on me and it said I didn't need to go to school any more, so I've just been hanging out at the farm, chillin' out, y'know.'

Did they even say 'chillin' out' any more? She had no idea.

When she was feeling particularly annoyed, as she did this morning, her imaginary conversation would be darker. She would hold out her hands, covered in the pale blue cotton gloves she hated so much, and say to her old best friend, 'I'm supposed to tell you that I'm allergic to everything now. But the truth is—'

She jumped at the sound of the van's horn. Had they seen her? She crouched lower, the dungy smell of a nearby cowpat horribly strong now the morning sun was heating the field up. A fox shot through the bars of the gate next to her and she realized the van had blown its horn to move it out of the road. Mandy's dad might be grumpy, but he would never run something over if he could avoid it.

Shaking, Kerry was caught between the relief that she hadn't been seen and the burning wish that she had been. Those hated blue gloves were in her pocket. She was tempted to push them into the cowpat with a stick, but as with all the other times she'd thought about it, she put them on instead. She was almost at her uncle's house, and she couldn't take the risk.

Kerry stood up once the chugging wheeze of the van's engine had faded away and watched the fox race to the opposite side of the field. She couldn't help but remember when Mandy's mum had taken them both to the cinema in that van, years ago, when they went to see *Toy Story 2*. She'd loved the trip there almost as much as the popcorn, the van seats high enough to see over the thick Cornish hedges that lined the roads. It had taken nearly an hour to get to the cinema, thanks to the winding roads and the way the ancient van struggled with the hills, but they'd chatted all the way there and all the way back.

She didn't want to remember it. It merely made her long for trips like that even more. If only she lived in a town, somewhere with a cinema and shops a walk away – or even a bus ride! There were no buses that served the nearest village and that was over two miles' walk away. The little shop there, where she used to get her Saturday morning treat, had closed down over a year ago, leaving just a pub and the village hall. It wasn't worth the risk to go there with nothing to do. Only one of her former classmates actually lived in that village and they had never really liked each other anyway. The rest were scattered over farms and other tiny villages. If only Mandy lived closer! Just one secret friendship would make everything easier to bear.

She wondered what Mandy looked like now. Was she spotty? It was one of the things she'd been warned about but so far she'd only had a couple of zits on her nose and chin. Did she still have her long brown hair or was that style too childish now? After all, the last time she had seen Mandy they had both worn vests beneath their school uniform, tied their hair back with bobble ties shaped like fruit and wore knee-high socks. Now she was wearing a bra – something she and Mandy had once giggled about – and wouldn't be seen dead in knee-high socks. Her hair was still just as black, curly and unruly as it ever was. She feared she wouldn't recognize Mandy now, but she knew her old best friend would know her a mile off.

Shoving her gloved hands deep in her jeans pockets, Kerry resumed her bad-tempered stomp across the field. She was already on her uncle's land, and never left it, but she was still out of sight of the farmhouse, nestled as it was in the valley below. Once it had felt as if the whole world was just two valleys and the fields that stretched over the hill between them. When she was younger, before everything changed, her uncle had owned all the fields she could see from her bedroom window. Since then he had sold off half of the land, but the hill was still his.

The day Uncle Cal came over to tell them about the sale was just as sunny and they had all stood on the patio at the back of the house, the adults with tea, she with apple juice. Uncle Cal hadn't been himself since he'd arrived. Instead of gathering her up into his arms as he normally did, he'd just patted her on the head and gone to find her parents in the studio, both of them covered in clay and dust up to their elbows.

'Let's 'ave a cuppa,' he'd said to them and like her, they'd known something was up.

He'd been expecting a fight. She knew that now, looking back. But her dad had just nodded at the news and said, 'You can still walk from our house to yours without leaving Tremaine land?' When Uncle Cal had nodded, he'd nodded too. 'Well then. That's not so bad. We've still got the hill.'

'I'll never sell the 'ill!' Uncle Cal said. 'And I put a rider on the sale, sayin' it has to stay dairy land. Don't want none of them property developers gettin' any ideas. I reckon Pentroath'll buy it. He's all right.'

In her family's eyes, the other local farmers that were 'all right' were the ones who helped each other out when the man from the government made them kill all the cows and burn them to stop the spread of foot-and-mouth disease. That had been the first time she'd seen her uncle cry. Mr Pentroath had helped him that day, and rested a hand on his shoulder when he broke down.

She could still remember the smell, even though it was over two years ago. Even now it made her shudder. That year had seen the last of her primary school education, the slaughter of the animals she knew by name and the end of her freedom. So many people said 2001 had been the worst year for farming since mad cow disease. For her, it was the worst year for a very different reason.

Cresting the hill, Kerry looked down into the neighbouring valley and saw her uncle's farmhouse. It was too big for him but he'd never leave it, even though it was draughty and damp and felt cold all year round. It had been in the family for generations, since her great-grandfather built it to replace the old cottage that *his* grandfather had built there before. The Tremaine family had owned the land she walked on for hundreds of years, but it didn't have the same magic for her as it seemed to for her uncle and father. Right now, the same fields they had played and worked in felt like an open-air prison.

The cows were in the next field. She knew all their names too and, even though she worried it would always be there, the fear that they too would be culled had passed. Unlike the herd before, she didn't head over to say good morning to them but instead moved as far away as she could. A couple headed towards her in the hope of a fuss so she picked up the pace and got through the next gate before they reached her.

From the last field before the farmhouse she could hear Damson barking. She made sure her gloves were on properly and tucked them into her sleeves so there was no gap exposing her skin. At least it wasn't too hot yet. She missed wearing T-shirts.

Damson was waiting for her on the other side of the last gate, the only one with chicken wire secured over it to stop her running through the widely spaced bars. Her mouth was too full of her favourite ball to bark now. She was mainly Border Collie, with enough German Shepherd in the mix to make her a little bigger, with black-and-white fur and the most gentle nature. The sight of her delight made Kerry's heart ache for Damson's sister, Plum. She checked the gloves again before reaching into her back pocket for one of Damson's favourite biscuits.

'Hello! Yes, I'm glad to see you too! But you know the rule. Sit. Calm down, now. I'll be through, dreckly, you just sit first. Then you get your treat.'

Damson sat and dropped the ball in front of her, long lines of drool stretching between it and her mouth as she spotted Kerry's closed fist.

'Now, you stay, Damson. Stay, there's a good girl.' Kerry dropped the treat over the top of the gate and then opened it as Damson gobbled the biscuit up. Once she was through to the other side and the gate was locked behind her, Damson was on her feet, nudging the ball with her nose, tail wagging. With a grin, Kerry picked it up and threw it as far down the yard as she could. Damson sped off, leaving a plume of dust, barking happily.

Kerry threw the ball three more times, grateful that Damson had learned to drop it at her feet and then back off after each retrieval. When it looked as if she was getting too excited to remember, Kerry reminded her to stay and placed a treat in front of her as a reward. She resisted the urge to fuss her, despite the gloves. It wasn't worth the risk. So she threw the ball one last time and hurried to the front door as Damson sped off again.

It was unlocked, as usual. 'Helloooo!' she called. 'Only me, Uncle Cal!'

She ate some scraps of crispy bacon left in the frying pan before rinsing it in the sink. Closing the heavy lid of the AGA oven, Kerry wondered where her uncle was and why he'd left the kitchen in such a mess. He was usually far tidier than this.

'Hello?' She peeped into the living room that was barely used and wrinkled her nose at the dust. It used to be her gran's favourite room and Uncle Cal kept it just as she'd liked it. She wouldn't have approved of this neglect.

'Uncle Cal?'

She had gone down the hallway to the bottom of the stairs, wondering if he was in the bathroom, when she heard his voice coming from the office. It used to be the dining room until her grandparents died and her uncle took over the farm. He said he was tired of carting boxes of receipts and paperwork up and down the stairs but they all knew how much he hated it when it was his turn to do Sunday lunch. At least her dad loved cooking, when he remembered to do it, and Mum didn't resent doing a roast every now and again.

Kerry paused, listening long enough to realize he was on the phone. He didn't sound happy. She heard something about being unreasonable and not having enough time before she hurried back to the kitchen. As much as she wanted to know what was going on, she knew better than to listen in. She'd only blush if something was said and then he'd know she'd eavesdropped.

Unable to go back home, Kerry put on the rubber gloves over her cotton ones and started washing up. It was clear that Uncle Cal was struggling to keep on top of things, even though it was well into June and all the calves had been born.

Just as she was starting to dry the dishes, the post was delivered. Wanting to be helpful, she gathered the letters from the mat to leave on the kitchen table ready for when he finished his call. She couldn't help but see the red words stamped on several of the envelopes.

FINAL DEMAND

Demand for what? Money? She flipped them over, seeing return addresses that were in London. She left them on the table and went back to the sink.

'Kerry? What are you doing here?'

She jumped at the sound of her uncle's voice. 'Mum said I had to come.'

'But I've got someone coming over. She knew . . .' he sighed. 'She must have forgotten.'

He looked tired. And he was wearing a tie and a plain white shirt with smart trousers, instead of a tatty T-shirt and jeans. 'You goin' somewhere after?' she asked.

He shook his head. 'They're comin' 'ere. I just said.'

The sharpness of his tone made her polish the plate she was holding harder. Uncle Cal was never snappish like this. If her mother hadn't told her she wasn't allowed home until lunchtime, she would have left then and there.

'I'm sorry, my 'andsome,' he said, crossing the kitchen to come and hug her before remembering himself and stopping a few feet away. 'I got things on my mind, s'all. But it might be best if you come back over later. I'll let you drive the biggun' if you like.'

She loved driving the tractor, but she could see it was a bribe. 'I can't go home. Dad's agent is there.'

His frown returned, deepening. 'T'int right,' he muttered, grabbing the kettle and filling it at the sink. 'Girl your age should be at school. Should be meetin' new people. When I were your age . . .' He flicked the kettle's switch, scowling at it.

'I don't need school, not when I'm inheritin' the farm. I don't need no exams to prove I know how to take care of it all. There ent no GCSE in muckin' out and silage, is there?' Kerry said, trying to lighten the atmosphere.

It didn't seem to work. If anything, it made her uncle's dark look even worse. 'There ent no future in farmin', Kerenza. No future at all.'

Steam plumed from the spout and the kettle clicked itself off. She watched her uncle making a cup of tea, feeling a tightening in her stomach. Her eyes flicked from the red-lettered envelopes to his poorly knotted tie and the dark patches of damp cotton at the armpits of his shirt. Who would he wear a suit for? Suits were for weddings and funerals and bank managers, he always said. But bank managers didn't visit farms. Did they?

'Are you in trouble, Uncle Cal?'

He stirred in the milk, keeping the spoon circling far longer than he needed to. 'Didn't that doctor do anything? I thought he was supposed to be the best in the country.'

The change in topic threw her. Doctor? Then she remembered the latest lie, one said in haste over Sunday lunch a few weeks before, when her uncle had started giving her parents a hard time about her 'allergies'. She'd hated her mother so much as she made up another pile of crap to throw Uncle Cal off the scent. Surely it was better to tell him the truth? When she said as much to her mother that evening, she'd been furious.

'You call me a liar when all I'm doing is protecting you?' Her voice sounded as harsh as a shovel scraping the concrete floor of the cowshed when mucking out. 'How can you think any good would come of people knowing what you are? You've seen them on the news—'

'I've seen them savin' people! There was that thing on the

telly about when Captain Flint caught those people who blew up that ship and—'

'Don't you be goin' on about that Captain Flint, he b'aint no natural thing! You want to end up like him? Being ordered about by the Queen and havin' no life of his own? That want you want, is it?'

'Mel . . .' her dad had said to her, gently, but when her mother got started, it took more than a gentle man to stop her.

'I don't want to keep lyin'!' Kerry had shouted back. 'And Uncle Cal wouldn't tell no one! Not if we asked him not to!'

'You think he'll just nod and smile and nothin' will change? Do you think he'll still love you when he knows what you are?'

Then the tears had come, hot and overwhelming, and she'd run from the room. Not even her dad's efforts to comfort her with his gentle voice had worked that night.

She looked at her uncle who was staring at her over the rim of his mug. Surely he would still love her if he knew the truth? He loved her even though he thought she was some freak allergic to the most unlikely things. But she couldn't find the courage to tell him, not after all this time. That would hurt him, finding out his own family hadn't trusted him, and she couldn't bear the thought of that.

'Oh, he said we were doin' all the right things and . . . and that it'll probably just get better when I'm older. Like asthma, y'know.'

'He did, did he? What was his name again?'

She shrugged. 'I can't remember.'

He glanced at the clock above her head. 'You can go and watch the telly upstairs if you like, but . . .' He paused, reconsidering. 'No, I'm sorry, Kerry, you need to go back 'ome. I can't . . . it wouldn't be a good idea for you to be here when she arrives.'

'Who?'

'Just someone from . . . the bank. Nothin' for you to worry about, but I'd never forgive myself if it made you ill. There's some fruit in the bowl, and the flask is under the sink. Make yourself a picnic if you like and go over to the north field, it's empty at the moment. Come back after lunch and I'll show you how to strip the Rover's engine. I've been puttin' it off. Gotta make sure you learn somethin' useful, eh?'

She put an apple and a banana in a bag, mainly to keep him happy, and left as he shoved the post into a drawer and muttered a goodbye. Maybe if she walked back over the hill slowly the agent would be gone by the time she got home.

'Oh! I forgot!' her uncle said, searching a pile of newspapers and then pulling one out. He rolled it up and handed it to her. 'Take this with you. Look on page twenty-five. I'll see you later, right?'

♣

In the north field there was a tree her great-grandmother had planted on her wedding day. The story handed down to each generation was that she had buried a pasty below its roots, so the piskies would be appeased, and poured beer over the newly planted sapling to keep the buccas happy, so the wedding night wouldn't be disturbed.

Of course, no one really believed in buccas or piskies any more, but she could remember her grandfather always telling her to break off a chunk of pasty crust and throw it into the hedge for the little magical creatures to eat. And even now, every time they had boiled eggs for breakfast they all turned the empty shells upside down afterwards and broke them at the bottom, so they couldn't be used by local witches to sail out to sea and sink the fishing boats. Even though she knew it was ridiculous, she still did it. Habits died hard.

Now the tree her great-grandmother had planted was a stout oak with a thick trunk perfect for sitting against and a generous shaded area that all manner of wildlife made use of in the hottest summers. There were little clumps of hair trapped in the gnarls of the bark where the cows had rubbed against it the day before.

She settled in a dusty hollow between two roots and flipped to page twenty-five of the *West Briton*. When she saw the pictures she clamped a hand over her mouth and looked away, unprepared for the shock.

It was a double-page spread about her father's sculptures and the renovation of Polgurnow village hall funded by his success. It was a simple 'local artist done good, hero of community' story, with one important omission: the truth.

The largest picture was of his first 'sculpture' of Plum, their old dog. Just the sight of it made her throat tighten and her chest feel as if it was being buried under a pile of bricks. Her gloved fingertips twitched at the memory of running her hands over Plum's fur and how, faster than she could register what was happening, the glossy coat had turned to stone beneath her fingertips. One moment she'd been fussing the dog for being such a clever girl, the next she was stroking a granite statue of her. Every little detail had been preserved in the freakish transformation, even the stitching in her collar that had changed too.

Her father had come rushing out of the studio at the sound of her screams and she had a vague sense of being comforted before the memory lost cohesion.

It was sheer luck that she hadn't done the same to her father by accident. It didn't occur to either of them that she had been responsible for what had happened to Plum. It wasn't a natural conclusion to leap to.

She could remember arguments that night as she lay in bed, the first time she'd ever heard her parents raise their voices to each other. Her father had wanted to take her to a doctor or contact the authorities, maybe even the Silver Helix, while Mother had argued that keeping it a secret was best for all of them. If they told anyone what had happened, their daughter would be taken away. Perhaps they would never let her come home again.

Kerry wasn't sure if she believed that any more and she certainly wasn't sure if it would be worse than being stuck on the farm. The newspaper article was singing her family's praises, describing how her father's success had rescued their tiny village from the brink of ruin, the village she wasn't even allowed to visit. She hadn't seen the village hall since her eleventh birthday, only a couple of months before her card had turned, as the people on the telly said.

Scanning the text, as much to stop herself from looking at the pictures, Kerry hunted for a mention of herself. She found it quickly, nothing but a throwaway mention of a daughter. It seemed that the journalist had actually listened to her mother's request for privacy.

She carried on reading. It told the story of a struggling pair of artists, one a potter, the other a sculptor, trying to survive. Then the breakthrough when her father tried 'a new technique' and created the most lifelike sculpture of a dog that Paul Wetherby had ever seen.

Kerry pressed her lips tight together at the sight of Wetherby's picture with her father at his gallery. Once a big deal in the London art scene, he'd retired to Cornwall and opened a little gallery in Penzance. It was for tourists, rather than locals, and her parents had minor success with a few pieces there. Then on a visit to their home, to see what they were working on in the studio, he'd seen Plum in the corner.

Then everything had got much worse.

It was obvious that Wetherby was visiting today because he wanted another 'sculpture' to sell. She hadn't made one for a few months, having cried for days after the last, a little hedgehog that her mother had found. There was a buyer in London, someone who collected hedgehog art apparently, who was willing to pay an absurd amount of money for a 'perfect reproduction'. She'd wondered if they would have been willing to pay that money if the buyer had known one of their favourite creatures had to die in the process.

'I know it's hard, pickle,' her mother had said as she held the cardboard box containing the hedgehog. 'But it's so quick they can't feel a thing. And that money could do so much good. That deer you changed last year fixed the village hall, didn't it? There are dozens of deer. One less doesn't make any difference, but that hall being saved has made all the difference to the village, hasn't it?'

'What will you spend the money on from this one?'

'We're going to give half to the RNLI and the rest will keep us going for a few months. You know how much the lifeboats need donations; they don't get any funding from the government. Just think, this little hedgehog could help save lives!'

Her mother always knew what to say to make it seem unreasonable not to obey her. Of course, refusing to kill a hedgehog seemed perfectly acceptable when held up against saving lives.

What really hurt was how much the animals she changed trusted her. She'd always found it easy to befriend them. Her father had once joked that she couldn't go outside without making a new friend. After they realized she had killed Plum, she'd chased away all the local wildlife – from ravens to rabbits – that used to visit her each day for titbits of food. She couldn't bear the thought of accidentally killing them. Weeping the whole time, she'd easily coaxed the hedgehog out of its protective ball to snuffle at her finger. The buyer didn't want a ball of spines, after all.

There was a picture of that damned hedgehog in the paper, with a caption beneath marvelling at how skilled her father was in creating those granite spines. Kerry slapped the pages shut and rolled the newspaper up again to stuff it between two branches, ready for when she went home. For a moment, she wondered whether to just run away rather than returning home and being asked to kill another helpless creature. But then where would she go? All of the family was here and she knew terrible things could happen to children who ran away.

Besides, her uncle was in trouble, she could tell. Then the most awful thought occurred to her. What if she could make a sculpture that would give him enough money to—

No! She covered her face with her hands. There had to be another way.

◆

Between messing about at the oak and then stripping the Rover's engine, Kerry managed to avoid her parents all day. She had dinner with her uncle, nothing more than baked beans on burnt toast eaten in silence. He looked ill with worry, now that there was no engine to distract him. She helped him bring in the herd for milking, taking care to have the broom handle ready in case any of them tried to get too close so she could gently push them back, and then went home as the sun set, her feet getting heavier with each step.

Her parents' modest house was so different to her uncle's farmhouse, being modern and much more comfortable to live in. It had two bedrooms and an annexe on the back that was her parents' studio. One half of the studio contained a kiln and her mother's pottery paraphernalia and the other her father's stone-working tools. He still sculpted sandstone as that was far easier to work than granite. It was one of the reasons her 'sculptures' commanded such high prices. It was a very difficult stone to work and far too hard to sculpt anything with the fine details as her curse could create. There were always a few blocks in the studio though, more as a sort of set dressing to satisfy Mr Wetherby when he visited. Thankfully his visits were rare.

When she entered the house she could hear her parents arguing again. Kerry slammed the door so that they would know she was home and the shouting stopped. 'Only me!' she called.

Her parents appeared at the doorway between the hall and the studio, all smiles and tense shoulders. 'Hello, pickle,' Mum said with a forced smile. 'Did you have a nice day with Uncle Cal?'

Kerry nodded. She hated the way they were smiling at her. It was worse than walking in on them fighting. She busied herself by taking off her shoes and putting them on the rack next to the door. 'I'm going to bed. I'm tired.'

'Don't you want to watch *X Factor* with me?' her dad called as she started up the stairs.

'No, thanks,' she said. 'Night.'

She wasn't tired at all. She just didn't want to have the inevitable conversation about the pressure the agent was putting on her father for another sculpture. Kerry went to her room, shut the door and sat on the bed. She looked at the dolls on the shelves that she hadn't played with for years and yet, somehow, she couldn't bring herself to get rid of them. She looked at the basket of cuddly toys in the corner and felt they were both childish and too dearly loved to give away. There were posters on the walls of a TV show she and Mandy had loved but that she hadn't watched for over a year now. These things didn't connect with her any more, but Kerry had no idea what to replace them with. It felt as if she was stuck in a life that didn't fit her any longer.

There was a gentle knock on the door. 'It's Mum. Can I come in?'

'I'm going to bed.' Kerry hurriedly took off her socks and gloves. The door opened anyway. 'Mum!'

'I need to talk to you about something important.'

Kerry threw her dirty socks into the corner just to annoy her. 'Can't it wait until tomorrow?'

'No. Look at this.'

Her mother sat on the bed an arm's length away. She was holding a newspaper clipping and with a jolt, Kerry remembered she'd left the copy of the *West Briton* in the tree by accident.

But when her mother unfolded the piece she held, Kerry realized it wasn't the same newspaper.

The headline was in large, bold letters:

PYGMALION BRINGS STATUE TO LIFE

Kerry's dread lifted. 'What's this?'

'There's an ace who works for that Captain Flint bloke, called Pygmalion,' Mum replied, handing over the article. 'He can make statues come to life.'

The name was familiar. She was certain she'd seen him on the telly, just a snippet about him before her father had marched in and turned it off. It had been something about the Silver Helix and she'd wanted to know more, but her father refused to let her watch it, muttering something about it being nothing to do with them.

Kerry read the article as quickly as she could. There had been some sort of attack in London and Pygmalion had made one of the lions in Trafalgar Square come to life and chase down one of the suspects, pinning him to the ground until a specialist armed unit arrived. 'It says he just touched the lion and it came to life. He's like me . . . but in reverse!'

Her mother smiled. 'That's exactly what I thought! And . . . well, I don't want to get your hopes up, my 'andsome, but I was wondering if he might be able to help us.'

'How?'

'Well . . . I was thinkin' . . . if he bring statues to life, maybe . . .'

Kerry gasped. 'What if he could bring my statues back to life?' She jumped up. 'What if he could bring Plum back to life?'

Her mother's smile widened. 'That's exactly what I was wonderin'!'

'We have to phone him! We have to find out the number . . . or email him. Uncle Cal has a computer!'

'We have to be careful though,' Mum said, patting the bed to encourage her to sit back down again. 'We need to find out if he can do this, but not let them know about you. Not yet.

You know how important it is to us to keep you safe. And Plum's statue was sold for a lot of money. We'd need to find the money to buy her back so it's a long way down the road yet. Sit down, darlin', and let me tell you what I think we should do.'

Kerry sat, trying to keep her body still as her thoughts ran ahead. If Pygmalion could bring Plum back it would change everything! She wouldn't be afraid any more!

'Now, the first thing we need to know is if he can even do it, right?'

Kerry nodded. 'But if we don't have Plum . . .' Her high spirits crashed. She could see where this was going.

'We need to test this Pygmalion,' Mum said. 'So you need to make a statue. Just one, darlin', just one.'

'But what if he can't do it?'

'Then we know. As soon as I saw that article I knew what we had to do, so I went over to Truro this afternoon. To the pet shop.'

Kerry's stomach cramped. She'd been expecting this, but it was still just as awful as she'd feared. She shook her head. 'No, Mum, I don't want to—'

'But we need to know, don't we? I know it's hard, I do, but you just need to be brave, one more time.' She left the room, no doubt to fetch the purchased pet. Turning a poor creature to stone didn't feel like being brave: it just felt evil. Like that snake-haired woman in the myths they'd studied at school in her last year. Medusa. Was that what the newspapers would call her, if they knew what she could do?

Her mother returned with a small pet carrier with a metal grille forming the door. Even before she could see it, Kerry could hear the mewling of a kitten and tears sprang to her eyes.

It was set on the bed, the door facing away from her. 'Now, darlin', you need to be strong. Just think about Plum. If this works, we can get her back, can't we?'

'And what if it doesn't?' Kerry sniffed as a tear broke free.

'Then . . . then we know.'

'And you'll have something new to sell.' The words sounded so much more bitter voiced aloud.

'We all have to do what we must to survive,' Mother replied. 'And now is not the time for that argument. Come on now, dry your eyes. Just this one, that's all I'm askin' for.'

Kerry swiped her sleeve across her nose as her mother opened the door of the carrier. The kitten looked like a fluffy black ball filling her mother's hand.

Her first instinct was to love it. To pick it up and cradle it to her chest and kiss the top of its little head. But she pushed that down as swiftly as she could, knowing what would happen if she didn't.

'He has little white fur boots,' her mum said, coaxing the kitten to uncurl and reveal them. 'See?'

Kerry's bottom lip juddered. Why was her mother pointing them out to her? It felt like the height of cruelty to make her admire the kitten like a new pet, rather than something she was being asked to kill.

The kitten stepped off Mother's hand and hesitantly explored the duvet with his paws. His squeaky meow made Kerry jump off the bed and back away.

'Oh, Kerry. I hate having to ask you to do this, I really do. You know that. But just imagine if that Pygmalion could change her back.'

'But won't you have to tell him about me?'

Her mother's gaze flicked away, focusing on the kitten. 'If that man can do this, I'm sure he will understand why we want to keep you safe. I'm going to ask him to help us protect you. He'll know what it's like to be . . . different.'

There was so much in that pause between the words. Was her mum thinking other words before she settled on that one?

She watched the kitten approach the edge of the bed, his booted legs stepping with the still-jerky movements of the very young. His eyes were a dazzling green and Kerry wanted nothing more in that moment than to be able to take care of him and love him as she had loved Plum.

Her mother's eyes were upon her, she knew it, just as she knew there was no way she could get out of this, short of running away. And she was too cowardly to do that. She glanced at the newspaper clipping again, wanting to hope so much, wanting to believe Pygmalion would help her even though they'd never met. But if she were him, and there was a girl who needed mistakes like these to be fixed, she'd do it without hesitation. She had to believe he would feel the same. It was the first time she'd had hope.

Forcing herself to move back to the bed, Kerry knelt down beside the kitten and sucked in a breath as she held out her fingertips, just as she would when meeting any new animal. She liked to give them the chance to come to her first, when they were ready, deciding for themselves if they liked the smell of her. As much as she didn't want the kitten's curiosity to bring him closer, she wanted it over as quickly as possible.

There was never any way to tell exactly when it would happen. Sometimes it was the first touch, sometimes it was a few moments later. The only mercy was that it was always quick, and quick enough that she was certain they didn't suffer.

The kitten mewed and loped towards her with his unsteady gait. Kerry held her breath, bracing herself for the inevitable and fearful that she could scare him away if the sob building inside her throat escaped.

She felt the warm brush of his tiny nose and as the fear peaked within her, the kitten froze, taking on the dull grey of granite before she had even blinked. She snatched her hand away as his little body tipped to the side, preserved with his neck outstretched, his curiosity given stony permanence.

Her mother picked the stone kitten up with great care, knowing full well that it would be so easy to break off one of the whiskers or the tip of an ear with its once-downy fur.

There was no black-and-white fur now, no brilliant green in his eyes. Now the only thing that caught the light was the occasional speck of mica trapped in the granite. She carried it out of her room, leaving the empty pet carrier on the bed. Kerry only had enough time to close its door before she returned.

'I know that was hard,' she said. 'Oh, I wish I could cuddle you. Maybe if we wrapped the duvet—'

'No,' Kerry said sharply. The other times she'd rejected the suggestion it had been out of fear. This time it was anger. She didn't want her mother to try and offer her comfort, being the one that had upset her! 'I just want to go to bed now.'

Her mother lingered in the doorway. 'I'm going to London tomorrow. To see that . . . man. There's hope, Kerenza, you have to hold on to that.'

But all Kerry could think of was that pause. What else was her mother tempted to call Pygmalion? She picked up the pet carrier, gave it to her mother, moving forward as she did so to push her out of the room. Closing the door in her mother's face, Kerry rested her head against it and finally allowed herself to cry.

♠

There was a message stuck to the fridge when Kerry went downstairs for breakfast, held on by the Nordic troll with a magnet in its back. No one in the house liked the thing, but no one had the heart to get rid of it either. She pulled it free and read that Uncle Cal was busy all day and it would be best if she stayed at home.

She could hear her father working in the studio, chipping away as some awful music from the seventies blared from his ancient stereo. Mum had obviously left; she would never let him have the music on that loud if she was working in there too. Drifting to the window, she could see the car was gone. London was at least six hours away, and that was on a good run. She wouldn't be back until late.

She made herself some toast and put extra jam on it, then hit upon the idea of scouring the news for any sign of Pygmalion. But she'd missed the breakfast shows and, with neither satellite TV nor a computer, there was nowhere else to look until the lunchtime news.

'Did you see the note?' her dad asked from the doorway. When she nodded, he came over and took the TV remote, switching it off. 'Seeing as you're free today, can you help with the shed? It needs to be painted and the weather's perfect.'

She couldn't think of a good enough excuse to get out of it. The day passed with a steady string of jobs in both the garden and the house. She missed the lunchtime news and the evening news too. Her father was full of energy, directing her in the midst of his own work. It wasn't until the evening, when they were watching the *X Factor* episode he'd taped for her the night before, that it occurred to her that he had been keeping her busy.

'Do you know when Mum will be home?'

'Late, pickle. Very late.'

'Have you spoken to her?'

He shook his head. 'I got a text saying she was setting off soon. You'll be in bed when she gets back.'

'Can't I stay up?'

'You might as well go to bed. If you're still awake when she gets back, you'll see her then.'

He didn't look away from the screen as he spoke. He was just as tense as she was. 'Have you seen that Pygmalion on the news?'

'You know I don't watch the news. Half of it's lies and the rest is propaganda.'

'But—'

'Everything we need to know about living our lives can be found right outside our door. Worryin' about what them politicians in London are doin' is bad for you.'

'But Pygmalion isn't a—'

'People worry too much about what other people are doin'.' He closed his eyes and sighed, then looked at her for the first time. 'I know you'm worried, my 'andsome, but there's nothing on the news that'll help with that. We just have to wait for your mother and see what's to do. A'right?'

Kerry sat back, cuddling a cushion, wishing they had a computer so she could find out about the ace online. She had so many questions that needed answers. Was she really an ace? She didn't look different but she could do something . . . unnatural. But what she did was horrible. Did that make her a knave? No, they looked different, didn't they?

She watched the singers on the TV, filled with a sudden loathing for the vacuous spectacle she and her dad used to love. It seemed stupid now. Empty. She closed her eyes and curled up as he commented on the latest performance. No matter what the news from her mother was, she'd go to Uncle Cal's tomorrow and ask to use the computer. She had to learn more about aces. And knaves. Just in case.

The sound of the front door closing woke her. She had fallen asleep on the sofa, and judging from her father's quiet groan he had done the same. They both scrabbled to their feet, Kerry delayed by the blanket that her father must have draped over her.

Just as she was reaching the hallway there was another sound – squeak of a meow – and she stopped, her body rigid as she listened for it again.

'It worked!' she heard her mother say. 'Look! He changed him back!'

For a moment, all Kerry could do was cover her face with her hands as the relief flooded through her. She hadn't realized how much she had needed this, until now. Then she dashed to the door to see her father pulling the little kitten out of the pet carrier, its white-booted legs splayed out in surprise.

'Look, Kez!' Dad said, holding him out towards her. 'He's right as rain!'

Kerry laughed and cried all at the same time. 'What was Pygmalion like, Mum?'

'Plump little fellow in a waistcoat. Nice enough, I s'pose. He was very understandin'. He said we were doin' the right thing, given how young you are.'

'Is he coming to visit?'

'No! He's got a job. Busy one at that. There are all sorts of dodgy wronguns that he and that Flint bloke have to catch, y'know. But he wishes you well and said that if an accident 'appens again, he'll 'elp us out.'

Kerry looked to her father to share her joy, but there was a frown which he quickly tried to hide. 'Good, good,' he said. 'I think we'll keep this little one in our bedroom tonight with the door closed.'

'What about Plum?' Kerry asked. 'Did you talk about getting Plum back?'

'Well, we know it's possible now,' Mum said and yawned. 'But not right away because of the money, like I said. It's past three. We should all get to bed and talk in the mornin'.'

Kerry looked at the kitten curling up in her father's palm and wished she could take him to her room. Even though there was the real chance of getting Plum back, there was something about the way her parents looked at each other before climbing the stairs that made her nervous. Something was being left unsaid, and she was certain it was because they didn't want her to hear it.

♥

Her mother's voice, high and strained, woke Kerry with a jolt. It was muffled by the bedroom wall, but still loud enough to penetrate. They were arguing again. It was mid-morning and she'd slept far later than usual. She worried about the kitten and whether the raised voices would be frightening him. What were they fighting about now? Surely the news about Pygmalion was a good thing?

She lay still for a moment, frustrated by how she couldn't make out the actual words, before getting out of bed and creeping out of her room. The door was thinner than the wall and she wanted to hear this one. Unlike all the other arguments that had filled the house over the past two years, something had actually changed. There was no cure for what she was – as far as they knew – but there was a safety net now. Had Pygmalion said something that caused this one?

'But it's not right!' her father was saying. 'How are we going to explain it to her? Bad enough that we've asked her to change all those animals. Asking her to do this is . . . it's going too far!'

'What choice do we 'ave?' was her mother's reply. 'We didn't ask for any of this! At least we made some good come out of it! I know it's . . . I don't want to do it either, but think of the money! God knows we need it!'

'So that's supposed to make it all okay then, is it?'

'We're talking about the farm! About Cal! If we don't help him it'll kill him, Crispin! You know that!'

Kerry opened the door. 'What's goin' on with Uncle Cal?'

Her dad was only wearing his pyjama bottoms, Mum was in her nightdress. At the sight of her they both froze. 'Nothin' that—' Dad started to say, when Mum shook her head at him.

'She should know.'

'Know what?'

Her mother came closer as Dad scooped the kitten off the bed and held it, in case it was tempted to go over to her. 'The farm's in trouble. Uncle Cal just can't make enough money any more. It looks like he has to sell it.'

'But he sells more milk than ever!'

'Times are changin', my 'andsome. Farmin' just int what it was. We've been tryin' to help but . . .'

'It's not enough,' Dad said. 'He hid how bad it was from us. He thought he could sort it out but he can't and now he needs a lot of money very quickly, else we'll all be thrown out.'

'But can't he just come and live here?'

'This land is part of the farm,' Mum said softly. 'That was the agreement. We gave up a big share of the farm after your grandparents died and in return Cal helped us to build this house. This was back when things were good. Before the foot and mouth and losing the herd. He had to sink so much money back in just to keep the farm goin' and it wasn't enough.'

Kerry wouldn't have believed a word of it if she hadn't seen those envelopes with the red writing on them, and the way Uncle Cal had been acting. Then she remembered what she'd heard through the door. 'What were you arguing about?'

Her parents merely looked at each other.

Kerry swallowed the lump in her throat away. 'Do you need me to make more sculptures? Is that it? To save the farm?'

'Let's go downstairs and have a nice cup of—'

'No, Mum, tell me now. Is that what I need to do? Were you scared of asking me because you think I'll want to send them to Pygmalion instead of that Mr Wetherby?'

Another silent look exchanged between her parents sent her temper soaring. 'Just tell me! I can't stand it when you're like this!'

'The animal sculptures make a lot of money, but not nearly enough for the farm. But, Pygmalion said . . . he knows that there are people who . . .' her mother looked up at the ceiling, '. . . who want to know what it's like to be a statue and then be changed back. It's . . . a weirdo thing. And . . . he said they ask him about it all the time and when he heard there was someone who—'

Kerry clamped a hand over her mouth, appalled. 'You want

me to turn a *person* to stone?' she whispered through her fingers. 'An actual person?'

'No,' said Dad, at exactly the same moment as her mother said 'Yes.' They looked at each other, something expressed without words between them, before her father walked away to the window and her mother took another step closer. 'Yes, darlin', that's what we need. Pygmalion knows some very, very rich people. Strange people who . . . who get excited about this sort of thing. He said if you change them into stone, he'll change them back. And we'll get a lot of money for it. Enough to keep the bank off Uncle Cal's back for a while, at least until he gets back on his feet.'

Kerry looked from her mother's desperate eyes to the kitten that had clawed its way onto her father's shoulder to survey the room. He was still turned away from her. 'But . . . that's just horrible. Why would anyone want that?'

'There's some weird people in the world, love,' her mother said.

'But what if it killed them?'

'It won't. Look at the kitten. He's fine.'

'I'm going to put the kettle on,' Dad said and she stepped aside as he went out, his face as white as the fur on the kitten's feet.

'But . . . people are different.'

'Pygmalion said it will work and he must know better than any of us, mustn't he? But we have to be very, very careful and keep it a secret. No one must ever know. A'right?'

'But how could he know? He can't have done it before.'

'He was very certain,' Mum snapped. Then she held her hands up. 'Sorry, love, sorry. I'm just so tired and I'm so worried about Uncle Cal and the farm and us, too. Where will we live if we can't save it? How will we be able to keep you safe if we don't have anywhere to live?'

It was hard to think when her mum looked at her that way and when all of her worries sloshed about inside. It felt wrong, totally wrong, but her mother wouldn't lie to her about something like this. It was too big and important. And she had to do something to help Uncle Cal. 'Will it save the farm if I do it?'

Her mother's eyes were welling with tears. 'Yes, darlin', yes, it will. You'll save the farm . . . all of us. Maybe even Plum, if we—'

'And Pygmalion will change them back?'

She nodded.

'Promise?'

'I promise, darlin', I promise he will.'

Kerry looked down at her toes, at the pyjama bottoms that were too short now. It still felt wrong, but she couldn't think of a way to say no that wouldn't sound selfish. If those people wanted it, if Pygmalion thought it was safe, if it meant saving the farm, then what else could she say to all that? 'A'right. I'll do it.'

♣

Kerry looked down from her bedroom window onto the roof of the art studio annexe below. The light shining through its doors spilled onto the garden and every now and again there was a shadow as her father moved around.

Her mother was down there too and Kerry was glad. She didn't want to be with either of them. They should have told her it would be today. They should have given her a chance to be ready. Mum said it was to stop her from getting nervous, which was fair enough, but it still annoyed her. She hated surprises and this was the worst sort.

She tried to imagine what kind of a person would pay someone to turn them into a statue and then back again. It made no sense to her. It would be the same as going to a hospital and asking the doctors to stop her heart and then start it again. How could there be any fun in dying?

There was one question that she just couldn't shake off; if the person died when they were turned to stone and Pygmalion brought them back to life, would their soul somehow come back to their body? It wasn't the sort of thing the experiment with the kitten could answer. She hadn't known his personality beforehand and he'd been taken back to the pet shop so she didn't know if there were any long-term effects. Did kittens have souls? Did people?

Uncle Cal said she wasn't allowed on his computer but didn't say why. He was grumpy and withdrawn and had sent her away early every day, even when there was still work to be done. She wanted to tell him they had a plan, that it would be okay, but she'd promised to keep it all a secret.

Kerry rested her forehead against the cool glass of her window, unable to look away from the studio roof. All of these questions and yet there was already someone down there, ready to take the risk. How could they not be asking the same ones?

Her mother came in without knocking. 'Are you ready?'

'Is the . . . are they really down there, right now?'

'She is.'

'What's her name?'

Folding her arms, her mother gave her a hard look. 'I thought I told you not to think about it too much.'

'Does she know that we've never done this before?'

'She talked it through with Pygmalion and he was happy. Now, your dad has set her up in the pose she wanted and it's set dressed. Like those classical statues in the book we showed you.'

'They didn't have any clothes on!'

'She has a veil, and a very simple dress. And we've done her hair too. She's been practising her pose and your dad has been sketching her. To help her relax and get used to being still, a'right? Now, we think it would be best if you just go in super quiet like, and just touch her back. Don't say anything to her. Don't tell her you're about to do it.'

'That doesn't seem right, Mum. Shouldn't she have some warning?'

With a smile fixed in place, her mother sat on the bed and patted a space near her. 'We talked it through and all three of us agreed that it's the best way. It's all to do with the way we hold our breath and get all tense if we're waitin' for something to happen. Like . . . imagine I was going to take a picture of you when a bucket of water was being thrown over you. If you knew it was comin', you'd hold your breath, and your shoulders would lift up a bit and you'd probably clench your fists, right? Well, this is the same. She wants to look absolutely natural as a statue. Not knowing the exact moment when it's goin' to happen will keep her relaxed, see? That's all it is. Now, let's not keep her waitin', eh?'

Like every time she felt nervous about something, her mother sounded so reasonable it felt silly to keep questioning it. There was nothing she could say that would stop this from happening. And if she refused, Pygmalion would be angry and then there would be no hope of getting Plum back at all. Besides, they needed to save the farm.

No matter how much Kerry tried to tell herself that it was up to the woman downstairs if she wanted to do something this stupid, it didn't stop her legs trembling as they went down the stairs. The sound of something operatic floated down the hallway from the studio's open door and she had the urge to just turn around and run from the house and never come back. She even half turned, only to see her mother standing at the bottom of the stairs, watching her.

Kerry managed a little smile as her mother raised her index finger and pressed it to her lips, urging her to be silent, before shooing her onwards with a couple of flicks of her hand.

The music grew louder with each step. Her father came into view, seated at the far end of the studio with the doors behind him. He was wearing his reading glasses and sketching. As Kerry approached the door, she saw a sort of plinth that wasn't usually there, like the big rostra blocks they had in the school hall that were used to make a temporary stage for the school play. It was covered in one of Grandma's fancy old tablecloths and lying down upon it, back to the door, was the lady who wanted to be turned into a statue.

Kerry froze at the sight of her. Her back was smooth and uncovered, the sheer gown she was wearing was very low cut. She had flowers in her hair shaped in a sort of crown, holding on a chiffon veil that covered her hair and shoulders. It was like looking at the back of an artist's model, posing as a medieval bride resting after her wedding.

When she reached the doorway her father looked up and then straight back down at his sketchpad without even reacting. The music was loud enough to mask her footsteps and she was only wearing socks anyway. Keeping her eyes fixed on the model's back, Kerry moved into the room without seeing any change in the woman's position. Certain that the model had no idea she was even there, Kerry stretched out her hand and leaned closer.

Her fingers were trembling and her heart was pounding so hard she could feel it in her throat. It felt wrong! How many times had she been desperate to touch someone else, to brush her fingers against her mother's hand as they walked, to reach out for a hug from her father? She'd worked so hard on quashing that need for touch that to do it now felt unnatural.

She wants to do this, Kerry reminded herself. *She wants this, and I need to save the farm and Uncle Cal.*

Besides, her mother was watching. She could feel her eyes on her back. With her lungs burning from having held her breath too long, Kerry lurched forward, touching the woman's back. For the briefest moment it felt warm and soft. Then it was cold, hardening before her eyes. The veil, the dress, the flowers, all turned to granite, taking on a new beauty of its own.

Her father tossed the sketchpad aside and rushed across the

room to inspect the transformation. Kerry, fearing she was going to be sick, heading for the patio doors instead, needing the fresh evening air and to move away from her parents who were both heading for the new statue.

'Oh my God,' her father whispered.

'It's what she wanted,' Mother said sternly, as if reminding him.

Kerry looked back at them, both touching the stone flowers of the crown, whispering to each other. She couldn't see the woman's face, obscured as it was by the thin layer of granite formed by the veil, only the hint of her cheekbones and the ridge of her nose. There was something so hauntingly beautiful about it and the way the delicate sweep of the granite dress described the curve of her hip.

She realized that she wasn't looking at the statue as if it were a real person. Suddenly cold, Kerry pulled her sleeves down over her hands and wrapped her arms around herself, silently praying that Pygmalion was right.

Otherwise, she really was a monster.

◆

Cornwall, 2005

The second statue was a man dressed like a Roman centurion complete with helm and spear. The third was another woman, painfully thin, dressed in a thick medieval gown and another veil. The fourth was a willowy, long-limbed woman who was dressed in a simple long white gown with angel wings on the back that her mother had made from real feathers and her hair brushed over her face like a strange sheet.

There was a gap of several months between them, long enough for the nightmares to subside between each one and the arguments to settle in the house. The first statue earned them enough money to pay off Uncle Cal's most urgent debt repayment. By the time the payment came for the fourth, the farm was out of danger. Uncle Cal was his old self again and even cooked them a Sunday roast.

Kerry took down the old posters in her room to make way for a new corkboard. She pinned the postcards and notes she received from the statue people on it, just to remind herself every morning that she hadn't done anything bad. Just like the kitten, Pygmalion had changed them back and asked them to write to her, reassuring the family that they were safe and well and very happy with their experience. He then forwarded on the mail. The postcard from the first lady showed Trafalgar Square and one of the huge stone lions. It was her favourite. She hadn't received a note from the latest one, but she'd only been turned into stone a week before.

They never addressed the notes to her, but Kerry understood that both Pygmalion and her parents never mentioned her to the statue people by name. She'd learned from her mother that they didn't even know where the studio was, having been brought there blindfolded as part of the agreement made with Pygmalion. They'd thought everything through, to keep her safe.

She wished she could write back to them though. Neither Pygmalion nor her parents agreed to it. She had so many questions. Did it hurt when they were changed back? Did they remember anything? Were they the same afterwards?

'Mum,' she said over dinner one evening, 'if another person wants to be a statue, can we afford to buy a computer if we buy Plum's statue back? Uncle Cal says his is broken.'

'We don't need one,' she replied.

'But I want to use the internet.'

'Nothin' on there for you,' her father muttered.

'But I could look things up. To teach myself. They're always readin' out website addresses at the end of TV shows. I'm missin' out! I'm fifteen next week and it's not fair!'

'What's not fair? Having a lovely home and a family who cares for you?' Mum said, gathering up the plates. 'Having an uncle who's happy to teach you a livin' and all the skills you need to—'

'He said himself there's no future in farmin'. And anyway, all I need to do to earn a livin' is turn weirdos to stone. I bet Pygmalion has got a computer.'

'What's that got to do with anythin'?' her father snorted.

'I'm just sayin' that—'

The phone rang and her mother answered it. 'It's Wetherby,' she whispered with her hand over the mouthpiece after a brief conversation. 'He wants to come over next week. Is there anything happening on Wednesday?'

As her father went to get the diary, Kerry left the table, angered by the way they kept trying to cocoon her. It was as if they didn't want anything ever to change, expecting her to still be happy with the same things she had done when she was twelve. Wanting to drown out the sound of her parents' voices, she put on the TV. With glee she realized she would actually catch the news, which was normally over by the time she was allowed to leave the table.

She'd missed the national news, so there was no chance of seeing Pygmalion or Captain Flint, but she kept it on anyway, just in case something really local came up in the regional segment.

There was something boring about some politician visiting Truro and she was about to change the channel when a picture of the lady she'd turned to stone the week before came onto the screen. 'Detective Inspector Pat Trelawny of the Devon and Cornwall Police has announced that they are treating the disappearance of Melanie Barker as suspicious.'

'Mum! Dad!' Kerry called. 'It's the lady who came last week! She's on the telly!'

They both ran in as the report continued. 'Miss Barker, known to the authorities as a vulnerable person, was last seen sleeping rough in Penzance two weeks ago. If you have any information on her whereabouts, please call the information line displayed below.'

'Quick, write it down!' Kerry said, wishing for the millionth time that her parents would get one of those new clever TV boxes that meant you could pause live TV. When neither of them moved, she dashed over to the little table in the corner with one of the phone handsets on it, and the notepad that sat beside it. Just as she'd got a pencil ready, her mother turned the TV off.

'Mum! We need to phone the police and tell them she's in London, with Pygmalion.'

'It wasn't her.'

'It was! She looked exactly the same!'

'You never saw her face,' Dad said quietly. 'It was a different lady.'

'It wasn't her face, I noticed. It was her chin, it was really pointy, just like hers was.' She pointed at the blank TV screen. 'And her ear was the same. The left one had a tear where an earring must have been caught on something and split it. I remember wondering if the scar would come out in the granite and it didn't and . . .'

It was as if someone had filled the room with ice and she shivered as she took in the expressions on her parents' faces. Her father looked ashamed, unable to meet her eyes, while her mother looked panicked. 'We have to tell her,' he said.

'It's all just a misunderstandin',' her mother said. 'They just looked alike, s'all. No need for any drama.'

'I never liked it,' Father muttered, shaking his head. 'Never wanted to lie. Never wanted any of this!'

As his voice rose, Mother's panicked expression mutated into one of anger. 'Don't you go makin' out you're some bloody victim in all this!'

'Why wouldn't you want to call the police about that lady?' Kerry asked but her father wouldn't even look at her. 'Oh God,' Kerry whispered as an answer occurred to her, staggering back until she bumped into the wall behind her.

Her mother turned to face her, trying to smooth out her

features with a fake smile. 'Now, Kerenza, there's no need to get upset.'

'Those people haven't been changed back, have they? It was all a bloody lie!' She clamped her hand over her mouth as her stomach heaved.

'Kerry,' her father began, but she ignored him, sending her mind back to the beginning of it all, the day her Mum brought the newspaper article about Pygmalion to her.

'But . . . the kitten. I turned it to stone and you brought him back alive. It had to be Pygmalion. I remember it! I remember that kitten so well! His little white fur boots. How else could you have . . .?'

She looked at her father and took in the guilt on his face, the way he kept looking at her mother.

Kerry squeezed her eyes shut, unravelling the lies. 'There were two kittens, weren't there? That's why you pointed out his boots! To make me think it was the same one! You never met Pygmalion at all! It was all . . . God, how could I have been so stupid! All those notes . . . you must have sent them all.'

It was so obvious! They'd made her think that Pygmalion was able to change them back when they had just really been sold as statues. That was why they wouldn't let her on the internet! So she wouldn't find anything about them being sold!

All of the nonsense about weird people who wanted to be statues and then changed back . . . it seemed so ridiculous now. She'd murdered them! That's why she was never allowed to meet them beforehand and why she always had to creep up from behind. Otherwise the victims would have asked questions and the careful poses that her father had arranged would have been spoiled.

'We needed the money!' her father said. 'And they were bad people, Kerry, people who did nothing good in the world.'

'Did you even see Pygmalion?' Kerry shouted at her mother. 'Or was that all bullshit too?'

'Don't you use that language with me, young lady!'

'What? You tricked me into murdering people and you're upset about my bloody language? Answer the question!'

'This is exactly what I told you would happen!' her father shouted at her mother. 'We should never have lied to her in the first place! We should have just lost the farm and made a new start!'

Then the tears came, violent in their assault, choking her throat as the full scale of her parents' deception hit her. How they must have lured those people to their home, promising a payment in return for being an artist's model, only to be murdered, turned into 'art' to be sold grotesquely as her father's work.

Beneath it all was the deepest rage at herself and her stupidity. All those times she had doubted, all those times she'd felt it was wrong and she didn't have the sense – no, the courage! – to stand up to her mother and say no.

She wiped her tears from her eyes, knowing she had to get away from them. She couldn't live another moment with people who thought that deceiving their child into murdering innocent people was justified by needing the money.

Kerry bolted from the living room, the hallway seeming to stretch as she threw herself towards the front door. It was dark outside but she knew the way across to Uncle Cal's so well she'd be able to find her way. There was enough time to form a route in her mind before a blinding pain at the back of her head snatched it all away and sent her tumbling into darkness.

♠

It was dark when she woke up and she was lying on something hard with strange edges that were digging into her ribs. A terrible dull ache throbbed through her skull and when she put her fingertips to her hair there, she could feel a tender lump where there hadn't been one before.

Her nose was blocked with mucus from the crying and her throat was scratchy and raw. She sat up and banged her head on a shelf, making something fall into her lap; an old plastic tennis bat from the set she'd played with as a small kid. She was in the cupboard under the stairs!

Kerry thought about the spiders she knew were in there. There was a light, somewhere, but then she remembered that the bulb had blown the week before. Hesitantly feeling her way, she made it to the door and pushed against it, only to find it wouldn't open. There wasn't a lock on it, not that she could recall anyway.

The realization that one of her parents had hit her, dragged her in there and barricaded the door dawned on her slowly, as if her thoughts were sticks being dragged through thick mud. She couldn't quite believe it, even though there was no other explanation. How could they be normal one moment and then hurting her the next?

Had they ever really loved her?

They were scared of her and had been ever since Plum died. And she understood that. She was afraid herself, constantly terrified she would accidentally touch something and turn it to granite. And they'd never been able to soothe that fear with hugs or even just a squeeze of the hand. That was the hardest thing. She craved touch more than anything, and now she wondered if the lack of it had led to her parents forgetting they had once loved her. Because they couldn't love her now, not really. This wasn't something you could do to someone you loved.

At first all she could do was cry and shake violently. It wasn't very heroic, not like in the countless TV shows she'd watched in which the hero immediately started fighting as soon as they realized they'd been captured. On the most basic level she couldn't equate her parents to the villains, despite what they'd done.

What they'd made her do.

She had to fight the urge to be sick with long, deep breaths and her arms wrapped tightly around herself. She twitched at a tickling sensation on her leg, then realized that if a spider did start crawling on her, it would soon be turned to stone. She didn't know whether to laugh or cry at that.

Kerry froze at the sound of a noise outside the door. A creak of the floorboard perhaps, or a chair?

'Kerenza?' It was her father's voice, softly spoken through the tiny gap between the door and the frame. 'Are you awake?'

At first she didn't answer. There was nothing but rage and tears. Words seemed impossible.

'I'm so sorry, my darlin',' he said, his voice cracking. 'I can hear you movin' and you must be scared and hurtin' and I should've . . . I should've stopped all of this happenin'. It's my fault. I didn't stand up to your mother when she suggested it. I was weak. I wanted to help Cal. And I wanted the farm to stay in the family, where it belongs. It was wrong, what we did.'

'You made me kill people!' she sobbed through the door. 'I never would've done it if . . . if I wasn't so stupid!'

'Lyin' to you were wrong, Kerry, it were wrong and I regret that, more than I can describe. But . . . those people being turned to stone, that's not something I regret.'

'What?' She dragged her sleeve across her nose, shocked out of her tears.

'I need to tell you about them, 'cos I think when you know what they were like, you'll feel better. I'm not sayin' the way we did this is right, not for a moment, but it's not what you think. They weren't innocent, good people, brought here and killed. They were awful, awful people, who did nothin' but spread misery to everyone around them. That man I dressed as a Roman soldier? He beat his wife and kids. Put her in hospital and broke his son's arm. The police told him to stay away but he kept harassin' her. Terrorized them, he did. And that skinny woman we made into a medieval princess? She stole money from a charity. The first one, she got drunk and ran over a child but her daddy was so rich, he got a lawyer and she got off scot-free. And the one we made into an angel? She killed her baby. Drowned it in Penzance harbour when she was high on drugs.'

'How do you know those things about them? Did Mum tell you? She could've made it all up to make you feel better.'

'It was in the paper, love. On the internet. She read about them getting away with it. That man got off scot-free too. The woman takin' from the charity got ten hours' community service and she had her hand in the till at the shop she worked at an' all. That woman who killed her baby was never even sent to court. They put her in an 'ospital for a while and she ran away and was livin' rough on the street, stealin', makin' a nuisance of herself. None of those people did anythin' good in the world, Kerry. So no, I don't regret what happened to them, not one bit. Uncle Cal never harmed a soul in his life, works hard. A gentle man, you know that. And he was goin' to lose everythin' and it would've killed him, Kerry. He never would've got over it. So the way I see it is that you made the world a better place. That mum and her kids are never goin' to be scared of that bastard comin' and beatin' them again. That rich cow is never goin' to kill another child when she gets drunk. Do you see? You made them into somethin' beautiful. You turned monsters into art!'

Kerry blew her nose into her jumper as she struggled to make it all fit in her head. 'If it was such a good thing, why didn't you tell me? Why did you trick me like that?'

'That there is what I regret. Your mum and I didn't think you was mature enough to see the good in it. We shouldn't have tricked you, pickle, we should've told you the truth. And the kitten . . . that was low. I argued with your mother for days over that. But I can't blame it all on her. We both done it.'

'So I was right? About Pygmalion?'

A long sigh came through the gap. 'You were. She never saw him. He don't know about you or any of this. I don't know how to say sorry about somethin' this bad. I . . . I can see it from your point of view and I can understand how you feel, I really can. All I can say is don't feel bad about those people. They were poisonous, makin' everyone's lives around them worse.'

'Why did you hit me?'

'Your mother panicked and threw that bookend at you, to make you stop. She didn't mean to knock you out, she just wanted to stop you from runnin' out in the dark in such a state. It's not like we can just put ourselves in front of you, is it, eh?'

'You locked me in here too!'

'Because we didn't know what you'd be like when you woke up, darlin'!'

'You're scared of me, aren't you?'

A long pause. 'Yes, my 'andsome, we are. And I hate to say that, but no more lies now. You can kill us so easily. And you were angry and upset – rightfully so! We wanted to have the chance to explain everythin' safely. To talk it through with you, without havin' to worry. Can you see that?'

It made sense. It always made sense, though, didn't it? They'd been lying to her so long she didn't know what to believe any more.

'We were scared you'd leave and the world out there . . . It's not for you, my darlin'. It's full of bad people and if anyone found out what you can do . . . I dread to think what would happen. We were scared that if you ran away, you might kill someone by accident.'

'Were you scared I'd tell the police what we've done?'

'Yes.'

She'd been expecting him to deny it. 'Because they wouldn't care if they were bad people or not, would they? We'd just be murderers.'

'That's right, darlin', that's right. That's why your mum panicked like that. We were scared for you and for us.' After another pause, he added, 'We still are.'

Kerry tried to imagine going to the police. How they might want to touch her, just to make her get into the car like she'd seen on TV shows. They always touched the top of the criminal's head to stop them banging it on the frame of the door. If she went to a police station instead, what if they wanted to take her fingerprints? Would they believe her without seeing the proof of her curse with their own eyes?

Even if she did make it through that without killing someone, it would end up with all three of them in prison. She'd be isolated. In a cell. Forever. Her throat started to close up again. 'I won't go to the police,' she croaked. 'I don't want any of us to go to prison.'

'Good. I want to open this door, Kerry. Can you come out slowly if I do that?'

'Yes.'

The tears had stopped, but not the shaking. There was too much to process, all at once, and she didn't know what to do about any of it, but she was certain she didn't want to stay in the cupboard a moment longer.

'Move back from the door then.'

It sounded as if a chair was moved away from the other side of it and then the door opened, casting a crack of horribly bright light across her and making her squint. Once he was sure she wasn't about to jump out on him, her father opened it wide and stood back.

Kerry stooped to get under the short door and was grateful to stand upright again. Her mother was standing at the far end of the hallway, face red and puffy with crying. Her father was still rather pale, his eyes red-rimmed.

'I'm sorry,' Mum whispered, starting to cry again. 'I didn't mean to hit your head, just your back, to make you stop. Are you . . . are you bleeding?'

Kerry looked at her fingertips and brushed the back of her head again to be sure. 'No. There's a lump though.'

Her mother started to sob into her hands, saying she was sorry over and over again. Kerry stood there, unable to go and comfort her and not even sure if she wanted to anyway.

'It's done now,' she said, hoping it would make her stop. 'I . . . I just want to go to bed.' She wanted to get away from them, wrap herself up tight in her duvet and try to work it all out. Not stand there, hurting, as her parents stared at her with frightened, guilty eyes.

'We'll talk it all through in the mornin',' Dad said, putting an arm around her mother. 'Clear the air. When we've all had a rest.'

'I don't need to talk about it,' Kerry said. 'I just want you both to promise me there won't be any more. No more people. No more animals. I won't turn anything into stone ever again. Not for you. Not for Uncle Cal. It's not right. Whatever way you want to think it is, it's not. Not for me.'

'Of course,' Dad said but her mother looked at him with a frown and in that instant, Kerry knew her mother would ask her again. Not for a few weeks, but she would, and she would make it seem like saying no was unreasonable.

'I'm goin' to bed.'

The last thing she had on her mind was to rest when she shut the bedroom door. She sat on the bed for a few moments, wiping her face and blowing her nose, wincing at the way it made her head throb even more.

Wanting some fresh air, she went to her window, only to find it was locked. The tiny little key that usually stayed in the security lock was gone.

Everything seemed to collapse into that one fact, that one missing key. They had locked her in. She looked down onto the roof of the studio and saw that the skylight was closed, no doubt locked, and the doors were shut too. It was night-time, she reminded herself, of course they were locked.

Then why did she feel as if she were in a prison?

A creak on the stairs sent her to the door of her bedroom and she pressed her ear to the gap between the door edge and the frame. There was no lock on her door, thankfully. She listened to her parents using the bathroom and when the footsteps approached her door she leapt into bed and drew the duvet right up to her ears. The door opened behind her for a few seconds and then closed again.

Her heart pounded in rhythm with the thumping in her skull. After a few minutes she could hear the creak of her parents' bed as they climbed into it and then the low murmur of a conversation.

Taking care to avoid all the squeaky boards, she opened her bedroom door silently and went into the hallway to listen in on her parents.

'I double-checked them all,' her father was saying. 'And I brought the keys up here.'

'We need to put a lock on the bedroom door.'

'I'm not lockin' her into her own room!'

'No, stupid, I mean for our room. I'll sleep better.'

They were afraid of her.

'Wetherby said it would be half a million for the next one. If we wait another six months, it'll go up to a million.'

'That makes no sense,' her father whispered back.

'It's a rarity thing,' her mother replied. 'The buyer in Dubai wants a male figure, something classical. They're minted over there. I reckon we could get more if we offered Wetherby a better cut. Just an extra five per cent. Then it's in his interest to make them pay even more, isn't it?'

Kerry pressed her lips tight together as her eyes welled with tears. She waited for her father to say something, to push back at last. 'I dunno, Mel. I dunno if Kerry will do another one. I don't know if it's right. And we can't tell her we'll be gettin' Plum back either, now she knows the truth.'

It wasn't an argument against. He just doubted her pliability.

'We need to tell Cal she knows. Before she does. We need to keep him onside.'

'How the bloody hell are we supposed to keep him onside after this?'

'He'll understand. He knows how dangerous she is.'

Kerry went back to her room and closed the door with great care, tears running down her cheeks.

Her uncle had known what they were doing. All this time, he'd never said anything to her, never once asked if she was happy with what her parents were asking her to do. He'd stopped pressing for news on allergy doctors before the first victim was turned to stone and now she knew why. Of course they'd had to tell him. He had access to the internet, he would have seen the news about her father's amazing new life-sized human sculptures. He was just as bad as them. Nothing was going to change. They were never going to let her go.

She stood, still as stone, feeling something shift within her. None of them loved her. She was just a freak to them, something terrifying to manipulate to make them money. Something to control.

No more.

♥

All she'd thought about for years was freedom but it had been a nebulous daydream, little more than images of running across the fields to the boundary of the farm and not turning back to go home again. Of watching the TV whenever she wanted to. Of having her own computer and using the internet.

Such childish visions of freedom. Her jailers had been so good at their job she hadn't even noticed the real bars they'd put around her, made of the promise of love, rather than of steel. They'd convinced her that staying away from the rest of the world was all about protecting her when it was really all about protecting their income.

She couldn't stop thinking about the moment her parents must have told Uncle Cal what she was, and more than that, about the sculptures and how they were made. He must have sat down with them, listened to the plan to save the farm and at some point nodded and agreed to it. He might not have liked it, but she couldn't care less about any moral doubts he might have had. The day he had decided that getting the money for the farm was more important than her was the day he stopped being her uncle and became another jailer.

Kerry knew that if she stayed in this house, this life, she would never be free. She could refuse but when they were desperate for more money what would they do to her? Hit her again? Deprive her of food? Water? She was dependent upon them for everything.

Getting away from them felt like an act of survival, even though the thought of going out into the world terrified her. They'd kept her sheltered and ignorant and she would have to learn the differences between the real world and what she'd seen of it on TV very quickly. She'd have to avoid people, but somehow buy food, find somewhere to live and a way to earn money that wasn't dependent on the death of an innocent creature or a human victim.

But even if she could achieve all of that, she knew that as long as her parents were alive, they would never stop looking for her. If she got out, their secret could too. It wasn't just about preserving their income, it was a matter of escaping justice too. But if she told the police what they'd done, she would be in just as much trouble, if not more. She'd been the one that actually killed those people, after all. They'd just be . . . what was the word? 'Accessories to murder'. That was it. And on the police shows she was allowed to watch, it was always the murderers that were punished the most.

Kerry went to the corkboard and took down the pinned notes, tearing each one into little pieces as she considered her options. She couldn't go to the police. She couldn't find somewhere to live and get a job without endangering the lives of others. She needed help and the only person she could think of approaching was Captain Flint, the one man she suspected would not only understand what she could do, but also be immune to her curse. He was already stone, after all. She had no idea how to find him, but if she could get onto the internet, perhaps she could find a way to contact him and ask for help.

Even if she did find him though, she was only fifteen. Her parents would have the right to make her come home. They were her legal guardians and she'd never be able to explain why they shouldn't be without incriminating herself.

The idea of freedom began to take on a new form. As long as her family lived, this would never be over. Her father had tried to convince her that the murders were some form of justice. That those people would have got away with their crimes unpunished if it wasn't for her. Just as they would, if she did nothing.

She would bring justice to her family and win her freedom in the process.

Kerry waited for over an hour until she could hear her father's snore. There was a chance her mother was still awake, so she packed her rucksack with clothes and used a trip to the bathroom to test whether her mother was asleep. She knew, given the events of the evening, that if her mother was awake, she would move at the sound of the bathroom door and make their bed creak. But there was no such noise as she returned to her room. She stuffed her toothbrush into the rucksack and went back into the hallway.

Kerry was surprised when she was able to open her parents' door. She thought they would have barricaded themselves in, and a part of her – the weak, childish part – was disappointed they hadn't. She crept inside the room that had always held a magical quality for her when she was young, before her card turned. She pushed aside memories of Sunday mornings when she would wriggle into the bed between them for lazy cuddles, and crept towards the foot of the bed.

Her mother was deeply asleep, mouth wide open and drooling onto her pillow, as her father's snore rumbled away beside her. Neither of them stirred during her approach.

Her mother's left foot poked from the duvet, her father's right foot next to it. Both were within her reach, but she couldn't move, assaulted by memories of happier times. But in each of those memories she was young. Normal. Still their little blessed child, born on St Piran's day and brought home the same day that the daffodils bloomed. A little girl who sang in the school choir, who loved her dog, and made friends easily.

That girl was gone. They hadn't loved her the same way since the day she had killed Plum and she had tried so hard to ignore how they had changed. But now, when she thought of recent times, it was easy to recall the way they stiffened whenever she walked into the room, the way they seemed relieved when she said she was going over to Uncle Cal's and how they tensed up when she returned. She'd stopped being their little girl years ago. And they had stopped being her parents.

Reaching out, she touched both of the exposed feet, holding her breath as the chill of stone replaced the warmth of their skin. When she released the stale air inside her, they were a study in repose, two sleepers beneath granite sheets far too realistic to have ever been shaped by a stonemason's tools.

The bed creaked loudly and then something in the base snapped and they crashed to the floor, making her yelp and leap back. As the dust settled, she became aware of a pain in her chest, as if something was trapped, but she swallowed the sob down. She wouldn't be sad for these monsters made into art. She wouldn't let herself be weakened by grief. It was easier to imagine her heart was stone, incapable of misplaced love and loyalty.

Kerry held up her hands, her thumbs at right angles from

her palms, placing the statues lying on the floor in an imaginary picture frame.

'"*Freedom*",' she whispered. '"A study in granite, by Kerenza
Tremaine".'

♣

The money was in the tin in Uncle Cal's desk, as it had always
been. She counted it out before folding it and tucking it into
the wallet she'd stolen from her father's studio. There was
almost a thousand pounds in cash and the Rover's diesel tank
was full. It would get her out of Cornwall.

She went back to her uncle's bedroom to look at him again,
just to be certain. Like her parents' bed, the rickety old bedframe
had broken, unable to support the weight of his granite body
and the stone sheets covering him. She didn't cry at the sight
of him either. She'd promised herself she would never cry ever
again. Her imagined granite heart was unfeeling, incapable of
being fooled a second time.

Her bag was waiting where she'd left it on her uncle's kitchen
table. The Rover was loaded with food and all the supplies she
could think of. No teddy bears. No dolls. All childish things
were behind her now.

A newspaper lay on the table, the word 'Flint' visible just
above the fold. He was going to be at a place called Ascot,
guarding Queen Margaret, the article said, following threats
to her life.

Ascot. Where the horses raced, she'd heard of it. There was
a map in the Rover and she knew how to drive well enough
to get there. She would find Flint and ask him for help.

She looked up Ascot on the computer, found a nearby hotel
and phoned them, booking a single room for the next two
nights under a false name.

Thinking ahead, she grabbed the notepad and wrote a note,
knowing that the security people around the Queen would

never let her near, but they might pass a note on if she was persuasive enough.

> *Dear Captain Flint,*
> *I am an ace. I need your help. I can turn people to stone and I have nowhere to go. I am staying at the Red Lion Hotel in Ascot for the next two nights under the name of Lisa Buckingham.*
> *My real name is*

She stopped, tapping her teeth with the pen. Not Medusa. She had to choose a name for herself before someone else did.

> *Stonemaiden.*

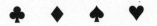

The
Visitor

by Mark Lawrence

Cambridge, 2017

'**I**'D RATHER BE DEAD than like that.'

The new girl was very pretty, Angela thought. She had long blonde hair and painted nails. Sometimes Betty would do Angela's nails and let her choose the colour. On those days she felt happy whatever happened, even if nobody noticed and nobody but Betty commented.

'If I ever get like that, shoot me.' The new girl was called Jenny and she chewed gum as she spoke. She didn't seem very happy to be at the home. She didn't like her uniform or the smell of the place or touching the residents. Angela knew all this because Jenny spoke as if she weren't there, complaining about one thing then the next. Angela wondered if maybe Jenny wanted to be in the movies instead. She looked as if she might have come from one with her highlights and make-up. She might have stepped into Carstons from another world where everything was better and more alive.

When Jenny left the room to fetch a feeding tube for Angela, Sarah Regan, who stayed to change Angela's pad, told her that the new girl was all silicone and hair extensions and only here because the job centre had sanctioned her benefits. Angela didn't really know what any of that meant but she was very interested in Jenny and so she made an effort to remember. Silicone, extensions, sanctioned. It amazed her to think that at nineteen the new girl was just two years older than she was. She looked like a princess and Angela wanted to know everything about her. Maybe Jenny would even be her friend like Betty was. Betty was very nice but also very old. Sarah Regan said Betty was a bag of bones and should have retired ten years ago. Angela loved Betty, more than her own mother if she was honest, which she tried to be, but she would very much like to have a friend of her own age.

'There, all done,' said Sarah. 'All changed.'

Angela would have said thank you but talking, like moving her limbs or being able to eat, was a skill that had always escaped her. Her mother said that she had been broken before she was born and that it was all part of God's plan but that none of us were clever enough to understand the plan and so often it looked like cruelty even though it was kindness. She would sit quietly after she said things like that and stare at her hands and her hands would be in fists with white knuckles. Angela preferred chatty people. When your side of the conversation is limited to smiles, eye pointing, and opening your mouth for 'yes' it's much better if the other person can talk the hind legs off a donkey, like Betty could.

'Nice dry pad,' Sarah said. Angela liked that she called them pads. Sarah wasn't always kind but she talked to Angela as if she understood, and that was worth more than kindness alone. She was a solid woman in her forties with a red slab of a face, big flabby arms and a sharp tongue, but she said that she called a spade a spade, and since she called a pad a pad Angela was prepared to believe her about spades. Some of the other staff called pads 'nappies' however old you were, as if you were a baby still, and Angela didn't like that.

Jenny returned with the feeding tube and Sarah attached it to the plastic button in Angela's belly.

'Urgh, that's so weird.' Jenny made the disgusted face she had made so often since arriving earlier in the week.

'The milk goes straight into her stomach,' Sarah said. 'It's all she has, special formula milk and water.' She gave Angela an unsmiling look. 'When you was little we used to feed you mush. Awful chore it was. Doctors told us to stop 'cos of the choking. Half of it was ending up in your lungs, Angie.'

Angela remembered the taste. They only ever gave her three things: apple puree, creamed potato, and vanilla yoghurt. She had loved them all. She wanted to have them again but nobody had ever asked her opinion on the matter and it had been two years since she last had a spoonful – apple, it was. Five years since she tasted something, ten years since her mother had brought her to the care home and said she might be staying a while.

'We always let Angie lie for a while before hoisting her back into her wheelchair,' Sarah explained. 'If you're in too much of a hurry you'll see that milk again and this time you'll be having to wipe it out of her hair, then hoisting her back onto the bed, changing her clothes, cleaning up her chair, then feeding her all over again. Better to be patient. It saves time in the long run.'

Jenny nodded, looking bored. 'At least she doesn't talk. The retards with a mouth on them just go on and on . . .'

'We call them special needs,' Sarah said. 'Management don't like to hear words like that. It's like they cross a new word off the list each year. Can't call 'em retarded. Can't call them spastics. They don't even like it if you say handicapped these days. It's disabled, thank you very much.' She shook her head as if minding her mouth was the worst of it. 'Let's have her up then.'

They rolled Angela back and forth to get her sling in place then used the mechanical hoist to lower her into her wheelchair. Sarah could lift Angela easily enough. She said she'd seen more meat on a butcher's apron. But there were rules.

And anyway, since the operation to straighten Angela's spine with a set of titanium rods and thirty-two screws to fix them in place, it hurt when someone picked her up wrong, so she preferred the hoist.

'We'll wheel her into the lounge. You can normally park her in front of the TV for a few hours before she starts whining. You like the telly, don't you, Angie?'

Sarah finished strapping Angela into the chair, a lap belt, harness, and headband all serving to keep her in place. She didn't look for an answer to her question. The truth was that Angela preferred conversation and having books read to her. But the television was definitely better than being left facing the wall. That was what Rose and Jimmy did with her if they were angry about something. It didn't have to be something Angela had done, though it was often a punishment for soiling herself on their shift. Jimmy called her Veggie instead of Angie. Rose laughed every time.

Sarah wheeled Angela into the common room with Jenny in tow, looking sullen.

'It smells in here. Something rotten.' Jenny wrinkled her nose.

Angela smiled around at the other residents whether they greeted her or not. Some could, some couldn't, some chose not to. The news was on so that meant Charlie Smithson had the control. Charlie always wanted the news though it seemed to Angela that he only wanted it on to establish his credentials as a news watcher, since he never paid it any attention. He sat in the armchair at the end of the room, gazing out of the big window across the rooftops of the old people's home next door. He wasn't old enough to join them over there, but he was old. A fat little man with a rim of grey hair and a shiny bald pate that he would slap at from time to time as if flies were constantly settling on it.

They would all watch the news now until Charlie went to sleep. If you tried to take the control from him he would bite, and if that didn't work he'd wail so loudly that you could never hear the new programme.

About two-thirds of the twenty residents at Carstons had some level of mental impairment to keep their physical disability company. Most of the staff acted as if all the residents were mentally incapable. They were like that even with Jordi, who could answer nearly every question on *Who Wants To Be A Millionaire?* and could explain how a television actually worked. They treated him like an idiot because his arms were small and twisted. Rose and Jimmy called him J-Rex because the dinosaur had useless little arms too. Sarah said he only knew the answers because they were repeats on UK Gold. But Angela thought that even if that were true then Jordi was very clever to remember them all.

The two cleverest residents were indisputably Renée and Shirley, both XTA since long before Angela was even born. The two old ladies had turned their cards when they were both girls of Angela's age. Xenovirus Takis-A had disfigured and disabled both of them. Renée claimed that they had been great beauties before the virus had struck them down. Shirley maintained that Renée had always looked rather horsey and that the virus had simply changed people's opinions about which end she most resembled. In America, Renée said, they would be called jokers and shunned, forced to live in ghetto communities. Shirley said that if she had to catch XTA then England was the best place to do it, and that if anyone called her a joker she would stick them with the bony spikes that had replaced her hands and which she referred to as her needles. Angela, who spent a lot of time listening and a lot of time thinking, though more through circumstance than inclination, thought that Carstons Residential Home was probably quite similar to a ghetto in many ways, and given that having any visitor was a great rarity they were being pretty well shunned here too. The main difference was that here they were being shunned alongside the victims of far less exotic viruses and injuries.

Charlie proved more resistant to sleep than usual, and in the third cycle of the news Naga Munchetty cut from the piece claiming that it was now *ten* portions of fruit or veg daily needed for health benefits to breaking news. The big screen flashed footage of Captain Flint involved in a dramatic rescue from a burning building. This of course set Shirley and Renée going. Any time an ace was mentioned, be it on the TV, radio, in a newspaper or just an offhand remark, the pair would launch into a who's who of yesteryear's aces, when superheroes were real superheroes, when taller buildings were leapt in single bounds, bullets pinged off with never a wince shown, and time was still found to save kittens from trees. The current breed, the ladies maintained, were all lazy good-for-nothings addicted to the internet, cocaine, and celebrity in equal measure. None of them were worth the dead and twisted that XTA left in its wake. All apart from that nice Redcoat of course. They both adored him.

Angela liked the two old women of course but she always felt they perhaps made too much of the hardships they endured. They had after all reached her age as perfectly normal girls, able to talk and eat and touch and walk and run, able to care for themselves, pursue their own interests, kiss boys and dance. And they could still do most of those things. Angela would swap lives with either one of them in a heartbeat, even now, even exchanging her seventeen for their seventies. She would swap a year of hers for a day of theirs.

Her aches roared rather than whispered today. She felt hot then cold. Ever since Sarah had come to hoist Angela out of bed that morning she'd been sweating then shivering. She didn't remember feeling so strange before or so bad.

♣

The evening shift came in as Charlie fell asleep and Mr Jenkins filched the control to change channel to *Strictly Come Dancing*, which was very popular at Carstons.

Rose and Jimmy came through the common room together. She was a hefty woman in her thirties with mean eyes and bitten lips, he a touch shorter, a touch younger, and a lot skinnier. Angela always thought Jimmy's face looked to be on the point of a smile that would light him up, but whenever she smiled at him she got a scowl in return, or that grin that meant one of Jimmy's cruel tricks was coming.

The residents kept their eyes down and their conversation to mutters as the pair passed by. Jordi called them Rosie and Jim rather than Rose and Jimmy, after a children's programme that was on TV when he was little. But he always waited until they'd left before he said it.

'Rosie and Jim!' Jordi operated on the principle that if something was funny once then it was funny a hundred times. He started to hum the theme tune.

'Now, now, Jordi!' Betty came through, glasses in hand as she wiped the rain from them. 'You'll catch more flies with honey.'

'I don't want any flies.' Jordi put his nose in the air.

'Angela, you're due a feed and medicines, aren't you, my lovely?'

Angela opened her mouth in a yes though she wasn't hungry. Betty never forgot her feeds. Betty had a kind word for everyone and she knew so many wise sayings. More flies with honey. Angela wasn't sure what it meant but she filed it into her memory. It sounded important. She didn't like flies. In the summer they would crawl on her face and she couldn't stop them. Once Jimmy had smeared jam on her cheeks and left her in her room by the open window. She had dozens of flies on her when Betty came looking for her.

'Oh dear! Oh dear!' she had said. 'Let Betty sort you out. Who's done this?'

But Angela knew that Betty knew who had done it. Over the years she had come to understand that Betty was afraid of Jimmy. He knew where she lived and had unpleasant friends on the estate. His younger brothers ran with a gang and Betty thought that Jimmy stole residents' medicines and sold them on the street through his tearaway siblings. Betty had once said that management had so much trouble getting staff that if she complained about the likes of Jimmy and Rose then the 'powers that be' would just insist that she retire. 'And then who would be here to keep all of you safe?'

Angela didn't like the mean things that Rose and some of the other staff did to her, but compared to the pain she suffered every hour of every day, and the difficulties confronting her at each turn, they were relatively minor inconveniences. She had rather suffer a thousand of Jimmy's casual cruelties than lose Betty. Betty loved her and she loved Betty.

Betty said that Jimmy was a bad seed, but more than that he was bored and frustrated. Rose too, she said, had never seen her lot in life as looking after disabled residents in a care home. Betty told Angela that Mrs Mason, the house manager, said most of the staff were at Carstons because they had run out of choices. They felt themselves stuck in a hard, dirty job for minimum wage because it was all that was on offer.

'When you put someone where they don't want to be they kick against it, Angela. And often as not it's the ones that can't defend themselves that get kicked.' Betty had shaken her head and tutted. 'It's not about the salary, dear.' She'd put her withered hand on Angela's permanently clenched fist. 'Though God knows a few more pounds would be very nice. It's a calling. You have to have love in your heart. You have to see the person before you.'

These were words Betty echoed now as she watched Angela make an effort to track Jenny across the room. 'Pretty girl, isn't she? It's paint, Angela, paint and skin. You have to *see* the person before you. Not just the wrapper they arrive in. I was a pretty one too, once. Not that anyone would believe it now.' A wry smile. She kept her voice low, just for the two of them.

Angela didn't answer. She felt strange, her heart pounding,

her flesh tingling as if a million flies were crawling over her. She tried to concentrate on Betty's words.

'Being too pretty twists how the world sees you and how you see the world. She's probably a decent girl in the middle of it all, but she's been spoiled. Don't you worry none about her.' Betty sniffed. 'Don't you go mistaking the crust for the pie. Take Renée, she's got a heart of gold if you get past that clever mouth of hers. And let's be honest, that XTA didn't do her any favours in the looks department. But she's worth ten of our new princess.'

Angela listened. Her hearing was the only part of her that had ever really worked well. All the while she struggled to keep her wandering eyes on Jenny, fighting to turn her head to follow the girl. She'd never seen anyone like her, not face to face. She wanted to be beautiful too. It didn't matter that everything Betty said was true.

'Angela! You're burning up!' Betty's hand was on Angela's forehead and it felt like a piece of ice. 'Are you okay, darling?'

Angela didn't know if she was okay. She knew that she did feel hot. She knew that Jenny had stopped at the archway to the kitchen corridor and was staring at her now, her eyes wide. She knew that the girl was everything she had ever wanted to be.

'Angela! You're shaking!' Beside her Betty was on her feet. 'Jordi! Get Mrs Mason! Now! Hurry. Tell her Angela's not well. Tell Sarah too—'

Angela didn't understand why she was falling. She had fallen twice before. Jimmy had dropped her on the bed once. But she should be in her chair. It was all very strange.

'Oh my G . . . Call an ambulance! NOW!' Betty sounded scared. Angela didn't want Betty to be scared. She didn't want to be on the ground either. Hitting the floor hadn't hurt at all. There were pieces of her wheelchair scattered all around her.

'She's having a fit.' Shirley's voice.

'A seizure.' Renée's voice. Both of them sounded frightened

too. Angela didn't know why. She had fits most weeks. They just gave her the meds and made sure she didn't choke.

Jenny stood where she was, not going for the phone, not coming to help, just frozen. She filled Angela's vision and for a moment Angela saw with a clarity that her damaged brain had never once allowed her in all her seventeen years. She saw Jenny's face with preternatural clarity. Every brush stroke of the foundation, every blemish beneath, every pore, she felt the beat of the girl's heart, the rush of her blood, the pulse of her fear.

'. . . turning blue . . .'

'. . . get her midazolam . . .'

'. . . off the floor!'

Betty's voice seemed to be coming from far away. 'You'll be all right, darling, you'll be all right. You gotta breathe, is all. Just take a breath. Let the air in, darling.'

Angela could see Betty crouched over her, on all fours with her face just above hers. Only she saw it all wrong, as if she were on the other side of the room, watching. She saw herself lying, twitching and twisted, with parts of her wheelchair still strapped to her and others scattered around her. The wheels lay on their side close by.

One of Angela's arms twitched and she saw Betty thrown aside.

'No!' The shout sounded in her chest. She saw herself lying there. Across the room. It made no sense and she wanted Betty, but the old lady looked hurt and Angela had done it. A blackness crowded her vision and for the second time in short order she was falling.

◆

What followed was darkness and confusion. There was pain too. Lots of that.

'Her organs are failing.'

That sentence reached in at some point and she chased it around in the darkness as it made tight little circles inside her skull.

'I've called her mother.' Betty said that and she sounded so sad that it made Angela want to cry.

'Coma.'

'It's not right. She deserved so much more than this.'

'Coma.'

'She'll be in a better place.'

'Coma.'

'We'll take her home.'

The darkness thickened and Angela understood that this was death and she wasn't scared.

And then she opened her eyes and daylight was streaming over her. She was in a bed. She struggled to focus. It was the hospice wing at Carstons. The home kept three medical beds for residents who were very ill. It wasn't unusual for residents to come back from hospital to spend their last few days here when there was nothing more to be done for them.

Angela drew in a deep breath. She didn't feel as though she was dying. She didn't feel any better or worse than normal. Betty! She remembered Betty being knocked aside and she struggled to turn. Somehow knowing that she couldn't turn over never stopped Angela trying. Her mother said that it was probably memory. When Angela had been very small she had been able to roll from side to side. Unlike most children whose skills increase as they grow, Angela's had only faded. It had taken just ten minutes without oxygen during her birth for the motor cortex of her brain to die. She had been expelled into the coldness of the world grey and limp and unable to howl about the indignity of it all. Any chance to speak or run or touch had been stolen from her by indifferent chance just before she was born. It had been ten years since she could even roll from her side to her back. That should be long enough to stop trying. But Angela tried again. And failed again.

She wanted to see someone, to know what had happened, so she began to cry out. She had no words but she could be loud when she wanted to. In her head she was calling for Betty. The noise she made was all vowels but it didn't take long for someone to come and the person who came was Betty.

'Angela! You're awake!' Betty came into her line of sight with a broad smile showing the even whiteness of her dentures. 'You're awake! And so loud!' She was having to shout to make herself audible over Angela's cries.

Angela stopped shouting. Her voice sounded very loud even to her.

'Let me get a chair.' Betty turned away to find one. 'I'm so pleased! So pleased. How do you feel?'

Angela felt hungry. She smiled. She had worried that Betty was injured. She wondered how long she had been asleep, and what a coma was, and if her organs had failed. She opened her mouth but of course her questions stayed on her tongue where they had always stayed.

'Let me have a look at you!' Betty scraped her chair closer. 'The doctors didn't know what you had, dear. A virus they thought. But with someone so complicated . . . Well. They sent you back to us.' Betty reached out to take Angela's hand.

The touch of flesh on flesh . . . there had always been a comfort in it. But this time it was electric. It was a sensation that rooted itself in Angela's bones. She felt a lurch. A physical yank. And a moment later she was looking at herself lying in the bed, blank-eyed and drooling from a wet mouth. It was as if someone had moved a mirror into the space where Betty had been sitting and instead of seeing the old woman she was seeing herself, red hair spread across the pillow, freckles stark across a skin so pale that it was hard to believe it full of blood.

In the next moment everything was moving. She was falling *again*. A chair clattered down beside her. She was on the floor between two of the three hospice beds. Angela tried to call to Betty for help. The sounds from her mouth were incoherent but they weren't all vowels and they didn't sound like her. She couldn't see Betty, not even her feet. She tried to roll and suddenly the room rotated around her. The heavy medical beds skittered away on their castered feet though the little wheels should have had their brakes locked. Angela found herself face down now, the cold linoleum beneath her cheek.

She lay motionless, shocked. Everything felt different. Everything. Even though she was scared Angela felt marvellous, as if liquid happiness had been poured into every limb, as if it had filled the marrow of her bones and suffused her skin. She tried to think, tried to understand what had happened. And then she knew. No part of her hurt any more. There was nothing, just tiny aches and niggles that were less than nothing. The structural agony that she had built her existence around, the pain that codeine and morphine nibbled at the edges . . . the great hurt that was deeper in her than her bones. It had gone.

Angela's eyes blurred with tears but she could still see better than on her best day. Slowly and with great care she moved her head, craning her neck. Betty's arm lay stretched out close by, the old woman's blouse, her wrinkled hand emerging from the cuff, the wedding ring worn for a husband twenty years in the grave. It was as if Betty were lying beneath Angela and her arm emerging from under her. Suddenly Angela was terrified that she had fallen on her friend somehow and was even now crushing her. She tried to turn and again the room spun. She glimpsed the chair Betty had brought over, this time flying through the air as though someone had thrown it.

When the rotation stopped, and Angela's head also stopped spinning, she found herself staring at the doorway. Sarah hurried into view and stopped, filling the entrance, her red face slack with astonishment. 'Dear Lord!' She turned back and shouted down the corridor. 'Rose! Rose! Jordi! I see you there! Tell Mrs Mason to call an ambulance.'

Sarah hurried in and knelt beside Angela. Nervously she

reached out and took hold of Angela's arm. As her fingers touched Angela's skin that strange sensation struck again. A pull as if Sarah were a magnet and Angela the iron filings that followed its invisible lines of force. She sensed the point of contact, but more than that, for an instant she was aware of the whole of Sarah, blood to bone, as though she had soaked into the woman, ink on blotting paper. The sensation was gone as swiftly as it came. And Angela had no time to ponder it. A larger question drove it from her mind. The arm Sarah lifted into Angela's view was Betty's, the skin on the hand wrinkled and stained, the knuckles large, veins prominent. But Angela could feel Sarah's fingers on her wrist.

'Lie still! You'll be fine.'

Angela tried to answer and again the wrong voice came, sounding out words that while nonsense were ones that Angela could never form. She looked at the hand in Sarah's grip and as she thought about the fingers they writhed before her.

'What's hap— Fuck me! What a mess!' Rose stopped short in the doorway, staring around the room.

'I think she's had a stroke,' Sarah said. 'I can't find a pulse. We need an ambulance.'

'She's got a pulse. She's grinning at you, for God's sake!' Rose came into the room. 'What happened to the beds? Betty couldn't move them by herself even with the brakes off. And they ain't off! Skid marks all across the floor!'

'That doesn't matter! Help me get her up!' Sarah reached for a better grip on Angela.

Together the two women lifted Angela between them. 'Can you stand? Betty? Can you stand?'

Angela didn't understand why Sarah was speaking to Betty but lifting her. But as they raised her level with the beds she saw that lying in the closest one, staring blankly at the ceiling . . . was her, Angela.

♠

It was too much. Angela screamed. Terror ran through her and her panic animated her as was never possible before. Sarah went staggering across the room, Rose fell back clutching her nose, blood flooding between her fingers.

'Bitch broke by dose!'

Angela fell again, hit the floor again, and again barely felt it.

♥

'She's in there! She's having a stroke or a fit or something!'

Sarah led the paramedics in.

'Oh Jesus! Help me with Angela first. She's nearly out of her bed.'

The two men followed Sarah not to where Angela lay sprawled on the ground but to one of the beds. 'All together . . . There, she's safe now.'

'Now, this is Betty.' They came to where Angela had fallen. She had her right arm in front of her and one by one she moved the wrinkled old fingers. In the back of her mind a small, confused voice seemed to be trying to talk to her but the fingers held all her attention. She had never in all her life seen something so wonderful, so complex, so beautiful, doing what she wanted it to do. Her own hands had balled into fists before she even knew she owned them. She could no more move her own fingers than she could tie a knot with her earlobe. But somehow in this dream she had hands that did what they were told and she was learning how to talk to them.

'Careful. She's stronger than she looks,' Sarah cautioned. She held her shoulder as if something might be broken inside.

'No worries, love.' The larger of the two paramedics gave a snort. He looked like the rugby players Mr Jenkins liked to watch on TV every Sunday. A huge man almost too bulky for his uniform, hands like bunches of bananas. 'We'll be careful with her.'

The other man shone a light in Angela's eyes and pressed two fingers to her neck. He tried to ask her questions but Angela ignored those just as she ignored the woman's voice at the back of her mind. She only wanted to look at her fingers move, one then the next then the next, each jumping to obey her will. It was the most marvellous and beautiful thing she had ever seen. She began to cry and found that she couldn't stop weeping any more than she could stop flexing and moving her fingers.

'Could be a stroke.' The smaller paramedic sounded doubtful. 'Or someone's slipped her some acid . . . I've seen them like this at Glastonbury. Either way, we need to get her in.'

The two paramedics put their stretcher down beside Angela and moved her gently onto it. They lifted her and carried her past Sarah, frowning and clutching her arm, past Mrs Mason fussing over Rose. Past Jordi and Renée and Shirley, their faces grave and full of worry. Past Jenny and a stocky young man she didn't know, a man with short dark hair and the line of a scar catching the corner of his mouth into a sneer. Doors opened and closed and suddenly there was daylight, a cold wind, the sounds of traffic.

Angela whipped her head around. They were loading her into an ambulance. Taking her away. She didn't want to go.

'Nnnnnnn' she drew a breath 'ooooooooo'

'It's OK, Bessy,' the big man said.

'Betty,' the other one said, climbing in beside her.

'Betty, sorry. We think you've had a stroke. It often affects people's language. You should remember how to speak as you recover. Just stay calm, love.'

They had her in the ambulance now on some kind of trolley. The big man banged on the back panel and the sirens started up, the vehicle lurching into motion.

'Nnnnooooo.' Angela's arms and legs began to flail.

'She's fitting again.'

'We have to hold you, Betty, so you don't hurt y—'

A wild swing of Angela's arm . . . Betty's old, stick-thin arm . . . sent the rugby player slamming into the side of the ambulance. The whole vehicle rocked to the side.

'Jeeeesus.' He levered himself up, wheezing. 'I think she broke my ribs.'

Angela.

A small, familiar voice.

Angela.

Angela went still, listening. The second paramedic began to strap her to the trolley, frightened fingers fumbling at the catches. 'You all right, Dave?' He tightened a strap and reached feverishly for the next. 'She threw you in the fucking air. She's just a little old lady and she—'

'I'm okay . . .'

Angela shifted and the first of the straps tore free with a loud retort.

'Jesus!' Both men drew back.

Angela, you don't want to hurt them.

It was true. She didn't want to hurt anyone. Also, it was Betty. Betty's voice. Angela wondered what she should do . . . what she *was* doing . . . she was in Betty's body. The proper Angela was lying in a bed back in Carstons, in the hospice, waiting to die. What should she do?

Let me back.

How could she do that?

Try.

Angela closed her eyes – Betty's eyes – and tried.

When she opened her eyes again it was to a white ceiling, and as the light flooded in the weight of her old pain settled on her once more. And though she had borne the burden all her life her moments of respite made it bite all the harder and she cried out at the hurt and the shock of it.

♣

'Won't the wonders cease?' A bored voice close at hand. A face moved into Angela's line of vision. The young man with the scar and the dark hair cut so short that his scalp gleamed beneath. 'The cripple awakes!' He moved in closer. 'Does it speak?'

Angela tried to answer but no sound would come from her open mouth. Had she been dreaming? Where was she?

'You must be Veggie,' the stranger said. 'James told me about you. James? Our mutual friend, little Jimmy. And I'm Booksie.' He leaned in closer, fixing her with an uncomfortable stare. 'And look at you, Veggie. You got dealt a shitty hand, swear down.'

Across the room a door banged open. 'Aren't you finished in here y— Oh, she's awake?' Sarah came across and Booksie relinquished his place with a last grin.

Sarah stood over Angela's bed, straightening the covers. 'Don't mind Booksie. I just asked him to get the beds back in line.' She had a frown on, though whether it was at the thought of the young man with the scar or from wondering how the beds had been moved in the first place Angela didn't know. 'Them doctors at the hospital, eh? What do they know? Coma, they said! And all it took to wake you up was a bloody great racket!'

With effort Angela turned her head to look across the room.

'Want something?' Sarah asked. 'Oh . . .' Her voice turned grave. 'Looking for Betty?'

Angela turned her head back, mouth open in a 'yes'.

'I'm so sorry, Angie. She was with you most days. As long as she could be. Mrs Mason had to shoo her out of here come evening. Betty was at your side just before you woke up. Like as not it was all her noise that brought you round!'
Sarah paused again, as if wrestling with the words. 'Betty took ill, very suddenly. I mean, she's looked ill for ages, if I'm honest, but she had a nasty turn. A stroke, we think. My aunt had one a few years back. Had her falling over and talking gibberish. All she could say for a week after was, "I don't know where

my keys are." Never got the use of her left arm back. Anyway, Betty's been taken to hospital and that's where she is. We're all hoping she gets well soon. But I don't expect we'll be seeing her again for quite a while.' She patted Angela on the shoulder. An uncharacteristically tender gesture for the woman. And again Angela felt that odd lurch as if even those gentle taps might somehow knock her out of herself.

◆

That night Angela's dreams were very strange. She saw Betty sleeping in a hospital bed just like hers. She saw Sarah sleeping beside a fat man with curly grey hair, both of them snoring beneath a duvet covered in large flower prints. She saw the smaller paramedic in an armchair, his head back, eyes closed, mouth open, open drinks cans around his feet, like the ones from the staff Christmas party. She knew his name was Simon. She saw the large paramedic sleeping beside a tiny woman beneath a duvet with zigzag patterns. He rolled over and winced in his sleep. Angela worried the tiny woman would be crushed. She knew the big man was Dave. And all night, as she skipped between her dreams, Angela held that aware-ness of the four sleepers as if they were close about her and all she had to do if she wanted to touch them was to reach out.

♠

Betty came back the next day. Angela was still alone in the hospice, staring at the ceiling, very bored and with her mind full of questions. She heard Betty's approach.

'No, I'm all right!' Her voice came closer. 'No, I'm fine. The doctors said so.' Closer still. 'A funny turn, that's all it was. I'm fine.' The door opened. 'Thank you, Mrs Mason. No, I don't want to take any days off. I want to see Angela.'

A moment later Betty entered Angela's line of sight, all smiles. 'And there she is! Awake at last! My angel Angela!'

The door closed and Mrs Mason retreated. Betty pulled up the chair she had used the day before, testing it first and pursing her lips at how rickety it had become.

'You and me, girl, we have to talk!'

Angela made a 'yes' mouth.

'That . . . thing . . . yesterday. That was like magic. That's what it was!' Betty always said she wasn't one to beat around the bush. 'I was in my head but you were there too, doing the driving. And not doing it very well it has to be said, dear.' Betty frowned. 'Is . . . is that something you could do again, do you think?'

Angela wasn't sure but she made her 'yes'.

'And this time would you not shout or throw yourself about? And leave when I ask you, and listen to me?'

Again, yes.

'Try then. Just for a little visit. And don't make me fall over and thrash around or they won't let me come back to work.' Betty reached for Angela's hand but before she could touch her it was Angela doing the reaching.

She sat dead still, every muscle tense, her old hand trembling before her. Angela could see herself lying before her. It wasn't like a mirror. Mirrors gave you one angle, the one she was used to. She didn't like this angle, it didn't look like her, not properly.

Betty? Angela asked it in her mind and her lips hardly moved.

A very faint reply came from somewhere far to the back of her. She couldn't make out the words but she knew it was a yes and that it was Betty. Slowly and with great care Angela tried to move the fingers of the hand before her. They wriggled to her will. She gave a wet gasp of amazement and nearly slumped off the chair. She curled one finger then the next, then moved the whole arm up, then down.

At the back of her mind Betty's voice came again, the words

still muffled. A reminder of something. Angela remembered. She was just to visit. With a sigh she pushed forward leaving the delicious lightness of Betty's body and tumbling back into the pain-haunted prison of her own. She found herself looking up at Betty as the old woman straightened in the chair and patted herself with both hands.

'Amazing! That was amazing!' Betty shook her head. 'You know what's happened don't you, dear?'

Angela really didn't. She had been too taken up with what had happened to her to wonder about the why or the how of it.

'It's the wild card virus, Angela, the XTA. You must have caught it. That's what put you in the hospital. You got it the same as Renée and Shirley, only you've gone and . . . what do they call it? . . . turned an ace!'

Angela blinked. It made sense. She opened her mouth for 'yes'.

'You've got powers, Angela! Powers!' Betty glanced around the room as if someone might be listening. 'I don't think we should tell anyone about them. Not now at least. And you have to be careful, Angela. Very careful.' She rubbed at her grey hair then folded her arms, looking pleased, excited, and twenty years younger. 'Now, what we have to do is work out what you can do!'

♥

The next few weeks were filled with more fun and excitement than Angela had experienced in her whole life. She found that she could possess or 'visit' Betty whenever the old lady touched her. She felt sure that she could do the same with anyone else who touched her though she didn't, partly because Betty had warned her about sharing her secret and partly because it seemed wrong to do a thing like that without asking and she had no way of asking.

Over the weeks she and Betty practised and slowly Angela learned first to sit without falling, then to stand without support, and later to move around the room, though she had to hold on to the bed or the wall because all of a sudden Betty seemed terribly tall and the floor awfully far away. She learned faster than any baby and Betty said it was because her old muscles already knew what to do and were just waiting for permission.

Learning to speak was an altogether more difficult process and one that had Betty's dentures falling out of her mouth on more than one occasion. Angela's main problem was that she wanted to say everything at once. All the words. All her thoughts. It took great resolve to slow down and practise 'aaaaaah' and 'bbbbbbh' and on through all the basic components. Slowly though, in the privacy of the hospice wing, Betty and Angela made progress.

The doctor from the local surgery came round eventually at Mrs Mason's request to remove the cannula from Angela's arm. The woman looked too young to be a GP and had an awful struggle to get the needle out of Angela's vein. She left red-faced and with a puzzled expression.

In addition to her power to visit Betty, Angela discovered that the gaps around her dreams had become crowded with an awareness of everyone who had touched her since that first day. At least if they were asleep too. She found that when the paramedics from the ambulance changed shift they left her dreams but if she concentrated during the day she could sense them sleeping too.

♣

'Ta da!' Sarah wheeled a new chair into Angela's room. 'It's a loaner, but it will have to do until wheelchair services come up with a replacement for your other one. They're still trying to say that you broke it and have to pay for a new one. Mrs

Mason has been telling them that's ridiculous and that you can't even move.' She parked the chair by the bed and shifted the hoist into position. 'I told her to say it was the chair collapsing that put you in hospital! Manufacturer's fault. You should sue them!'

Sarah struggled to get Angela into the new chair. She had always been able to bend Angela's stiff legs into the necessary angles. Now she puffed and panted and had to get Jordi and Jimmy to help her. Jordi shouldn't even have been asked, he was a resident not staff. Even then with all three of them straining and Jimmy turning the air blue with curses they could only move Angela's legs when she did her utmost to relax them. Finally she was in and they wheeled her into the common room.

That night Jordi and Jimmy were added to her dreams. Jordi peaceful in his narrow bed in the room four doors down. Jimmy sleeping open-mouthed on a sofa that looked as old and as worn as Betty.

◆

Angela's return to the common room was greeted by a round of applause and she grinned around at the smiling faces, her eyes blurring with tears. Fat old Charlie relinquished the control and returned to his chair slapping at his bald head. Jordi put on an animal show for her because they all knew she liked them, and everyone sat and watched the varied challenges of the African honey badger for the next twenty minutes.

Shirley and Renée came across the room to welcome Angela back, and thereafter she became aware of their eyes on her more often, as if they somehow sensed a fellow XTA. But if they did then neither of them said a word. Both joined Angela's night-time crowd, though Shirley had barely touched her, just brushing the side of her shoulder with one of the dangerous-looking spikes that served in place of hands. Great for picking up litter, Shirley always said, picking your nose . . . not so much.

♠

Betty and Angela's experiments were limited now to the times when Betty could visit Angela in her room. The old lady announced herself intrigued by the trouble the doctor had experienced getting the needle from Angela's arm and by the efforts Sarah had reported as necessary to get her into her chair.

'Some of those aces are as strong as an ox. Tough as old leather too.' Betty reached for a stainless steel bedpan. 'Just . . . let me . . .' She managed to slide it between Angela's arm and side. 'See if you can give it a squeeze, dear.'

Angela tensed, an action which always pressed her arms tight against her. Betty's eyebrows rose above her glasses. 'R-relax now, dear.' She reached forward and a moment later brought the crumpled remains of the pan into view. The faint pattern of indentations across the curved and flattened pan looked like the marks a rib cage might impress.

'I'm just going to try something else, Angela. It won't hurt.' Betty took a pair of nail scissors from her bag and gently traced the point across the back of Angela's hand. She frowned and tried again. 'Not a mark!' She put some effort into the action. 'Well . . . dear. The good news is that I can't put a scratch on you. The not so good news is that if you need another operation or an injection we could be in trouble . . .'

They carried on with their experiments. Angela concentrated on learning to talk. At Betty's insistence she also checked on how strong she was when visiting Betty. It seemed that some of her strength manifested while she was visiting, but far from all of it. In Betty's hands the stainless steel bowl, which Angie had crushed without the slightest effort, was stiff and difficult to untwist, but she could do it, and when the metal tore and left a jagged edge it scored a red line across her hand that hurt but didn't bleed.

♥

Two days after Angela's return to society a strange irritation at the back of her mind during *Strictly Come Dancing* caused her to concentrate on what she now called her list of 'contacts'. She quickly became aware of the smaller ambulance man, Simon, lying amid a veritable sea of beer cans. He was asleep but choking, with vomit bubbling from his mouth. Without thinking she reached out to him and a heartbeat later she found herself choking on a mouthful of sour puke. She rolled over coughing and spitting. Oddly, the first thought that occurred to her was that she hadn't used any of her time in Betty to eat anything. This horrible stuff drooling from Simon's lips was the first thing she had tasted in years. It wasn't in the top ten things she would have put on her list. Or the top thousand.

Groaning, Angela stood Simon up, finding him to be even harder to balance than Betty, and backed him into his armchair. The strength she brought to Betty didn't manifest here and every action was a struggle. She wiped his mouth with his hands and wiped the hands on the arms of the chair. There was no voice at the back of her mind. Wherever Simon was he wasn't watching her or his body. A sudden and marvellous understanding struck her. She could reach for any of the sleepers. As long as they were dreaming she could reach for them across whatever distance stood between them and visit!

Angela spat more of the taste from her mouth and looked around the darkened room. Enough daylight bled through the heavy curtains to show that every surface lay cluttered with cans or books or magazines, half-eaten meals, everywhere crowded with rubbish of one sort or another. Angela felt more like an intruder than a visitor. She hadn't been invited. Simon wouldn't want her sitting there in his man's body looking at his room, tasting his vomit. But she knew he could have died. Sally Jenks had choked on her own sick at Carstons the year before. There was supposed to have been an inquiry. Rose was supposed to have checked on her and have her on a monitor. Somehow it had all gone away. Hushed up, Betty had whispered. And only the empty chair in the common room had remained to remind them that there had ever been a Sally Jenks.

'I should leave,' Angela said with Simon's mouth. The words came out slurred and funny. She wanted to help him, but she didn't know how. It made her sad. Maybe his big friend Dave would help him. 'Goodbye.'

She reached for her body and a moment later was seeing from her own eyes.

'Angie?' Jordi was bending over her. 'Are you all right?'

Angela made her 'yes'.

'Away with the fairies was she?' Shirley called from across the room.

'Back with us now.' Jordi returned to his seat. 'Well, don't go having a fit, Angie. I don't think there's any midazolam left!'

Angela had heard as much from Betty. On Angela's care plan it said to give her point five of a millilitre of midazolam if she had a fit, and then point five more if she hadn't recovered after ten minutes, and then to call the ambulance. The stuff was a powerful sedative and for reasons Angela didn't understand there were people who would pay to suffer its numbing confusion. This meant that for the best part of two years Jimmy had been helping himself to bottles of the stuff from the stores, along with diazepam tablets, morphine in solution, and anything else with a street value. There was a strict accounting system of course but Rose just signed the medicines off against the names of the patients for whom they were prescribed, fictitiously increasing the discretionary component of their doses. Of late, things had grown much worse. Jordi had been the one to explain it to Angela, whispering his observations beneath the strains of *The Great British Bake Off* on Channel 4.

'You know who Booksie is, don't you?' Angela didn't and Jordi didn't wait for an answer. 'He runs that gang, the one that owns Southerns Estate and Green Road down to Thrush Oaks. He's hardcore. Been in prison for glassing a bloke down at the Ram's Head. Anyway, he got sick of Jimmy lording it about and taking such a big cut out of what he steals from here. So he signed up for a job as care assistant. Helps with his parole officer or something. He got Jimmy to get Rose to fix the paperwork so Mason took him on. So now there's no middleman and Jimmy is just Little Jim again, and Booksie goes straight to the source and takes what he wants. Only what he wants is a lot more than what Jimmy used to take. He's eating into the standard meds. Charlie hasn't had a tranquillizer in three days, that's why they've got him locked in his room. And Renée's had nothing for her pain. That's why she's crying. And—' Jordi fell silent as Booksie crossed the room with an armload of blankets. 'He's got that Jenny working for him too now. She doesn't look very happy about it but she's too scared to say no.'

Angela stared at the doorway through which Booksie had departed. Jenny had been looking worried rather than sulky since Angela woke up. Angela knew Betty was right about seeing the real person not the face they showed to the world. She'd looked out from Betty's eyes and that didn't make her Betty any more than Jenny looking at the world from the face of a fairytale princess made her something special. But even so, despite all that common-sense stuff . . . it hurt Angela to think of the girl being frightened or sad. She had no Prince Charming to save her, so maybe Angela would have to do it.

♣

Booksie was a problem for the future though, and Angela's future had always been crowded with problems, most of them due to her own body's relentless assault on itself. For now Angela's priority was to rid herself of the memory of a mouthful of vomit by creating better memories. Her visit had alerted her to the opportunity to taste again. And not only to taste the things she had loved before they started to feed her through a tube but to taste the forbidden foods. The stuff that wasn't mush. The stuff that had to be chewed and whose aroma had driven her to distraction over the years.

When Betty came into Angela's room that evening their practice led in a very different direction. It was easiest to explain it to Betty with her own mouth, the words still awkwardly shaped even though the tongue that spoke them had been doing so for decades longer than Angela had been alive.

'I want to eat.'

Angela listened hard for Betty's answer, tingling at the back of her mind. Hearing Betty when Angela was visiting her had always been difficult but they were getting better at it. It seemed as though Betty wanted her to wait, but her mouth was watering and the hunger that had been gnawing at Angela all day seemed suddenly larger than her stomach, larger than the room.

Angela lurched to her feet and walked Betty towards the door, her gait ungainly and over-cautious. Betty sounded as if she were disagreeing but it was hard to hear above the roar of Angela's appetite.

For the first time ever Angela left her room on two feet. She tottered down the half-lit hall to the kitchen. The door opened with an alarming splintering noise that reminded Angela that Jordi had told her they kept it locked to stop him helping himself to sugar at night. Betty's cry of protest rang out in the back of Angela's mind but the damage had been done now and she could smell something incredible that drew her through the doorway with irresistible force.

Sniffing hard and with drool running down her chin – Betty's chin – Angela located the source of the aroma. A large two-handled stainless steel saucepan . . . and revealed within when she lifted the lid, the leftover stew from that evening's meal.

Angela reached in, dipped Betty's gnarled fingers into the cold slop and began to feast.

At first it was difficult to remember to chew, and although swallowing seemed to take care of itself Angela choked several times simply through trying to devour the stew too quickly. The taste was beyond anything she had ever imagined, so rich, complex, bursting with so many flavours. Sensations overwhelmed her. She ate without thought, revelling in every mouthful, tears rolling down her cheeks. The stew told stories to her tongue. The primal joy of chewing hypnotized her. She could do this forever. This and nothing else. Just sit right here and eat and eat and eat until she was as old as Betty.

It was only the lights going on and Jordi's gasp of astonishment behind her that brought Angela's feasting to a halt. With a cry of dismay around a full mouth she fled for her own body.

◆

Experiments with food thereafter were rather more controlled and limited in duration. Betty accepted Angela's tearful apologies and genuine contrition, and was always sure thereafter to bring something with her to Angela's room for a taste test. Humbugs proved to be a favourite!

♠

On Friday Jenny came in on the morning shift looking subdued. She kept her gaze on the floor and avoided the residents. She had been starting to warm to Shirley but today she wouldn't look at the old lady. Angela watched her the whole time and when at last she briefly raised her head the girl revealed a black eye. Angela watched enough television to know that men hit women but somehow she had thought that only happened on the shows, like people getting shot, or billionaires marrying prostitutes. It was no mystery who had done it though. Angela knew the answer to that one even before she heard Renée say it to Shirley. Booksie had done it.

♥

That Sunday Betty had the night shift with Sarah and a Filipino woman called Mai who only ever worked nights. Management called it the graveyard shift but Carstons was anything but quiet after lights out. Residents needed to be turned, to be changed, to have meds, to be reassured, to have new linens . . . any number of tasks.

Jacey Lomas needed new sheets and Betty, finding the linen cupboard bare, was about to go down to the laundry for more when a door down the corridor banged open.

'Jordi?' She squinted. 'Jordi Barron! What are you doing out of bed at this hour, young man?' Jordi was one of the good sleepers but now he lurched down the corridor like something from the *Night of the Living Dead* in plaid pyjamas.

'We have to tell,' Jordi slurred.

'What are you talking about now?' Betty took his shoulders and steered him back towards his room.

'Booksie, we have to tell about Booksie,' Jordi said. Then as Betty got him back into his room. 'It's me, Angela. Jordi is asleep.'

'Dear Lord! You can do that?'

'Yes.' Jordi took hold of the headboard and tried to lift his bed. 'He's not very strong though. I think the better the bond is the more of my strength comes through. Anyway . . .' Angela gave up on lifting the bed and sat Jordi down on it. '. . . we have to tell the police about Booksie.' Angela had watched a great many police shows on television and had considerable faith in their ability to deal with the likes of Booksie.

'We can't, dear.' Betty took Jordi's hand in hers. Angela saw that she was trembling. 'You don't know these people. They'll follow you home and put bricks through your window. And that's just the start of it. They don't care about the police. Half of them are too young to charge anyway.'

'I can do it,' Angela said.

'You, dear?' Betty shook her head. 'How are you going to tell them? Not like this, surely? You'll only end up getting poor Jordi into trouble.'

'Get me my word cards and a policeman and someone to hold them for me. I can do it. Booksie can't hurt me.' The word cards were very slow and laborious but if someone held them up and paid close attention they could tell which of the four sections on the card Angela was staring at, and gradually, piece by piece she could build simple sentences.

♣

Betty called the local police on the following morning and told them that a resident at the care home wanted to report a crime. A day passed in which Angela could settle to nothing. She visited the paramedic Simon and raised him from the fetid pit of his bed to tidy the flat while he slept. She reasoned that it was okay to invade his privacy when he clearly needed so much help.

In the end she barely dented the mess, but she did get all the cans and bottles off the sides and floor and into the correct recycling bags. She left those by the front door and was considering how she might leave a message for Simon when the alarm by his bed began to blare. She hurried him back to bed and tumbled him on top of the duvet just as he started to wake. She was gone before he realized she had been visiting.

Back in her chair at Carstons, Angela came to her senses with a shudder. It was a strange thing to wear a man's body and she didn't like the smell in that flat or the plates of congealed food. Betty said her husband had been a drinker.

Angela hoped Simon would stop soon or he might join Betty's husband in the graveyard over by the Westland Bridge. It seemed a strange thing to have a body that worked and didn't hurt and then to want to poison it.

'Angela?' Shirley's voice. The old lady had taken the seat beside her. 'Off dancing with moonbeams again?'

Angela made her 'yes'.

'You've been doing a lot of that, dear, since your illness.' Shirley leaned in close. 'Thick as thieves with Betty too. That's all right with me, dear. You keep your cards close to your chest. It's not always wise to show anyone what card you've turned.' She tapped her nose with her left spike. Angela was always afraid the old lady was going to put her eye out or something, but of course Shirley never did. She'd had fifty years to practise with the 'gift' that XTA brought her. She told a story that for years she'd had to wear special plastic covers on her two spikes 'for public safety'. In the end though she had argued and won the case that they were part of her body and not subject to restrictions any more than Muhammed Ali was expected to keep his fists in an iron box. What the *powers that be* might do to Angela though if they knew what tricks she could perform . . . Angela didn't like to think of it. She agreed with Shirley. Hers was a card to keep hidden.

◆

'I have to go, dear, I'm sorry.' Betty looked worried. 'I thought they would come within the hour but this is ridiculous. I called ten hours ago. I rang them just now and they said an officer had been assigned but couldn't say when we might see him. The woman asked if I could bring you to the station. I asked her if they had a wheelchair ramp for those steps yet. That shut her up.'

The shift had ended two hours ago and the next set of staff were there, Booksie, Sarah, and Jenny. The girl shuffled around as if trying to be unnoticed, shooting nervous glances at Booksie when his back was turned. It hurt Angela to see that. It seemed like stamping on a flower.

'I'd stay, of course I would, but he might not show up until tomorrow and Benjy hasn't been fed and I said I'd help Mrs Ellard at Number 11 give her Robin a bath.'

Benjy was Betty's cat about whom she worried to a degree that made Angela doubt all portrayals of cats as independent and self-sufficient predators. Robin was the son of an elderly neighbour and had Down Syndrome, which meant that at the age of twenty-nine bathing him seemed to require two other adults. Or perhaps that Robin was just a handful.

'I've asked Sarah to tell anyone who comes asking for you to come back tomorrow during my shift.' Betty looked at her watch. 'I have to go.' She gave Angela's hand one last pat and hurried away. Angela watched her go. Betty wouldn't be far away. She only lived two streets from the home. Sometimes when she stood by the common room window she swore she could hear Benjy meowing for his dinner.

♠

'You have a visitor, Angela.' Booksie walked into the common room just as Sarah and Jenny left, pushing two of the residents off to bed in their wheelchairs. It was five to nine and everyone was supposed to be tucked up by quarter past. 'Officer Reynolds says he had a message that you wanted to report a crime.' Booksie had a fixed and slanted grin, hooked at the edge by that scar of his which looked very pale at the moment. His eyes burned with a dark fury that made Angela want to look away. She forced herself to be brave and smiled for them both.

Officer Reynolds stood a head taller than Booksie and just as broad. He had full red cheeks, a neat moustache, and a touch of grey in his black hair. He looked nothing like the policemen on the television and glanced around the common room with a poorly disguised sneer.

'Maybe I should take you both somewhere private?' Booksie asked.

'Yes,' the policeman said. 'That would be better. Thank you, Mr . . .?'

'Booker. Joseph Booker. At your service, Officer.' Booksie clicked his heels together. 'Would I be right in saying you're new to this beat?' He started to wheel Angela towards the residents' rooms.

'Came over from the Met last month. My wife's got family round here.' The policeman followed Booksie and Angela along the corridor and into her room.

'Now, Miss Leighton, you had something to report?' Officer Reynolds stood in front of Angela and although she craned her neck she couldn't raise her eyes enough to see his face. She became deeply aware that she was drooling and that the neckerchief Betty had left her with was spotted with wet patches. Of all the things her visiting had shown her the thing she liked least was seeing herself from the outside. She tried to tell herself that she looked so vacant because she was gone from her body, but a large part of her worried that what she saw of herself while visiting Betty was what others saw all the time. 'Miss Leighton?'

Angela made a moan. Learning to shape words in Betty's mouth had done nothing for her abilities with her own.

'She can't talk,' Booksie said. 'I think someone's been playing games. She can't have called you herself. Did they leave a name, whoever it was that did call?' His eyes flashed towards Angela and for a second he showed his teeth.

Angela tried to stop them, she called out 'no' but nothing escaped save a louder moan. The policeman glanced at her, disgusted, and consulted his notebook. 'A Betty Parkins. Do you know her? Does she work here?'

'Ah, Betty!' Booksie grinned and raised his voice over Angela's shouts. 'Lovely old lady. Gets a bit confused.' He tapped the side of his head. 'Had a funny turn the other day and was taken to hospital yelling nonsense. I'll have a word. Maybe it was supposed to be someone else who wanted to make a report. The residents have their little rows.' Booksie shared a smile with Officer Reynolds. 'She stole my shawl, he took my stick. There's an old dear who's always threatening to sue. We'll sort it all out, don't worry.'

Booksie led the policeman away from Angela's protests. A coffee and a biscuit were mentioned. Officer Reynolds didn't say goodbye, or even look back. Booksie flicked the lights off as he left.

♥

A long time passed before Booksie returned to Angela, sitting alone in her dark room. She had searched for her contacts but none of them were sleeping. She had flexed against the chair and heard the support struts groan, but breaking free wouldn't help her, so she stopped. She sat blind and waited, her worries chasing around her skull. Would Booksie go after Betty? Would he do it straight away?

When he pushed open the door and flicked the lights back on she flinched and her chair groaned again.

'Well,' Booksie said. 'Well, well, well.' He took the visitors' chair and positioned it opposite Angela then sat in it. 'You wanted to report something to the police, did you?' He showed his teeth. 'Do you know what? I don't even care what it was you wanted to say. The main thing here is that nobody in this shithole is *ever* to call the police about anything. Understand, Veggie?'

Angela met his dark eyes and wondered how deep the well of fury behind them was.

'Understand?' And with the question Booksie slapped her, hard, across the face, swinging with his arm extended. A second later he was out of his chair doing a dance of pain, the hand under his other arm. 'Motherfucker! Motherfucker!' He stopped dancing and shook the hand in front of him as if trying to rattle the hurt out of it. 'What the hell?'

He returned his gaze to Angela. She smiled at him. Puzzled and flexing his hand, Booksie moved in closer. He punched her in the face with his left hand and less enthusiasm behind it than the first blow.

'Ow! Jesus!' He danced away, shaking that hand. 'Oh, you bitch!' Booksie glanced around the room. His eyes fixed on the oxygen cylinder at the foot of the bed. At night an oxygen machine helped Angela to breathe. The cylinder was there in case the machine broke. Booksie picked it up, a steel tube two feet long and thicker than his arm. 'This'll do.' He seemed so far gone in his outrage that he hadn't even questioned why punching Angela in the nose had hurt his hand and left her unbothered. Something in the redness of his face, and the white scar cutting across it, gave Angela pause. She had never seen hate before. Disdain, distaste, casual cruelty, all of those, but not the raw, unhinged hate burning in Joseph Booker's eyes.

He swung the cylinder from his hip, two-handed, arms out. A killing blow. A blow to shatter a skull and splatter the wall beside it with brains. The heavy steel hit Angela's cheek bone and . . . rebounded, flying free of Booksie's grasp. Her head jerked fractionally to the side. It felt like a tap. But it was a tap that rocked her in her chair.

'Is . . . is everything okay in there?' Jenny's scared voice, rising above the clatter of the cylinder as it skittered across the floor and hit the wall.

'Fuck off!' Booksie didn't even look round.

It amazed Angela that the man could give so little thought to the consequences of his actions. What if he had killed her? How would he explain that? She supposed the same madness had held sway when he had smashed a beer glass and jammed the jagged edges into a man's face in the middle of a crowded pub.

'Oh. You. Fucking. Bitch.' Booksie pulled a knife from his back pocket and unfolded the blade. He came forward at a rush, stabbing at her chest, neck, and face, knocking her chair over onto its back, snarling like a frenzied animal.

His rage terrified Angela. She screamed as she fell, screwed her eyes tight, screamed some more. The knife blows felt like pinpricks. Once he stabbed her eye. It made her wince. The attack seemed to last forever. Eventually though, Booksie's energy failed him and he lay across her, panting. Angela opened her eyes. Booksie's hands were covered in blood and for a moment she wondered if she were dying. But then she saw the cut on his palm and the darker blood welling from it and realized that he had somehow cut himself, his grip slipping from the hilt to the blade.

Angela started to laugh. She couldn't stop herself. She lay there, awkward in her fallen chair, giggling helplessly.

'You fucking monster!' Booksie reached up and took a pillow from the bed. A moment later it was over her face with all of the man's weight pushing down on it.

In the soft darkness Angela's giggles faded to chuckles and then stopped. She guessed that Booksie was trying to stop her breathing but she felt fine. Her strength might be all but useless in a crippled body but her lungs could suck air through a pillow without difficulty.

'Booksie? What's going on in there?' Sarah's voice at the door. Knocking followed. 'Booksie?' Sarah was scared of him too or she would have come in. The door wasn't locked.

'Just a game. A fucking game. That's all. You heard her laughing.' Cursing, Booksie tossed the pillow aside and got up, clutching his wounded hand. 'This isn't over, bitch.'

Moments later he was gone and Sarah was in his place, clucking and fussing. 'What on earth's been going on here, Angie? How'd that stupid boy cut himself? And what a mess he's made!'

With Jenny's help Sarah got Angela's chair upright and then

hoisted her into bed. They changed her into her night clothes, changed her pad, set up her oxygen, and found her a clean pillow. Jenny mopped up the blood, all the while casting unread-able glances at Angela. Angela smiled back, wanting to see an echo on Jenny's face, but the girl looked away.

Sarah stayed after Jenny left. Her brutal features hadn't been designed with shame in mind and the expression looked odd on her. She opened her mouth as if to say something, then shook her head and patted Angela's hand. 'What a world we live in, Angie. What a world.'

Sarah left and turned off the lights. Angela lay, mind racing, not sure how she felt. Scared, exhilarated, alive, victorious. None of them covered it but each had a part to play. She lay for a long time thinking through what had happened, trying to understand what went on in a mind like Booksie's. The thought of Betty, lying in her bed not two streets away, struck Angela in the middle of replaying the hit with the oxygen cylinder. Immediately she focused in on her friend and found the old woman sleeping in her fussy little bedroom. Angela paid the lightest of visits, just enough to listen through Betty's ears. Nothing but night sounds, the creak of the house, the traffic muffled by glass. Betty winced, murmured and turned in her sleep. Angela felt a stab of pain from somewhere under the old lady's ribs. She visited a little deeper and took the pain herself so Betty could sleep. It wasn't a nice ache but she would return to worse and Betty needed her sleep.

What it was that brought Angela back to her own body she couldn't say but suddenly she was there staring at the darkness. And then a light swept the wall and it wasn't darkness. Booksie was there with a torch.

'Awake, are we? Good. I wanted you to be awake for this, freak.' He came closer, playing the torch beam across her face and dazzling her. 'You're one of those joker fucks, aintcha? A very special special needs case. A fucking joker and you think the joke's on me!' He lifted a red plastic . . . thing, a carton with a handle, and a long yellow spout. It looked a bit like what the cooking oil in the kitchens came in, and it smelled very strong. 'Let's find out how you burn, shall we? I brought Mr Petrol to help!'

Booksie seemed calm now, and somehow that made it worse. When he was raging Angela could almost understand his readiness to hurt. But calm, and grinning. That was something alien.

'Before we go too far though . . . a little test.' Booksie put the petrol can down. 'No point making a big mess if you're just going to laugh it off. I'll do time for you, but you gotta do your part and die screaming.' He produced a cigarette lighter and made a flame. He took Angela's fist and lifted it. She could see the slightest tremor in his fingers, vibrating the flame. A sign that his rage was still there perhaps, burning at the core.

'Now . . .' He held the flame under her wrist.

At first Angela felt nothing, then heat, a hot spot, uncomfortable, seconds passed, the heat moved past uncomfortable. Booksie stared into her eyes the whole time and now she turned her head away. It hurt. She could smell burning and it was her.

'Success!' He withdrew the flame. 'Now for the main show!'

Angela began to scream. She didn't want to die. She didn't want to suffer in the flames. Terror flooded her and she shook her traitor limbs, the arms and legs that had never once done what she asked of them.

Booksie leaned over her, petrol can in hand. 'Hold still now. You don't want to miss anything. It's the last thing you'll do, Veggie.'

It was his grin that turned her fear into anger. And it was her anger she threw at him.

From one heartbeat to the next she moved from her body to Booksie's and in that instant found herself staring down at herself, proud for once to see her own face, snarling, teeth bared. She dropped the petrol can and started to walk stiff-legged towards the window.

'You . . . should . . . never have . . . touched me.' She formed the words with his mouth even as he fought and raged at the back of her mind.

Keeping Booksie from regaining control of his body took every ounce of Angela's will and she knew she wouldn't be able to fight him for long. She had never had to contest owner-ship before. She was a visitor, not an invader.

Two more steps and she had him standing before the window. 'Fucker.' She bent him double and slammed his face into the windowsill. The tiled corner hammered into his mouth, shat-tering teeth and breaking his jaw with a loud snap. The pain was considerable but Angela had lived with pain all her life. And besides, when she left, it would be Booksie's to own. She let him fall to his knees, gripped the windowsill in both hands, and smashed his face into it a second time.

The impact knocked her back into her own body. She could hear feet in the corridor outside, running towards her. The door banged open and Sarah was there, Jenny behind her. After that there was light, shouting, confusion, an ambulance. Simon was there, and Dave. They stopped to look at her before they carried Booksie off on the stretcher, and both of them returned her smile.

Angela lay in the darkness afterwards, her smile still in place. Maybe, she thought, I'm not a good person. But nobody said I have to be. Just because my body doesn't work doesn't make me a saint . . . Betty wouldn't have hurt him. Not like that. But I'm not sorry. Not one bit.

♣

An inquiry followed. The press became involved. Betty saw to that. Angela wasn't sure where Betty's extra courage had come from. She didn't know why the old lady wasn't scared of bricks through her window any more, or of the 'worse'. But Betty got the *Cambridge Evening News* on the case and before long there were almost more policemen, inspectors from the parent company, reporters, and auditors from the Care Quality Commission at Carstons than there were residents.

◆

It took a good six months for everything to settle down and by that time Angela's contact list had grown to scores. One of the reporters got sent to cover the civil war in Syria and Angela paid a quiet visit one night. She took a short sleepwalk to the balcony of the Turkish hotel serving as their headquarters and got to look out over the lights of Istanbul and smell the air of another world. One of the policewomen went on holiday to Lanzarote and again Angela paid a quiet visit too.

♠

Betty announced that she was going on holiday as well. Angela couldn't remember Betty ever taking a holiday. Who would help bathe Robin at Number 11?

Betty made a special effort to go around everyone in the common room and to say a proper goodbye, which Angela thought was very nice of her since she was only going on holiday.

Angela didn't know what Betty had said to Shirley and Renée but both the old ladies seemed to be dabbing their eyes when Betty left them. She gave Jordi a hug and a kiss then came to Angela.

'I won't say goodbye to you, dear. Because you can always visit.' She patted Angela's hand and gave a wink. 'Leave it to the weekend though, eh?'

Angela made a big smile then a 'yes'. Betty had asked her not to visit after the incident with Booksie. She said she wasn't angry or anything and that she loved Angela more than anything except maybe Benjy (and even then she winked) but that she needed her privacy. And Angela had agreed even though she missed walking around Carstons in Betty's body and eating ice cream in the kitchen and finding toffees in her pocket.

Angela watched Betty leave at a slow shuffle, leaning on her stick, and somehow she found herself wanting to cry too. Betty looked so old these days. More than anything Angela wanted her to have a lovely holiday.

♥

The wait for that weekend seemed endless but eventually it arrived and Angela visited Betty that night. It took forever to find her, almost the whole night, and Angela grew very worried, but at last she felt her friend and reached for her.

Angela opened Betty's eyes and was surprised to find herself in a bed very like the one she had just left. There were lines in her arm just like when Angela had her coma. And monitors bleeping quietly to themselves, jagged green lines tracing across screens.

'This isn't a holiday.'

Across the dim room someone turned around in surprise. 'Did you just . . .'

Angela turned Betty's head for a better look. A young nurse with a torch and a clipboard stepped back in astonishment. 'W . . . Wait there, Mrs Parkins!' She left at a run.

'Wake up, Betty!' Angela sat up in her bed. Looking down she saw to her surprise that bandages wrapped the whole of Betty from just below her chest to her hips and clear tubes led out from under the dressings. The whole area hurt quite a bit. 'Betty!'

Something fluttered at the back of her mind. 'Betty?'

Hello, dear.

'Betty! You're sick. You didn't tell me you were going to

hospital. You said a holiday!' She tried to keep the anger from her voice.

Well . . . I didn't want you to worry, darling. And it is a holiday I'm going on. They can't mend me, and I'm very tired, and it hurts so m— . . . actually it doesn't hurt at all now. Did they give me more morphine?

'I think so.' Angela didn't say she was looking after the pain or Betty might ask her to leave. It did hurt, but Angela had dealt with worse. 'Can't you come home now? I don't like it here.'

I can't, dear. I should have told you before. I know. But I didn't want to see you cry. I wasn't brave enough for that.

'You're very brave. You're the bravest—'

I won't be coming home, dear. The doctors said so when they thought I was too drugged up to hear. They don't think I'll last until morning. It's a shame. I don't even remember when I last saw the sun come up. I would have liked to watch one more dawn. I would have liked a room with a view. You know what you can see from that window? A brick wall, that's what. A sigh. It's very good to have you here, Angela. I had no idea how lonely this all would be.

The door banged open and a doctor filled the doorway, the nurse from before standing on tiptoes to see over his shoulder.

'Good God!' He took a step forward. 'Mrs Parkins? How are you even . . .'

'We're going to find a view.' Angela swung Betty's bare legs over the edge of the bed.

'Absolutely not! You're . . . you should be heavily sedated! There's internal bleeding—'

Angela bit through the tubes in her arm and pulled loose some of the others. She slipped from the bed and put her weight on both bare feet. The pain made her bite her lip but it wasn't so much. She had had as bad before.

'I simply can't let—'

Angela pushed the doctor aside. He went staggering across

the room and fell over a drip stand. She hadn't meant to be so rough but the pain made it difficult to judge.

Angela! Be nice. Are you okay, dear?

'I'm fine.' Spoken through gritted teeth.

Angela walked Betty out past the astonished nurse and into the corridor beyond. At several points on the way to the lifts nurses asked her if she was all right or whether she was supposed to be out of bed. Their tone implied that she was neither of these things. Angela ignored them. In her head she could hear Betty making good natured comments and trying to set the nurses' minds at ease. *I do feel much better.*

Angela reached the lifts with three nurses in tow and a handful of others off looking for help. Two of the nurses followed her into a lift.

'You've clearly had a major operation, my dear . . .' the older of the two said, a lady with a kind face and curly grey hair.

'Mrs Parkins . . .' the other read from the band on Betty's wrist. She straightened up. 'Mrs Betty Parkins.'

'And she's the nicest lady in the whole world. So you two leave her alone,' Angela said. She had tears making her eyes blurry so she couldn't see the floor numbers properly. Both nurses exchanged glances.

After a number of stops and starts they reached the top floor and Angela began to look for access to the roof. It took a while with the nurses fluttering about her trying to convince her to go with them. The older one pointed to the bright crimson blossoming through the layers of bandage around Betty's waist.

'You are putting yourself in serious danger, Betty!'

Down the corridor more nurses waited and with them two hefty orderlies. Angela ignored them all and went to the steps leading up to a blue door marked 'Roof'. Before she got to it the two big men came and took her arms. Neither of them were as big as Dave the paramedic but they were much bigger than any other men Angela knew. She took a handful of each man's shirt and lifted them up so their toes were off the ground then carried them back to the nurses, one in each hand to balance her.

'Stay here,' she told them and went back up to the blue door. It might have been locked, she couldn't tell. The roof was dark and windy. Angela took some of the metal rail that went around the edge and used it to tie the door shut. She didn't want to talk to any more nurses. She went back to sit where the rail had been, dangling Betty's feet over the edge and looking out to where the sky at the horizon was just turning grey.

'We'll have our view soon, Betty.' The wind whistled through the cables holding an antenna nearby. 'Betty?'

Yes, dear. She sounded distant now. Faint. *I was just looking at the view. I think that new medicine has really helped. I feel marvellous. You can't imagine how much it hurt . . .*

'No.'

They sat in silence for a while. Somewhere behind them there was a muffled banging on the blue door but it didn't matter.

Look. A new dawn. All those houses. And the sun glinting on the river.

'It's very pretty.' Angela could feel the sunlight on her legs now. Even with all the pain filling her like broken glass she could feel the sunlight. 'Betty?'

Yes, dear? So far back in her mind that she could hardly hear her.

'Don't go.'

I have to, darling. All of us are just visiting after all. We come when we're invited and after a while it's time to go. You know that, Angela.

'I know it.' Angela found that she was crying again.

♣

Too faint to hear, but somehow there was happiness in it and kindness. And then nothing.

◆

With a sharp inhalation of breath Angela was back in her body and for once the pain she found there was less than what she had left behind. She searched for Betty but Betty had gone and all she found were memories of the old lady's smile.

♠

All of us are just visiting. That's what Betty had said and Angela supposed that it was true. Maybe Betty had gone somewhere better. The world, after all, was random and cruel, just as the virus that had given Angela the chance to visit and taken so much in turn from people like Shirley and Renée was random and cruel.

Angela's last thought as the sunlight found her curtains and she slipped into a long-delayed sleep was that what the world needed rather than a virus that handed out superpowers was a virus that handed out kindness. One that made sure there were more Bettys and fewer Booksies.

She slipped into her dreams surrounded by scores of those who had touched her and whose lives she could touch in turn. Windows on a world long denied to her. Windows on a world she wanted to change.

♣   ◆   ♠   ♥

Feeding on the Entrails

by Peadar Ó Guilín

Belfast, 2017

AH, THE EUROPA! THE most bombed hotel on the continent since the Second World War. Only the government could afford to run it now, terrified of the bad press if ever it closed its doors for good. And so here it was, opening to the public after its third rebuilding. Stronger than ever. Indestructible.

Cameras watched the streets outside for suspicious activities, with Artificial Intelligences analysing, cross-referencing and parsing each image. No suitcase made it into the lobby until electronic sniffers had checked it for Semtex or the tiniest traces of fertilizer. Nothing could go wrong – this was Belfast, after all, where the *Titanic* was built.

But now, with the security trade show starting, arriving guests were to be treated to even higher levels of protection. Random checks and thumb-prints; a pair of aces on standby from the Silver Helix and much, much more. And so it was that when Billy Little, a paunchy, balding, bespectacled gentleman in his early fifties, rolled a coffin right into the lobby, a uniformed woman stopped him at once. 'We'll have to check that, sir.'

He sighed, his breathing asthmatic. 'You have no idea how many checks I've already been through with this thing.'

'Are you resisting?' she asked hopefully while a cluster of bored and jealous colleagues shuffled closer.

'No,' he raised his hands in surrender, causing a dozen Tasers to leap from tooled-leather holsters.

The guard made him lift the lid off the coffin. Red satin lined the interior, with a walking stick lying on top of it. 'My company can sell you one with a sword inside,' she said, having confirmed that this one was exactly what it looked like.

'No, thanks.' Billy dabbed at his forehead. Seven checks so far, but not one person had asked him why he needed to bring an empty coffin into the hotel. He'd hardly slept all night worrying about it, inventing stories about sudden deaths and trade show delegates with strange sexual fetishes. And throughout it all, he wondered if it might not be such a bad thing to get caught.

But nobody cared. Honest to God, it was almost as bad as getting on a plane.

Finally, after checking under the trolley with mirrors, they brought forward a pair of German Shepherds, while an excited man boasted for all to hear, 'They can be trained to find any drug you can think of! Chemicals! *Very* sensitive animals!' He made a great show of walking them up to the coffin while a crowd of early delegates stood around watching. But no sooner had the dogs taken one sniff than they each let loose a jet of urine before jerking free of their handlers. They ran off into the ballroom while delegates jeered and laughed.

Everybody drifted away and finally Billy was free to move on.

His room looked out over Glengall Street, with a flock of crows on the roof of the Opera House below him. But he wasted no time on the view. Instead, using every ounce of strength he possessed, he lifted up one end of the massive coffin. God, he was getting too old for this! And, as always, he couldn't help the jolt of nausea that accompanied the sight of the old woman jammed underneath it these last two hours. The false bottom had protected her from most of the weight, but even the little she'd had to bear had squeezed blood out of her so that now she lay in a pool of it.

'My muscles have locked,' she rasped. 'Lift me out.'

He obeyed, his stomach rebelling yet again when his skin came into contact with her sticky clothing. 'I don't want to do this any more,' he said, at last. 'I can't. I'm . . . I'm a respectable businessman.'

'Granddaughter,' she said.

He dropped his head, defeated. It was the only word she needed. Billy Little had never married, never even wanted to. He had only ever loved one woman: a bizarre mirage of a creature that had appeared to him every few months for the last thirty years. Even now, with his body flabby from a lifetime of Ulster Frys, his voice hoarse from acid reflux, his hair gone and his nipples as foul-mouthed as ever, she still gave every appearance of being in love with him. He would do anything for her. But instead, he did it for 'Grandmother'.

Sometimes he carted her around as he was doing today. Sometimes his job was simply to drive his hearse down a particular street at a particular time of night, or to hand an envelope to somebody who blanched at the sight of it. Billy understood none of it. But he felt sure that if he did, he'd never be able to live with himself. She was up to something, something unspeakable.

Whatever it was, he didn't want to know. It would break him. 'I'm away to the bar,' he said.

She wasted no breath on an answer and Billy breathed a sigh of relief.

Downstairs again. More delegates were arriving, all rumpled suits and red faces from the indignity of a dozen searches. They queued to check in, watching the latest drones from competing companies swoop and glide, catching in the fancy new chandeliers until a ladder might be fetched to get them down.

Unsure what to do, he pretended to look at his phone. He had games on it that would take him away from all this for a while.

'Are you real?'

Billy jumped. He looked down to see a pretty young woman in a wheelchair with the brightest lipstick he'd ever seen. She sounded Spanish to his ears. 'Real?'

'Look around you,' she waved an arm. The bar heaved with men and women in suits, smiles plastered on their faces, phones in their hands, business cards flying about like confetti at a wedding. And Billy couldn't help smiling. 'Real,' he said. 'Aye, I am. Not like this lot.'

'Buy you a drink?'

'Um . . .'

'Oh, you think I'm trying to seduce you? I *could* seduce you,' she winked. 'I'm *very* bad, but no. My editor wants me to do a piece on Northern Ireland and—'

He froze. Most people knew better than to talk to foreign journos. Her dark, sparkling eyes turned serious at once. 'No names,' she said, 'and nothing serious anyway. Just background stuff that everybody says, yes? Come,' she wheeled around, then beckoned him to follow. Her nail varnish was the same bright shade as her lipstick.

He obeyed, sheepishly, finding a chair beside her. 'What, uh, what is your article about?'

'The peace process. Why it always fails here. Wait!' she whistled loud enough to halt every conversation in the lounge. Heads turned, but the only one she was interested in was the waiter's. 'Two whiskeys,' she said. 'At least twenty years old.' Then, she turned back. 'You ever hear of a paper called the *Corriere della Sera?*'

He shook his head. He didn't read them, couldn't even look at them. Or the news on TV for that matter. Thirty years ago his entire family had been murdered, one after another over the course of a single month. If it weren't for his ace lover, the grief would have killed him too. She was the only family he had left now. Her and Grandmother. They had become his entire life.

'My editor sent me to follow a *very* particular rumour. And good for you! Because it means he pays to get us drunk. I'm Francesca,' she squeezed his hand. 'I don't need your family name, but I'd like to call you something.'

'Billy,' he said.

'Billy. Good for you.' She produced an expensive tablet from under the wheelchair. 'Now, why does the peace process keep failing here?'

'Uh, the Nationalists won't recognize that the Province is British. They'll never make us surrender what's ours.'

She rolled her dark eyes. 'You are going to give me slogans, Billy? In exchange for good whiskey? Look, here it comes. Just smell it and then try to tell me the same old shit I can see written on the walls of the city. Taste!'

He couldn't help smiling at her. Francesca was so much fun. She said she wasn't here to seduce him, but Billy had been born good-looking, and while he'd lost most of that, he still recognized flirting when he saw it, even if it was less than half-serious. Still, though. Still. A desperate part of him suddenly wanted her. Not for sex! But just . . . just to go with her back to Spain or wherever she'd come from. *To be free. Oh, to be free!*

And the whiskey *was* good. Mostly, he bought cheap vodka and guzzled it before bed in front of the wild cards gossip channel.

Francesca leaned forward, lowering her voice. 'Every time somebody tries to make peace here, they are destroyed, yes? Like when John Hume was shot in '93 in Omagh. Do you remember that?'

Billy's breath caught. He had only ever been to Omagh once in his life. In 1993, as it happens. And the very next day, his lover had come to him. 'Aye, I remember.'

'Or what about that Loyalist man, Hutchinson? Blown to bits carrying a coffin at a funeral?'

Billy felt nauseous all of a sudden, because he remembered that too.

'I have . . . I have to go.'

'No, Billy! Stay! We'll talk about something else. Even sport! I would lower myself to that!'

But he was already stumbling away towards the exit.

♣

Eventually, and with much guidance, the bird slipped out of the air vent and onto the bathroom floor. It trembled, exhausted and filthy from its ordeal.

The goddess ignored it. She had work to do. First, she voided her bowels onto the tiles, and then she fumbled through the mess with arthritic fingers until she found the plastic bag. She might have been able to carry it with her under the coffin, but if she'd been caught coming into the hotel with such a substance, the consequences would have been . . . awkward.

When the time came to turn her attention to the crow, it was to make it swallow some capsules.

Finally, she taped the bird to her armpit, and taking the walking stick from the coffin, she hobbled out of the room.

Badb could see herself through one of the windows at the end of the corridor. The lighting was subtle here. The designers of this latest build had placed energy-saving bulbs into elaborate metal frames along the walls so that it looked as if the light was coming from brass bowls of burning oil. It wasn't flattering: her face became a jigsaw of random shadows.

She forced the elevator to take her to the top floor with a special card. Nothing stopped her until she emerged into another corridor to find large men in bulky, bulging suits halfway down it.

'Stop right there!' one of them called.

She walked on.

None of the lights were working here, but there was no mistaking the white man in charge, with his goatee and his bespoke suit. Glanville, a lesser ace, but an ace all the same. He stared in shock at her as slowly, so slowly, she hobbled towards him along the corridor.

'McNulty,' he breathed. At the sound of his dismay, other guards behind him reached carefully into their jackets. Not one of them was local and Badb doubted that any of them on waking that morning had the slightest idea where they would be working. *Fascinating.*

'You are not invited,' Glanville growled. 'There's a conference on the ground floor that's more your style.'

'I'm here for the meeting,' she said. 'Although, you have gone to great lengths to keep all of us at the FRU out of it. You even tried to hide from us that it was taking place. Putting it on during the trade show.'

He drew himself up, his chest broad as a drum. Glanville was the reason none of the lighting was working on this floor except down near the elevator. Frying electronics was about all he was good for, but his presence at a meeting signified the tightest levels of both security and paranoia.

'The FRU is too compromised,' he said. 'You can't be trusted. Four of your own bosses have been murdered in the last decade alone!'

'You too have leaks,' she replied, deliberately raising her voice, 'how else did I find out about your charade?'

Behind Glanville, a door sprang open and a man wearing a red jacket and a tricorn hat looked out. The latest Redcoat, of course. The men who adopted that ridiculous name kept getting killed, but fresh men always appeared to take their places.

Badb perceived no more heroism in this one than the last she had met. That didn't mean he could never achieve glory. Let him suffer a few horrors. Then, he might be willing to die for something larger than his own ego. Especially if a goddess nudged him in the right direction, engineering 'coincidences' and 'chance encounters' with strangers. It could be done. Even working with the most base materials. She was fattening a hero right now.

But it wasn't Redcoat. This new one showed even less intelligence than his predecessors: he had just revealed the meeting room. 'Very well,' Badb said, using a voice that indicated outrage, 'I'm leaving. But my superiors will hear of this.'

Glanville sneered. 'What age are you anyway? Seventy? You look more like ninety. Why haven't you retired? And you smell like shit.' He turned to a colleague. 'She really does! Literally. Shit.'

Badb waved her stick and opened her mouth as if to shout at him. It was a mistake. Rather, it *looked* like a mistake, because she fell against one of the light fittings on the wall, holding on to it for dear life, before tumbling onto the floor.

'*Don't* help her up,' said Glanville. 'Seriously, she should be in a home.'

Badb fought back to her feet. She returned to the elevator, muttering all the while.

Once out of sight, she closed her eyes. Yes, the crow that had been strapped to her armpit now nestled safely in the bowl-shaped light fitting she had fallen against.

Very satisfactory.

◆

The following morning, Billy stepped outside to find crows lining rooftops all along the road. For all that he claimed to be a businessman, the funeral parlour did very little work indeed. Yet, money appeared regularly in his account, more than he needed and none of it ever audited or questioned.

The birds cawed and pecked.

When he'd been a boy, people called informers 'touts', but now locals used the word 'crows'. And instead of warning a bigmouth that 'walls have ears', they'd mutter, 'black feathers' and the talker would quickly shut his yap.

Who knew why the language had changed? Not Billy, that was for sure, but the sight of the creatures in such abundance made his guts twist for some reason, and many a time he'd come across dead birds of other species just lying in piles on the street.

In the distance, wailing sirens twisted his stomach again. They were another constant presence; so common that these days locals just got on with their business. But not today. Right now, the city held itself still. Curtains were closed. Cars remained parked all along the kerb, as though today were Sunday and not the middle of the week.

Billy fondled the phone in his pocket. He never checked the news, but maybe . . . maybe this one time . . . He performed a quick search, and there it was, like acid at the back of his throat: the Europa Hotel.

Twenty-two people had been poisoned. Twenty-two! Capsules of ricin powder had been opened in the room's air conditioning unit and everybody had breathed it in.

And among the victims were members of the IRA who'd been sitting in the same room as their sworn enemies in the Ulster Unionist Party. There'd been government ministers present from both Britain and Ireland. There'd been a personal envoy of the US president. And all were found face down on the table where they were planning to negotiate peace. Whoever the murderers were, they'd even gone to the trouble of killing a crow with the same substance and leaving it behind as a gruesome calling card.

The phone clattered to the ground, its screen fractured beyond repair.

What have I done? And not just this time. But the other times too. It was he, after all, who had supplied the coffin that blew the leader of the Progressive Unionist Party to smithereens. Grandmother had told him to do it and he hadn't questioned her. Not that there had been explosives in the casket when Billy had handed it over! But he'd always been surprised the police had never asked him about it.

Then, there was Omagh. And Lisburn after that. How strange that tragedy dogged his every footstep!

He looked at the phone on the ground. Cracks webbed the screen, but not enough of them that he couldn't still see the words. He sobbed. *This! This is why he shouldn't read the news!* He ground the device with the heel of his shoe until the accusations flickered and died.

♠

Billy didn't see Grandmother again for a fortnight.

In just a few weeks she had aged years. She was a hundred if she was a day, her skin a coat of blisters, her body little more than a layer of bandages and warped bone. Even the corners of her eyes dripped ruby tears that lost themselves quickly among the scabs on her cheeks.

'You will put me under the coffin,' she whispered. She couldn't climb up on the table herself. Even her lips and tongue were bleeding. 'You will leave the coffin in the sacristy of St Malachy's church and drive home.'

'I've told you,' he said. 'I've had . . . I've had enough. I can't.'

'Do this, and two days from now, *she* will visit.'

He didn't need to ask who.

So diminished was the crone, he could have lifted her with one hand, but his skin recoiled from the touch of her clothing. His gorge rose and his eyes watered. She must have noticed, yet she didn't care. When he laid the coffin on top of her, he heard the distinct *snap* of a breaking bone. She made no sound of protest. She never did.

Billy was the one who was shaking. Now, he really did need to retch and he ran to the downstairs bathroom to do so, heaving and weeping, opening a window with trembling hands to let the smell out. Finally, he crawled back to the trolley.

'I'll be back,' he said. 'In a second.'

The hearse waited outside, unlocked as always. Nobody had ever tried to steal it. He jumped in, fumbling for the keys, still tasting the puke at the back of his throat, as rain pattered on the windscreen. He'd go somewhere. Away. Down south even! Or catch a ferry over to Scotland. It didn't matter, none of it mattered.

It was a Sunday night in late summer and the whole city felt dead. Flags were still up from the recent parades. Fresh red, white, and blue paint had been lovingly applied to the footpaths, with every gable end bearing the face of a masked man or a murdered hero.

'What am I doing?' he muttered. Had he really left an old woman under a coffin to die of thirst? A joker like himself? He put his foot down on the accelerator. He was never going back to Grandmother, that's all there was to it. He couldn't hide from it any more: from who she was. What she was. A monster, and he her accomplice in slaughter. Maybe he'd go all the way to Spain to visit Francesca. She'd make him laugh and he had a story to tell her, the likes of which she'd never heard.

Faster and faster he drove. He was doing it! He was finally doing it!

BANG!

Billy jumped, losing control of the wheel. The entire windscreen turned white with cracks. Then he jerked violently forward against the seatbelt, rocking back again as the hearse came to halt. *What . . .?*

He staggered out. His neck felt like it had been wrung by a giant. A single pebble lay jammed in the windscreen. He stared at it under the rain, wondering where it could possibly have come from with no other cars on the road to kick it up. *The sky?* Or had some child thrown it?

Nobody came to help him. It just wasn't healthy in these parts to examine strange goings-on in the night. So Billy stood in the rain, lost, bewildered. 'A taxi,' he thought, finally. 'That's what I need.'

He had yet to replace the phone, but there'd be an office around here somewhere. But just as he turned to look, there came a flap of wings and a sudden blow to his shoulder. He screamed with the shock of it, staggering against the wall behind him. *I've been shot!* It was the only thing that made sense, except that right then, a rain of pebbles scythed down from the sky, smacking into the metal of the hearse, bouncing from the footpath, striking his arms and calves, killing streetlights and setting off car alarms.

The darkness above his head seemed to writhe.

Billy ran. Stones and pebbles clattered along the street behind him. Something flew at his head, leaving a burning line of agony behind it.

He stumbled up to a door, banging on it for all he was worth. 'Let me in! Let me in!'

'Wait!' came a quavering voice behind it. 'I'm trying!' But even as his saviour fumbled at the locks, a bird slammed into Billy's head and savaged his ear. He screamed and screamed.

He found himself in the street again. There were birds everywhere, black as night, utterly silent but for the slap of their wings. They came after him when he tried hiding under a truck. They ignored their losses when he picked up an old brush in the street and swung at them until his strength failed.

'All right,' he said, weeping, because it was obvious now that they were herding him. 'All right. I'm away home.'

Ten minutes later, he stood once more in the basement of the funeral parlour, in front of the coffin. But he wasn't alone this time. A hundred crows filled the room around him. He could smell their damp feathers. Their wings rustled. They lined the empty bookshelves and crowded the backs of chairs. *She* had to be controlling them.

It took him several minutes more to gather his courage to speak.

'I know you can hear me, Grandmother,' he said. His voice cracked, his breath wheezed and rattled in his chest. 'I'm guessing you had my family killed. Armi too, before that.'

Nothing.

'And ever since then, all I have left is you and her. You and her. You think I don't know you're the same? I mean, I remember when I saw her that first night. Dancing near the Island . . .' And as he spoke the words, he pictured his lover again, the perfection of her, an explosion of joy. 'She was ripping off bandages. Aye. Like the ones you need for your bleeding . . .' He felt sick again and had to lean on the coffin for support. 'It would take an idiot not to know you were the one person, but I . . . I made myself that idiot. Well, no more!' His voice rose and rose until he was screaming the words. 'No more! *No . . . more!*' He battered at the wood of the casket, making bloody lumps of his fists. His face was all snot and tears. 'I know it now, you see? I can't pretend I don't. A thousand people are dead 'cos I never stopped you.' He swallowed, looking around at the crows, his ear stinging from where it had been slashed earlier by a beak. Then, he straightened his shoulders. 'You're stayin' under that coffin, so y'are!' His voice barely quavered. 'You'll never hurt anybody again.'

A crow on the back of a chair opened its beak and he flinched. '*Release . . .*' it said distinctly, and another immediately added, '*. . . me.*' Then, two more birds at opposite ends of the room spoke a word each.

'*Release . . .*'   '*. . . me.*'

Then, a hundred other throats took up the command so that they echoed and re-echoed around the basement, now to his left, now his right. Above him, behind him, between his feet. '*RELEASE ME!*' '*RELEASE ME!*'

Billy's bladder chose that moment to let go, but strangely,

it didn't matter. He felt as if he was outside his own body. He took a shuddering breath just as they all fell suddenly silent.

'No amount of birds will ever shift that coffin,' he said. 'Release yourself, murderer. If you can.'

Every beak pointed right at him, at his face. At his eyes. The implication was obvious. Obey, or die. He didn't want that. To experience the pain. Or to leave nothing behind him but a wasted life as the collaborator of a monster. Nevertheless, he raised his chin, forcing himself, for once in his life, to look fate in the eye. 'For . . . for Belfast,' he said. 'For Ulster. For Peace.'

And they chorused back at him:

'You . . .

are . . .

glorious . . .

Billy . . .

Little.'

'What? What do you mean? I—'

The crows attacked.

♥

The Screeching Ace returned that night. They say a hundred people were admitted to hospital with burst eardrums. But that the doctors had to work on them by candlelight, because all generators had ground to a halt and everywhere fuses had burned themselves out. From the beaches of Waterford to the bogs of Donegal, flocks of crows tore themselves bloody. Milk soured on the shelves. Crops withered under ravenous swarms.

And then . . . then, the violence returned. The land is thirsty, after all, and it will drink.

♣ ♦ ♠ ♥